"Yu men held up Neece thet night an' robbed him of his money. An' yu-all sicked this girl on me 'cause none of yu had the nerve to meet me face to face. . . . Wal, thet's my say. An' after all yu're meetin' me face to face!"

As Brazos stopped speaking, he read the desperate intent in Orcutt's eyes and beat him to a gun. Orcutt's heart was split even as he pulled the trigger and his bullet hissed hotly by Brazos' ear.

That left one more man—and a woman—before Brazos settled the score!

**TWIN SOMBREROS**
was originally published by
Harper & Row, Publishers, Inc.

*Are there paperbound books you want but cannot find in your retail stores?*

You can get any title in print in **POCKET BOOK** editions. Simply send retail price, local sales tax, if any, plus 25¢ (50¢ if you order two or more books) to cover mailing and handling costs to:

MAIL SERVICE DEPARTMENT
POCKET BOOKS • A Division of Simon & Schuster, Inc.
1 West 39th Street • New York, New York 10018

Please send check or money order. We cannot be responsible for cash.                         *Catalogue sent free on request.*

Titles in this series are also available at discounts in quantity lots for industrial or sales-promotional use. For details write our Special Projects Agency: The Benjamin Company, Inc., 485 Madison Avenue, New York, New York 10022.

# ZANE GREY

# Twin Sombreros

PUBLISHED BY POCKET BOOKS NEW YORK

TWIN SOMBREROS

Harper & Row edition published 1941

POCKET BOOK edition published May, 1976

This POCKET BOOK edition includes every word contained in
the original, higher-priced edition. It is printed from brand-
new plates made from completely reset, clear, easy-to-read type.
POCKET BOOK editions are published by
POCKET BOOKS,
a division of Simon & Schuster, Inc.,
A GULF+WESTERN COMPANY
630 Fifth Avenue,
New York, N.Y. 10020.
Trademarks registered in the United States
and other countries.

Standard Book Number: 671-80447-2.

Printed in the U.S.A.

## Chapter One

THE SUN hung gold and red above the saw-toothed, snow-tipped ramparts of the Colorado Rockies. On a bluff across the sunset-flushed Purgatory River a group of Indians sat their mustangs watching the slow, winding course of a railroad train climbing toward the foothills. Five years had passed since first the iron trail and smoke devil had crossed out of Kansas to the slopes of Colorado; and still the Indians watched and wondered, doubtful of the future, fearful of this clattering whistling monster on wheels that might spell doom to the red man. Had they not seen train after train loaded with buffalo hides steam eastward across the plains?

A lithe rider, dusty and worn, mounted on a superb bay horse, halted on the south side of the river to watch the Indians.

"Utes, I reckon," he said, answering to the habit of soliloquy that loneliness had fostered in him. "Like the Kiowas they shore die hard. Doggone me if I don't feel sorry for them! The beaver an' the buffalo aboot gone! The white man rangin' with his cattle wherever grass grows! . . . Wal, Reddies, if yu air wise, yu'll go way back in some mountain valley an' stay there."

The rumble of the railroad train died away and the black snakelike string of cars wound out of sight between bold gray bluffs. A moment longer the Indians lingered, their lean and wild shapes silhouetted against the sky, then they wheeled their ragged mustangs and disappeared in red dust clouds over the ridge.

"Wal, come to think aboot it," mused the lone rider, "they're not so bad off as me. . . . No money. No job. No home. . . . Ridin' a grub line, an' half starved. Nothin' but a hawse an' a gun."

Brazos Keene's usual cool and reckless insouciance had suffered a blight. The outcast state he had bitterly avowed

5

was far from new to him. It had been his fate for years to ride the trails from cow camp to ranch, from one cattle town to another. He could not stay long in one place. Always he had been driven. Wherefore the sadness of the hour scarcely had its source in this cowboy wandering. He put a slow hand inside his open vest to draw forth a thick letter, its fresh whiteness marred by fingerprints and sundry soiled spots. He had wept over that letter. Marveling again, with a ghost of the shock which had first attended sight of that beautiful handwriting, he reread the postmark and the address. Lincoln, New Mexico, May 3, 1880. Mr. Brazos Keene, Latimer, Colorado, c/o Two-bar X Ranch. The Latimer postmark read a day later.

"My Gawd, but this heah railroad can fetch a man trouble pronto," he complained, and swallowing a lump in his throat he stuck the letter back. "What in the hell made me go into thet post office for? Old cowboy habit! Always lookin' for letters thet never came. I wish to Gawd this one had been like all the others. . . . But aw no! . . . Holly Ripple remembers me—has still the old faith in me . . . An' she named her boy Brazos—after me. Aw! thet hurts somethin' sweet an' turrible! Shore as I'm forkin' this hawse heah thet'll be bad for me . . . or mebbe good!"

Lost in memory Brazos saw the green river brawling between its gray banks where the willows had a reddish tinge not all from the sunset. A brace of wild ducks winged swift flight over the water; coyotes watched the rider from the slope opposite; the willows shook with the movement of deer or cattle working down to the river; far across the valley on a rising slope black horses showed against the gray. The cold keen air, the fresh odor of the swollen river, the faint color along the brush-lined banks told that the time was early spring. Beyond the Purgatory the land climbed in level benches row on row, always higher and rougher, leading to the gray-ledged ridges, and these in turn to the shaggy foothills that ended abruptly in the mountain wall of slate cliffs and russet slopes and black belts above which the snow crown gleamed white and rose.

"Only five years!" mused the rider, with unseeing eyes on the west. "Five years since I rode along heah down the old trail from Don Carlos' Rancho . . . An' what have I done with my life?"

A savage shake of his head was Brazos' answer to that disturbing query as also it was a passionate repudiation of memory. It had been his wont in dark hours like this to seek oblivion in the bottle. But with that letter heavy against his heart, with the past vivid and stingingly sweet on him, with the indisputable proof that Holly Ripple's faith in him would never die, he could not be so base, so treacherous. Not in the hour of his remorse and shame! If he could destroy the letter and forget . . . but that was vain and futile.

Brazos rode on down the river trail toward Las Animas. He did not know how far it was in to town. His horse was lame and weary. This stretch along the Purgatory was not prolific of cow camps; nevertheless, Brazos hoped to run into one before nightfall.

The sun set, a nipping wind blew down from the heights, the winding river lost its glow of rose to shade dark and steely under the high banks opposite. A coyote wailed out its piercing mournful cry.

"Purgatory, huh?" muttered Brazos, somberly. "Wal, the son-of-a-gun Spaniard thet named this heah creek shore hit it plumb center. Purgatory? River of Lost Souls! . . . Doggone it thet doesn't fit me proper. I'm shore a ridin' fool—a gone goslin'—a lost soul!"

The trail worked up from the river to an intersection with a road. In the gathering darkness, Brazos' quick eye caught sight of three horsemen riding out from a clump of dead trees which only partly obscured a dark cabin. The riders wheeled back apparently thinking Brazos had not seen them.

"Ump-um," muttered Brazos to himself. "Yu gotta be cuter'n thet, my bocos. . . . Now, I just wonder what'n hell kind of a move yu call thet."

All the instincts and faculties of a range rider had been remarkably magnified in Brazos Keene. He reined his horse some rods before passing in front of that clump of trees.

Brazos heard a sibilant hissing *"hold thar!"* and a sound that seemed like a gloved hand slapped on metal. A hoarse voice, thick tongued from liquor, rasped low. Then came a young high-pitched answer: "But Bard, I'm not risking. . . ." The violent gloved hand cut that speech short. To Brazos the name that had been mentioned sounded like Bard, but it might have been Bart or even Brad.

"Hey, riders," called Brazos, curtly. "I seen yu before yu seen me."

After a moment of silence, Brazos heard the word "Texan" whispered significantly. Then one of the three rode out.

"What if you did, stranger?" he asked.

"Nothin'. I just wanted yu to know all riders ain't blind an' deaf."

Brazos' interrogator halted just so far away that his features were indistinguishable. But Brazos registered the deep matured voice, the sloping shoulders, the bull neck.

"Thar's been some holdups along hyar lately," he said.

"Ahuh. An' thet's why yu acted so queer?"

"Queer?"

"Shore. I said queer."

"Playin' safe, stranger."

"Yeah?—Wal, if yu took me for a bandit yu're way off."

"Glad to hear thet.—An' who might you be?"

"I'm a grub-line ridin' cowboy. I'm tired an' hungry, an' my hawse is lame."

"Whar you from?"

"Texas."

"Hell! A deaf man could tell thet. Whar you ridin' from?"

"Montana. Straight as a crow flies."

"An' whar you makin' for?"

"Mister, if I wasn't hungry an' tired I wouldn't like yore pert questions. I'm not goin' anywhere in particular. How far to Las Animas?"

"All night drill fer a tired hoss."

"Any cow camp near?"

"Nope. Nearest ranch is Twin Sombreros, three miles from town."

"Excuse me for askin'," went on Brazos, with sarcasm, "but do yu fellars belong to an ootfit thet'll feed a hungry cowpuncher?"

"My boss hasn't any use fer grub-line riders."

"Yu don't say. Wal, I reckon I don't eat. Small matter. But would yu tell me if there's any grass heahaboots for my hawse?"

"Good grass right hyar, stranger. An' you can bunk in the old cabin thar."

"Thanks," returned Brazos, dryly.

The burly rider turned to his silent companions, just discernible in the gloom. "Come on, men. If we're makin' Lamar tonight we got to rustle."

The couple joined him and they rode by Brazos too swiftly for him to distinguish anything. They took to the north, soon passing out of sight. Brazos kept staring in the direction they had gone. The thing that struck him on the moment was the fact of his insatiable curiosity. These three riders had not acted out of order, considering the time and place. They had a perfect right to be suspicious of him, as he likewise had of them. But there had been something wrong about them, something insincere, something hidden. A meeting with strangers on the ranges was nothing unusual for Brazos Keene. He had an uncanny instinct for recognizing dishonest men. That was one reason why he rode so many grub-line trails. He was honest himself, flaming of spirit, bitter toward the outlaws, the rustlers, and crooked cowmen who dominated the ranges from the Little Big Horn to the Rio Grande.

"Surely hombre," soliloquized Brazos, ponderingly. "He wanted to be shore I *was* a stranger. Now I wonder why? An' if he didn't stop one of them from takin' a pot shot at me, I'll eat my sombrero. . . . An' thet one I heahed clear an' shore. . . . 'Bard, I'm not risking!' Thet's a stumper. Thet hombre was goin' to bore me. What wasn't he riskin'? Why shore it was my ridin' in on them. Doggone queer! But he had been hittin' the bottle. I heahed liquor in his voice. An' it's no use tryin' to figger oot any deal thet has to do with red-eye."

Brazos dismissed the incident from mind. Dismounting, he led his horse off the road to the clump of trees.

Long bleached grass of last year's growth appeared to be plentiful, and this fact relieved Brazos from worry about feed for his animal. The cabin proved to be close at hand. Brazos peeped in the open door. It was pitch dark inside and smelled dry. He removed saddle and bridle from the bay and turned him loose. Brazos carried his paraphernalia inside and deposited it upon the floor. He felt in his pockets for matches. He had none. Then he groped around, hands outstretched, until he bumped into a bench made of boughs. This, with his saddle blankets, would furnish a better bed than many to which he had of late been accustomed. Lastly, he went to the door to look out.

Bay was cropping the grass near by. The sky had become overcast with dark clouds and the cold air had moderated. Brazos felt rain or snow in it. Coyotes were wailing. A few dead leaves rustled on the trees. The black melancholy range seemed to envelop the cabin. Brazos did not like the place, the night, the nameless oppression. But how many times had that very mood weighed upon him? He groped his way back to the bench where, heartsick and hungry, too bitter to care what happened, too weary to think longer, he lay down and fell asleep.

Some time in the night he awoke. At first he imagined he had awakened from a vague grotesgue dream, details of which he could not remember. Usually a light sleeper, he thought nothing of being aroused. But after a moment he felt that this was different. And he attended to outside sensations.

He heard a drip, drip, drip of rain on the floor. Evidently the roof of this shack leaked. A low moaning wind swept by under the cabin eaves. The night was so black that he could not locate either door or window. Mice rustled the rubbish in a corner. The dry musty smell of the cabin appeared to have been permeated with a damp odor, which, of course, came from the rain. Drip—drip—drip—slowly the dropping sounds faded in his consciousness.

From that hour on he slept fitfully, restlessly, harassed by strange dreams. One by one these increased in their morbid vagaries until finally a ghastly climax brought him awake, wet with cold sweat.

Dawn was at hand. Through the window he discerned a faint blue of sky. Apparently the weather had cleared. But all of a sudden—drip—drip—drip. The drops of rain water were slow and heavy. They spattered on the earthen floor. It was now light enough in the cabin to make out a ladder leading up to a loft. The old yellowstone chimney and fireplace had crumbled out of shape. How gloomy and still this square within its four log walls! Brazos wondered what had happened there. But for that matter, no log cabin in the West could be without its history, much of which was dark, violent and bloody.

All at once a cold chill crept over his skin. That dank odor, dominating the pungent dry smell of the cabin, assailed his nostrils. Drip—drip—drip! Brazos was wide awake now, on the verge of being startled by he knew not what. Like his sight and hearing his olfactory sense had been abnormally developed by an outdoor life. Drip —drip! The odor he had connected with this sound did not come from dropping rain water. It was blood. Fresh blood! Brazos seemed suddenly transfixed with a sickening icy clutch at his vitals. He had smelled human blood far too often ever to mistake it.

In a single action, he slid upright off the bench. That drip came from the loft just about the center of the cabin. Brazos could not see the drops, but by their sound, he located them—stretched out his upturned palm. Spat! Despite his steely nerve the heavy wet contact on his hand gave him a shock. He strode to the light of the doorway, there to confirm his suspicion.

"Blood!" he ejaculated, his eyes fixed on the red splotch in his palm. "Cold an' thick. . . . There's a daid man up in thet loft. . . . Aha! them three hombres last night! . . . Brazos, I reckon yu better be rustlin' oot of heah pronto."

Hurrying back to the bench, Brazos wiped the blood on his saddle blankets, and carried these with his saddle to the door. Dawn had given way to daylight with a ruddy tinge in the eastern sky. And at that moment a clattering roar of hoofs swept up like a storm before the wind, and a group of riders pulled their horses to a sliding halt before the cabin.

"Ahuh. Jig aboot up! I savvy," muttered Brazos, and stepping out of the door he flung down the saddle and blankets to stand at attention. He needed not to see the rifles to grasp that this was a posse and that he was the object of their onslaught upon the cabin.

"Hands up, cowboy!" came a harsh command.

"They're up," replied Brazos, laconically, suiting action to words. The leveled guns and grim visages of this outfit showed that they meant business. Brazos had seen many posses and had been a member of not a few. Most of these riders had the cowboy stripe, but some of them, particularly the harsh-voiced, hard-faced leader, appeared to be matured men.

"Pile off, Stuke, an' you, Segel," ordered this leader. Whereupon two riders flung themselves out of their saddles to rush at Brazos from each side. "Grab his guns! Search him. . . . Take everythin'."

"Heah!" flashed Brazos, hotly. "Don't take thet letter!"

"Careful, cowboy, or we'll bore you. . . . Search the cabin. . . . Jim, rustle up his hoss."

Brazos' rage had burst from his cool mien owing to the rude theft of his precious letter. But he was quick to recognize real peril and on the instant became his old self. He surveyed the group of horsemen to ascertain that they were all strangers to him and no different from any hard determined outfit of Westerners. In a moment, he made certain that not one of them had ever seen him. He had not been in that vicinity for six years, which was a long time on the range.

"Bodkin," called a rider from within the cabin, his voice queer.

"What! You found him?" queried the leader, sharply.

"Yes. Up in the loft. Send someone in to help us let him down."

Brazos listened with strained ears to the sounds and husky voices inside the cabin. Murder had been perpetrated. And he was to be held for it. The situation was critical and his life depended upon his nerve and wit. Presently three of the posse came out of the cabin, carrying the body, which they deposited upon the grass. Brazos' startled gaze bent down upon a handsome youth scarcely

12

twenty years old, evidently a cowboy from his garb, dark-haired and dark-skinned. He had been shot through the back. All his pockets were turned inside out.

"Allen Neece," burst out Bodkin, in surprise. He had not expected to see the owner of that name.

"Shot in the back."

"Robbed!"

"Purty cold-blooded, I'd say."

"Bod, I reckon we might jest as wal string this hombre up."

These and various other comments greeted Brazos' ears, and drew from Bodkin the harsh decree:

"Cowboy, you're under arrest."

"Hell! I'm not blind or deaf," retorted Brazos, sarcastically. "May I ask who yu air?"

"I'm Deputy Sheriff Bodkin of Las Animas, actin' under Kiskadden's orders."

"An' what's yore charge?"

"Murder."

Brazos laughed outright. "My Gawd, man, air yu loco? Do I look like I am drunk or crazy?"

"I reckon you don't," replied Bodkin, with glinting eyes taking stock of Brazos.

"Do I look like a hombre who'd shoot a boy in the back, rob him, an' hang aboot waitin' for an ootfit to come get me?"

"You can't never tell what a cowboy will do from his looks."

"Aw, the hell yu cain't," replied Brazos, contemptuously, with piercing glance of scorn flashing from Bodkin to his men. "What kind of Westerners air yu?"

Brazos' scornful stand, his cool nerve in the face of a critical situation obviously impressed some of the riders.

"Bod, I'd recommend a fair trial fer this feller," said one.

"It shore has a queer look, this whole deal," interposed another. "Kiskadden has grown testy of late. Better let him be the jedge."

"Wal, if you-all ain't fer hangin' him pronto, I'll hev to take him into town," said Bodkin, in gruff reluctance.

"See heah, Mister Deputy," spoke up Brazos, keen to

13

catch his advantage. "Last night aboot dark I was held up by three men. I saw them first, pullin' their hawses behind the trees there. One of them was goin' to shoot me when another knocked up his arm. I'll shore remember his voice an' the name he called thet man. . . . Wal, I hailed them an' one fellar rode oot. Never mind what he said. But by Gawd! his dodge is clear to me now. They rode away, an' I turned my hawse loose an' went to bed in the cabin heah. Sometime in the night I woke up. I heahed what I thought was rain drippin'. Aboot daybreak I woke again an' heahed thet same drip—drip—drip. Then I smelled blood. I got up an' caught some of thet drip on my hand. It *was* blood. I was carryin' my saddle oot when yu rode up."

"Haw! Haw!" laughed Bodkin, with a leering sneer, "An' what way was you goin' to ride, cowboy?"

"Hot for Las Animas, Mister Deputy Bodkin, yu can bet yore life on thet," rang out Brazos.

"You expect me to believe that?"

"I don't care a damn what yu believe. I'm *tellin'* yu, thet's all. It's my way of given' yu a hunch."

"Say, I'm an officer of the law an' you're one of these rowdy windy cowboys, of which this hyar range is too thickly populated."

"Wrong again, officer. You may have the law behind yu, but yu're not very bright. I don't resist arrest. But I'm innocent of this charge. I want a fair trial an' a chance to prove it. What's more, if yu knew me yu'd be most damn shore of yore proofs before yu pressed this charge."

"I would, huh? Suppose you acquaint us with your name an' status in Colorado."

Brazos made no reply to the deputy, and spent the following interval in a hard scrutiny of the members of this posse. It was significant that two of them in the background moved to hide behind those in front.

"Bod, you cain't hang this Texan on such heahsay evidence," advised the slow-spoken member.

"Why not? Cause you're a Texan yourself?"

"Wal, as to thet, Texans, whether they're guilty of crime or not, ain't very often hanged. Personally, I reckon this cowboy is innocent as I am of this murder. An'

14

mebbe I'm not the only one. If you hang him, Kiskadden will be sore. An' if by any chance he ain't guilty an' it comes oot—wal, it'd kind of heat up the stink thet hasn't died oot cold yet."

During the brief duration of that quiet speech Brazos gauged both men—the sandy-haired, sallow-faced Texan whose looks and words were significant—and the swarthy Bodkin, dark-browed, shifty of gaze, chafing under the other's cool arraignment of the case, and intense with some feeling hardly justified by the facts herein presented.

"All right, Inskip," rejoined Bodkin, with suppressed anger. "We'll take him before Kiskadden. . . . Prod him to his hoss, men. An' if he bolts, blow his towhead off."

Brazos' captors shoved him forward. Bay had been found and saddled. He did not like this crowd and pulled at his bit, held hard by one of the posse. Brazos mounted. The body of the boy Neece was lifted over a saddle and covered with a slicker. The rider of this horse essayed to walk, which gave Brazos the impression that Las Animas was not far distant. Presently the cavalcade started toward the road, with Brazos riding in the center.

For a while, Brazos was too busy scrutinizing the faces of Bodkin's men to pay much attention to the lay of the land. When he did look beyond them, however, it was to see the Purgatory River winding down through a beautiful stretch which he remembered. At its extreme eastern terminus the sunrise over the horizon flooded the range with a soft rose light. Vast gray prairie lands rolled away to the north. Dots and strings and herds of cattle dominated the landscape. Columns of smoke rising about green field and red and white houses marked the location of Las Animas. Manifestly the town had grown since Brazos' last visit there six years and more ago. At that time the railroad had just reached it.

Brazos inquired of the rider on his left as to the size of Las Animas, but received no response from that worthy. The posse appeared to be a surly lot, not given to much talk.

"Say, pardner," he ventured, accosting the young man on his right, "how big is Las Animas now?"

"Right pert town. About twenty-five hundred, I'd reckon," was the civil reply.

"Gee! Thet's shore a metropolis. Wide open like it used to be?"

"Purty wide. I've only been there a year. Folks say it's slow now."

Bodkin turned to glare at the young rider. "Shet up. This man is under arrest fer murder."

Brazos felt the old gusty fire thrill along his veins, and he had to bite his tongue to keep from a sharp retort. But he would bide his time. He had seen numberless Westerners of Bodkin's type. His knowledge of them equaled his contempt. There would be men in Las Animas who would remember Brazos Keene and who would be certain to give this fourflush deputy a jar.

The cavacade traveled on at a slow trot and at length reached a site strangely familiar to Brazos. It was the head of the valley. He identified a grove of cottonwoods stretching far on each side of the river. Many a time had he camped there. The difference consisted in that the wildness of the sylvan spot had given place to a ranch that would have gladdened the eye of any cowboy. A long, low, red-roofed, red-walled adobe ranch house stood upon the north bank of the river, and below it, where the cottonwoods trooped into the valley, spread barns and sheds, corrals and racks in picturesque confusion. The droves of horses in the pastures, the squares of alfalfa, and the herds of cattle dotting the valley and the adjacent slopes attested to the prosperity of some cattle baron.

"Doggone!" ejaculated Brazos in the enthusiastic appreciation of his kind. "Whose ootfit is thet?"

Inskip, the Texan, riding second on Brazos' left, took it upon himself to reply.

"Twin Sombreros Ranch," he replied, his dry drawl significant of something more than information. "Operated now by Raine Surface, runnin' eighty thousand haid of the Twin Sombreros brand. Used to belong to Abe Neece, father of the daid boy we're packin' to town. Abe is livin' still, but a broken man over the loss of thet ranch."

"Wal, I don't wonder," returned Brazos, feelingly. "Gosh, I'd rather be a grub-line-ridin' cowboy."

Bodkin turned again with malignance in his visage. "You'll be a swingin' cowboy before sundown."

"Yeah?" drawled Brazos in his cool slow speech. "Bodkin, I savvy thet if I don't swing, it shore won't be owin' to yore kind offices."

It so happened that when the cavalcade reached the crossroad to the ranch a sextette of riders, some of them cowboys, rode down from above to halt their mounts at sight of the posse. Brazos espied two young women riders and he burned both inwardly and outwardly. His proud, fiery nature rebelled at the indignity Bodkin had forced upon him.

"What's this, Bodkin?" demanded the leader.

"Mornin', Mr. Surface," replied Bodkin, with both importance and servility. "We been out arrestin' a cowboy. Charged with murder. An' I've got the proofs on him."

"Murder! You don't say? Who?"

"No other than Abe Neece's boy—young Allen Neece."

"Open up here!" ordered Surface, and in another moment a few feet of unobstructed lane intervened between the rancher and Brazos Keene. For Brazos it was one of those instinctively potent meetings of which his life on the ranges had been so full. He turned from his long glance at the two girls, the older of whom had hair as red as flame, a strikingly beautiful face, with blue-green eyes just now dilated in horror.

"Who are you?" demanded Surface, with intense curiosity, not one iota of which denoted sympathy.

Brazos gave the rancher a long stare. Among Brazos' gifts was the rare one of an almost superhuman perspicuity. The time had long passed in his eventful career when he distrusted that peculiar faculty. Surface fell under a category of Westerners far removed from the open-faced, eagle-eyed, great-hearted pioneers whom Brazos revered.

"Wal, who I am is shore none of yore business," replied Brazos, coldly.

"Cowboy, I'm Raine Surface, an' I have a good deal to

17

say with the business of this county," returned the rancher, plainly nettled.

"I reckon. Do you happen to be in cahoots with this fourflush, Deputy Bodkin?"

The sharp unexpected query disconcerted Surface and elicited a roar from Bodkin.

"I put Kiskadden in office," said the rancher stiffly, putting forward a fact Brazos could see no reason for mentioning. "I recommended to the Cattlemen's Association that we appoint deputies to help rid this range of desperadoes an' rustlers—an' rowdy cowboys."

"Wal, Mr. Surface, yu shore impress me powerful," drawled Brazos, scornfully.

"What's your name?"

"Wal, I'm not advisin' yu to ride into town an' find oot. Yu might, along with yore deputy hired hand heah, find yoreself disappointed."

"You insolent ragamuffin of a Texan!" fumed Surface, evidently resenting his failure to be given due importance.

"See heah, Surface," flashed Brazos, his piercing tenor stiffening his hearers. "I am a Texan an' one of the breed thet don't forget insult or injustice. You're a hell of a fine Westerner—a big-hearted cattleman who was on the square wouldn't condemn me without askin' for proofs. You take this Bodkin's word. If he hasn't got some queer reason to fasten this crime on me, it's a shore bet he itches to hang someone. . . . Wal, I happen to be innocent an' I can prove it. I could choke up an' spit fire at the idee of my bein' taken for a low-down greaser who'd shoot a boy in the back to rob him. . . . An' swallow this, Mister Raine Surface—you'll rue the day you insulted a ragamuffin of a cowboy who was only huntin' for a job."

The silence which followed Brazos' arraignment was broken by Inskip.

"Surface," he said caustically, to the pale-faced rancher. "You're new to this range. All you Kansas cattlemen need to be reminded thet this is western Colorado. Which is to say the border of New Mexico. An' mebbe yore years oot heah air too few for you to know what thet means. All the same, Bodkin an' you should have given this cowboy the benefit of a doubt."

18

"Bodkin said he had proofs," rejoined Surface, testily. "I took his word."

"Texans hang together," tartly interposed the deputy sheriff, giving a double meaning to the verb. "Inskip wanted to ride out on this hunt. I reckon he had a hunch. I really didn't want him."

"Bodkin, I'm given' you a hunch," drawled Inskip, with tone and glance that warmed Brazos. "Kiskadden is a Texan. Mebbe you didn't know thet."

At this juncture, when a strong argument seemed imminent, the redheaded girl moved her horse close to Surface and put a hand on his shoulder.

"Dad, don't say any more," she implored. "There must be a mistake. You stay out of it. *That* cowboy never murdered Allen Neece."

"Lura, don't interfere here," snapped her father, impatiently.

"Mr. Surface, we'll ride on in," said Bodkin, and gave his men a peremptory order to move on.

Before the riders closed in on Brazos, he gave the redheaded girl an intent look and a smile of gratitude for her championship. Her big eyes, still wide and dark, appeared to engulf him. Then the cavalcade started. Brazos soon regained his composure. Presently, it occurred to him that this situation had approached a provoking complexity. He cursed his luck. It was bad enough to fall into a perilous predicament without having it assume irresistible interest. He would fight that, and the hour he was freed, he would ride away from Las Animas.

Before they had ridden many paces a clatter of hoofs behind and a call for Bodkin again halted the riders. The rancher Surface followed.

"A word with you, Bodkin," he said, reining his mount.

"Sartinly, Mister Surface," returned the deputy, hastening to fall out of line.

"About that suit of mine against—" he began, with something of pomposity. But Brazos made quick note of the fact that that was all he could hear. Bodkin and Surface walked their horses out of hearing. Brazos was not missing anything. The two riders who had the disagreeable task of holding the corpse in the saddle and

19

keeping it covered swore openly at this second loss of time. As Brazos turned to face forward again, he met Inskip's deep gray eyes in which there flashed a bright steely glint that could be interpreted in only one way. Brazos' blood took a hot leap, then receded to leave him cold. This halt boded ill to him. Sight of Bodkin's grim visage, as he came riding back from his short colloquy with Surface, warned Brazos of the unexpected and the worst.

But Bodkin took the lead of the cavalcade again without a word other than a command to ride. His tenseness seemed to be communicated to all. Their faces set away from the prisoner. Inskip took off his heavy coat and laid it back across the cantle of his saddle—an action Bodkin might have taken as thought-provoking had he noticed it. Brazos' reaction revolved around sight of the two big gun butts sticking out of Inskip's belt. They spoke a language to Brazos as clear as had been the gray lightning in Inskip's eyes.

The outskirts of Las Animas lay just ahead, beyond a bridge over a brook that brawled down to the Purgatory. Oaks and cottonwoods lined the west bank.

"Stop hyar, man," ordered Bodkin, wheeling his horse. "Inskip, you ride on in an' report."

The Texan made no reply nor any move to act upon the deputy's command.

"Segel, you an' Bill wait hyar with Neece," went on Bodkin. "The rest of you come with me."

He turned to ride off the road. "Inskip," he said, suddenly, halting again. "Are you takin' orders?"

"Not when it doesn't suit me," replied the Texan. "What you up to, Bodkin?"

"I'm goin' to finish this job right hyar," rejoined the deputy, fiercely. "An' if you don't want your Texas pride hurt, you'd better not see what's comin' off."

"Wal, I ain't so sensitive as all thet," drawled Inskip.

Brazos realized the game now and what a slim chance he had for his life. That chance was vested in Inskip. An awful instant he fought the shuddering clutch on his vitals, the appalling check to his thought. It was succeeded by the desperate will and nerve, the unlimited re-

20

sourcefulness of the cowboy whose flame-spirit had been engendered by such terrible situations as this. There would be one chance for him and when it came he must grasp it with the speed of lightning.

Bodkin led down the west bank of the brook. The trees and rocks broke up the formation of the posse. Brazos' sharp eye caught the rider behind Bodkin bending forward to untie his lasso from his saddle. They entered a rocky glade comminated by an old cottonwood tree with spreading branches and a dead top. Brazos had been under that tree before.

"Open up," shouted Bodkin. "Prod his hoss out hyar."

A moment of cracking ironshod hoofs on rock and Brazos' horse champed his bit under a widespreading arm of the cottonwood. All the men faced Brazos, pale, with thin lips set.

"Boss," spoke up one of them, hoarsely. "I'm bound to speak out. This deal is too raw fer my stomach."

"Rustle then. Git out of hyar," yelled the leader, livid with passion.

"I sure will. Come on, Ben. We didn't join this outfit to hang a cowboy thet ain't proved guilty."

The lean rider addressed detached himself from the group.

"Bodkin," he said, forcefully. "You're too damn keen on this necktie party. Frank an' me are slopin'."

"Yellow, huh?" shouted the deputy, as the couple rode off. "All right. I'll bear it in mind."

"See heah, Bodkin," interposed Inskip, "did you ride all this way to have yore mine changed by Surface?"

"Inskip, you go to hell!" hissed Bodkin, enraged at the sarcastic implication. Nevertheless, it could scarcely have been rage that paled the redness out of his malignant visage.

Brazos read in Inskip's eyes what Bodkin failed to see; and it was that intelligence which sustained him. The Texan might have a trump card up his sleeve, but Brazos could only think of two desperate chances, one of which he was sure would be presented.

"Flip thet noose, Barsh," ordered Bodkin, sardonically, addressing a lean rider whose hat shaded his face. He had a coiled rope in his left hand. He gave the coil a toss. The loop spread to fall over Brazos' head and lodge on his shoulders. Another flip and the noose closed round his neck. The feel of the hard smooth hemp against Brazos' bare flesh liberated in him the devil that he had kept leashed. Brazos had never before suffered the odium of this phase of border law. Barsh plainly quailed before Brazos' steady gaze.

"Pile off, all of you," shouted Bodkin, stridently, dismounting to lean his rifle against the tree. "Barsh, throw the end of your rope over thet branch."

*"Hold on!"*

This order issued from the Texan, whose hand obstructed Barsh's arm in his effort to toss up the rope.

"Wha-at?" bawled Bodkin, rudely disrupted, glaring at Inskip.

Bodkin was the only rider beside Brazos who had not dismounted. The others had laid aside their rifles and shotguns to crowd back of Barsh, nervously hurrying to get the gruesome job done.

Inskip deliberately rode between them and Brazos. "Bodkin, he might have a mother or sweetheart. An' he'll want to send some word."

"Aw, hell! Let him blab it pronto then."

"Cowboy, do you want to tell me who you air an' send some message?" queried Inskip, calmly.

"I shore do. But I don't want this skunk to heah it."

"Wal, you can tell me," returned Inskip, and pulled his horse toward Brazos.

"Hyar, Inskip . . . *not so close!*" shrieked Bodkin.

The Texan leaned toward Brazos to whisper swift and low: "Grab my guns, but don't kill onless you have to."

Brazos' clawlike hands swept out. As he jerked loose the two big guns, Inskip spurred his horse to lunge away.

*"Freeze!* —— yu!" pealed out Brazos, as he covered Bodkin and the startled posse.

# Chapter Two

BRAZOS heard Inskip's horse pound over the rocks and plow the brook. The Texan was racing for town. Bodkin turned a ghastly hue. Barsh gasped and dropped the rope. The others stood stiff, surely expecting those menacing guns to belch fire and death.

"Hands up! . . . Turn yore backs!" ordered Brazos, his voice ice-edged. "Bodkin, tell yore men to fork their hawses. One move for a gun means I'll kill you first."

"Fellars—he's got—me cold," rejoined the deputy, huskily. "Fer Gawd's sake—lay off your hardware. . . . Climb on."

While they mounted stiffly, Brazos hauled the lasso in with his left hand and wound it around the pommel.

"Ride oot, you hombres. . . . Yu go last, Bodkin. An' when we hit the road yell for Segel an' yore other man to go ahaid."

When the riders emerged from the grove Bodkin bawled to the couple on guard with the dead man.

"Ride on, you fellars—an' don't look back!"

It might have been only a few moments and it might have been longer before the strange cavalcade entered the outskirts of Las Animas—Brazos never knew. But once having passed the portal of the town, he drew a deep breath and sat back in his saddle, lowering the big guns to rest on his knees. Bodkin had treasured his swarthy skin too dearly to make any false move, and his men evidently were not forcing any deadly issue.

The wide long main street was familiar to Brazos, despite the many new buildings. Las Animas had doubled its population in five years. The old gray clapboard and brown adobe structures stood side by side with new ones of more imposing front. Brazos' roving gaze caught sight of a sign: *Mexican Joe. Hot Tamales.* And his heart leaped. If old Joe happened to come out of his restaurant now, there would be a recognition somewhat disconcerting to Bodkin and his posse. But Joe was not one of the many to see the strange procession ride down the street. Brazos was aware of a quickly augmenting crowd in his rear. Before half a block had been traversed, Brazos saw to his left a building and a sign that had not been there in his day. Both sheriff and jail had come to the cattle town.

"Turn in, yu-all, an' set tight," called Brazos. A quick glance assured him that either he or something unusual was expected. Men were grouped about, and out in front stood a tall bareheaded man in his shirt sleeves. He had a silver star on his black vest. He stood significantly sidewise toward the street, his right hand low. Brazos breasted the hitching rail to see a broad lined face, deep piercing eyes, a thin-lipped, close-shut mouth, and bulging chin. Texas was written all over that wonderful visage.

"Wal, Bodkin," he drawled, in a dry crisp voice, "you ride away in the daid of night without orders from this office, an' you ride back with a daid man haidin' yore parade an' a shore enough live cowboy with guns at yore back. What the hell kind of deputy air you?"

"Boss—I had this cowboy arrested fer murder," panted Bodkin, "an' thet —— Inskip double-crossed me——"

"Shut up, Bodkin," interposed Brazos. "I still want to bore yu awful bad. It's shore only oot of respect for this office thet I haven't shot yu long ago."

"Cowboy, talk to me," said the man with the star.

Brazos had not looked into many as clear hawk eyes as those with which this Texan took stock of him.

"Air yu Kiskadden?" queried Brazos, sharply.

"Thet's me," came the curt reply.

"Did Inskip give yu a hunch aboot this?"

"He told me you'd be likely to ride in, but I'm bound to admit I didn't expect you."

"Sheriff, will yu give me a square deal?"

"You can rest assured of thet, cowboy. I'm the law heah."

"My Gawd, but it's a relief to pass these over. Heah!" burst out Brazos, and with a dexterous flip of the guns, he turned them in the air to catch them by the barrels

24

and hand them to the sheriff. "Sheriff, I shore haven't had many deals where I was more justified in throwin' guns than in this one. But when Inskip gave me a chance to use them, he whispered for me not to shoot unless I had to. So I bluffed yore deputy an' his posse."

"So I see. Wal, if you bluffed them, why didn't you ride the other way, instead of insultin' my office this heah way?"

"I happen to be a Texan an' I'm sore."

"I seen thet long ago. Go on. Why'd you come?"

"Last night I was held up oot heah by three men. I'll tell yu in private how they acted, what they said, an' the lie they told me. . . . It was aboot night. I was cold an' tired. Bay heah was lame. So when the three hombres rode away, I went to sleep in the cabin there. In the mawnin' I found too I'd been sleepin' with a daid man. An' I'd just got ootside the cabin when Bodkin with his posse came tearin' up. I had no idee what they wanted an' they'd covered me before I found oot. Wal, they arrested me for the murder of the young man they found in the cabin, shot in the back. Sheriff, you can bet yore life thet those three hombres last night an' Bodkin's ootfit this mawnin' knew the daid boy was in the cabin nine hours before I knew. . . . There was nothin' for me to do but go along. I went. Bodkin is a surly hombre, an' he's a hell of a queer deputy sheriff. First off it didn't look like he had any idee of hangin' me. But he stopped at this Twin Sombreros Ranch oot heah, held up by the rancher Surface. An' from thet moment Bodkin grew hell-bent to hang me. Inskip saw it comin' an' he tried to reason with Bodkin. But yu cain't reason with a bull-haided, fourflush, notoriety-huntin' deputy sheriff who for some queer twist was daid-set to hang me. When they had the lariat aboot my neck, Inskip rode in so I could grab his guns. Thet saved my life, sheriff. I'm innocent an' I can prove it. I want my name cleared. Thet's why I took the risk of holdin' up yore ootfit an' ridin' in heah to surrender."

"Who air you, cowboy?" queried Kiskadden, searchingly.

"Thet'll have to come oot, I reckon," returned Brazos,

reluctantly. "I haven't been in Lás Animas for six years. But there'll be men heah who'll vouch for me."

"All right. Get down, cowboy. . . . Bodkin, you look burstin' with yore side of this story. Mebbe you'd better hold in——"

"Aw hell!" interrupted the deputy, his face working. "Wait till you hear my side. He's a slick-tongued fellar, believe me. I'll gamble he turns out to be a range-ridin' desperado. An' it's a thousand to one thet he murdered young Neece."

"Neece! Not Abe Neece's boy?" exclaimed Kiskadden, shocked out of his composure.

"Yes. Young Allen Neece."

"Aw, too bad—too bad!" rejoined the sheriff, in profound regret. "As if poor Abe had not had enough trouble!"

"Boss, you just bet it's too bad. It'll sure go hard with Allen's twin sisters. Them gurls thought the world of him."

"Fetch Neece in," ended Kiskadden, and taking Brazo's arm he led him into the office.

"An' see heah, sheriff," spoke up Brazos. "Will yu have my hawse taken good care of? An' Bodkin took my gun, watch, penknife—an' a personal letter. Thet's all I had, an' the letter means most to me."

"Cowboy, I'll be responsible for your hawse an' your belongings."

"Thanks. Thet's a load off my mind. An' one thing more," said Brazos, lowering his voice so that the men carrying in the body of Neece could not hear him. "I reckon thet letter will prove my innocence. I got it yesterday mawnin' at Latimer, which you shore know is a hell of a long day's ride. An' if I know anythin' aboot daid men, young Neece was killed durin' the day. Hold an inquest, sheriff, an' make shore what hour thet pore boy was murdered. 'Cause the whole deal has a look of murder."

"You're a cool hand," replied Kiskadden, admiringly. "I kinda like you. From Texas, eh?"

"Shore. I was born in Uvalde."

"How old air you?"

"Twenty-five."

"Wal, you don't look thet. Any folks livin'?"

"There was—a few years ago. But I've been too unhappy lately to write home."

"Air you straight, cowboy?"

"I am, sheriff, so help me Gawd!" answered Brazos, passionately, meeting full the penetrating gray eyes, that had something of shadow in them.

"Wal, I promised you a square deal," concluded Kiskadden. "Come with me. I'll have to lock you up."

A corridor opened from the office. Kiskadden unlocked the first door on the right, to disclose a small room with one barred window. The only article Brazos could see at quick glance was a blanketed couch. Kiskadden escorted Brazos in and halted in the doorway.

"Cowboy, one thing bothers me. In case you air innocent, which Inskip swore you was, an' I substantiate thet, you're liable to hold somethin' against Bodkin an' mebbe his men."

"Hell! Thet bothers me," flashed Brazos, sitting down heavily on the couch. "Bodkin? I didn't know aboot him. . . . An' thet Barsh, who put a rope around my neck. Only man who ever did thet! . . . But, Kiskadden, I'll be more interested in the three hombres who tricked me into this mess."

"Cowboy, you don't seem to concern yourself aboot why I'm lockin' you up."

"Concern? Say, I'm tickled to death. What have I got to worry aboot now? You're a Texan an' a man. You'll see through my part in this deal. . . . But when I get oot . . . Sheriff, I'm askin' yu—please get possession of my letter an' please don't let anybody but yu read it. I shore couldn't stand thet."

"We'll see." The sheriff went out to close and lock the heavy door.

Brazos lay down on the couch. As he composed himself, the sound of heavy boots and indistinct voices came through the walls from the sheriff's office. The window of his cell opened on the back.

After a while, his blood ceased to race and his thoughts to whirl. "Doggone!" soliloquized Brazos. "When did I ever have a closer shave than thet?" He was well off in jail for a few days. He would be well fed and have a bed to sleep on. And meanwhile, he would piece the fragments of this case together. Something more would come out at his trial, or at least the perfunctory hearing Kiskadden would have to give him.

He had not the least doubt that Kiskadden would not only release him, but establish his innocence. This Texan recalled other denizens of the Lone Star State that he had known—Cap Britt, for one, for whom he had ridden and shot himself into notoriety some years before. Inskip was another. These men knew their kind. Brazos wondered if this Abe Neece had come from the Lone Star State. Surface was certainly not a Texan. Brazos tried to sidetrack an insidious impression of intrigue involving the three riders who had accosted him out at the cabin, this deputy Bodkin, and the young man Barsh, who had been afraid to show his face, and Surface. Brazos had only slim pegs on which to hang these suspicions. But a remarkable career on the ranges had given him an experience far beyond his years. Always he had been thrown against a background of cattle dealing, with its multiplicity of angles. The vast plains of Texas, the Panhandle and the Llano Estacado, the silver-grassed ranges of New Mexico, the Colorado steppes and the many valleys of Wyoming—these he knew as well as any cowboy who had ever ridden them. Rustlers, outlaws, desperadoes, bandits, and the ever-increasing number of cowboys gone wrong—these had multiplied with the building of the cattle empire. Likewise, the strange fact of apparently honest cattlemen being in league with the evil forces had flourished since the first great herds of longhorns had been driven north from Texas. Brazos recalled a few he had known, the most notable of whom, though not the last—Sewall McCoy—brought a cold jerk along Brazos' nerves.

The redheaded daughter of Surface came back to mind —Lura Surface. She had certainly made him a target for wonderful blue-green hungry eyes. "I know her kind," muttered Brazos. "A flirt—for whom cowboys air apple pie. I'll shore have to see her again, risk or no risk. She saw I was no low-down murderer. An' I'll have to remember thet."

28

Brazos had innumerable questions to ask somebody about this Twin Sombreros Ranch, the Surfaces, and the Neeces. At this point he was interrupted by footsteps out in the hall. He heard a heavy bolt or lock shot back. The door opened to admit a man carrying a tray.

"Hyar's some grub, cowboy," he said gruffly, setting the tray down on the couch.

Brazos rolled to a sitting posture, his boots clanging on the floor.

"Say, yu're one hombre I'm gonna treat white in this burg," sang out Brazos. "Hungry? Wal, look at thet grub! . . . Stay an' talk to me, pardner."

"Agin' orders," rejoined the guard, who went out to lock Brazos in again.

Brazos made the most of that generous meal. A starved condition was not conducive to optimism and clear thinking. He felt vastly better. Pacing the narrow confines of his cell, he lived his experience over again and realized that he got more out of it. Then he lay down to rest, and anon, he stood up on the bed to peep out of the small window. It opened out upon a high-fenced compound rather than corral, at the back of which ran a long shed of stalls. He saw the flank of his horse Bay.

The afternoon passed far from tediously for Brazos. Those heavy footfalls in the office and on the flagstone sidewalk had meaning for him. Unless Las Animas had more than doubled the population of his day, he estimated that very nearly every man in the town had visited Kiskadden. Late in the afternoon, two guards brought his supper.

"We've orders to take you out back fer a little exercise, if you want," announced one.

"Wal, in the mawnin," replied Brazos. "An' if yu'll fetch me water, soap an' towel, an' a razor, I'll consider myself obligated."

"Glad to, cowboy." They went out in the gathering dusk.

Brazos took off his clothes and went to bed, his eyes shutting as with glue. That night he made up lost sleep, and it was very late when he awoke. The stars told him that the dark hour before dawn was close at hand. The lonely silent hour Brazos had always chosen to guard the herd!

If he could not sleep, that had always been a bad hour for him. His reckless life always spread out for him to review, the ghosts of dead men haunted him, the many opportunities for betterment that he had missed, the many times he had had to ride away from ranges and cowboys he loved, and lastly the dark-eyed lovely girl who had made him a wandering, line-riding cowboy.

From now on his torture would be relentless and unabatable. That letter! He felt for it against his heart. Gone! And a wrench of pain and fury shook him. Would the sheriff read that letter aloud at the trial? Brazos did not believe the Texan would subject him to that ordeal.

That letter had wrenched Brazos' soul. And he had not dared to read it all or go back to it. He had been flayed. The bitter anguish of the past had softened. What hurt so terribly was to find that his name had been revered, that love and faith still abided out there beyond the Cimarron, that Holly Ripple had named her boy for him, that her husband Frayne and her foreman Britt and all that hard-riding, hard-shooting outfit of cowboys the like of which had never been known on the ranges, all swore by him, made him a tradition, and never ceased to believe he would end his reckless wandering and come back to them.

"Aw, I cain't ever go back," moaned Brazos into the silent blackness of the night. "An' I cain't ever drink no more—to make me forget—an' fight—an' ride on some place new. . . . Thet boy will find me some day, unless I'm daid—*she* will send him—an' then he'd see true. . . . By Gawd, it's tough! I'm drove to be what *she* trusted me to become—what thet boy thinks I am."

Daylight brought a cessation of Brazos' unhappy memories and resolves. But he divined that a leaning to evil had passed out of him during his dark hour. He felt himself transformed, gone back to the old gay cool Brazos Keene with something inexplicable added.

The guards brought his breakfast, and the necessary articles with which to wash and shave, and make himself presentable.

"Your trial is comin' off today," the kindly one of the

two announced. "An' I reckon you needn't be ondue worried."

"Thanks, pardner. Thet's fine. Take me ootside for a stretch."

All morning, however, he was left alone, waiting for a footfall that did not come. The fact of the omission of his noonday meal augured further for his release. Brazos paced his cell, finally achieving patience. At last a slow clinking step in the corridor ended his wait. That was the step of a Texan.

Brazos was not disappointed. The door opened to admit Kiskadden, who closed and locked it.

"Wal, Brazos," he drawled, "I'm missin' my dinner to have a confab with you."

"Yu know my name?" queried Brazos, sharply.

"Shore. It's on the back of this letter. Brazos Keene. Wrote small an' pretty, but I read thet much anyway. I'm glad to tell you no one else has seen it. I reckon Bodkin's man, Segel, put no store on it. An' heah it is, cowboy."

"My Gawd, sheriff, but I could die for yu—savin' me the shame of disgracin' a girl I once loved," replied Brazos, in grateful emotion.

"Wal, I'm glad if it means as much as thet," returned Kiskadden, and he sat down on the couch to take out a black pipe. "I always figger better when I smoke. Not thet I'm not shore you'll go free. It's a pore case agin' you, Brazos, an' has some queer angles."

"Ha! I had thet hunch. Yu wouldn't be a Texan sheriff if yu hadn't seen thet."

"You got this letter the mawnin' of day before yestiddy, at Latimer, didn't you?"

"Yes, sir. An' all by accident, or mebbe a hunch. I was ridin' through aboot eight o'clock. I went in the post office an' was paralyzed to get it. I rode oot of town scared to death. But finally I sloped off under a tree. . . . Gosh, I must have been there for hours but I didn't have the nerve to read it all. But the sun was high an' hot when I rode on again."

"Wal, we had two doctors make the inquest on young Neece," went on Kiskadden. "Our Doc Williamson, who lives heah, an' a surgeon from Denver, who was on a train. Williamson seen him an' dragged him off. They found young Neece had been killed early in the evenin' of thet day you rode oot of Latimer. The bullet hole in his back was shot there after Neece was daid. Both doctors agreed thet he had been roped—there were abrasions on his arms above his elbows—an' jerked off his hawse on his haid. Thet caused his death."

"Wal, my Gawd!" ejaculated Brazos, in wondering fire. "I had no rope on my saddle."

"Brazos, I was convinced of yore innocence yestiddy, an' now I know it. But for yore good, I reckon you better stay for the hearin'. It'll show Bodkin up an' I'll discharge him pronto. Another angle, it leaked oot somewhere thet Surface would jest as lief see you hanged, along with all the grub-line cowboys thet ride through."

"Hell yu say?" queried Brazos, thoughtfully. "Sheriff, I shore didn't take a shine to him."

"Surface is new heah. Claims to be from Nebraska. But he's from Kansas. Rich cattleman—an' has a lot of stock. Same as all of us, for thet matter."

"Ahuh. How'd Surface get thet Twin Sombreros Ranch from Neece?"

"Wal, thet's kind of complicated, an' never was cleared up to suit me. Neece was operatin' big. He had five thousand haid comin' up from Texas for Surface. The cash for this herd was paid Neece at the Cattleman's Bank in Dodge. More than fifty thousand dollars. Neece was fetchin' thet sum over heah to our bank. But he got held up by three masked men, an' robbed. Wal, the queer angle is thet the big herd jest vanished off the range. Neither hoof nor hair of them was ever found."

"But the cow ootfit!" exclaimed Brazos, aghast.

"Same as the herd. They vanished. Neece made a blunder at Dodge. He hired a foreman thet he didn't know, let him pick an ootfit, an' sent them south after the herd."

"Thet ootfit was bought off," said Brazos, abruptly.

"Wal, there was no proof of anythin' except the longhorns were gone. Neece couldn't deliver to Surface. An' he had been robbed of the money. Twin Sombreros was mortgaged an' the banks wouldn't advance more. Neece lost all to Surface. He's a broken man now, livin' oot of town down the Purgatory. An' the twin gurls, Neece's joy an' pride, air running a restaurant over by the railroad station."

"Twin girls!"

"Shore. Eighteen years old—the prettiest gurls in all the West. An' you cain't tell them apart—not to save yore life. June an' Janis, they're called. Neece was powerful proud of them twins. He sent them back to Kansas City to go to school. Thet was ten years ago. An' he didn't see them often an' not atall of late years. He developed this Twin Sombreros Ranch for them. Thet was his brand. Two high-peaked sombreros. Wal, the gurls just got heah when the crash came. Hard luck fer them, everybody swore, an' was sorry. But them gurls had spunk. They borrowed money an' started a restaurant. Old Abe's Mexican cook stuck to them. An' say, thet little restaurant is packed every mealtime, with a crowd waitin' ootside. They've paid back what they borrowed an' now they're makin' money."

"Stampedin' mavericks!" burst out Brazos. "I reckoned I'd heahed some range yarns in my day. But this one takes the cake. . . . I'll bet thet Lura Surface sticks up her nose at the Neece twins, huh?"

"Wal, the wimmen folks all say Lura is a cat an' powerful jealous of the twins. You see, she queened it over the range till Neece's gurls got heah. An' now she's not got it all her own way."

"Kiskadden, what yu tellin' me all this for?" suddenly queried Brazos, sharp with suspicion.

"Aw, just range gossip, cowboy," drawled the Texan, with an evasive smile.

"Yeah? Wal, it's shore powerful interestin' an' yu don't strike me as the gossipin' kind. . . . I figure Inskip's a friend of yores?"

"Yes. We're pardners in a cattle business, but I'm the silent one. . . . Wal, to come back to yore hearin', which is set fer two o'clock, I'd like you to read that letter to me."

"Aw! Sheriff, you didn't open it?"

"No."

"What yu want me to read it for?"

"Brazos, I really don't have to heah it, if yu object. But

33

it'll strengthen my conviction, I'm shore. An' I may have to talk turkey to Surface an' some of his cattle association. All the same, I'll respect yore confidence."

"Shore. I—I'll read it to yu," replied Brazos, soberly, and as he opened the thick letter his lean brown hands shook slightly.

> Don Carlos' Rancho
> Cimarron, N. M.
> May 2, 1880

Dear Brazos:

This is the third letter I have written you since you left us over five years ago. I am sure the others never reached you else you would have written. They were sent at a venture. This time, however, I know you will receive this one, and I am writing much that I omitted before. We have a railroad mail service now, *caballero mio;* and this epistle should reach your post-office in less than two days. So near yet so far, Brazos!

We heard quite by accident that you had lately ridden down from Wyoming to a job with the Two-bar X outfit. A cattleman neighbor of ours, Calhoun, had just returned from Latimer, and he met Britt at the station. Wherever Brazos Keene rides, it will be known! Calhoun told Britt a lot of range gossip, including your latest exploit at Casper, Wyoming (which *I* did not believe) and poor Britt came home like a man who had seen ghosts. He told the cowboys and Nigger Johnson (bless his white heart ) told me. Not one of the other boys mentioned it to me. You'll be amazed, Brazos, and I hope hurt a little to learn that every single one of the old outfit you once lorded it over so gayly is still riding for me. They were a sick bunch of cowboys. How they loved you, Brazos! I'd have given much to have been hidden in the bunkhouse when Britt told them about you.

They are spoiling little Brazos Ripple Frayne, your namesake, who is nearly five years old. He is a little devil and drives me frantic. He favors his father, Renn, more than me. But he has a little of my

34

Spanish. He never tires of stories about rustlers, gun-men, bandits, buffalo and cattle stampedes. And *your* name makes his eyes grow big and round. You should see Brazos roll a gun and hear him say: "When I grow up, I'm gonna bore that Billy the Kid!" Oh! it is dreadful, the propensities he shows already. His father does not seem to mind. Britt, who worships the lad, says that when Brazos takes to riding the range, the hard years of the New Mexican border will be past.

Since you and your outfit broke up the Slaughter gang and did away with Sewall McCoy, Clements and their tools, we have no rustling on a big scale. Strange to say, we were never drawn into Lincoln County War, which was in its incipiency when you rode for Don Carlos' Rancho. That terrible feud accounted for the lives of three hundred men, surely the bloodiest war the West ever knew. Billy the Kid came out of it alive. He and a few of his desperado allies still actively rustle cattle and find a ready market. Billy has more friends than enemies. He has visited Don Carlos' Rancho twice during the last year. He is twenty years old and has killed twenty men, not including Indians and Mexicans. Billy would not be bad looking but for his buck tooth. He is a quiet little fellow. Such eyes! They are like forked blue lightning. Pat Garrett is on Billy's trail. They are expected to meet any day. The range is speculating. Britt and Renn both say Garrett will never risk an even break with Billy. If he does, he'll get killed. Renn said once: "I've seen the day I could beat that little hombre to a gun!" And Britt said: "Brazos could do it *now*!" . . . Oh, you border ruffians! You strange cold Westerners! I confess to a little weakness for Billy the Kid. That's not strange, considering my Spanish heritage, and the fact that before I married an outlaw gunman, I had a soft spot in my heart for a gunman cowboy, one Señor Brazos Keene.

So far as we know, Billy's outfit never stole a steer off our range. After my father's custom here, I had Billy and his gang to dinner. He told me he remem-

35

bered my father and evidently cherished that memory. Well, the good, bad old days are over, at least for Don Carlos' Rancho. We are running over seventy thousand head. The railroad has simplified cattle-raising. The long hard drives are a thing of the past in this territory. Chisum, the old rustler baron with his jingle-bobbed cattle, survived the Lincoln County War. Billy the Kid, who rode for Chisum once, had sworn to kill him. But the old man still holds forth at Seven Rivers, surrounded by a hard outfit, and a hundred thousand head of longhorns. Brazos, he once asked me to marry him. I've never forgotten the shock of that. Right now I can see you shake your handsome curly head and say as you did once: "Wal, who'n hell hasn't asked Holly Ripple thet?"

Brazos, I am wonderfully happy. Renn has more than justified the faith I placed in him. He is a big man on the New Mexico ranges and long ago has lived down that vague hard name that came with him from Dodge and Abilene. My father's traditions and work have been carried on. We have our darling little boy and—dare I confess it?—expect another little Frayne at no distant date. May it be a girl— Señorita Holly Ripple Frayne! Our material riches do not mean very much. I forgot to tell you that my riders have a share in our cattle business. In fact, Brazos, there is only one drop of bitterness to taint the sweet cup of Don Carlos' Rancho. And that is your loss, your wandering, rolling-stone life, your bitter fiery spirit and your fate to throw a gun, your inevitable fall.

We have heard of you often. You know range gossip—how cowboys love to talk, to carry tales. If I believed all I have heard, my heart would be broken. But I *know* you would never be crooked. Still all my faith in you cannot change the fact that haunts me. If you persist in your lone wolf wandering from bad cow-camps to hard cow-towns, always with that chip on your shoulder, it will not be long until you too, like many of your old pards, find a grave on the "lone prairie." That would be a pity, Brazos. You

36

are such a fine boy. You have such splendid possibilities.

Britt tells me that I broke your heart. Oh, how I have prayed that was untrue! I know you loved me. But you were a wild boy, Brazos. You were only nineteen years old—my own age. I felt like a mother to you. Indeed I did love you, but it was as a sister. That, of course, I did not know until Renn came into our lives. He was my man, Brazos.

If you loved me so deeply as Britt and the cowboys seem to believe, you could never go to the bad. The greatest grief can be a source of joy. I don't believe you loved me greatly. If you had, you would have paid me the honor of being better for it. You were just disappointed, cut to the soul, and instead of letting the goodness, the sweetness in you dominate your future, you rode away with that proud, passionate, devilish side uppermost.

Brazos, in this letter, which I am certain you will receive, you have come to the end of your rope. You will stop your wandering—your drinking. You were never a drunkard, but you could easily have become one. You must find a steady job—*if you refuse to return to Don Carlos' Rancho*—and you will be worthy of my faith, and Renn's regard, and the love of these cowboys.

There are hundreds of pretty lovable western girls just aching, just eating their hearts out for a man like you. Find one of them, and love her. (Oh, don't tell me you couldn't. You *could*. Didn't you have a case on Señorita Dolores Mendozo, while you were courting me?) Ah, Brazos! . . . Love her and marry her and settle down to deserve the reward that should come to all cowboys like you—who have made this glorious West habitable for us—made its empire possible.

Fetch her out here to live. To be my friend! And if in the fulness of time you and she were to be blessed with a little girl, let us pledge her and little Brazos to each other.

This is the last letter I shall ever write you, my

37

friend. I hope and pray you take it as I have written it, and that you will consider my husband's proposition, which follows in a postscript.

*Adios Señor*

Ever yours faithfully,

Holly Ripple Frayne

P.S.

Dear Cowboy Old Timer.

I am adding a few words to Holly's letter, which I have read. But she will not get to see what I write you.

Britt wants you to come back to Don Carlos' Rancho. So do I. So does the outfit. We are going to need you.

Brazos, let me hurry to get rid of things hard to express. I know how you felt about Holly. I know because I felt the same. If she had chosen you, I still would have stayed on. I would never have expected—never have wanted to get over it. Loving such a woman changed me from an outlaw to a man. For years, I have worried about you. Britt and I, all the cowboys, have never stopped looking for you to come back. But the deeper hope, of course, is that you would go straight and true, wherever you were.

That's that.

Brazos, Holly's letter might mislead you about affairs of the range out here. Well, as a matter of fact, the rustling business is as good as the cattle business. There's a new outfit up in the hills where Slaughter used to hide out. And Britt doesn't like the prospects one damn little bit.

I could tell you several queer looking deals, but one will go to show you the old game is kicking back, as we always expected it'd do. Not so long ago, the biggest herd of longhorns Britt ever saw drifted up the Cimarron—a gaunted bunch that had seen long and hard travel. The outfit worked them across the valley, avoiding the cow-camps, taking scarce enough time to fatten up, and they split the herd and drove to the railroad, shipping from Maxwell and Hebron to Kansas City.

Britt, the old fox, thought the drive had a queer look and took pains to get these details. They were all the facts obtainable. But somewhere along this trail to the railroad, the name Surface leaked out. You know how strange things happen in this cattle game. It's a safe bet, Brazos, that this drive was a steal, as big a one as we ever saw come out of Texas. And naturally we're passing the buck with a hunch to you. Britt swears he never knew a cowboy in your class to scent and follow crooked tracks. Keep this under your hat, old timer, and look around over your Colorado way. There probably is another Sewall McCoy cropping up. These cattlemen rustlers are the bane of the ranges. A real honest to God rustler was always easy to contend with, till it came to the fight, and then you could gamble on hell and bullets. But these respectable buyers and sellers of cattle, while all the while they have outfits rustling for them —these are the tough nuts to crack.

It's Britt's hunch and mine that this man Surface might turn out to belong to the class mentioned above. No need to tell you, Brazos, what a delicate matter such suspicion is. It's something you just can't speak out loud in the West. Every rancher has stolen cattle, knowingly or not, and he's testy about it. As for the crooked rancher—at the least hint he goes for his gun, and roars to the law and his associations afterward. Ride down this man Surface, and write to us, Brazos.

And, cowboy, while you're doing it, consider coming back to be my foreman of the outfit running the Ripple brand. On shares!

Yours truly,
Renn Frayne.

At the conclusion of this reading, Kiskadden strode to and fro in the cell, while Brazos sat with bowed head over the letter. Once the sheriff laid a heavy hand on the cowboy's clustering chestnut curls, beginning faintly to show silver at his temples. The tread of boots outside brought Kiskadden to a halt.

"Aboot time for yore trial, Brazos," he said, consulting his watch.

"Sheriff, as I told you, I never read all this letter—first time," replied Brazos, gravely, as he carefully folded the pages and put them back into the envelope. "Honest I didn't."

"Cowboy, I'm shore glad Bodkin didn't read it. . . . Brazos, there ain't much I can say, except I'm glad I trusted you. If I hadn't an' you'd sprung thet letter on me, I'd shore been ashamed. . . . It's a wonderful letter. Brazos. I'd like you to know I rode fer Colonel Ripple when I was yore age. I knew Cap Britt. We were Texas Rangers under McKelvy. An' I shore have heahed of Frayne."

"Aw! Yu don't say?" burst out Brazos, gladly. "All my agonizin' fer nothin'! When I heahed the name Kiskadden —Las Animas sheriff—I reckoned yu might be one of them hangin' sheriffs an' I was shore sick."

"Don't blame you, cowboy . . . Wal, we'll go oot now an' I'll be settin' you free pronto. What then, Brazos? . . . Tell me, on the square, cowboy, air Holly Ripple's love for you an' her faith—an' Frayne's an' all of them—air they justified?"

"Hell no!" ejaculated Brazos, with a wrench. "But, sheriff, I could look Holly in the eye an' Frayne an' Britt —all thet tough ootfit of pards—an' swear to Gawd I've never done a crooked thing since I left them."

"Wal, I ask no more," returned the Texan, feelingly.

"All the same, I'm gonna tell yu more," flashed Brazos. "This day marks a change in my life. It's been comin' a long time. Somethin's busted inside me like a million sparks. I'll be what Holly Ripple thought I was or I'll die tryin'."

"Wal, now, cowboy, I reckon thet's to say you've wiped oot the five years. Good! You've got much to live up to an' I believe you're equal to it."

"Thanks, Kiskadden. . . . An' heah we air forgettin' the most important thing in thet letter. The hunch aboot Surface!"

"No, Brazos. I'm lettin' thet ride fer the present. All aboot you was personal. Frayne's hunch is business. An' believe me, damn serious."

40

# Chapter Three

THE sheriff's office appeared rather cramped quarters with the dozen or more occupants standing and sitting around. Outside a considerable crowd had collected. With few exceptions, notably the dark-garbed Surface and some close associates at his elbow, the assembly was composed of dusty-booted, roughly clad cattlemen.

Brazos took a swift survey of these spectators, more to sense their attitude than to look for some one who knew him. That there would be old acquaintances present he felt sure. For the time being the feeling in general seemed one of curious hostility.

"Set there, Keene," said Kiskadden indicating one of two chairs back of his desk. Brazos saw his gun and belt, his watch and penknife, lying on some papers. The desk drawer was half open, showing the dark butts of several Colts.

"Let everybody in, if there's room," called the sheriff, to the guard at the door. Presently Kiskadden pounded on his desk to stop the talking. He stood erect. "Fellow citizens," he said. "My mind aboot this case is made up. But I'll hold a hearin' so thet you-all can get the facts."

Surface took a step out from the group of ranchmen evidently accompanying him. His mien was forceful, arrogant, suggestive of power. His bland face appeared to Brazos to be a mask. Not since Brazos had taken to the cattle trails had he trusted eyes like these.

"Sheriff, I move we try this man before twelve jurors. I will serve along with the members of the Cattlemen's Association. We can pick the others from businessmen here."

"What's the idee of thet?" demanded Kiskadden.

"Your declaration that you had already come to a decision proves the consensus of opinion correct."

41

"An' what's thet opinion, Mister Raine Surface?" queried the sheriff, sarcastically.

"You wouldn't hang a Texas cowboy. This murderer would already have swung but for Inskip, who's another of your Texas breed."

"Wal, Surface, thet Texas breed opened up this cattle empire. An' the strange fact is you seldom heah of one of them gettin' hanged. Thet might come from their gun-throwin' proclivity, an' then again it might be thet few Texans deserve to swing. In this case, I'm refusin' your offer of a jury. The law of this county is invested in me."

"Kiskadden, you may rest assured your authority will not last long," rejoined Surface, heatedly.

Brazos took in this byplay with a thrilled interest and keen observation. Surface certainly had no conception of Texas character. Evidently, he was rich, powerful, sure of himself. He seemed utterly blind to the fact that he himself was on trial there, before at least three cool Texans.

"I'm as shore as you air of thet," drawled Kiskadden, his narrowed eyes like slits of gray on the rancher. "An' I'm also shore of somethin' else. It's goin' to look damn queer presently, when I prove this cowboy innocent, thet you're so keen on hangin' him."

Surface turned a dark red. His collar appeared to be too tight for his bulging neck.

"You insulting Texan. I'll run you—out of office for that!" he exclaimed, stridently.

"Run an' be damned. Yore action an' yore talk air not regular in this deal. They look fishy to this court. To be lousy with money an' haid of this new Cattle Association shore doesn't entitle you to run me an' my office. . . . Do I make myself clear, Mister Surface?"

If the rancher did not take the hint at that, his associates surely did, for they drew him back and shut his mouth.

"All right. The hearin's on," called out Kiskadden, loudly. "Deputy Bodkin, step forward."

"Yes, sir," replied the burly officer, coming up to the desk.

"Take off yore hat when you testify to the court. . . ."

Place yore hand on this Bible an' swear to tell the truth an' nothin' but the truth."

Bodkin took the oath.

"Now proceed with yore testimony."

"Wal, sir, it was late after two o'clock, night before last," began Bodkin, glib with importance. "I'd been playin' cards an' had hardly got asleep when I was woke by somebody at my winder. I seen two men. It was too dark to see their faces plain. They was strangers. One of them told me they'd watched a cowboy shoot another off his horse, search him and drag him into the cabin. Thet was the old Hill cabin, long empty, six miles west of town. My informant told me the cowboy came out of the cabin, unsaddled the horses, an' turned them loose. Then he went back. It was rainin' an' cold. He'd likely stay in the cabin till daybreak. Then the two fellars rustled off in the dark. I heerd their horses. . . . Wal, I got up, dressed an' rustled out fer a posse. At thet hour, it wasn't easy. I had to take who I could get. It was near dawn when I'd collected ten men. Inskip come along on his own accord. I didn't want him. He heerd me wake his riders. He told them to saddle his hoss. . . . Wal, we rode out fast, an' arrived at the cabin jest at daybreak. The prisoner thar had jest stepped out the door. We held him up, took his gun an' what he had in his pockets. He was a cool one. I seen blood on his hand. I sent men inside to search the cabin. They found the dead man in the cabin an' fetched him out. It was Allen Neece. Thet was sure a surprise to me. His pockets was turned inside out. I heerd today thet Neece won a hundred dollars at faro the afternoon before he rode out of town. He was goin' to see some girl. . . . Wal, the prisoner hyar sure went white an' sick when the dead boy was carried out an' laid on the grass. A blind man could have seen thet he'd murdered him. We found one hoss, the prisoner's. An' Segel packed the dead boy in on his saddle. . . . All the way in I was debatin' on hangin' the murderer. An' when I got to it, this side of Twin Sombreros Ranch, Inskip crowded in front of us an' gave the cowboy a chance to grab his two guns. . . . We got held up pronto an' drove into town. An' I'm fer arrestin' Inskip——"

43

"When Surface called you back, what did he say?" interrupted Kiskadden.

"What?" queried Bodkin, disconcerted for the first time.

"Surface halted you at his ranch, then followed you an' stopped you. He drew you out of hearin' of yore men. This court is powerful interested in what Surface said."

"Wal—sir," exploded the deputy, his swarthy visage turning yellow. "He advised hangin' the cowboy right then an' thar. Said he distrusted this office. Too much red tape an' favor to Texans."

"Surface advised hangin' the prisoner without trial?"

"Yes, sir. An' I was just set to do it. Barsh had the rope around his neck when Inskip broke up the game."

"Thet will do, Bodkin," said the sheriff. "Doctor Williamson, will you please step forward an' make yore report."

A stout middle-aged man, with ruddy face, approached the desk.

"Mister Sheriff," he began, "and gentlemen. My fellow practitioner and I find that young Neece came to his violent death not later than the middle of the afternoon of day before yesterday. We find that death was caused by a compound fracture of the skull with consequent concussion of the brain. The bullet hole in his back was made long after he was dead. He had been roped and jerked heavily to the ground, probably from a horse."

"Thank you, Doctor," replied the sheriff. "Now, gentlemen, let me read you a telegram received heah this mawnin'. It is dated Latimer, Colorado, an' it reads: 'Sheriff Steve Kiskadden, Las Animas. The letter addressed to Brazos Keene was delivered to him in person at eight-ten o'clock day before yesterday morning. May fifth. Signed Postmaster John Hilton.'"

"Brazos Keene!" ejaculated Bodkin, as if the name stirred vague associations. A murmur ran through the standing crowd. But it was certain that Raine Surface had never heard the name.

"Yes, Brazos Keene," drawled the Texas sheriff, not without a dry satisfaction. "Gentlemen, you all know thet Latimer is a long way from Las Animas. Much too far for the hardest of hard-ridin' cowboys to get to the Hill

44

cabin in the afternoon—an' murder an' rob young Allen Neece. The letter Keene has in his possession absolutely clears him of any implication whatever in this tragedy. It was physically impossible for Brazos Keene to be there. What is more, Brazos Keene is not the breed of cowboy who would perpetrate such a cowardly job. For the benefit of those present who could not possibly have heard of Brazos Keene, an' further, to clear his name in every way this court has power, I suppose to heah from men who *do* know him. . . . Mr. Hutchinson, will you please step forward. I need hardly tell the courtroom who an' what Randolph Hutchinson is."

A stalwart man, long past sixty, yet erect and keen-eyed, stood out from the crowd.

"Mr. Sheriff an' fellow citizens," he said. "I have known Brazos Keene for years, in fact since his first trail trip up from Texas to Dodge City. He was a wild cowboy, as indeed all those boys had to be to survive those days. After that I gave him many an important job. Long after that time Brazos rode for the Ripple outfit at Don Carlos' Rancho. He often rode into Las Animas. I am sure many of our merchants and cattlemen will remember him, and join me in saying no finer, straighter, squarer cowboy than Brazos Keene ever straddled a horse in the interest of the honest cattle business of the range."

Next, without being called, a little wizen-faced, bright-eyed Mexican rushed to take Hutchinson's place.

"Mexican Joe—he know thees Señor Brazos Keene," he began, dramatically. "Joe run leetle restaurants here many years. Joe lend the moneys many times to thees cowboy. He ees always pay. One time he save my girl from the drunk hombres. Señor Brazos es un caballero grande!"

This eloquent tribute elicited a smile from many of the sober-faced spectators. Then the crowd parted to let out a stooped, gray, hawk-faced, bowlegged man who had grown bent and stiff in the saddle.

Brazos gave a violent start. "Hank Bilyen! . . . Aw, sheriff, don't let thet son-of-a-gun talk aboot me!" cried Brazos, appealingly.

"Howdy, Brazos," drawled Bilyen, as he hobbled up

to offer his hand. Brazos wrung it heartily. "Hank, you old geezer! I clean forgot aboot you."

"Wal, I ain't forgot you, cowboy, as you'll get a hunch pronto," replied Bilyen, stepping up to Kiskadden. "Sheriff, I take pleasure in accommodatin' you with some facts about this cowboy you've had the nerve to arrest."

"No, Hank, you've got it wrong," drawled Kiskadden. "My bright deputy arrested him. Keene rode in heah with the whole posse in front of him. An' he gave himself up for trial. I'll take it as a personal favor to me if you testify to yore estimate of him."

"Wal, gentlemen," said Bilyen, with a dry chuckle, as he faced the gaping crowd. "It jest occurs to me how orful long five years is. Fer it's been thet long since Brazos Keene used to give us somethin' to talk about round the campfires. An' in thet time the railroad has come, with many new people, an' most of the old-timers have passed on. So to most of you, Brazos Keene is a stranger. An' to the newcomers, like Surface an' Bodkin, an' the rest of you, I'd say you're lucky to see one of the real cowboys who made this range safe. Brazos Keene was one of Cap Britt's outfit. An' if thet means little to you, let me add thet Britt was Colonel Ripple's righthand man. An' Ripple was one of the greatest ranchers the West ever knew. Some years back, the Colonel fetched his daughter Holly Ripple up from the South, an' about thet time the bad men of the border concentrated in New Mexico from the Cimarron to Glorietta Pass. Britt had a hundred thousand steers. To hold them he got together the greatest outfit of riders ever runnin' fer one brand. Chisum's bunch wasn't a marker to Britt's. An' Brazos Keene was the leader of thet outfit. . . . It ill becomes a Westerner to speak of another's gun record. An' Brazos Keene might be offended. But I'll risk a little. He was the swiftest man with a gun, the fiercest in spirit, the most relentless tracker any of us old-timers ever knew. It was Keene's cunnin', his hound-scent on a trail, an' last, his skill with a gun thet broke up the associated bands of rustlers in New Mexico. Sewall McCoy—sure you've all heard his name—he was one of these rich, smooth, respectable, office-seekin', social-prominent cattlemen who behind all thet was the blackest, craftiest, bloodiest rustler baron we ever had out heah. McCoy believed dead cowboys told no tales. If he could not corrupt honest boys he had them ambushed an' shot. Brazos got this gentleman to rights—an' he killed him. . . . Also he killed Williams, another cattleman followin' in McCoy's tracks. An' he fetched the boss rustler Slaughter before McCoy—packin' him over a saddle, hanged before he was bored full of holes—an' he confronted Mr. McCoy with the little book thet rustler kept, an' he called McCoy all the turrible names the range ever heerd of. Exposed him before two outfits, dared him, cussed him to draw, an' killed him! . . . Thet, gentlemen, was only one of the little deals Brazos Keene is known by. . . . An' this is the Brazos Keene our clever deputy had the gall to arrest, an' our new neighbor Mr. Raine Surface, had the nerve to want hanged, an' our smart young citizen, one Barsh, had the—Gawd! I don't know what to call it, but for want of a better word I'll say insanity—this Barsh had the insanity to throw a noose around Brazos Keene's neck. . . . If I haven't lived all these last twenty years on the frontier in vain, if Hank Bilyen hasn't lost his sense of Western creed, an' his memory for historical facts—then it's a thousand to one thet Brazos Keene will find the murderer of Allen Neece, an' he'll get to the bottom of Mr. Surface's queer hankerin' to hang him—an' as for Bodkin an' Barsh— Wal! I ain't predictin' in these days of onsartin life, but I wouldn't be in their boots for a million dollars!"

Once in his life Brazos had stood for frank eulogy about himself and for blunt reference to his career. The crowd stood silent under Bilyen's harangue, and at the thundering end, it gave further proof of how the truth had sunk in, especially in the case of the cowering Barsh, the pallid sweating Bodkin, and the pale Surface.

Brazos wrestled up out of his seat. "Hank, old-timer, thet'll be aboot all," he drawled in his cool dry way. "If you think so doggone much of me as thet, stake me to a sack full of pesos, will yu? I'm broke an' it's shore embarrassin'."

"Come to the bank with me," replied Bilyen, grinning, shaken out of his passionate earnestness.

47

Kiskadden pounded on the table to stop the talking, laughing and shuffling of boots.

"This hearin' ain't quite over yet," he explained. "Brazos, I'm returnin' yore gun. . . . There! An' I'm apologizin' as a man if I cain't as a sheriff."

"Thanks, Kiskadden," replied Brazos, as he buckled on the heavy belt. "Gosh, thet's good! You know I sorta feel undressed withoot it. . . . Ahuh! Wal, I had a hunch. Some slick law-abidin' hombre took the shells oot. I'll just load up again—to be ready in case I meet any skunks in the street."

The humorous speech of the cowboy contrasted strangely with the singular dexterity with which he reloaded the weapon, and then rolled it in a flashing steely wheel. One of the onlookers burst into a nervous laugh, but the majority seemed fascinated by that action of Brazos'. On the frontier, the six-shooter was supreme, law or no law.

"Bodkin," called out the sheriff, drastically. "I never did cotton to you. How I ever hired you to represent me in this community is hard to explain an' impossible to swallow. But I reckon you was forced on my hands by Surface an' some of his Cattle Association friends. . . . You're the blunderin'est—not to say wuss—excuse for a deputy thet I ever seen. Why, down in Texas you'd last aboot as long as it took you to walk oot from yore appointment. An' my last official act as sheriff heah is to discharge you. Get oot! You're fired. It'd be a good idee for you an' Barsh to hide. . . . Open up there. Let 'em oot! . . . Now, gentlemen, the Brazos Keene hearin' is ended, an' I'm resignin' as sheriff."

A response approaching uproar succeeded this dramatic climax of the trial. Brazos caught a general disapproval in the assembly. There appeared to be immediate discord in the Cattlemen's Association. Kiskadden would not hear those who approached him to disclaim against the turn of affairs. He forced these men to follow the others out to the street. Brazos and Bilyen were left alone with the sheriff.

"Wal, mebbe I wasn't glad of a chance like thet!" he exclaimed, his face shining.

"Don't blame you. But the county will be hot over it," replied Bilyen.

"What yu got up yore sleeve, Texas Jack?" queried Brazos, shrewdly.

"I'll tell you later. Brazos, you ain't slopin' off, by any chance? . . . Haw! Haw! Excuse me. . . . Wal, I want to move oot. What you want done with thet fine bay hawse?"

"Doggone if I know."

"Tell you what," interposed Bilyen. "I'll send a boy over to fetch your hoss an' saddle to where I keep mine. Later I'll be takin' you out to meet my boss."

"An' who's he?"

"No less than Abe Neece—a grand old man, Brazos. I was his foreman at Twin Sombreros, an' after the crash, I jest couldn't leave him. Brazos, you'll be so sorry fer him thet you'll go gunnin' fer trouble."

"Will I? Doggone it! Oot of the fryin' pan into the fire! . . . At thet, I'm sorry enough now for these Neeces. Hank, it was like yu to stick. I kinda think yu're a real fellar."

At the door they were accosted by a lithe young man in rider's garb much the worse for wear. He had a clean-cut, youthful face, tanned by exposure, and fine eyes.

"I'd like to shake your hand, Keene," he said hesitatingly, but with a winning smile.

"Shore. An' who're yu?" returned Brazos, slowly, as he returned the smile. He was the easiest cowboy on the ranges to approach—when he happened to meet this type.

"Jack Sain. Hank knows me. I've been pretty friendly with the Neeces. Allen was my pard. It plumb busted me all up—what happened to him."

"Ahuh. Wal, I'm darned glad to meet yu, Jack."

"Brazos, it was Jack's friendship for the Neeces thet cost him his job. He rode fer Surface. You see there ain't any love lost between the Surfaces an' the Neeces."

"Wal, Jack, I'll be wantin' to hobnob with yu some," said Brazos, thoughtfully. "Where yu workin' now?"

"Nowhere. I can't get a job. Surface is strong in the association an' he's queered me."

"Doggone!" mused Brazos. "Thet's interestin'. Surface

'pears to be playin' a high hand around heah. . . . Jack, where can I find yu later in the afternoon?"

"Meet me at the Twin Sombreros Restaurant, up by the railroad station. About suppertime."

"Thet the place run by the Neece girls? Won't they be kinda nervous—seein' me?"

"Janis was with me in the sheriff's office. She slipped out just after Hank's speech. Before she went she said: 'Jack, I'd never believe that cowboy murdered Allen.' . . . Both the girls are dead game, Brazos, an' they'll be glad to see you."

"All right, Jack. I'll be there."

They parted, and Bilyen led Brazos slowly up the wide street. "Fine lad thet," Bilyen was saying. "Down on his luck now. I reckon he didn't tell you everythin'. Lura Surface was sweet on Jack. She throws herself at every fellar who strikes her fancy. But when Jack met June Neece, he went loco. You never seen a cowboy so deep in love. An' June leans to him a lot, though she's not a hell of a flirt at all like Janis."

"My Gawd! . . . Hank, is this a story yu're readin' me? The next think yu'll tell me these sisters will be pretty an' sweet an'—wal, Jack said they were daid game."

"Cowboy, wait till you see them."

"What am I gonna wait for? Tell me, man. An' then if it's bad news I can fork my hawse an' ride."

"It's good news, Brazos," replied Bilyen, soberly, taking him seriously. "June an' Jan Neece are the wonderfullest girls this range ever saw. Pretty! Hell, thet ain't no word! What's more they're sweet an' true—an' game? Say! . . . Old Abe developed thet ranch for them—sent them east to school to be educated—to do him proud. Ten years ago! They came back with trunks of stylish clothes an' crazy to make joy at Twin Sombreros. Only they never got there! Folks love these girls because they're unspoiled. An' when their fortunes fell, they went plumb to work."

"Hank, I reckon I better climb Bay an' race for Montana," declared Brazos, ruefully.

"Why, you darn fool?"

"Cause I have a turrible weakness."

"Haw! Haw! You haven't outgrowed thet. Wal, Brazos, I reckon it's on the cairds fer you to stay here."

"On the cairds? Hell, yes! They always run thet way for me. Same old—deal! If I've got any sense atall, I'll rustle."

"Since when did Brazos Keene grow selfish?" queried Bilyen, with subtle scorn.

"Selfish? Me! What's eatin' you, Hank Bilyen?"

"Think of thet pore murdered boy—an' his broken-hearted dad—an' them fine girls workin' from daylight to midnight."

"Thet's what I am thinkin' aboot!" protested Brazos.

Bilyen halted in front of a bank and spoke low in Brazos' ear. "They've lost their brother. An' the beautiful home thet was built fer them. Their father is dyin' of grief. . . . They've been cheated, robbed, ruined. . . . An' last, Brazos, young Allen Neece was givin' his time to ferretin' out the secret of thet ruin. *An' thet's why he was murdered!*"

Brazos leaned back against the rough stone wall of the bank and drew a deep breath, that whistled at the intake. His narrowed gaze fastened down the wide street, with its wagons and horses and busy sidewalks, out to the gray rangeland and the purple mountains. There was no use for him to rail at destiny or to try to run away from the inevitable. He pressed a steel-like hand against his breast where his precious letter lay in his pocket. He remembered.

"Shore, Hank, I savvy yu," he answered, with the old cool drawl. "Let's go in an' rob the bank. Then yu can take me oot to meet Abe Neece. An' after thet, I'll see the twins. . . . Doggone! Only yesterday or thereaboots, I was a friendless, grub-line ridin' cowboy. Funny aboot life! But it's worth livin'."

A few minutes later, Brazos stood outside the bank again, feeling a compact bulge in his pocket not altogether made by his precious letter.

"Hank, I only wanted a little money," expostulated Brazos. "How'n hell will I ever pay it back?"

"Holy mackerel, Brazos, ask me an easy one. But I know you will," rejoined Bilyen, with a laugh. "I can spare thet. Before I went to work fer Neece, I sold my herd to him, an' I've saved my money an' wages. Lucky I did. I'm takin' care of the old man now an' I lent the twins enough to start their restaurant."

"Wal, yu always was a good friend, Hank. Yu deserve to be a big rancher. . . . Say, who's this gazabo comin'?"

"Thet's Sam Mannin'. Still has his store down the street. Sure, you remember Sam."

"No, I shore wouldn't have known him," said Brazos. "Gosh, what a few years can do!"

A spare gray Westerner of venerable and kindly aspect came up to them, his lined face breaking into a smile.

"Hello, Brazos," he said, heartily, extending his hand. "I heard you were in town, but I didn't see any smoke. Glad to see you again. An' just about the same!"

"Howdy, Sam. It's just fine to shake yore hand. I'm gonna run in pronto an' buy oot yore store. Have you any of those red silk scarfs Louise used to sell me?"

"Plenty, cowboy. My store an' business have grown with the years."

"Thet's fine. An' how's Louise?"

"Married long ago, Brazos. She has two children."

"I'll be doggoned! You tell Louise Mannin' I swore she'd wait for me."

"I will. An' if I remember Louise in your day, she'll be fussed. Be sure to drop over. . . . How are you, Hank?"

"Wal, Sam, I was feelin' low till Brazos rode to town. Things will pick up now."

"I shouldn't wonder," responded Manning, wagging his gray head, and he passed on into the bank.

"Hank, let's duck down an alley, or somethin'. If I meet any more old friends I'll bust."

"Stand your ground, cowboy. I got to buy some grub. . . . Haw! Haw! Look who's spotted you. Has she got eyes? Aw no———"

"Save me, Hank. Who'n hell? I'll bet it's thet Surface girl."

"Right, Brazos. I'll duck in the store. Hope some of you'll be left when I come out."

Brazos had attention only for the stunningly handsome

52

and strikingly attired young woman who bore down upon him, face flushed and eyes alight. She was taller than she had appeared astride a horse, beautifully proportioned, and several years beyond her teens.

"I congratulate you, Mr. Brazos Keene," she said, graciously offering her hand. "I'm very glad indeed. It was a stupid blunder."

"Wal, thet's shore nice of yu, Miss Surface," replied Brazos, as he bowed bareheaded to take her hand. "Considerin' how keen yore father was to see me hanged, I'm more'n grateful to see yu wasn't."

"Oh, Dad is impossible," she declared, impatiently. "He seems to suspect every cowboy who rides in from the West. If one happens to come along from Kansas, he'll hire him."

"Shore does seem unreasonable an' hard on us Western riders," drawled Brazos, his gaze strong on her. "I was aboot to shake the dust of Las Animas. But now, I just reckon I'll hang around. Do you think I might get to see yu again?"

"You might," she replied, blushing very becomingly. "I'd like nothing better."

"But Mr. Surface wouldn't like it."

"I'm over twenty-one."

"Wal, you shore don't look it. . . . I wonder where I was all the time yu've been growin' up into such a lovely girl."

"I've wasted a good deal of it on cowboys less appreciative than you," she replied, accepting his nonchalant challenge with a dark flash in her green-blue eyes.

"Most cowboys air dumb. . . . When an' how can I see yu, Lura?"

"When do you want to, Brazos?" she returned, brightly, the red spots playing prettily in her cheeks.

"Wal, I want to right now. But I've got to go with Hank. Would tomorrow be too soon? I reckon I can wait thet long."

"I imagine you will find that long time very trying," she said, quizzically, watching him with amused wonder. Yet she had the soft light in her eyes that usually shone in women's eyes for Brazos.

53

"I'll just aboot die. . . . I'm afraid it happened to me oot at yore ranch the other day—when yu told yore father thet I never murdered Allen Neece."

"What happened?"

"I don't know what yet. But I felt powerful strange around heah," replied Brazos, putting his hand to his heart.

"You *are* sudden. . . . Brazos Keene, I believe all I've heard about you today, except that you were crooked."

"Wal, in thet case, I'll forgive yu."

"I'll bet it's true you've been a perfect devil with women."

"If havin' my heart broke a lot of times proves thet— wal, I'm guilty."

"There's Dad down the street," she returned, coolly. "Meet me tomorrow afternoon about three in the grove on the east bank of the brook that runs into the Purgatory about a mile out of town. Can you remember all that?"

"I'll be there," promised Brazos.

She rewarded him with a dazzling smile and swept on down the street.

"Brimstone an' chain lightnin'," soliloquized Brazos, watching the superb form depart. "Turrible took with herself. Crazy aboot men. An' I cain't savvy what else. But doggone it! I like her."

Bilyen emerged from the store burdened with bags, of which he gave Brazos a generous share.

"You look kinda sheepish," he observed. "I'd be some worried if I didn't know you was goin' to meet June Neece today."

"Yeah. An' why June if she's got a twin sister you cain't tell from her?"

"Oh, you can—if *they* help you. . . . I said June because she's warm. Janis got the nickname Jan, meanin' January. An' you ought to remember this range in winter."

"Jan cause she's cold an' June cause she's hot! Say, Hank, this plot is thickenin' too darn deep. Suppose *they* wouldn't tip a fellar off which one he happened to be makin'—to be talkin' to?"

"In thet case he'd be in deep, believe me."

They walked to a stable and corral on the outskirts of town, where Hank sent a boy after Brazos' horse and saddle. In due time, the two were riding out over country that brought thrilling memories to Brazos. And what interesting historical facts Brazos did not remember or never knew, Hank glibly supplied.

"Brazos, you should remember Fort Lyon. You once had a fight there, I reckon about seven years ago. Wal, there's the old fort. It was abandoned by the army two years ago. Kit Carson stayed there a good deal in the sixties, as also did Buffalo Bill, supplyin' buffalo meat to the fort. West of town about ten miles is the ruins of Fort William Bent, built by the Bent brothers in 1874, the same year I come to Las Animas. Them was the good old wild days, Brazos. When there was roundups of great cattle herds from the Panhandle, an' huge shipments of buffalo meat an' hides to the east. Wagon trains, prairie schooners, stage coaches. All gone—them days of romance!"

"Yeah? Wal, it strikes me *all* the romance an' *all* the wild days ain't gone. Look what's happened to me in two days!"

Bilyen had a little ten-acre ranch on the Purgatory. A gray shack faced the rocky, swift-running stream, and the splendid vista of plains to the south and the noble slopes of foothills rising to the Rockies on the west.

"I can set on my doorstep an' ketch trout," boasted Hank. "An' look at thet!"

"Wal, I reckon I'll buy this place from yu an' settle down," drawled Brazos, dreamily.

He was leaning over the rocky bank, still dreaming, when Hank came out of the shack accompanied by a man whose lean gray visage denoted the havoc of trouble if not of years. Brazos leaped erect, galvanized with an instinct in this meeting. It was to meet the penetrating gaze of tawny shadowed eyes.

"Howdy, Brazos Keene," was the man's greeting. "Hank has told me about you. I'm glad you were cleared of that trumped-up charge."

"Shore happy to meet you, Mr. Neece," responded Brazos, warmly.

"Cowboy, you've got the cut of my son Allen. . . . Only you're older—an' there's something proved about you. Allen was young, reckless, inexperienced."

"Let's set down on the bank heah. Nice view. I'm gonna buy this place from Hank."

"Have you met my twin girls?"

"Not yet. I've heahed all aboot them, though. An' I gotta hand it to them, Mr. Neece. I shore look forward to meetin' them."

Neece sighed and gazed out across the greening brakes and swales to the open range. He was not old, nor feeble, but it appeared plain that the shock of disaster had broken him.

"Brazos, is what Bilyen tells me true?" he queried presently, with an effort.

"Gosh, I'd trust Hank every way 'cept talkin' aboot me."

At this juncture Brazos fell from humor to earnestness, changed by the dark meaning fire in Hank's eye.

"Hank says you're goin' to stay here an' look into the deal we Neeces have had."

"I shore am. It looks queer to me," declared Brazos, realizing that he was not averse to being drawn into the Neece mystery.

"That's good of you, cowboy. But why do you interest yourself in our troubles? You never knew Allen. You have not met my girls. Surface, who ruined us, is at the head of the strong combine of cattlemen in east Colorado. You're takin' a large order on yourself."

"Wal, thet's easy to answer," declared Brazos, coolly. "Bodkin arrested me because he needed to hang the crime on somebody. He thought I was a stranger—a cowboy down on his luck. Surface wanted me hanged. For reasons I'm gonna find oot. If thet wasn't enough to rile Brazos Keene—wal, this rotten deal handed to yu an' yore three kids shore would be. Thet's all, Neece. I don't want to brag, but the ootfit chalked up some bad marks for themselves."

"You insinuate Surface is in some way connected with Bodkin?"

"Insinuate nothin'. I'm tellin' you, Mr. Neece. But did yu need to be told thet Surface doesn't ring true—thet Bodkin was a fourflush shady deputy sheriff? Wal, Kiskadden knew it an' he was damn glad thet I rode along to blow this ootfit up. Kiskadden resigned pronto."

"He did? Well!" ejaculated Neece, beginning to grow intense.

"I don't just savvy Kiskadden. Shore he's a Texan an' would have backed me to the throwin' of guns. I seen them in his desk. All easy to snatch! . . . But he's got somethin' up his sleeve beside the deal given me. Shore I reckon on surrenderin' to him——'

"Surrenderin'? I thought you were arrested an' jailed."

"Not exactly," drawled Brazos. "Bodkin an' his posse arrested me, shore. But when we rode into Las Animas an' up to the sheriff's office, I had thet posse in front of me, sittin' their saddles stiff."

"How, for heaven's sake?"

Brazos gave a brief account of the fray and how Inskip had helped him come out on top.

"Inskip? So he was in the posse. Brazos Keene, I note the real Westerners take to you."

"Wal, Kiskadden shore has somethin' up his sleeve beside takin' to me. . . . Neece, I have a letter thet cleared me of implication in the—the murder of yore son. It's from New Mexico. Now I read it to Kiskadden. An' I'm gonna read a little of it to yu an' Hank heah. When I ran into Surface, I hadn't even read that part of it, an' it came as a surprise to me. Yu air to keep mum aboot it, see?"

Brazos took out Holly's letter, carefully opened and smoothed and sorted the pages until he came to Renn Frayne's postscript. The passage that related to Surface he slowly and gravely read.

Neece showed that he still had flint in him to strike fire from. Manifestly deeply stirred, he controlled himself admirably and very probably found his real self for the first time since disaster and grief had overcome him.

"No coincidence! That was my herd. It was last seen on the Canadian."

"Wal, I had thet hunch myself. What yu think, Hank?"

"Brazos Keene! So you dropped out of the sky with thet letter? Same old Brazos! . . . By Gawd, I'm riled. I can see light an' it's red. Haw! Haw! There's some of us left. . . . Surface, the——"

"Cheese it, Hank," interposed Brazos. "You're turrible profane. An' after all it may be a pore steer. Only it cain't be! But we gotta be shore. My idee is thet Frayne has tipped me a hunch damn important to eastern Colorado. . . . Neece, I've heahed yore story from Hank. Just now, I only want to put one question. How an' when did yu lose thet money of Surface's yu got in Dodge?"

"Simple as a, b, c. I wanted cash. Got it, an' took it on the train in a satchel. The train was late. It didn't get into Las Animas till after midnight. Jerry, my stableboy, met me with the buckboard. We drove out toward the ranch. At the turn of the road, where the brook crosses an' the cottonwoods grow thick, I was held up by three men an' robbed."

"Ahuh. An' they shore knew where yu'd been an' what you had."

"You bet they did."

"Was there anythin' at all familiar aboot them?"

"No. Strangers. They wore masks. But I never forget a voice, once I hear it. One of the three had a young nervous high-pitched voice almost womanish. He called the burly man what sounded like 'Brad,' an' got cussed for doin' it. They were rough, tough range riders."

"Brad," echoed Brazos, with a wild leap of his pulse. "Was thet all you heahed?"

"Yes, One of them batted me on the head. Jerry is not well yet from the beatin' they gave him."

"Did yu ever tell thet you heahed the name Brad—spoke by a young nervous high-pitched voice?"

"Come to think of it, I don't believe I ever did except maybe to Allen. How about that, Hank?"

"You never told me."

"It must have slipped my mind after I told Allen. You excite me so it all comes back clear."

"Wal, thet's all I want to heah this time. I'll walk aboot a bit an' think. Then I'll ride back to town an' keep my appointment with Jack Sain. . . . Neece, do you like thet cowboy?"

"Jack Sain? Yes, I do, though I've only known him since the girls came home. He and Allen were friends, and . . ." Neece's voice broke.

"Ahuh. Wal, I liked him too. . . . Hank, I'll be heah in the mawnin'. An' Mr. Neece, don't get het up overly aboot this. I might be loco, but I swear we're on as black an' bloody a trail as I ever took up. So it behooves us to use our haids. Adios."

## Chapter Four

BRAZOS KEENE rode slowly into Las Animas, oblivious of the glorious red and gold sunset, and the numerous riders who passed by. He was still wrestling with that familiar old urge to ride away. Always the safest thing to do! Yet all the while he knew he had committed himself to a stern duty that could only end in bloodshed—all the while he admitted the damnable fascination of the intriguing tragedy of the Neeces. Nevertheless, he still wanted the flaming spark.

When he arrived at the railroad station it was near the supper hour. The restaurant he sought had more prominence than the station itself and had been remodeled from an old adobe building he had difficulty in remembering. A second story had been added and the whole given a coat of whitewash. The building, the location and the neat sign were all attractive. A hitching rail ran along in front. Brazos dismounted, still too soberly pondering his predicament to awake to the momentous meeting at hand. Tying Bay to the rail, he stalked with his clinking step into the restaurant, expecting to see the cowboy with whom he had an appointment. But Jack Sain was not there. So far as he could see at a moment's notice, the place was empty.

Brazos slid a long leg over the bench and leaning upon the counter, looked about him. The restaurant had windows on three sides. Evidently the entrance into the kitchen was through the other side. There appeared to be a double counter in the center with benches all around, and small tables with chairs next to windows. The inside of this new restaurant only added to the spotless white attractiveness of the outside.

"Doggone! This is shore a hash joint. Cowboys shore will stuff themselves heah. Wonder who runs——"

At this juncture, two things happened simultaneously —Brazos remembered the Neece twins, and a door opened to admit a girl. Brazos never figured out what gave him such a shock, but the fact was that never in his life before had any girl produced the effect this one had on him.

She was slight and graceful of form, fair-haired, but not blonde, and her face was white, sweet, sad. She had seen him before she entered and it struck Brazos she did not act like a waitress. She approached him, and putting her hands on the counter, she leaned forward. Her eyes were a tawny light brown. They engulfed Brazos. They searched his very soul. They appeared to Brazos to be the loveliest, saddest, most accusing eyes that ever shook the heart out of a poor cowboy. A long unfamiliar trouble suddenly fermented in Brazos' breast, but disturbing as it was, it was not so torturing as the fear her dark and troubled gaze aroused. Brazos was about to blurt out, to swear by heaven that he had not murdered Allen Neece.

"Brazos Keene," she affirmed.

"Wal, I—I was thet pore hombre when I come in heah," he said, fighting to smile, "but I cain't say now for shore."

"I am—June Neece," she returned, her low voice breaking a little.

"Aw, I wish I could say," floundered Brazos. He did not know what he wanted to say.

"We are sorry you were arrested and locked up on——"

"Thet was nothin' atall, Miss Neece," interrupted

Brazos, with unconscious pathos. "Shore I hardly ever ride into a town but somethin' like thet happens. I'm a marked man. . . . As for the cause this time, wal, I oughtn't to remind you aboot . . . but I swear to Gawd I'm innocent . . ."

"Don't," she interposed, earnestly. "If you had not been proved innocent, *I* would have known you were innocent." And she pressed a warm little hand in Brazos' upturned palm and left it there while she turned to call: "Jan, come here."

Then it appeared to the bewildered and thrilled cowboy that another June Neece walked into his heart. He was keen enough then to realize the nature of the malady that for once shunted aside his cool nonchalant self.

"Jan, this is he," said the first tawny-eyed vision to the second, and then to him, with a little smile: "My sister, Janis."

There was absolutely no telling these twin sisters apart. The one called Janis blushed and a bright glow suddenly burned out the shadow in her eyes.

"Brazos Keene? Oh, I am glad to meet you!" she exclaimed, and repeating her sister's action, she put her hand in his other as it lay on the counter.

"Wal, I shore am happy to meet yu-all," responded Brazos, coming to himself. There they stood, these unfortunate twins, holding his hands. It was a beautiful wonderful fact. Two pairs of tawny eyes instead of one pair gazed up at him with a soft warm light of faith, of sympathy. That was the moment Brazos Keene had wanted; that was the spark which set him afire.

Brazos enfolded both of these little white hands in his own hard ones and held them tight. "June an' Janis," he said, intensely. "I didn't just happen to ride along heah. There's somethin' back of it. I've met yore friend Jack Sain. Hank Bilyen is an old pard of mine. He took me oot to meet yore Dad. An' I've heahed yore story."

"Oh, I hope Dad was not unjust to you," interposed June. "He's so strange—so dazed——"

"Yore father is a fine man—a real Westerner. He's not old or broken. Only down, heartbroken under these

61

blows. . . . Would it make yu glad, girls, to know he shore wasn't strange or dazed when I left him?"

"Oh!" cried June.

"Brazos Keene! We've heard all about you," cried Janis. "We wouldn't wonder at anything. But if you woke Dad out of his lethargy—if you roused his old fighting spirit— cheered him a little, as Allen tried so hard to do and couldn't do. . . . Oh, Brazos Keene, June and I will worship you!"

"Wal, it looks like I done thet already—so yu may just begin thet worshipin' right heah," drawled Brazos, with the slow smile that so transformed him.

"You have!" they cried, in unison.

"I told yore Dad I was pretty shore aboot what had become of the herd of Texas longhorns he sold to Surface, but lost on the trail north."

"Oh, are you sure?" entreated Janis, squeezing his hand. June gazed at him mutely, as if he were a phenomenon too good to be true.

"Wal, I'd gamble on it."

"That is what Allen was trying to find out. He confided in me."

"Ahuh. Then yore brother was workin' on this deal?" rejoined Brazos ponderingly.

"Allen swore he'd never rest until he'd got our—our Twin Sombreros Ranch back again," answered Janis, with tears brimming her eyes.

Brazos succumbed to the moment, realizing its inevitableness, and that perhaps he was swearing away his life. But the bewitching nearness of these girls, the sense of a great part he had been destined to play in their lives, magnified all his old spirit to do, his reckless disregard of self. He drew the girls closer over the counter, while he flashed a wary look around.

"Listen," he whispered. "An' keep this secret in yore pretty haids. . . . I'm gonna track down the murderers of yore brother—an' kill them! An' what's more, I'm gonna run Surface oot of the ranch he stole from yore Dad an' put yu back there!"

Brazos, inspired by what he felt and much he could not understand, had exaggerated hope, daring, resolve.

Once spoken aloud, the pledge seemed outrageous. But the girls gave him no reprieve, no chance to make provisions. They took him intensely, with deadly earnest, their faces paling to pearl hue and their eyes dilating. He might have been looking at just one girl, so incredibly similar were they. Neece's daughters were new to the West, but they were part of it. They had been east long enough to share the tenderfoot's glamorous regard for a cowbow desperado, but were Western enough not to doubt or fear it.

The street door banged, interrupting whatever eloquent acceptance appeared to tremble on the sweet lips of the Neece twins. Jack Sain came tramping in, his sleepy eyes alight, his smile infectious.

"Howdy, Brazos. I see you've got acquainted without my help," he remarked, as the girls withdrew their hands from Brazos' grip.

"Jack, we introduced ourselves all around," replied Janis, gayly. June was silent, though she smiled at the young man.

"Wal, Sain, heah yu air, an' I clean forgot yu," drawled Brazos. "Yes, I've met yore friends an' am I glad? I've been tellin' them what tough luck I'd been playin' in not to be heah long ago. An' thet I'd shore make up for it."

"Jack, this Brazos cowboy is not so slow," said Janis, teasingly.

"Slow! Never in this world could you apply that word to Brazos Keene. I see he's perked you up already. An' I'm darned glad."

"Wal, I'm kinda glad myself," said Brazos.

"Let's get our order in before the gang comes rollin' along," suggested Sain.

"Order? Gang? Say, am I loco?" ejaculated Brazos, mildly.

"You are, an' it tickles me. I'll bet you couldn't ask June or Jan to serve you ham an' eggs—not to save your life."

"Ham an' eggs? Wal, I'll be doggoned! No, I cain't."

"Boys, what will you have?" asked one of the twins. The other had turned to the vanguard of hungry visitors now flocking from all directions.

"Aw, air you June or Janis?" queried Brazos, helplessly.

"Never mind. Either of us can serve you. But hurry. We will be swamped soon."

"I was starvin' to death when I come in, but now I cain't eat," declared Brazos, eloquently.

"Ha! Ha! Didn't I have a hunch?" laughed Sain, evidently delighted at something not apparent to Brazos. "I'll order double. Steak medium, mashed potatoes an' gravy, bread an' butter, coffee. . . . An' tell that Mexican cook Billy the Kid is out here."

While the restaurant rapidly filled with a crowd of various types and the young waitresses flitted to and fro from customers to kitchen and back again Brazos listened to his voluble friend and eagerly watched for June without any hope whatever of being able to tell which of the twins really was June.

When, however, Sain gave Brazos a dig in the ribs with his elbow, Brazos came out of his trance.

"Say, cowboy, go easy. I've been pitched off hawses too often to have ribs of iron."

"Look behind you—at thet handsome dressed-up dude rancher," whispered Sain. "At the table."

"Ahuh. Wal . . ." replied Brazos, leisurely complying. "Kinda spick an' span, at thet. But he's got a nice face. Who is he?"

"Henry Sisk, an' he has a nice face I'm bound to admit. Too damn nice! Women like him a heap."

"Don't blame them. How aboot June an' Janis heah?"

"June couldn't see him with a telescope. But I got a hunch Jan likes him. Anyway, it's Jan he 'pears to be courtin' ."

"How'n hell does he know which one he's courtin'?"

"He doesn't, unless they tell him, you can bet your roll on thet."

"How do yu tell, cowboy?" asked Brazos.

Sain reddened perceptibly, but was not ashamed of it. "I don't. Only the girls are decent enough to give me a hunch."

"Gosh! What'd yu do if they didn't steer yu?"

"Brazos, I'd be a plumb crazy cowboy, believe me. But

don't get a wrong notion. Both June an' Janis have been friendly to me. Thet's all. I never even had nerve enough to hold June's hand. They're not the flirtin' kind, Brazos."

"So I see. Wal, how aboot this Henry Sisk? Is he a decent hombre?"

"Yes. I'm jealous, I reckon. Henry is young, good-lookin', rich, an' a fine fellow."

"Wal, I'll see if *I* approve of him," drawled Brazos, coolly, as he swung sidewise over the bench. "Jack, yu order apple pie an' milk for me, if yu get a chance."

Brazos gave his heavy belt a hitch and took several slow strides over to the table where young Sisk sat, glowering at no one in particular. His frank face and dark eyes impressed Brazos favorably.

"Howdy, Sisk," said Brazos. "My pard heah told me who yu air. I'm Brazos Keene."

"How do. I saw you when I came in," returned the young rancher, not exactly incivilly though certainly awkwardly. He was surprised and aghast. But he put out a hand willingly enough.

"I'm wonderin' if yu need a rider," replied Brazos, after the grip.

"I always need a rider who can work."

"Doggone! Work isn't my long suit," drawled Brazos, with his captivating smile. "I cain't rope very wal, an' I'm no good atall at most cowboy jobs, an' I'd just starve before I'd dig fence-post holes. . . . But if I do say it myself, I'm pretty fair with guns."

"Brazos, you're that thing impossible to find—a modest cowboy," said Sisk, laughing. "If you're serious, ride out to see me."

"Thanks, I'll do thet some day," concluded Brazos, and returned to his seat beside young Sain. That worthy gave Brazos an inquiring look. At this moment one of the girls brought a generous golden slice of apple pie and a large glass of creamy milk. Brazos stared from these to the charming waitress.

"Do my pore eyes deceive me?"

"Didn't you order apple pie and milk?" she asked, regretfully.

"I shore did. But I never even dreamed of such pie an' milk. Will yu duplicate the order, Miss Janis?"

Brazos found his favorite dessert and drink even more delicious than they looked. Both had disappeared as if by magic when the girl returned to set another plate of pie and brimming glass of milk before him.

"Miss Janis, all I want to know is can I come in heah as often as I want an' get a gorgeous supper like what I've had?" asked Brazos, most impressively.

"Why, certainly—so long as you pay for it," she replied, trying to keep her face straight.

"But I'm broke a good deal. Money slips right through my fingers."

"This is a strictly cash business, Mr. Keene," she said, demurely.

"Mexican Joe trusts me," importuned Brazos. "Aw, Miss Janis, I shore wouldn't want to be exclooded from this heah lovely place just on account of bein' financially embarrassed now an' then."

"Have you any references as to—to good credit and character?" she asked, mischievously. "If you will bring these, we shall be glad to trust you. . . . And by the way, I am not Janis, but June."

"Help!" prayed Brazos, fervently, throwing up his hands.

Sain had heard this byplay, and he was all grin. "There ain't any help," he said.

"What's a fellow gonna do?" implored Brazos, honestly aghast at an unparalleled situation.

"I reckon the only thing a fellar can do is impossible," returned Sain, sagely, from which cryptic remark Brazos gathered no solace. They finished their dessert and had to wait to pay their bill. "Wal, June," said Brazos, taking a chance on this sister and apparently hitting it right, "how much do we owe for thet scrumptious supper—an' do we have to stand around on the corner ootside till mawnin' to see yu again?"

"Dollar eighty," replied June, as she took the bill he extended. "Twenty! Yes, you're broke."

"Gosh, is thet a twenty?"

While June went to get change, Brazos saw Janis carry a tray to Sisk's table. There was no trouble in ascertaining the state of that young man's mind. Janis might have been in the solitude of the outside prairie for all he cared. He raised a strong earnest appealing face to the girl. And when she had set the several dishes before him, Brazos' sharp eye caught him plucking at her hand. Janis smiled down upon him, but shook her head and left him.

"Heah you air, Mister Brazos Keene," drawled June at Brazos' elbow. She imitated his Texas accent perfectly, and did it with a straight face. Brazos held out his hand to take the change.

"Say, Lady, I've handled girls turrible rough for less than thet," he said.

"Pooh! . . . There's your change. I hope you will become a good customer."

"June, I'll eat myself to death," he rejoined, softly. "When can I see yu again?"

"Breakfast time."

"But listen. There's nothin' for me to do heah. Only the saloons an' cairds. An' yu know, I'm Brazos Keene, doggone it! There's always some hombre layin' to shoot me in the back."

That was a happy lead for the cunning Brazos to take. It was no falsehood and he had worked it often. June's eyes dilated. She gazed up at him, unconscious that she had already taken possession of him.

"We are off at ten. I'd like you to meet my aunt. She is Dad's sister, and lives with us upstairs."

"Thet's just fine. I'll come."

"Jack, you'll come, too?"

"I'm sorry, June. I can't tonight."

When they got outside and Brazos went to the hitching rail to untie Bay, he glanced back into the restaurant. June still stood there, as if alone in the crowded room, her big eyes dark upon him. They made Brazos' heart leap, and then they sobered him out of selfish exultation. Had he misled this girl and her sister to hope vainly? He cursed himself for a reckless cowboy.

"Jack, where's yore hawse?" he asked, gruffly.

"I don't own one."

"Hell! A cowboy without a hawse! . . . We gotta remedy thet. I'll get one from Hank. Where yu live?"

"Out of town. Not far," replied Sain, evasively.

"It was doggone good to meet you, Jack. I kinda like yu," said Brazos, as he tightened his cinch. "We gotta see a lot of each other."

"Well, cowboy, if you have ever been withoot a job or a hoss or a friend, you'll know how I feel," rejoined Sain, and bidding Brazos good night, he strode away up the dimly lighted street.

"Wal. Thet boy's in trouble more'n aboot a girl," soliloquized Brazos, as he swung up on Bay. "Doggone it, there's nothin' but trouble in this world. Heah I am deep in again an' lovin' it!"

Brazos rode out to the stable where Bilyen kept his horse while in town, and turning Bay over to the boy there, he drifted slowly up the street. Brazos could never control his heart but he had long been absolute master over his mind. And it behooved him to relegate this sweet insidious emotion to the background and begin cudgeling his brains.

The main street of Las Animas had always boasted of its numerous saloons, gambling dens and dance halls. These did not appear to be so numerous or so prosperous as during the cattle drives of 1874 and later, but there were plenty left, Brazos thought, and some as disreputable looking as they had ever been.

Brazos strolled up one side of the long wide street and down on the other. It took him just the half-hour required for this walk to decide on his line of procedure. After all, it seemed to Brazos, vital things were decided for him. With how many thousand crooked men had he rubbed elbows? What was it that made him gravitate toward the crux of a situation? Brazos asked himself many questions that he never answered. He had a supreme faith in something that led him on. All he had to do was to ride the range, and walk this wide street of Las Animas, and hang around the drinking dives and gambling dens, and the stores and corners. Watching and listening had become second nature with Brazos. When he got a scent he would track it like a hound. Allen Neece had been murdered. His father had been robbed. These black deeds seemed bracketed together. There had been a plot against the Neeces, whether simple or complex Brazos had not clarified in his mind. On the moment it looked pretty simple to Brazos. All he had to do was to find a man named Brad or Bard and a companion with a high-pitched nervous voice. That might happen any time, but Brazos did not delude himself. A rotten deal like this would have many little clues, all leading to the main issue, which was the theft of cattle on a gigantic scale.

At length, Brazos entered a saloon named Happy Days, which was a new one to him. But the garish furnishings, the noisy drinkers and the smell of rum were far from unfamiliar. The hour was too early for the gamesters. Brazos' entrance did not appear to be noted, but though he held aloof from bar and guests, he was seen and recognized. He did not need to pretend that he was looking for someone. He actually was, though he did not know whom, and his presence had a quieting effect upon the inmates.

From this place he passed along the street taking in the several saloons. Returning on the opposite side, he entered the Call You gambling den, a house that had once been pretentious and patronized by the range elect, but which now was the most sordid he had seen. He found the bar crowded and the gaming tables mostly occupied. At one sat a gambler who would have attracted a less keen eye than Brazos'. His pale cold face, enhanced by his dark frock coat, drew attention to himself in a saloon full of range-garbed men. He espied Brazos not many seconds after Brazos singled him out. His glance held more than the cold curiosity of the gambler. Brazos accosted a cowboy on the way out.

"Say, bud, who's the cairdsharp?" he asked.

"Reckon they're all sharps in this camp. . . . Thet's Howard."

"Where does he hail from?"

"Denver, they say."

"Howard. . . . Is he the only flash gambler hereaboots?"

"You don't see many like him. An' he drops in from the train pretty often."

"I'm a stranger heah," explained Brazos.

"Wal, if you wasn't you wouldn't be askin' questions about Howard."

"Yeah? An' why not?"

"He ain't partial to curiosity."

"Aw, I see. Ladies' man, huh?"

"Cowboy, he's a killer in more ways than one. Haw! Haw!"

Brazos strolled unobtrusively around until he reached a point behind Howard. The gambler sat at a table with three cowboys, playing poker, and he appeared to be ahead of the game.

"Excuse me, but I object to any one standing behind me," presently spoke up the gambler, politely.

"Wal, thet's no wonder," drawled Brazos. "I'll go around on this side."

"What you hintin' at, cowboy?" growled one of the three youths at the table, gazing irritably up at Brazos.

"Gosh, I wasn't hintin'."

"Hell you wasn't. You better——"

"Shut up, before you say somethin'," fiercely interrupted the player next to the disgruntled one. "Don't you have no idee who you're talkin' to?"

After that the three cowboys were apparently blind to Brazos' presence, but the gambler was not, though he did not look up directly. Brazos watched him steadily, studied his features, his frock coat, his white, wonderfully dexterous hands. At length the gambler queried sarcastically:

"Don't you want to sit in?"

"Game's too slow for me."

"You appear mighty interested in watching it. I must ask you to sit in or get out."

"Wal, I'll tell you, mister," replied Brazos. "I'd like to join yu, but it sorta riles me to play cairds with a cairdsharp when he's got a little gun hid high up under his coat on the left side."

The gambler dropped his cards, and his hand quivered while his eyes blazed cold fury upon Brazos.

"Careful, Howard," interposed the eldest of the three cowboys. "Don't be crazy enough to draw on thet fellar."

70

"Who is he?" snapped the gambler, perceptibly relaxing.

"Wal, I ain't sayin'. He might be Billy the Kid."

"Brazos Keene's my name, if you want to know," said Brazos.

At this juncture, the losing member of the cowboy triangle leaped up, red of face, to slam his cards down on the table. "Whoever he is, he's busted up this game," he said.

"An' a damn good thing," agreed the third.

They abruptly left the gambler sitting alone. He raked in the few chips and little silver that his fellow players had abandoned. It was obvious that the presence of Brazos and the attention thus attracted to himself were distinctly unwelcome.

"Brazos Keene, eh?" he queried at length, sitting back to flash brilliant icy eyes upon Brazos.

"Yeah. An' I heahed one of yore victims call you Howard."

"That's my name," replied the gambler, curtly.

"From up Denver way, I heah?"

"Where I hail from and what I do doesn't concern you, cowboy."

"Wal, I'm not so damn shore aboot the last."

"Were those fellows friends of yours?"

"Never saw them before. It was the way yu hide the little derringer gun thet riled me. I just naturally get cussed when I see thet kind of gun-packin'."

"So you broke up my game."

"I didn't intend to do thet. Yu talked powerful sarcastic, so I thought I'd call yu an' see if yu'd throw yore toy pistol," drawled Brazos, with glinting eyes that did not match his soft voice.

The gambler's face turned a shade grayer, either from anger or realization of what he had escaped.

"Curiosity has cost many men their lives."

"Shore. But not men like me. An' now I'll tell yu thet I had another reason for tryin' yu oot."

"I had a hunch you did. And what is it, Mister Keene?"

Brazos leaned close to the thin-lipped cold face and answered low:

71

"Ask Lura Surface."

It was a random shot that Brazos hazarded, but it went home. Howard growled his surprise and wrath, and turning on his heel strode by the watching line of curious men to the bar, where he ordered whisky.

Brazos backed against the wall and leaned there. He kept a narrowed gaze upon the gambler until he left the saloon. From sundry remarks which came to Brazos' ears he gathered that he had not hurt his status there by offending Howard. Brazos pondered over the amaze and rancor Howard had evidenced. Indeed there must be something between Lura Surface and this handsome cardsharp who secreted a small gun in his breast pocket where he could snatch it swiftly. Something that probably was to Miss Surface's discredit. Brazos had nothing against her. He really liked her for her defense of him. Nevertheless, in his cunning speculative mind she was being relegated to a place where she could not be considered with feeling. Brazos decided, however, to give her the benefit of a doubt.

A little before ten o'clock, Brazos wended a reluctant and yet impelled way toward the Twin Sombreros Restaurant. He could not have resisted the urge if he had wanted to. And he fought off the presage of calamity. When he arrived at the corner, he espied one of the twins talking to Henry Sisk. Indeed the two were arguing if not actually quarreling, from which fact Brazos deduced that this was Janis. There appeared to be several customers who were being waited upon by a Mexican girl.

Brazos mounted the side stairway leading up to the second story and knocked on the door, sure of the trepidation and another nameless sensation obsessing him. The door opened as if someone had heard his step outside. June stood there, in a white dress that had never been made in Las Animas. This apparition smiled upon him and Brazos dated his abject enthrallment from that moment. As always with him, when a thing was settled, inevitable, he found his cool easy poise.

"Evenin', Miss June. I reckon I'm ahaid of time," he said.

"No. You are late. Come in."

She ushered Brazos into a cosy bright little sitting room.

72

"Aunte, this is our new-found friend, Mr. Brazos Keene," she said to a gray-haired woman who sat beside the lamp table. "My Aunt Mattie, Miss Neece—Daddy's sister."

Brazos made the lady a recipient of his most gallant bow and pleasantest smile. "I shore am glad to meet yu, Miss Neece," he drawled, as he bent to take the hand she hesitatingly offered. "Yu favor yore brother an' I'd have known yu."

"For the land's sake! . . . June, this nice-looking boy can't be your terrible Brazos Keene," exclaimed the aunt.

"Yes, he is, Auntie."

"Aw, Miss Neece, don't believe everythin' yu heah," implored Brazos, honestly. "I'm not turrible atall."

"I don't believe you are. I'm glad to meet you. Janis filled my old head with nonsense. Said you were a black-browed giant—very fierce to see."

"Air yu shore it was Janis?" inquired Brazos.

"Yes, indeed. June has been telling me the . . . well, I'll not give her away. But your ears must have burned. . . . Take his hat, June. . . . And hadn't you better lay aside that cumbersome gun?"

"Wal, Lady, I wouldn't feel dressed proper if I did thet. . . . There, I'll slip it around so you cain't see it."

"Thank you, I—I guess that's better," she replied, rising. "Mr. Keene, you met my brother Abraham?"

"I did, an' I shore like him."

"June tells me you cheered him up," she went on, in hurried earnestness. "And Dave Wesley called on me this afternoon. He had just ridden by Bilyen's ranch. He said he had not seen my brother so near like his old self. Oh, if you are responsible for that, I thank you."

"Lady, I'm afraid I am responsible," rejoined Brazos, seriously. "An' I shore hope I didn't overdo it."

"Have you any ground to believe Abraham's loss can be retrieved?" she asked, beseechingly.

"I cain't explain. It's what a cowboy calls a hunch. I've trailed up a good many of my hunches an' never lost oot on one yet."

"Only a hunch! Oh, I had prayed you might have really learned something," she returned, sadly.

"Miss Neece, I cain't talk aboot it now. All I can say is for yu to go on hopin' and prayin', too."

"Perhaps Abraham will tell me. I'll see him tomorrow. Good night, Mr. Brazos Keene. Somehow you inspire me strangely. . . . June, I'll leave you young folks alone. Good night, dear."

Brazos found himself alone with June Neece; and his five endless years of wandering for he knew not what were as if they had never been.

"You must understand Auntie, and Jan and me," said June, gravely. "It is not the loss of Dad's fortune, and Twin Sombreros Ranch that hurts so terribly. It was Dad's broken heart. All these years he had worked for us. The blow crushed him. And he was sinking under it. . . . Then Allen's sudden ghastly death . . ."

Her face was white and her big eyes shone darkly tragic up at him.

"Never mind, June," interposed Brazos, feelingly. "I reckon I understand. It's hard. But you must bear up. . . . I've had my grief. An' I'm a livin' proof thet grief passes—an' thet joy an' hope come back."

"You have had trouble?" she asked, softly.

"For five years I've been a driven cowboy . . . an' my trouble came to an end today—when I met yu."

"Me? . . . Oh!" She warmed wonderingly to that. "Tell me your story."

"Some day, when I reckon I dare."

They stood by the table, with glances locked, and constraint overcoming the simplicity of that meeting. June turned away with a blush, only to be drawn again to look at him, as if to make sure the situation was real.

"Brazos Keene! . . . To think I'm alone with *him!* Oh, I've heard who and what you are. It has been on the lips of everybody all day long."

"Wal, I hope it's goin' to be good for yu thet I am Brazos Keene," returned he, mournfully. "But maybe if I was Henry Sisk or Jack Sain I would have more chance for you to like me."

"Brazos, don't be hurt," she said, hurriedly, and put an appealing hand on his arm. "I'm glad. I've always dreamed I'd . . ." she broke off, blushing. "I'm Western,

74

you know. And I saw a good deal of the life here before Dad sent me away to school. I've a weakness for—for desperadoes. So has Janis. . . . Only it seems so strange to be with you—to *know*. Who would ever take you for—what they call you? No wonder Auntie could not believe her eyes! You do not look it."

"Wal, what do I look, then?" he queried, a little gruffly, for once weakening to permit discussion of this delicate subject.

"I haven't really dared to look at you—close," she rejoined, shyly. "Come here, your back is to the light. . . . There. Brazos, at the risk of seeming a flatterer like Lura Surface, I must say you're a stunning-looking cowboy. You've a clean tanned, boyish, handsome face—nice curly hair almost blond, the kind any girl would like to run her fingers through. . . . Oh, Brazos! It's a little gray over your temples! . . . And your eyes take something from your winning smile and soft Southern drawl."

"My Gawd, June, you must have kissed the blarney stone. Now, what's wrong with my eyes?"

"Nothing. Janis said they were gray. Now I see they're blue. You're making sheep's eyes at me now, Brazos Keene. But you can't fool me. Those eyes could be terrible."

"Could they? But I'm comin' back at yu, June Neece. There's nothin' wrong with yu atall. An' to say yu're the prettiest girl I ever saw in my life isn't sayin' what I mean. I reckon it's the class yu was born with an' somethin' yu got away at school."

"We' *are* getting on," she replied, demurely.

"Yu mean we're gettin' some place where I've no right to be?"

"Come sit here," she returned, and led him to a little sofa in the corner. They gazed at each other again, questioningly, yet with no hint of doubt or uncertainty. There was something vital, compelling, drawing, that made no allowance for short acquaintance.

"June, I'm gonna be honest. Meetin' yu has thrown me plumb oot of my saddle."

"It means much to me, Brazos—I don't know what."

75

"Yu're countin' on yore hopes of what I can do for yore Dad?"

"Yes. But if we were out home—at Twin Sombreros— and if we had not trouble—I—think I would feel the same."

"Girl, yu cain't be in love with Jack Sain?"

"Who said I was?" she answered, smiling. "I like Jack. We played together when we were kids."

"Wal, I was afraid—I reckon I thought yu might care more'n thet. Jack is crazy aboot yu, which is no wonder."

"I'm sorry, Brazos. But I didn't flirt with him as Jan did with Henry Sisk. I'm sorry for Jack in more ways than one. He has had one misfortune after another. And the last is too bad. He had just found a good job after being idle for months, then lost it."

"How'd he lose it?"

"Al said he was running after Lura Surface. Her father caught them meeting on the road one night. He raised Cain and had Jack discharged."

"Ahuh. The Surfaces don't mix up in this thing— Aw, no, not atall. . . . June, I'm gonna meet thet young lady oot along the road, tomorrow afternoon. But I'm not runnin' after her."

"Already! You? I thought you might be one man proof——"

Brazos took June's hands in his and bent to interrupt her.

"Listen, June. If I hadn't met yu, I'd have flirted with Lura Surface. But I have met yu—an' thet's all the difference in the world. . . . Raine Surface is one of these respectable crooked cattlemen. I've met a few like him— to their sorrow, an' my idee in meetin' this girl is to get at things. Thet's my way, June. I cain't explain. But I follow my hunches. Please believe me, June."

"They said you *were* a devil with the women," retorted June, unconscious of jealousy.

"Never mind what I was. It's what I am now thet should count with yu. Trust me, June."

"It's none of my business," said June, distantly, her face averted.

Brazos gave her a little shake and pulled her closer,

76

scarcely master of himself under the sweet and bewildering feelings she had betrayed. She had made no attempt to withdraw her hands, and when he drew her so close that her cheek brushed his shoulder still she did not repulse him.

"June, it's all yore business. If yu won't trust me aboot this Surface girl I'll never go near her. An' by thet we might lose time. For Lura Surface, withoot knowin', will give me hunches."

"But she hates Jan an' me," declared June, with heat. "Jan hates her—and I'm going to hate her."

"Why does Janis hate her?"

"She made a fool out of Allen. That happened before we came home."

"Was Allen in love with her?"

"Yes."

"Wal, thet lady 'pears to have a trade rat's instinct to collect—only she doesn't trade."

"There you're wrong, Brazos. She does trade—if you mean kiss for kiss, and all that."

"How do yu know?"

"Women don't have to be told such things. We just know."

"Ahuh," rejoined Brazos. He was thrillingly aware of June resting her cheek ever so slightly against his shoulder, and yearned to prolong the disturbing contact.

"Jan and I tried to be decent to Lura Surface," went on June. "We didn't hold anything against her because she lived in our home. And she is pretty and fascinating, even to girls. But she stuck up her nose at us. One day she came into the restaurant with Henry Sisk. Jan and I ignored them. Would not wait upon them. Then Henry came to the counter and wanted to know why he could not get any service. It was Jan he approached. And did Jan tell him? Right then and there Lura Surface lost him."

"A handsome cat," muttered Brazos, to himself.

"It's catty of *me*—to talk this way," replied June, turning to face Brazos. "But, Brazos, think of my—of our side of it. Jan and I have been deeply hurt by Lura Surface. But we have been taking our medicine, as Westerners say.

Here *you* come along and fill me—us—with some new wild hope. Suppose *you* . . . Oh, I wouldn't say it."

"June, yu'd hate me, I reckon. An' shore with reason. But isn't this because of the new hope thet I may be able to help yore Dad?"

"Yes. Yet it's only fair to tell you that's not the only reason." She had paled again and her eyes were eloquent.

Brazos dared not ask that reason. The sweeter she grew, the more restraint he put upon himself. Then June withdrew her hands.

"We are talking like old friends. I declare I don't quite recognize myself," said June, with a nervous laugh, trying to throw off the spell. "I wouldn't want you to think *any* cowboy could hold my hands and—and——"

"Wal, I wouldn't," interposed Brazos, smiling. "Shore yu've been sweet an' gracious. Yu make me proud, June. An' I'm askin' yu. Yore brother Allen was a cowboy. Now if he'd swore on his honor, wouldn't yu have trusted him?"

"Indeed I would have, Brazos. Allen didn't make many promises, but you could rely on him."

"Wal, I'm like Allen, June. I give yu my word. An' if yu won't take it, I'll be hurt powerful deep."

"Your word for what?" she flashed, dark eyes bright and solemn on his.

"To fight yore Dad's battle. . . . June, thet means, in the first place, workin' every way to find things oot. An' if I pretend to be loco about Lura Surface, an' to drink an' gamble aboot town, or to do *anythin'*—yu gotta know I'm playin' a deep game. I'll be one lyin' deceitful hombre. To all but yu, June!"

"Oh, I wouldn't want Dad to think——"

"I couldn't fool Hank Bilyen, an' he'll explain to Neece. I reckon Kiskadden will savvy, too. An' thet Texan will help me, June. . . . Give me a free rein, girl."

"Is it so—so personal, Brazos?" she inquired, wistfully. "Wouldn't you help Dad to get his property back even if there were no June Neece?"

"I shore would. But there *is* a June Neece. An' I've—I'm gonna fall powerful hard in thet quarter. Don't let thet worry yu. It'll be an anchor for me."

"How could I help worry? Suppose by some miracle

you reinstated Dad at Twin Sombreros Ranch. What would you ask of me?"

"Nothin', June. Yu've already paid me for thet."

"How?"

"Why—by bein' so sweet an'—an' all. I feel what I mean, but cain't explain. . . . An' June, yu forget I'm Brazos Keene—gunman an' killer."

"Oh, you're either the most wonderful fellow in the world—or the most brazen devil," she exclaimed, in a quandary.

"June, I'm shore not the first."

"Yes, you are, Brazos, I don't care what you've been," she declared suddenly glowing. "I don't do things by halves. I'll believe in you, Brazos Keene."

Brazos put his hand inside his vest and took out his precious letter.

"June, shore thet'll be aboot all." Brazos' drawl could not entirely subdue the emotion in his voice. "Another girl believed in me once. I helped her all I could, but I failed her in thet I never lived up to what she thought me. . . . I want yu to read this letter from her. Kiskadden had me read it to him. An' thet's why he set me free. It'll prove some things to yu, June—the things yu believed true of me. Maybe yu're the girl Holly speaks of in this letter. I hope to Gawd yu air an' thet I can be worthy. But for the job in hand, I'm yore man."

"Holly who?" questioned June, wondering, as she received the letter.

"Did yu ever heah of Holly Ripple?"

"Indeed I did. I remember hearing about her years ago before Jan and I went away to school. She lived out in New Mexico—on a vast Spanish grant. . . . Oh, Allen wrote me five or six years ago—all about Holly Ripple's ranch and her terrible riders. Brazos, could you have been one of them?"

"Wal, I reckon."

"Holly Ripple!" June beheld him with searching woman's eyes.

"Yes . . . I rode with that ootfit, June. She called us her Knights of the Range. . . . Wal—wal—we were all in love with her, yu savvy. An' the best of us, Renn Frayne, won

79

her love an' married her. They have a boy they call Brazos, after me. . . . But read the letter some time, an' keep it safe till yu see me again. . . . An' now let's get down to practical things."

"Oh, Brazos, can we ever be practical?"

"I've got to be if yu cain't. . . . I want to ask some questions aboot Allen. Were yu in his confidence, June?"

"Yes. Allen was afraid to tell Dad what he was doing. And he didn't even tell Jan."

"Ahuh. Wal, if I figure Allen correct, he was trackin' the ootfit thet ruined yore father."

"He was on the trail of the three men who held Dad up that night and robbed him."

"Did he tell yu anythin'?"

"Not much. Oh, let me recall it," she went on, excitedly. "They did not belong around Las Animas. But they rode here often. He had nothing to go by except—except the night they robbed Dad, one of them—a boy with a girl's voice called another of the three by the name Brad. Allen said Dad told him that."

"Yes, June, your Dad told me. And here's the funny part of it. One of the three hombres who held me up thet night called his pard Brad, or a name thet sounded like thet. By Gawd! Those men murdered Allen. He was on their trail. . . . Did any one else but yu know Allen was workin' on yore father's case?"

"Yes. It was found out. I remember Allen was sore because the loungers around town called him the cowboy detective. Allen kept the secret of what he suspected and had learned—except from me—but any one could have guessed what he was doing. He was so dark and grim and determined."

"June, do yu reckon Raine Surface heahed what Allen was up to?"

"Lura would have heard it, surely."

"Shore, she'd tell her father. . . . June, can yu remember any more Allen told yu?"

"Let me think. Yes. . . . The night before Allen was killed he had supper with me downstairs. It was late, almost time for Jan and me to come off duty. Allen asked me if I'd seen a handsome hard-faced cowgirl, small and slim with eyes like black diamonds. She looked the real thing in riders, he said. I told Allen no girl of that description had come into the restaurant. Then he said she had made up to him in the Happy Days saloon. He seemed curious, yet distrustful. But he didn't tell me any more."

"A cowgirl . . . Wal, now I wonder. . . . An' thet's all, June?"

"I wouldn't say all by any means. Only it's all I can remember now. Perhaps when I see you again——"

"Thet'll be in the mawnin', I reckon. But don't worry aboot me. I'm takin' over Allen's job of huntin' for the three hombres who robbed yore Dad—an' murdered Allen —an' held me up. . . . An' shore as death, one of thet three was a girl with a high-keyed voice!"

## Chapter Five

BRAZOS espied Lura Surface's white horse tied among the pine saplings before he turned in off the road. He found her most effectively placed in a green-shaded, brown-matted nook opening upon the bank of the swift brook. Bareheaded, her red hair flaming, her strange eyes alight, her lissome full-breasted figure displayed to advantage in her riding habit, she made a picture that struck fire in Brazos, despite his cool preconception.

"Good afternoon, Miss Surface. I shore am sorry to be late," he drawled, and throwing aside his sombrero he sat down and slid to his elbow beside her.

The green eyes devoured him, for nothing except her effect upon him. Yet her quick breath, and the quick rise of her breast, betrayed a little shock at his nearness. She was used to men, but not of his stripe, Brazos thought. His gun had bumped her knee.

"Howdy, Brazos Keene," she said, with a smile that enhanced her hard bright charm.

81

"Wal, I do pretty good, considerin'," returned Brazos. "Cowboys don't often fall into such luck as this."

"I came early. Had a quarrel with father. But I thought yu'd never get here."

"Wild hawses couldn't have kept me away from yu, Lura."

"Same old cowboy blarney."

"Ump-um. If yu take me for any other cowboy, wal, we won't get nowhere atall."

"Where will we get if I take you as I did yesterday?"

"An' how was thet?"

"A lonely cowboy, down on his luck, unjustly jailed, suspicious of men—an' needing a friend."

"Thet's takin' me true, Lura. But I cain't say I'm without friends altogether."

"You could always get women friends, Brazos."

"Shore. Thet's my trouble. I almost didn't come today."

"Why?"

"Wal, yu shore took my eye. An' I knew if I saw yu again I'd go loco."

"Loco? What's that? I've heard the word."

"Loco is a weed hawses eat sometimes an' go oot of their haids."

"Humph! I can just see *you* going loco!" she ejaculated. "Why, you're the coolest cowboy I ever met. And Lord knows I've met some cool ones."

"Wal, suppose at thet I did go loco?"

"I'd be delighted. You're different, Brazos. Oh, I was sorry when I thought they'd hang you! And what a thrill I had yesterday! Scared too? Brazos Keene—the notorious Brazos Keene! . . . But I'm not so scared now."

"Gosh, Lady, I'm as harmless as a kitten. . . . So yu'd be delighted if I went plumb loco about yu?"

"I'd love it," she said, slyly, yet with a catch in her voice. Her brazen coquetry had not heretofore been used to subjugate gunmen.

"Lura Surface, I'm not gonna do it. I reckon I'll get over this meetin' with yu. But I won't risk another."

"Oh," she pouted, blushing becomingly. "And why not?"

"Yu're just my dish of a woman an' if I tasted yu once I'd have nothin' to look forward to but starvation."

"I never satisfied any man's hunger yet. But I might—yours."

Brazos sat up, and with swift strong arms he drew her back so that she lay almost flat with her head on his breast. Then he held her, gazing down upon a suddenly paling face and eyes that dilated strangely between fear and desire. Her red lips parted. But she was thoroughbred in that, as she had invited this onslaught, she would not show the white feather.

"Lura, yu shore oughtn't play at love with a hombre like me."

"Who says I'm playing?"

"Shore yu air. An' I've got sense enough to see it an' decency enough to spare yu what many a cowboy I've known would take."

"You think I'm a flirt?"

"Wal, I never call women names, onless they're nice names. . . . Yu're powerful seductive, Lura, turrible appealin', an' pretty isn't the word. Yu've got a devastatin' kind of beauty. . . . If I let go of myself now, an' fell to kissin' yu, as I reckon I might do by force, I'd be a gone goslin'. I might fall stark ravin' mad in love with yu. An' where'd thet get me, Lura? I'm Brazos Keene, only a notch or two behind Billy the Kid in range standin'. Yu're daughter of Raine Surface, rich rancher, an' yu're the belle of this corner of Colorado. Suppose such a wild thing as yore fallin' in love with me. Yu couldn't never marry me."

"I could run away with you," she panted, her eyes like green stars.

"Wal, thet's too wild for even me to reckon with an' yu wouldn't. . . . So when it comes to Brazos Keene just yu figure thet he's not gonna dream such dreams. At the same time, I'd like yu to know it'd be damn sweet an' wonderful to tear yu to pieces."

"Well, since you're not going to try—please let me up," she said, serious over what seemed a greater conquest than she had hoped for. If he resisted her, at least he paid tribute to her charm. And perhaps he grew all the more desirable for that. She sat up, scarlet of face.

"I wouldn't let yu off thet easy next time," he warned.

"You are a queer one. What'd you meet me for, if not to make love? Who ever heard of a cowboy who didn't?"

"Wal, heah's one. Lura, could yu give me a job ridin' for yore Dad?"

"Oh, I'd like that. In fact I thought of it. I said to father: 'Why not get this Keene cowboy to ride for us?' He flouted the idea. 'That gun-throwing desperado from New Mexico! I guess not!' And I said: 'But, father, you never care how tough cowboys are coming from Dodge or Abilene.' And he shut me up."

"Ahuh. He's got a grudge against Western riders, I reckon. Wal, thet's tough on us from over the divide."

"I can't understand it, Brazos," she replied, as she straightened her disheveled hair. "Riders like you are not tough or low-down. You may be wild, dangerous, and all that. But father's excuse is queer. Why, he has hired rustlers and even outlaws when we ranched outside of Abilene. He had some bad outfits—bad in another sense. That's why he sold out and came to Colorado."

"Reckon I savvy thet. Bad outfits sometimes hurt a cattleman's reputation," replied Brazos, casually.

"Indeed they do. Father lost friends in Kansas. He had one serious lawsuit during which some pretty raw things were hinted against him. He shot a cattleman named Stearns."

"Kill him?" queried Brazos, as if shocked.

"No. Stearns recovered, I'm glad to say."

"Wal, yore Dad didn't strike me as the shootin' kind."

"He's not," the girl returned, with some note akin to contempt. "Unless he's got the edge on the other man. Why, he was scared to go into town for fear he'd run into Allen Neece."

"Neece? Thet was the cowboy I was accused of killin'. Did yu know him, Lura?"

"Yes. I liked him better than any boy I knew. I was terribly shocked at his death."

"Reckon yu would be. From all I heah, Neece was a nice chap. Did he ever ride for yu?"

"No. Father not only wouldn't have Allen but ran him out of the job he had."

84

"What for?"

"Allen was in love with me."

"Aw, I see. Shore tough for Allen—an' then gettin' murdered in the bargain. Who could have done thet job, Lura? Some cowboy jealous of yore likin' for Allen?"

"Hardly. No cowboy ever liked me *that* well."

"When did yu see Allen last?" asked Brazos, apparently growing interested.

"The very night he was murdered. I was in town. I met him coming out of the Show Down Saloon. He was half drunk. Allen took to drink after the Neeces lost Twin Sombreros. He didn't see me. And I didn't stop him for the good reason that he was with a little black-eyed wench in boy's pants. She was hanging on to Allen as if she'd lose him. I had seen her once before somewhere. I think on the street in Dodge. Not the dancehall type, but a pretty hard-faced hussy. I'll always remember her and think she had something to do with Allen's murder."

"Shore thet might be. She scraped acquaintance with Allen, got him to drinkin' an' had a couple of hombres ootside, maybe, waitin' to rob him. I've known thet to happen to many a cowboy."

"It'll never happen to Allen Neece again, poor devil. If it hadn't been for that black-eyed girl my conscience would hurt me."

"Yore what?" drawled Brazos, with his slow smile.

"I daresay you think I have no conscience—or any womanly virtues."

"Nope. But yu don't need anythin' with yore good looks. . . . Lura, yu've made me doggone interested in young Neece's case."

"Have you seen his doll-faced sisters—the twins?" she asked, quickly, and the green eyes showed her true nature.

"Did he have sisters? I didn't know. Tough on them, I reckon."

"Humph! They didn't seem to take it so hard. They didn't even stop slinging hash—not for a day."

"Wal, yu cain't never tell," said Brazos, dropping his head. What little regard he had left for Lura Surface went into eclipse.

"I mustn't stay longer, Brazos," said the girl, consulting her watch. "Father watches me closely and times my rides. I told him I wanted to ride into town, but he wouldn't hear of it. . . . Here we have spent an hour—the last of which didn't keep the promise of the first. . . . When shall we meet again?"

"I reckon never, Lura. But thanks for this once. When I'm far away, I'll think I might have kissed yu, an' kick myself."

"Oh, don't go away. Why, I've only met you! . . . Tell me, when?"

"Wal, maybe some day I'll meet yu in town an' weaken. But, Lady, yu've been warned."

"I'll take the risk. . . . It has been different from—well, other times I've met boys here." She mounted gracefully to her saddle, aware of his appreciation, and said with dark-green provocative eyes on him: "Adios, Brazos Keene."

Brazos watched her ride away with only one regret—that he liked her well enough to be sorry she was innocently involved in a sinister plot that dimly shadowed her father, and which she had unwittingly made clearer.

Brazos rode back to town, for once not seeing the afternoon sun flooding the range with golden glory. Long past was the day when he had distrusted his intuition. A pending tragedy of oncoming events vied in his mind with the consideration of the callousness of the acts which he had sworn to reveal. Despite his spirit of flame, and in this case the irresistible incentive, he felt as never before the reluctance of the intelligent and normal gunman to force issues. In times past, wild youth, sometimes inflamed by the bottle, had needed little spurring on. But he was a man now; he was through with rum; and he hated the trail that led inevitably to bloodspilling. Yet here he was, unalterably committed; he did not want to draw back; and still the passion needed held aloof. Brazos longed for the incident or the revelation that would make him a tiger.

When he dismounted at the corral where Bilyen had first taken him, and turned Bay over to the stableboy, he suddenly had an inspiration:

"Pedro, did yu know Allen Neece?"

"Si, señor," replied the Mexican.

Further queries rewarded Brazos with some significant facts. Allen Neece had come to the stable on the night he was murdered. He was on foot and under the influence of drink though not by any means drunk. He had to wake Pedro to get his horse. It was not until Neece had mounted and ridden off that Pedro had noted a companion—a boy on a black horse, waiting. This last information seemed of tremendous importance to Brazos. That boy was the cowgirl June Neece had mentioned and the girl in rider's garb that Lura Surface had seen with Allen.

Brazos strode uptown to the restaurant. The hour was early and only a few customers were at supper. One of the twins came to Brazos and though he thought he could trust her smile and bright eye, he would not take a chance.

"Wal, which one air yu?"

"Brazos, what has happened?" she whispered, leaning over the counter.

He answered low: "June, I've been oot to meet Lura Surface an' the hunch I got from her riled me."

"Oh—what——"

"Never mind now. But don't worry aboot me or yore Dad. Please fetch me some supper."

That night Brazos haunted the main street and the saloons. The cowboys and cattlemen on the street, coming in or going home, the drinkers and bartenders in the saloons, the gamblers at the tables and the loungers around, and more than one dark-garbed group who drank by themselves—all heard that Brazos Keene was hunting for some one. It was spoken first by a man who had seen Keene enter Las Animas' saloons in years gone by. Then it passed from lip to lip.

Brazos' stalk was no pose, yet he did it deliberately. Nevertheless he had little hope that he would encounter the trio who now loomed large in the mystery of Allen Neece's murder. They would be out on the range, hidden in the hills, or back east in the gambling dens of Dodge or Abilene. They would be in close touch with the man or men who were back of this crime. It might well be that they would be summoned presently to do away with Brazos Keene.

In the Happy Days saloon Brazos came unexpectedly

upon Bodkin, whom he had not seen since the day of his release by Kiskadden. The ex-deputy had just set down his glass on the bar. Sight of Brazos cut short words he was speaking to a companion.

"Hey, Bodkin, heah yu air," called Brazos, so ringingly that the inmates of the crowded saloon went silent. "Where yu been?"

"I've been around town as usual," replied Bodkin, turning a dirty white under his swarthy skin.

"Like hell yu have. I been lookin' for yu. Have yu been put back as deputy sheriff of this heah town?"

"No. Kiskadden fired me, you know, an' then he resigned. The Cattlemen's Association haven't made no appointment yet. But I'm expectin' it."

"Yu're expectin' what?" drawled Brazos, with scathing insolence.

"To be elected sheriff."

"Aw, hell! Elected? Who's electin' yu? Not the citizens of this heah town. They won't be asked. If they would be, yu'd never get a vote, onless from some of yore hired hands. . . . An' who's yore Cattlemen's Associaion ootside of Raine Surface?"

"Miller, Henderson, Sprague—all big cattlemen," returned Bodkin, hurriedly. "Inskip was one—but he quit."

"Ahuh. An' when does this ootfit aim to settle yore appointment—an' also yore hash?"

"They meet tomorrow night."

"Wal, tell them I'll call an' cast one vote against yu."

"I'll do thet, Keene."

"An' while yu're carryin' messages from me, take this for yoreself. If yu're appointed sheriff I'm gonna see red. . . . An' this for yore hired hand, Barsh. He better keep oot of my way."

Thus Brazos talked himself to a verge of the passion he required of himself. Seldom was he a talker until the cumulation of events propelled disaster.

"I reckon Joel won't invite any meetin' with you, Keene. You oughtn't to have it in fer him 'cause he was only actin' on orders."

"But he threw thet noose round my neck," flashed Brazos, as if the mere fact brooked no pardon.

88

Backing through the swinging doors, Brazos left that saloon to break its silence with a subdued sound of excited voices, and then an angry protesting roar from Bodkin. Brazos had scarcely turned up the street when the doors banged behind him.

"Hold on, Brazos. It's Hank." And Bilyen, keen and glinting of eye, joined him. "My Gawd, cowboy, but you burned Bodkin up! What's the deal?"

"Howdy, Hank. Aw, I was only bluffin' Bodkin, an' takin' thet chance to set the town talkin' aboot Surface an' his Cattlemen's Association."

"Brazos, you've got goin'," rejoined Bilyen, shrewdly. "You shore are. You never was one to talk wild. Mebbe you were throwin' a bluff, but you had somethin' behind it."

"Wal, enough to want to rile myself up. . . . Hank, I was wantin' to see yu. If yu cain't give me the lowdown on rustlin' in eastern Colorado, find oot for me pronto."

"I know, Brazos. Got thet this very day. Kiskadden an' Inskip told me. They're shore interested. As a matter of fact, I was surprised. I reckon you won't be though. . . . Brazos, there 'pears to be considerable cattle stealin' in small numbers, takin' in all the big brands on this range. Too slick an' bold to be the work of any gang but real rustlers under a smart leader. Kiskadden an' Inskip lost three hundred haid last month. The Star Brand not so many. Small ootfits down the Purgatory none at all. Henderson's ootfit rarin' aboot a big drive on their Circle Dot Brand. Miller has lost considerable haid. Sprague an' the big cattlemen up on the slopes hard hit for these times. All this last month, an' the herds driven over into Kansas an' shipped east."

"Ha! Ha!" laughed Brazos, mirthlessly.

"Say, what's so funny about thet?" demanded Bilyen, affronted.

"Struck me funny."

"What did?"

"The way my hunches work oot," returned Brazos, grimly. "But for some men it's aboot as funny as death. . . . Hank, will yu meet me oot west of town at sunup in the mawnin' ?"

"Yes, I will, cowboy. Where?" answered Bilyen soberly.

"At thet old cabin on the hill—where Allen Neece was murdered," said Brazos, tersely, and abruptly strode away toward Mexican Joe's place, where he had a room.

Next morning Brazos rode out of Las Animas at the break of day. Nine out of ten mornings for fifteen years he had been in a saddle at this hour. But he was not trail driving today, or guarding the herd, or riding a grub line from one camp to another. He felt a keen cold exhilaration that was not entirely engendered by the morning crispness from the mountain heights.

When he rode by Twin Sombreros Ranch the sun was just rising red and glorious over the range. Two cowboys espied him from the lane that led down to the big barns, and they halted to watch him. It never occurred to Brazos that they did not recognize him. Their dark intent gaze seemed prophetic of the shadow which hovered over that beautiful ranch.

What a property to lose! No wonder Abe Neece, at his age, had seen the fruit of a lifetime pass from him with inconsolable grief! But then, Brazos reflected, Neece had worked and planned for those lovely twin daughters. It was the kind of ranch Brazos would have liked to own, and, failing that, ride for. The ideal location on the talking river, the groves and lines and clumps of trees, the peeled-log fences, and the cabins, and the low-roofed rambling ranch house, white amid the green—they left a picture in Brazos' mind. And they created another—of the chestnut-haired girls waving to him from the porch.

"Doggone! Thet was a funny idee," soliloquized Brazos, puzzled. "Wās I ridin' in or ridin' oot? . . . But it's nothin' like Don Carlos' Rancho. Thet was un grande hacienda española. . . . I can see Holly now, ridin' down from the hill. My Gawd, wasn't she lovely? . . . I just gotta see thet little boy they call Brazos. . . . An' Cap Britt, the old Texas son of a gun! An' thet wild ootfit of mine!"

But the past was gone irrevocably, and for the first time since Brazos had ridden away from the Ripple Ranch he could remember without pain. Some magic had charmed away that old sadness. Never would what he had done for Holly Ripple be forgotten by her or her husband or her

90

men! He had had help on that hard job—a bunch of the wildest and keenest riders who ever forked a horse. Some of them had died by his side, fighting for the señorita of Don Carlos' Rancho. But in this Neece job he had started practically alone. He thought he had better go it alone, unless the trail led into the stronghold of a gang of plains rustlers. That Brazos believed was possible and probable, in which case he would need some riders.

Trotting west, Brazos' mind was crowded and active. Yet as he cleared the timber and began the long ascent that led up to the hill, he had an eye for the country. The whole eastern range was flooded with crimson light—a rolling undulating land of shining grass, bisected by a winding green-bordered river. He could see tens of thousands of cattle, black acreage near at hand and twin dots in the distance. With cattle at forty dollars a head and a boundless range, what a harvest for a bold well-led band of rustlers! That harvest would come. It always did come. It would be a quick short one, and then the gang would ride north or east or south. Not west! That led into New Mexico, and the ranges there dealt summarily with wholesale cattle thieves. Yet even in New Mexico, just so long as cattle black-spotted the valleys and plateaus, just that long would the rustler flourish.

Brazos reached the top of the hill and halted. The cabin and grove of trees he sought lay off the road to the left and a little farther on. What halted Brazos was the prospect to the west. He looked across the Colorado line into New Mexico, and next to Texas he loved that country of black-belted, snow-capped mountains, of silver-grassed valleys, of wide shining ranges encompassed by protecting walls. Spring had almost ended, and the warm sun had made inroads upon the snowy south slopes of the Rockies. But the peaks were still white, glistening rose, still impervious to the lord of summer.

Pikes Peak in the north rose dim and grand; the closer Spanish Peaks dominated the scene; and the great red and black wall, leading south, hid the base of the range beyond. If there were any cattle along this last heave of the Great Plains into the Continental Divide they were lost in gullies and swales between the foothills, or the valley of the

91

Purgatory. The rough, gray, rocky foothills harbored little grass and they led into the fastnesses of the mountains.

Southwest from where Brazos sat astride his saddle, gazing raptly at old familiar landmarks, yawned the gap in the range, where the Old Trail led up and over into New Mexico. It had a tremendous fascination for Brazos, not all of which came from the fact that he had ridden it and fought on it all the way from Dodge to Lincoln. Three hundred years before, the French fur traders had walked that trail, and the Spanish padres and explorers after them, and then the American fur men, down to the time of Kit Carson, and then the freighters in their covered wagons with their guards of soldiers, and the tide of gold hunters and pioneers, and lastly those other empire builders of whom Brazos counted himself one—the cowboys with their herds of longhorn cattle from Texas. It was a grand scene to Brazos, knowing as he did know so well what had taken place there down the long years. He had a melancholy feeling that he was a part of the West which had vanished. The noble wilderness appeared the same, despite the iron track he could see curving between the hills; the sun rose as always to gild those unassailable ramparts, and to shine on the rugged red walls, the black belts, the canyons of white, and the beckoning dim range. But the glory and the dream—that was to say the wildness and the romance—seemed to be passing away.

Then as a clip-clop of a trotting horse disrupted Brazos' thoughts and he turned to see Hank Bilyen coming, he remembered his errand and he laughed outright. The robbery of Neece and the murder of his son, the mysterious workings of a hard outfit, and the recent raids on cattle herds—these were far from tame and bereft of romance. Brazos realized that June and Janis Neece could furnish enough of that disturbing element to satisfy a whole range of cowboys.

"Mawnin', Hank," was Brazos' greeting.

"Howdy, Texas. Seen you a long way back. What's the idee, Brazos?"

"Wal, I want yu to help me go over this ground with a fine tooth comb."

"Tracks, eh? I ain't takin' any back seat for you, Brazos Keene. Never was one to hobble hawses."

They rode into the clump of trees and tied their horses.

"Allen Neece was found in thet cabin. But accordin' to the doctors he wasn't killed there. What I want powerful to find an' shore expect to find is a small boot track."

"Ahuh. Wal, let's get goin'."

They entered the cabin, with riders' eyes searching the ground for tracks. Hank got down on his knees to scrutinize those just inside the door. He was slow.

"Reckon them was made the mawnin' Bodkin found you heah," he said, at length.

"An' heah's my track, goin' an' comin' back. I slept on thet bunk."

They searched the musty dry cabin as hunters of treasure might have. "Well, nothin' heah," said Brazos. "If thet little boot marked the dust heah it's been tracked over. Let's go up in the loft."

The loft covered half the space under the roof and had been built of peeled poles laid close together. It shook under their weight. The light was dull up there, but they could distinguish objects. Bilyen concluded that the murderers had climbed the ladder up to a point level with the loft and had shoved the body headfirst back upon the poles. A dark smear of blood ran along one of them.

"What's thet in the corner?" asked Brazos, and crawled carefully back. He found a rope, a lasso, that had evidently been hurriedly flung there without being coiled. He crawled back to Bilyen with it.

"Look, Hank. . . . Must have been the rope which made the marks on his arms," said Brazos. "Take it down, Bilyen, while I investigate some more."

Brazos went over every inch of that loft without further discovery. When he got down he found Hank sitting in the door, studying the rope. Brazos knelt to scrutinize with him. They were tense and silent. Next to a gun and a horse, the lasso was a cowboy's most treasured possession.

"Wal, what you make oot?" queried the Texan gruffly of Brazos.

"Lasso all right. Manila, wal made. Same as any one of a hundred."

"Yes, an' what else, cowboy?"

"It shore never was used on a calf or a cow or a steer."

"Hell no. Brazos, it ain't new. It's been tied on a saddle fer a long time. A cowboy riata never used by a cowboy! . . . Does thet say anythin' to you?"

"Ump-umm. Don't talk so much, Hank. Let's go all over the ground heah."

Every path and bare spot and thin-grassed bit of ground out to the road and along the road to east and west they carefully inspected.

"Now thet clump of trees," said Brazos. "Hank, heah's where I run into the three hombres." He related the incident, laying stress on the name he had heard and the nervous young high-pitched voice. Bilyen's silence attested to the impression Brazos' story made on him. They proceeded to the patch of timber. "Aboot heah is where their hawses stood."

It appeared to be a scraggy bit of dead and dying timber, extending back a considerable distance. Brazos directed Hank to search there, while he began at the farther end. Brazos had something in his mind. At the farthest point, under the largest and thickest-foliaged of the trees, he found a bare spot of ground. At sight of hoof tracks and tiny boot tracks his blood leaped. Down he knelt and almost smelt at the boot tracks. Of all the innumerable imprints by riders' boots that Brazos had ever studied these were the smallest. No cowboy ever had small enough feet to take a boot that made these tracks. Ten-year-old boys did not wear boots made to order. These had been left by a girl. Brazos knelt there as if he were reading a dark page of the book of life.

"What'n hell air you porin' over, cowboy?" asked Bilyen, curiously, as he came upon Brazos.

"There! My hunch was true."

Bilyen did not utter a word but made a careful inspection of the spot, and then faced Brazos with a curious fire in his eye.

"Cowboy, there's a girl mixed in this deal."

"Shore."

"An' she come way back heah to be far from thet

94

cabin. . . . An' she set her hawse for a while. . . . An' she got off heah—an' heah she walked to and fro. . . . *Nervous!* An' heah she stood still, her heels diggin' in. Rooted to the spot, hey, Brazos? . . . An' there she got on again, light-footed an' quick. . . . Wal, Brazos, I'll be ——!"

"So will I, Hank," rejoined Brazos, ponderingly. "Get me some little sticks so I can measure this track."

"Brazos, I reckon you won't be lookin' for a cowgirl answerin' to this boot track? . . . Not much!"

"Not any at all," returned Brazos, with a cold steely note in his voice.

"She was the one of them three hombres with the young nervous high-pitched voice. . . . She was afraid of the risk. . . . She was goin' to bore you, Brazos!"

"I shore gotta meet thet sweet little lady."

"How you goin' aboot thet, Brazos?" asked Hank, scratching his scrubby beard.

"Ride the line an' take a look at the gamblin' halls."

"They got cash an' they ain't cowmen. Wal, when you find out where their money comes from you'll be gettin' hot."

"Hot? Say, old-timer, I'm burnin' right now. . . . But I'll cool off. I don't like the idee of a hard nut of a cowgirl in this deal. I might have to wing her. I did thet once to a woman who was drawin' on me an' I'll never forget her scream."

"How you figure her part in this?"

"How do yu?"

"Plain as print. She an' her two pards air from oot of town—she's a good-looker an' likely enticin' to cowboys. Allen Neece was easy took in by girls. He liked a drink, too, same as all the boys. Wal, this gang of three was after him, for reasons that bear strong in this deal. She got to Allen—an' the rest was easy."

"I figure aboot like thet, Hank," returned Brazos, thoughtfully. "Beside I know more'n yu. The night Allen was killed he walked down to the barns to get his hawse. Pedro said there was a boy with him—a boy on a black hawse—an' they hung ootside. They rode away. Now what happened is this. If I remember correct thet night

95

was nice an' warm, with a moon an' the frogs peepin'—just the night for a rendezvous oot heah. But they never got heah. Thet Brad an' his other pard roped Allen an' dragged him off his hawse. The fall killed Allen, but they didn't know it. They packed him up heah, shot him—an' left him in the cabin."

"While the girl waited heah under this tree nervous an' sick," added Hank.

"Nervous, anyhow. Wal, she had—good reason to be nervous," declared Brazos, darkly. "Just aboot then I rode into the deal."

"Funny how things work oot. It shore don't pay to be crooked. . . . Brazos, who's behind all this?"

"Hank, yu're a curious cuss," drawled Brazos, carefully depositing in his pocket the little sticks with which he had measured the foot track. "Let's go back to town an' have breakfast."

On the return they did not exchange another word until they got by Twin Sombreros Ranch, when Bilyen curtly asked Brazos: "Did you see Surface standin' in the door?"

"Shore. He looked big as a hill."

"Must be one of these early birds, eh?" rejoined Bilyen, sarcastically.

From there on into town Brazos found his tongue and asked his comrade many questions regarding the possibility of one of the big cattlemen of the range being the genius and backer of a bold and clever gang of rustlers.

"Kinda hipped on thet idee, ain't you?" rejoined Bilyen, who seemed nettled that Brazos did not tell all he knew.

"Reckon I am. It's a great idee."

"Wal, it wasn't born with you, Brazos. I had thet long ago."

"Hank, yu're from Texas an' no fool," mused Brazos, as if apologizing for Bilyen. "Will yu swear to it?"

"I shore will—to you. But I wouldn't want to yell it oot loud in the Happy Days or the post office."

"Why wouldn't yu, old-timer?"

"I want to live long enough to see Abe an' the twins back at their ranch."

"Ahuh. Wal, I'll yell it—tonight at thet Cattlemen's Association meetin'."

"By Gawd, you've a nerve, Brazos! An' you're cunnin', too. Wonder I didn't think you'd do just thet. . . . Shore we figger the same. You'd egg one of them cattlemen an' whoever's in with him to sic the cowgirl an' her hombres on to you, eh?"

"Eggs-ack-ly, Hank," drawled Brazos.

"Hell! It's no good. If they wasn't too smart to trail you they'd be too scairt."

"Wal, maybe they never heahed of me."

"They're livin' west of the Mississippi, ain't they?"

'It's a good idee anyhow, Hank. An' heah's where we eat."

"I'll ride oot home an' get breakfast for Abe. See you pronto."

In a few more moments Brazos was gazing across the counter into a pair of lovely hazel-brown eyes that shone upon him.

"Mawnin', June—if yu're June," he said, with a smile.

"Good mawnin', Brazos," she replied, mimicking his accent.

A perverse devil in Brazos led him to whisper: "What would I get—if I'd found oot somethin' important for yu?"

Her eyes dilated and the rose of her cheek faded. "What would you like—flapjacks or lamb chops?" she queried, meeting him in spirit.

"Aw, no! . . . Would I get a kiss?"

She blushed scarlet and the hint of humor fled. "Certainly, you would."

The surprise of that quick assent shocked Brazos into a realization of his bold levity.

"Forgive thet. I'm loco this mawnin'," he added, hurriedly, lowering his eyes. He knew that his remorse was not going to live long in the light of her consent. Presently under his lowered gaze he saw both flapjacks and lamb chops set before him, and mumbling his thanks he began to eat. Presently his ears were assailed by a sweet voice: "No coffee and biscuits this morning?"

"Aw, I forgot. Shore I do," replied Brazos, nonplussed at he did not know what. Until he looked up!

"So that is the secret of your heroics?"

"Wha-at?" blurted Brazos, dumbfounded.

"You would extract a kiss from Janis for some little service to the Neeces?"

"June! . . . So help me heaven I swear I thought she was yu."

"Cowboy!"

At that Brazos flushed deeply. To be relegated to the rank and file of ordinary cowboys was something he could not tolerate.

"Look heah, Lady," he said, coolly, "I thought she was yu. Thet's a mistake I cain't help. It just popped oot—thet aboot askin' for a kiss. I shore didn't mean it an' I apologized to her. An' I do to yu. I was loco."

"Why were you so—so loco this morning?" she asked, dubiously, a little less aloof.

Brazos cautiously made certain no one could hear his reply. "June, this mawnin' I found a real clue to Allen's murderers. I can't tell yu now, but I will tonight, if yu'll see me."

"Come after ten," she replied, in earnest eagerness. "Oh, I can hardly wait. . . . Brazos, I'm ashamed. I—I doubted you again."

"Again? I didn't know you'd already done thet."

"Yes, again. I may as well confess it. I—I'm horribly jealous of Jan. She gets all the boys and men, too."

"Ha! Ha! I'd shore like a tintype picture of thet. Wal, I can forgive yu doubtin' me, but I'm not so shore aboot yore callin' me 'cowboy,' the way yu said it."

"How did I say it, Brazos?"

"Turrible full of contempt. An' see heah, June Neece. Hard name I have, I gotta admit. But all the same I don't belong to thet cowboy brand."

"I am sorry. It's my turn to beg pardon. . . . Then I'm to tell Jan you took her for me—and you were only teasing about the kiss?" Heightened color and rather abashed eyes accompanied this query.

"Please do, June. An' tell her I know she was teasin' too —aboot givin' me the kiss."

"Not Jan! She meant that."

"O Lord, what am I missin'!" burst out Brazos, frankly. There were times when he had to be deadly honest.

"If you really took Jan for me—you will miss nothing," replied June, tilting her chin.

"I really did. An' what yu mean, June Neece—thet I'll miss nothin'?"

"Because I will give you two!" she flashed, merrily and fled.

Brazos rode twenty miles that day and visited a spring roundup, two cow camps, and a ranch with a shadowy reputation. At each place he introduced himself with a question.

"Have yu-all seen a bald-faced thoroughbred hawse with three white feet? I'm Brazos Keene an' my hawse was stole. Last seen goin' north with two men an' a kid—maybe a girl in boy's clothes—on a black hawse."

His inquiry elicited sympathy everywhere except at a ranch where the burly dark-browed rancher, Sneed, betrayed a glint of curiosity that the keen Brazos did not fail to record.

"No, Keene, I hain't seen any hoss marked like that," he replied, slowly.

"But yu did see the two men an' the kid—who's a cowgirl?" swiftly followed Brazos.

"What you givin' me? I didn't say so."

"Aw, the hell yu didn't. Sneed, if yu want to tell me when an' where yu seen thet ootfit, wal an' good. But if yu don't yu're shore gonna be watched."

"Watched! An' who by, an' what fer, Mister Keene?"

"Ask yoreself. Air yu tellin' me, Sneed?"

"I hain't seen no two men an' a kid," repeated Sneed, stoutly.

"How aboot cattle?" hazarded Brazos, like a hound on the scent. "Seen any herds of mixed brands drove along neah toward the Kansas line?"

"No," replied Sneed, harshly.

"Then yu must have been wearin' blinders . . . or maybe yu couldn't see for dust. . . . Good, day, Sneed. I'll be seein' yu again."

Brazos would never have ventured such bold and scarcely veiled remarks as these, had he not intuitively caught this cattleman over on the wrong side of the fence. Brazos had found out that Sneed had a bad name in the first place, and secondly, he had not been equal to Brazos' sharp interrogation. There might have been only a little wrong with Sneed and then again there might have been a great deal. Brazos added another tiny link to his chain.

"Wal, in the next month or so," he soliloquized, as he rode back toward Las Animas, "if somebody takes a pot shot at me or I find myself trailed—I'll be doggoned shore I'm on a hot scent. An' it behooves little Brazos to move careful."

Brazos avoided the restaurant that night and had his supper at Mexican Joe's. Afterwards he began the gamut of the saloons, where he pretended to drink. And at nine o'clock, when he mounted the steps up to the Odd Fellows Hall, he pounded on the door with the butt of his gun.

"Open up heah!" he shouted.

The door was promptly unlocked, allowing Brazos to enter, a little unsteady on his feet. But seldom had Brazos Keene been any more sober and cool than at this moment. He needed the sharpness of vision and wit of a dozen cowboys. Much might depend on this venture.

"Excuse me, gennelmen, for intrudin' heah. I'll leave it to yu whether what I say is important or not."

A dozen or perhaps fifteen men sat around a long table, upon which stood bottles and glasses and a box of cigars. Brazos swept the group in one glance, to recognize Henderson and Surface. He had never seen Sprague, but identified him from Bilyen's description. Other faces were familiar. And lastly, to his surprise, he saw Inskip.

"It's that cowboy, Brazos Keene," spoke up one of the men.

"Drunk! Put him out," called Surface, rising from his seat.

"Go slow, Mister Surface, aboot puttin' me oot," drawled Brazos, his eyes on the rancher like slits of fire. "I'm not drunk. Shore I've had a few nips just to make me talky. But yu'll find me level-haided enough."

"Let him have his say, Surface," advised Henderson, intensely interested.

100

"Go ahaid, Brazos," interposed Inskip, dryly.

"But the intrusion of a drunken cowboy! Intolerable," protested Surface, and as he sank back into his seat it was not anger alone that marked his sallow visage.

"Speak up, Keene," ordered Henderson. "Be brief and to the point."

Brazos, having gained his point of entrance, changed visibly, and sheathed his gun, though he left his hand on the butt.

"Gentlemen, I picked oot this meetin' as the proper place an' time to make a statement shore to be interestin' to all Colorado cattlemen," began Brazos, swiftly, with his glance roving as swiftly. "It so happens thet events kinda gravitate to me. An honor I never cared for but was thrust on me! The cattle situation heah on this range from the Spanish Peaks down to the Old Trail is nothin' new to me. I recall five situations like it. Yu all know what caused the Lincoln County War in New Mexico. Yu all shore have heahed of the Sewall McCoy combine with Russ Slaughter. On the one hand there was the educated rich smooth cunnin' gentleman-rancher, an' on the other the dyed-in-the-wool rustler, hard as flint, an' leader of as bloody an ootfit of cattle thieves as ever forked hawses. Yu-all may have heahed too, what I had to do with the trailin' an' breakin' thet double ootfit. I mention it heah, not to brag, but to give some importance to what I'm aboot to tell yu."

Brazos let that sink in. He did not rest his gaze upon any one of the fascinated faces of his listeners, but he missed nothing of the effect of his words.

"Yu cattlemen face the same situation heah on this range," he went on impressively. "An' if yu don't break it up there's no tellin' how powerful an' all-embracin' it'll grow. . . . Short an' sweet then, gentlemen, there's a cattleman on this range who's workin' like Sewall McCoy. He's yore friend an' maybe pardner. I'm not insultin' any of yu heah or any citizen of Las Animas. 'Cause what I know cain't be proved at this tellin'. But it's the truth yu can gamble on. . . . Thet's all gentlemen. Take it for what its' worth."

Slowly Brazos, while ending this biting speech, backed to the door, limning on his mind's eye the strangely contrasting visages there. Then with a leap he was out of the door, to bound down the stairs.

## Chapter Six

As THE train whistled for Las Animas the conductor observed Brazos Keene buckling a heavy gun belt around his slim waist. And the several passengers who had scraped acquaintance with the handsome cowboy in his new suit stared aghast.

"That nice curly-haired cowboy!" whispered one, a girl in her teens.

"Who would have thought it!" ejaculated her mother.

"Cowboy, it's two days yet till July Fourth," remarked the conductor.

"Wal, heah at Las Animas I don't feel right withoot my hardware on," drawled Brazos, smiling at the girl.

"Who are you?" she asked, eagerly.

"Sorry to confess, Lady. But I been sailin' under false colors. I'm Curly Keene, bandit, an' all around desperado. . . . Adios."

Brazos picked up his bag and made for the platform. As the train slowed to a halt he espied Bilyen foremost of the waiting bystanders. Before Brazos stepped down he swept the platform with searching gaze. Bilyen beckoned for him to come off.

"Howdy, Hank," drawled Brazos. "Kinda like old times to see yu packin' thet gun."

"Wal, you dressed-up son of a gun," ejaculated Hank, delighted. "Brazos, you shore look fine."

"How about things heah?"

"Not so good. But no hurry tellin'. I hope you had better luck than me."

"Hank, I shore learned a heap. But what good it'd do I

cain't say. . . . Come with me. I've got somethin' for the twins."

They entered the restaurant to find June and Janis excited and glowing, for once forgetting their duties. Brazos made them a gallant bow, and then gazed from one to the other in exceeding great earnestness, and back again.

"Aw! Three weeks makes no difference. I cain't tell yu apart. I cain't tell nothin' 'cept yu air lovelier," he said. "Heah' I fetched yu somethin' from Kansas City." And opening his bag he drew forth two large beribboned boxes of candy and presented them.

"Oh, Brazos—you look grand!" exclaimed one, taking him in with rapt eyes. If she were June she neglected the little identifying mannerism she had agreed to adopt for Brazos' sake.

"Thanks, cowboy. We thought you'd never, never get back," murmured the other.

"And almost prayed you wouldn't!"

That would be June, Brazos thought, and thrilled to the soft dark shadow in her tawny eyes.

"Aw, thet wasn't kind. . . . Has anyone been lookin' for me?"

"Brazos, we try not to hear talk across the counter—but we did . . . and Jack is worried."

"Wal, girls, don't worry none, now I'm back. See yu later. I'm goin' oot with Hank. Got some news for yore Dad."

Outside Brazos turned to his faithful comrade and voiced a sharp query: "What's come off? June an' Janis look a little strained."

"Worry about you, I reckon. The damn burg has been full of talk."

"Ahuh. Wal, let's walk down to Joe's. I'll leave my bag. Did yu fetch my hawse in?"

"No. I drove in for supplies. You can ride oot on the wagon with me."

Brazos gave attention to the street and pedestrians ahead. Las Animas showed the stimulus due to the near approach of the Fourth. It was scarcely likely that any one on the street saw Brazos first. Mexican Joe, at sight of him, beamed all over his seamed and swarthy face. "Ah,

Señor Brazos. Now thees good old time she come back!" Hank turned a corner with Brazos and led him to a side street.

"Did yu savvy thet damn greaser?" growled Brazos.

"Shore. Joe reckons yu'll find oot pronto who's lookin' for yu. Nobody seems to know."

"Did Bodkin get put in as sheriff?"

"Not yet. The Cattlemen's Association split. Henderson an' Surface had a hell of a row. Henderson resigned."

"Ahuh. Henderson? I reckoned thet night when I busted up the meetin' he was gettin' leary."

"Brazos, he shore had reason. Not long after thet row Henderson lost a thousand haid of steers an' his best hawses. The two cowboys on guard were shot. An' the rest of the ootfit didn't know till mornin'."

"Hell yu say!" ejaculated Brazos. "Pretty bold an' raw. It's gettin' hot, Hank."

"Kinda queer, don't you reckon, right after thet row with Surface?"

"I'd say so—*if* anyone but Surface is responsible. He might be smart enough to see thet very thing."

"Wal, damn if I see it," rejoined Hank, stoutly. "You're onsartin' then of Surface's guilt?"

"Hell no! An' thet's what's eatin' me. I'm shore aboot Surface, but cain't prove it."

"Boy, you caint get proof in a minnit."

"Yu can stop a bullet, though. Hank, if there *is* any ootfit lookin' for me *they'll* know me an' I won't know them. Too many odds! I cain't stack against thet. I swear if it was any other kind of a deal—if it wasn't for the twins an' Neece—I'd pull leather for Texas."

"Not to be thought of."

"I'm gettin' sore. An' thet's good. It'll do what a bottle of red likker used to do. . . . Wal, what'd yu find oot?"

"Nary a thing. I took train to Hebron an' talked with the railroad men there. Got no satisfaction. They'd shipped cattle train after cattle train east. An' one bunch was no different from another. 'It's no mix of ours if some of them cattle was rustled,' said the station agent. Billy the Kid's ootfit is sellin' cattle to the beef buyers from the Indian reservations. Nobody talkin'."

Brazos had no more to say until he and Hank met Neece at the cabin. It pleased Brazos to see that Neece was a changed man. He had pulled out of hopelessness. He had gained.

"Wal, Neece, I've news thet I shore hope yu'll find somethin' in," began Brazos. "My job at Kansas City, yu know, was to get track of the cattle people Surface ships to. I couldn't find oot. This may have been regular an' then again it may have been queer. Thet fact alone is queer. Their interest is in buyin' an' sellin' beef an' *not* in where it comes from. A big per cent of cattle herds shipped there is shore rustled. An' nobody's tellin'. But I spent three days loafin' aboot the stockyards, an' I found oot from the yardmen aboot two big trainloads of long-horns thet was shipped in early spring. Longhorns an' mixed brands, from New Mexico. One trainload went into the stockyards an' was drove oot of there in small bunches. The other trainload went east. Yu cain't track unbranded cattle any more'n yu can cattle wearin' brands yu don't know. Shore them big trains carried yore herd. An' thet herd just faded. . . . Wal, on the way back I stopped over at Abilene. I was plumb nervous aboot it as aboot seven years ago I shot up thet burg. But shucks, everybody I ever knew was long daid. Funny how short-lived we Westerners air! Abilene has growed some an' it was still pretty hot. I mixed with cowboys, cattlemen, gamblers an' town folks. Naturally, yu know yu never get anywhere askin' one Westerner aboot another. But I finally met a cowboy who once rode for Surface. He was not my kind an' he was mum as an oyster. Then I met a cattleman who spit fire when I asked aboot Surface. What I got oot of him might have pertained to any rancher. It 'peared this cattleman was kin to one who had been a pardner of Surface. . . . Heah, I have the names. Stokes, the pardner was. Wal, Stokes an' Surface operated big in cattle. Surface bought an' Stokes sold. One day they quarreled an' Surface shot Stokes. Nobody saw the fight. Surface claimed Stokes drew first. Some people said the trouble was over money, an' some said Stokes had been heahed to question Surface aboot where

105

he got his cattle. Anyway Surface left Abilene. Thet was over a year ago. An' thet's aboot all."

"I reckon it's significant," declared Neece, soberly.

"My idee is it strengthens our case," added Bilyen.

"Wal, I agree," said Brazos. "But what we air convinced of might not be worth a whoop in court. Surface has money an' influence. He'd beat us. An' we don't want any court decision against us. This deal will never go before a Denver court."

"You are daid right, Brazos," returned Bilyen.

"Yes, an' what I want is to get Surface daid to rights. Let me get thet in my own way. All the same I won't overlook the littlest hunch yu can give me. Anythin' could be a hunch."

"Lura Surface has left Twin Sombreros, so I heah," put in Hank. "She's stayin' with a friend, Delia Ross. An' lettin' thet gambler Howard run around with her."

"Yu don't say? Wal!"

"Brazos, did Hank tell you Henderson called on me?" queried Neece. "Well, he did. An' though he didn't mention Surface I took it as an expression of regret an' sympathy. Henderson is head of the bank that wouldn't lend me the money to save my ranch."

"Ahuh. Wal, thet is a hunch. Rustle my hawse, Hank. I'm ridin' to town."

Henderson received Brazos with a veiled surprise not unmixed with interest.

"I called to ask a couple of questions, Mr. Henderson, an' maybe one is in the nature of a favor," said Brazos, frankly.

"Well, shoot, cowboy," replied the banker, with an encouraging smile.

"Do you know Jack Sain?"

"By sight, only."

"Could yu give him a job ridin'? From all I heahed since I came back yu need some riders. I'll stand for Jack."

"Very well. That is recommendation enough. Send him in."

"Thet's fine of yu, Mr. Henderson. Jack's down in the mouth, he's had such bad luck. He took the Neeces' trouble to heart. . . . My other question is kinda personal an' I hope yu excuse it."

"What is it, Keene?"

"Air yu for or against Raine Surface?" asked Brazos, deliberately.

"Is that any business of yours?"

"Not onless yu make it mine. But I'm against him. I'm on Abe Neece's side in this deal."

"Keene! So that is what Inskip meant?"

"Mr. Henderson, yu know me an' I make bold enough to think yu have confidence in me. If Cap Britt was heah in yore place he'd put me on this job."

"What job?"

"Why, yu're a Westerner, Mr. Henderson."

"Yes. And you're a clever cowboy, Keene. . . . Did you know that Raine Surface killed a cattleman named Stokes for insinuating things?"

"Shore, I heahed thet."

"Keene, I won't say anything. But you can make your own conclusions."

"Will yu respect my confidence?"

"Absolutely."

"Wal, I reckon Raine Surface is another Sewall Mc-Coy."

"Aha! That was behind your little address to the Cattlemen's Association some weeks ago? Inskip told me that very thing."

"Yes, it was an' is."

"Ticklish business, even for a Brazos Keene. Surface has many interests, riders galore, and according to range gossip a tough outfit somewhere up in the hills."

"All powerful interestin' to me, Mr. Henderson. If Surface didn't have them, he wouldn't class with Sewall McCoy. At thet I reckon McCoy had what Surface doesn't show to me. An' thet's brains. McCoy lasted for years in New Mexico. An' if it hadn't been for my suspicion aboot a cowboy rider in my ootfit, why McCoy might be playin' a high hand yet. But Surface won't last the month oot. He just doesn't savvy us."

"Us? And who are us?" queried Henderson, tersely.

"Wal, Kiskadden an' Inskip an' Neece an' Bilyen an'

me—an' *yu,* Mr. Henderson," drawled Brazos. "I'm obliged to yu for seein' me an' more especial for yore bolsterin' up of my hunch aboot Surface."

"See here, Keene, I didn't say—I didn't intimate—" stammered the banker-cattleman, much perturbed.

"All I needed was to talk to yu a little. I know what yu think. But yu didn't tell me an' yu can rest safe in thet assurance. Keep oot of Surface's way. He might try to bore yu to strengthen his stand."

Brazos strode out of the bank, glad to be in the open air, where he wanted to whoop and swear. But all he did do was to stand with apparent carelessness watching the passers-by. Presently he turned the corner, down the side street and went around to Mexican Joe's. From the little window of his room upstairs he bent a keen and penetrating eye upon the men on the street.

Henderson knew Surface was crooked and yet he dared not betray him. That was one of the strange angles peculiar to the West. He swallowed his loss and waited for some one else to risk calling the cattle baron a rustler. Brazos' original hunch, almost at sight of Surface, had been true as a compass needle pointed to the north. Raine Surface was a thief, a leader of rustlers, a counterfeit rancher, an instigator of murder if not actually a murderer, an ingratiating man of important affairs and movements, a man who would show yellow in the face of death. He was not a master rustler. For that matter neither had been Sewall McCoy. But Russ Slaughter had been as game and desperate as the frontier bred them. He had to be shot full of holes before a rope had twanged around his neck.

"Wal, I've got the cairds an' I can shore play them," soliloquized Brazos, as broodingly he watched the passers-by and grew dark in the mood that held him aloof. "All I gotta do is lay for some of these hombres who're oot to cash me in. . . . An' Bodkin is one of them. . . . An' thet trio of hombres includin' the cowgirl with the little feet. . . . An' maybe some others I gotta savvy. . . . An' by Gawd, I'll bore some of them—an' cripple one who'll squeal. . . . Failin' all thet I'll corner Surface himself—make him crawl or kill him!"

It was a harsh decision, but relentlessly welcome. And Brazos now had something more authentic to justify his personal suspicion—the moral backing of a man whose loss at Surface's hands had not rendered him unsound.

Brazos stayed by that little window all afternoon until dusk. Of the many strangers he watched there were a few to whom he would ever turn his back.

When Brazos ventured forth again he felt that he had eyes in the back of his head—that he could see through doors and walls—into the very brains where skulked the villainous purposes to his undoing.

When he entered the restaurant he chose a seat where he could watch the door.

"Wal, air yu shore yu're Janis?" he asked, in dubious admiration, as he looked up into the pretty face above him.

"Brazos, why do you want to make so sure I *am* Janis?" she asked.

"I don't want to offend June," he replied, truthfully, not dreaming of the interpretation the girl might put upon that. The quick brightening flash of her did not alarm him.

"Have you offended her?"

"I shore have," admitted Brazos, remorsefully.

"Brazos, you went away without collecting something I owed you," she said, with subtle charm.

"Aw Janis, I was only foolin'."

"You shouldn't fool with *two* girls, Brazos Keene."

While she went to fetch his supper Brazos pondered that satiric statement. He failed to find anything of January in Janis Neece. She seemed warm, responsive, not in the least shy like June, and altogether alluring and provocative. All at once Brazos saw her in the same light wherein he saw June, which was to admit that they were as like as two peas. What was the matter with this Janis Neece? Did she not know that he was in love with June? It was most disturbingly sweet to see and hear Janis as she had been then. What a quandary to be in! To feel the same tumultuous wave go over him for either when the other charmer was absent! Brazos vowed he would dare an understanding with June, or if that did not seem

109

politic, to postpone his courting until the grave issue with Surface and his minions had been settled. And the next moment Brazos cursed himself for a sentimental fool, realizing that even with death on his trail he could no more stop making love to June Neece than he could stop breathing. He might, however, be able to stay away from the restaurant, which course would enable him to give all his thought and nerve to the purpose he had set himself.

That night after supper Brazos began his stalk, as stealthily as if he were deer hunting, though, with the wary intensity which accompanied the blood pursuit of man.

He kept to the shadow close to the sides of the buildings and he proceeded slowly. He was seen, but never by any pedestrian or lounger whom he had not seen first. One of Brazos' uncanny faculties—that which had always been a part of any gunman who survived long—was to sense in any person the mood which now gripped him. Wherever possible, Brazos had a long look into a saloon before he entered. When he went in, it was with sudden stride, to stand facing the whole assembly, with a keen and menacing front. On these occasions there were indeed few occupants whom he did not see. And always, after a few moments, when the significance of his stand had permeated to the farthest corner, he would back out. This bold maneuver had its telling effect. It made the crowd aware Brazos Keene was on the rampage, all the more dangerous because he was sober. It told his enemies, if any were present, that it was not possible to shoot him in the back, that a false move on the part of any man would precipitate a flashing gunplay, that he was ready for an even break. This procedure was a wall of advantage for any gunman. Buck Duane, King Fisher, Wild Bill—most of the celebrated gunmen lived and dominated by that sole act of defiant hardihood. Billy the Kid, youthful desperado of the period, walked coolly before a crowd of men all itching to kill him and he lived to be assassinated by a sheriff who feared to meet him in the open. The secret of this strength lay in its strange effect upon men who revered nerve above all else in an opponent—

upon the obvious fact that the first who attempted to draw upon the gunman would almost certainly perish for his brazen pains.

Brazos left that impression behind him in all the saloons and gambling dens of Las Animas. He left more— an intense curiosity as to whom he was so boldly seeking. Those who had seen him had not the least idea that Brazos himself did not know. He guessed they would whisper the names of Bodkin, Barsh, possibly Surface, though hardly the last named, for the rancher did not frequent these disreputable halls. Lastly, the act itself affected Brazos deeply, almost equivalently to the stimulus of hard liquor, from which fire and violence of spirit he would not recover until this bloody business had run its course.

Contrary to Brazos' earlier consideration of what he thought he had better do, he presented himself at the door of the Neeces' apartment over the restaurant and knocked solidly. The door opened quickly, to disclose one of the twins in a dressing gown, most bewitching in the dim lamplight.

"Sorry—but I gotta see June," announced Brazos, with a deep breath.

"Come in. I've been waiting. I knew you'd come. Janis and Auntie have gone to bed," she replied, in a low voice a little hurried.

Brazos strode in with his clinking tread and dropped his sombrero on the floor. Almost, the sweetness of June's presence, the intimacy she granted, burned away that dark mood. He flinched at a thought of his brazenness—at his stubborn need to end misunderstanding. But a second thought reassured Brazos. It was only fair to him that she should hear his honest intentions. He might not be able to come back again.

June stood before him, turning up the lamp ever so little. She looked at him with dark wide eyes.

"Had I not better run to my room and slip on a dress? I'm quite—quite——"

"Quite distractin'—an' thet's what I need," he interrupted her gloomily.

"Brazos!" She came close to catch the lapels of his coat

and look up anxiously. "What has happened? I never saw you look like this."

"Nothin' happened yet, June. But it's gonna happen—an' pronto. There air men in town—I don't know how many—come to kill me. An' I just been goin' the rounds to let them see I won't be so easy to kill."

Flattered by her anxiety, Brazos had reacted to the desire to carry it still farther. Though his statement was not in the least exaggerated, it was yet one he would not have made except under the stimulus of those troubled eyes.

"Oh, mercy! I feared—this," whispered June, unsteadily, and leaned shaking against him.

"June, I reckoned yu'd better heah it from me," he said, earnestly. " 'Cause no matter if I am Brazos Keene—somethin' might happen. But I've been in a heap tighter place—to come oot safe. An' so it'll be this time."

"And it's all because you want to help us," she said, eloquently.

"Never mind thet," he rejoined hastily. "June, it's shore hard to say the rest. My chest's cavin' in. . . . Yu remember the night I left for Kansas City—how I was mad enough to take them—them two kisses yu was mad enough to say yu owed me?"

"I'll never forget, Brazos!"

"Wal, I was so scairt thet I ran off withoot declarin' myself. An' it's kinda haunted me since. . . . June, I cain't have yu misunderstandin' me. It wasn't thet I was askin' anythin' of yu then. I just couldn't go withoot them kisses. . . . An' the reason is yu—I—I— Aw! I love yu turrible, June. Thet's all. . . . An' if I come oot of this mess alive I'll shore ask yu to marry me. . . . Somethin' I'd better ask now—'cause when yu go home to live at Twin Sombreros an' be an heiress—why I just couldn't have the nerve."

She lifted her face flushed and radiant. "Brazos," she whispered shyly, "I've loved you from the very first minute you looked at me."

"Aw, June—thet cain't be so!" he implored, and took her into his arms.

"It is so," she whispered, hiding her face on his shoulder. "It has nearly—driven me crazy. . . . I was afraid—I thought you—you loved Janis best."

"Good Lord!" breathed Brazos, over her clustering hair. But the nearness of her, the surrender of her soft palpitating person to him, the maddening fact that her white arms were slipping round his neck—these drove away the appalling thought of Janis.

"Brazos—did you ask me—anything?" she murmured.

"I said I would—if—when I come oot of this mess alive."

"Better ask me—now."

He was overcome and happier than he had ever hoped to be in his life.

"Darlin' June. I'm turrible unworthy of yu. But I love yu. . . . An' I ask yu to—to be my wife."

"You have my promise," she said, simply, and lifted her face from his shoulder, and then blushing scarlet—her lips to his.

"There! Ah, no more! . . . Brazos!" she whispered, and slipped shyly from his arms, to close the opened dressing gown around her neck. "Go now, Brazos. It's late. And here I am—forgetting my modesty! But you've made me happy. . . . I'm not afraid *now,* Brazos. Adios, my cowboy!"

## Chapter Seven

THAT night Brazos lay a long time awake, the first hours in wondering bliss, elated, exalted, transformed, and the later hours wearing toward a realization of his appalling responsibility. In the morning when he awoke again it seemed into an enchanted land. But the light of day and the sounds outside told him that dreams must give place to the sternest, coldest rationality and cunning of his life. Brazos drove love, June, future out of his mind. He knew his job and that he was big enough for it. The

113

harder he was, the more brazen in nerve, the quicker to recognize and outguess his enemies, the greater his chances to win. That was the West.

At breakfast in Mexican Joe's, Brazos met a rough cattleman whom he engaged in conversation.

"Howdy. How's tricks oot yore way?"

"Too many tricks," returned the other, gruffly.

"Which way is thet?"

"Over toward Spanish Peaks."

"Losin' cattle?"

"Didn't have many an' wouldn't have minded the loss, but I got a note to meet at the bank."

"Cain't yu get more time?"

"I haven't tried, stranger."

"Wal, tell me who rustled yu oot an' I'll get yore time extended."

"Who might you happen to be?" deliberately asked the cattleman.

"I might happen to be anybody to yu, but to these rustlin's—I'm plain Brazos Keene."

"I'm Jim Blake, an' glad to meet you, Keene."

"Do yu know who's stealin' yore stock?"

"No."

"Have any ideas?"

"I used to have. They've been routed lately. Rustlers hadn't bothered me much this last year, up till lately. There are a couple of two-bit outfits workin' back under the Peaks. But they never raided me. My cattle was runnin' with the Arrow Brand, most of which was rustled last month."

"Arrow Brand. Whose is thet?"

"Belongs to Patterson who recently throwed in with Surface."

"Ahuh. Now we're gettin' somewhere. Pretty slick. Rustlin' their own stock."

The cattleman stared mutely at Brazos, amazed and perturbed.

"Shore *yu* didn't say thet, Blake," added Brazos. "But *I* did. Thet's what I think."

"Every man can't say what he thinks. Reckon you can."

"Suppose yu could?"

114

"You're a cool hand, Keene. I don't wonder no more."

"Wal, I'm gamblin' I've guessed what you think. . . . Yu go to Henderson, the banker, an' ask him to renew yore note. Yu can mention me."

"Thanks, Keene. I'll do it. . . . An' listen—if I didn't have a wife an' kids I'd talk freer. Savvy thet?"

"Jim, have yu got any cowboys?"

"Two. One's my son."

"Tell them I'll ride oot to see them some day soon. Much obliged for tellin' me so much. Adios."

That morning Brazos began patrolling Las Animas much in the same mood as that in which he had accosted Blake. It was Saturday, and the influx of cowboys and other ranch folk had noticeably begun. Brazos stalked by the Twin Sombreros restaurant looking out of the corner of his eye. Across the railroad tracks the station platform showed the usual crowd and bustle incident to the arrival of a train. Inside the station Brazos encountered Lura Surface just turning away from the ticket window. She was dressed for a journey and her appearance was striking. She carried a satchel and evidently the larger bag at her feet belonged to her.

"Mawnin', Lura Surface. Air yu runnin' away on me?" drawled Brazos, doffing his sombrero.

"Brazos Keene!" she exclaimed. Then she gave him a glance from superb green eyes that was not particularly flattering. "Yes, I *am* running away, and for good—if it's anything to you."

"Yu don't say. Aw, I'm sorry. I been wantin' to see yu powerful bad."

"Yes, you have," she rejoined, with scorn.

"Honest Injun, Lura."

"Why didn't you then? I wrote you. I wanted to ask you to—to help me. I went to the place where we met before. But you didn't come. And you never wrote."

"Lura, thet's too bad. I'm sorry. I never got yore letter. Fact is I haven't been to the post office. Don't never want to get another letter! An' I've been away for weeks."

"I heard you had—only yesterday. Too late to save my hard feelings toward you."

"Lura, yu make me feel bad. What'd I do to hurt yu?"

115

"The nerve of you! To ask that."

"Wal, I'm askin'," he returned, with his frank smile. As a matter of fact Brazos remembered very well, and also the regret he had felt at the time.

"It's too late, Brazos," she said, a little bitterly. "I'm going to Denver to marry Hal Howard."

"Aw! . . . yu don't say? Wal, I'm shore congratulatin' thet hombre."

"But you don't congratulate me?" she flashed.

"Hardly. I just cain't see yu throwin' yoreself away on a cairdsharp. Why, Lura, yu got all the girls oot heah skinned to a frazzle."

"For what? Playing at love?"

"For downright good looks. Yu're shore the handsomest girl I know, ootside of bein' an heiress."

"If you thought so—so much of me why did . . ." she asked, softening under his warm praise, and faltering to a close. Her hard green eyes misted over. Then she went on, "Was it because you'd heard things about my love affairs?"

"No, it shore wasn't," he replied, bluntly, realizing that he had met her at a singularly opportune moment.

"I was a flirt. But I would have told *you* . . . I had to have a man, Brazos. . . . If you don't want me to hate you forever, tell me why—why you started so sweetly—and left me flat?"

"Lura, I reckon I don't know how sweet I started, but I shore know I fell flat," said Brazos, earnestly. It was only a half truth, but it did not lack sincerity. "An' if I'd gone on, meetin' yu, I'd fall'n so turrible in love with yu thet I'd half died. But I swear, Lura, it wasn't thet which made me back oot."

A perfect blaze of glow and color suffused her face and warmed it to genuine beauty. That betrayed the insatiate need of her soul—the food and drink of love without which it would starve; and her eyes shone with glad comprehension, and forgiveness. Thus she faced Brazos a moment, the truest of her womanhood possessing her, while impulsively she squeezed his hand. Then a dark intelligence succeeded all this feeling in her glance, with

116

a swift reversion to the fact that they were not alone in a railroad station.

"Brazos! You were afraid of Dad?" she whispered.

"No. Not thet. . . . Lura, I'm not afraid of any man. But it was because *he* was *yore* father."

She met his piercing gaze with understanding, and a visible shudder.

"I can forgive you now, Brazos. And I can return your confidence. . . . Dad wanted you hanged. And you didn't want me to break my heart over a cowboy who knew why Dad wanted him out of the way. . . . Howard figured it all out. He had that hold on father—so we played it for all it was worth—while I was still an heiress."

The train whistled for the stop. Lura designated her bag, which Brazos took up. They went out on the platform, where Brazos reverted to the man who was not going to be surprised by any enemy. The engine rumbled past; the train halted with squeak and jar; and there followed the bustle incident to its arrival. Brazos helped Lura on, found a seat for her, and depositing her bag he held out his hand, finding speech difficult.

"Good-by an' good luck," he said. "Yu're game, Lura. . . . I'm gonna risk a word of advice. Stop Howard's caird playin'."

"He will not need to gamble," she flashed, with a smile.

"Ahuh. Thet's fine. . . . Doggone it, Lura. I wish now I hadn't been so—so cold thet day."

"Cowboy devil! Maybe *I* don't. Too late, Brazos. But oh, I'm glad I know. . . . There! You must run. One last word, Brazos Keene. Lean closer." She put her cool lips to his ear, in what certainly was a caress as well as an act of secrecy. "For my sake, spare Dad the rope!"

Brazos could find no answer. He clasped her hand hard, bent over it and then let go to stand erect. The train was moving. One last glance he took at her eyes, brimming with tears, and dark with pain. Then he wheeled to run back to the platform, and jump off. He stood till the train passed by, and then, absorbed in thought, he moved to stand back against the high wooden platform of the freight house. And whirling thoughts occupied his mind.

The crowd cleared away; the station platform grew

117

vacant except for a blanketed Mexican; the boy with the mail bags went off toward the post office; horses and wagons moved down the main street of Las Animas.

Out of the welter of his thoughts Brazos attained a clear thread of fact and reasoning. It came only after regret and admiration for Lura Surface had had their sway.

Despite his first conception of her and the succeeding estimates to which he had listened, Brazos preferred to believe in her genuine interest in him. Perhaps he flattered his masculine vanity. He knew that many women had an instinct to collect men as an Indian brave had to collect scalps. For his own duplicity he suffered a modicum of shame, but he excused it on the score of necessity, and felt glad that he had left her the impression that not personality but circumstances had disrupted her love affair with him. That had done no harm; it had pleased and mollified her, and had moved her to a startling confession and plea.

Lura Surface had learned what a great scoundrel her father was. She had then visualized or had been told of his inevitable downfall. She and Howard had frightened him or forced him to give them a considerable sum of money, and they were eloping. And Lura, in reward to Brazos for his sentimental assurance, had verified his suspicions about her father, though not as a betrayal. She had wanted Brazos to know that she knew that he knew. And lastly, with a true Western girl's knowledge of what her father deserved, she had implored Brazos to spare him the deepest degradation of a cattleman.

Brazos wended a pondering watchful way down the street. At the corner where the bank stood an idea struck him. He went in to see Henderson.

Without any greeting or other preliminary Brazos flung a query at the keen-eyed banker.

"Did this heah bank get held up yesterday or maybe day before?"

"By a bandit?" replied Henderson, laughing despite his surprise.

"I reckon one man might think thet. . . . A bandit with green eyes an' red hair."

118

"Keene, you're a wizard. You beat me all hollow."

"Wal, come oot with it then. Didn't Raine Surface draw a big sum of money?"

"All he had in cash."

"How much was thet?"

"Close to forty thousand dollars."

"Doggone! . . . An' wasn't Howard with him?"

"Yes. Surface claimed it was a gambling debt. He didn't strike me as good a loser as usual."

"Gamblin' debt yore eye!" retorted Brazos, scornfully. "Henderson, thet was the price of Howard's silence. The gambler sold oot cheap. But still he got the girl."

"Lura!"

"Who else?"

"Good heavens!" ejaculated the banker, intensely astonished. "I begin to see light."

"Yu been wearin' blinders long enough, Henderson. Keep this under yore hat for the present."

"Wait, Keene," said the other, as Brazos turned to go. "That little matter of putting Bodkin in as sheriff has come up. What'll I do about it?"

"Air yu still in Surface's Cattle Association?"

"I resigned."

"Wal, if I was yu, Mr. Henderson, I'd say pretty pert thet I was for savin' the town Bodkin's burial expenses by not electin' him sheriff."

"That's certainly pert. I'll do it, Brazos. But let me give you a hunch. They'll make Bodkin sheriff."

"Shore they will—if he's crazy enough to accept it. I guess I better throw a scare into him."

Brazos left the bank to stalk down the street. The business of this important day was in full swing. All available space along the sidewalks was occupied by wagons, buckboards and saddle horses. It was dusty and hot. Shirt-sleeved Westerners of every class moved along the walks or stood at doors or corners. It was noticeable to Brazos that as he approached, some of them froze and most of them attempted to conceal restraint. None of them met his glance. But when he passed they turned to watch him.

Passing the open door of the largest merchandise store

119

Las Animas could boast of, Brazos had a glimpse of Bodkin holding forth to a group of men, some of them dusty yellow-booted visitors from the range. Brazos passed on and halted. What could he make out of an encounter with Bodkin? The man would not draw. But he could be made a target for speech that would sweep over town like fire in prairie grass.

Brazos turned back to enter the store. He assumed a swinging forward crouch and the sullen mein of a cowboy who had been tilting the bottle. The little group spread from a circle to a line, leaving Bodkin in the center and apart. The action was like clockwork. Bodkin showed no marked effect at sight of Brazos. As the cowboy had let him off before, he would again. This time, however, the ex-deputy packed a gun at his hip.

"Bodkin, I been lookin' all over this heah town for yu," declared Brazos, in a surly voice.

"Keene, I haven't been hidin'," complained Bodkin.

"Wal, yu're damn hard to find, an' yu shore got thet Barsh hombre hid somewhere."

"He's out of town."

"When's he comin' back?"

"I don't know. Probably soon."

"Can yu get word to him?"

"I could if I wanted to."

"Ahuh. Wal, yu better want to. Yu tell yore ropin' hombre thet he'd be wise to stay away from heah or else do some tall figgerin' how he's gonna keep me from borin' him."

"Keene, Barsh wouldn't dare meet you in an even break. He's only a boy. He never shot a man. An' you wouldn't shoot him in cold blood."

"Hell I wouldn't! Hasn't there been a lot of shootin' in cold blood goin' on aboot heah? . . . I'm sore, Bodkin. I'm spittin' fire."

"So I see. That's your game. It's none of my business. Everybody knows you're rarin' to fight, but you don't shoot men who're tryin' to keep out of your way."

"What's to keep me from shootin' Barsh's laig off?" demanded Brazos, swaggering a little. He had his sombrero pulled down over his eyes so that they were in shadow.

"Your bein' Brazos Keene, I reckon."

"An' what's to keep me from shootin' *yore* laig off?"

"I'm not worryin' none," returned Bodkin, but the fading of his healthy tan attested to another state of mind. The interview had begun to be painful to him. He seemed to catch a point in it.

"Ahuh. I reckon yu got me figgered good. . . . Wal, then, yu're so damn smart what's to keep me from shootin' Raine Surface's laig off?"

Bodkin's start and expression were peculiar, and he did not reply. All the other men stood spellbound. The business of the big store ceased, clerks and customers standing amazed in their tracks.

"Answer thet, Bodkin. Talk, damn yu! Wasn't yu loud-mouthed when I dropped in on yu?" shouted Brazos, in a loud sullen voice that halted pedestrians outside. "What's to keep me from shootin' Raine Surface's laig off?"

"Nothin', Keene—nothin'," ejaculated the other, harassed and impotent. He knew what was coming and he could not ward it off. Only a gun could do that! "But you couldn't do it—any more than to Barsh. . . . Mr. Surface is out of your reach. He's a big man on this range. You're loco, Keene. You're drunk."

"Not so drunk as yu reckon, Bodkin. . . . An' yu're defendin' Surface from a likker-soakin', fire-spittin', gun-throwin' cowboy?"

"I'm tryin' to talk sense. You might as well bust in on Henderson in the bank, or Mr. Jones here at his desk—as Raine Surface. Why, it's outlandish. . . . Mr. Surface is a generous, big-hearted gentleman, a power in this town, a fine citizen who has the best interests of the community——"

"Haw! Haw!" interrupted Brazos, in harsh mockery. "Bodkin, yu must be a fool as wal as the other things yu air. I reckon next yu'll say Surface never did anythin' against *me*."

"Sure he—never did," panted Bodkin, loyally, beginning to sweat. He was caught in a trap of his own setting.

"The hell's fire he didn't! How aboot ridin' after yu

thet day an' orderin'—*I say orderin'*—yu to hang me right then an' there?"

"He didn't order me. I was actin' under orders from Kiskadden."

"Yu lyin' tool of thet two-faced cattleman." Brazos fairly hurled the epithet. "An' next yu'll be sayin' thet Surface didn't beat Abe Neece oot of Twin Sombreros Ranch. . . . He didn't steal the herd of Texas longhorns that Neece had comin' north. Aw, no—not atall! He didn't have his tools buy off or kill Neece's ootfit of riders an' drive thet herd west along the Cimarron, over the Dry Trail, across New Mexico to the railroad? Aw, no— not atall! . . . Surface didn't have his tools—one of which *you* air, damn yore yellow skin! He didn't have them hold Neece up thet night late an' rob him of the money Neece was takin' to the bank next mawnin'. . . . Aw, hell no! not atall! . . . An' yore big-hearted respectable fine boss didn't have nothin' to do with Allen Neece's murder?"

"My Gawd—no!" gasped Bodkin, huskily. "Keene—all I cay say is—you're drunk—or crazy."

"Yu're the crazy one, Bodkin," rasped Brazos, in a voice no drunken man could have used. "An' yore boss, Surface, is wuss than crazy. He's new heah. An' yu're not so damn old. Why, man, this corner of Colorado is close to New Mexico. There air Texans on this range. . . . Yu're lookin' at one now."

"Brazos Keene—Texan or no—you'll be run out of Las Animas," blustered Bodkin, haggardly, fighting for wit and courage.

"An' who's goin' to do thet little job?" queried Brazos, scornfully.

"Surface will. The Cattlemen's Association. . . . The business men of this town. . . . They can't stand for such ravin'——"

"Cheese it, Bodkin," cut in Brazos, piercingly. "Yu heahed me. An' yore little audience heahed me. . . . Just what yu air ootside of a monumental liar I haven't figgered yet. But yu're crooked. Yu heah thet? . . . Yu're crooked. An' if yore crooked boss puts yu in as sheriff of Las Animas I'll kill yu!"

Brazos ended that ringing denunciation in a silence which could be felt. Bodkin's terrified visage satisfied Brazos that he had driven his point home. The spectators equally satisfied Brazos that his incredible affront would fly swiftly as the wind on a thousand tongues to every corner of the range. His New Mexico friends, Holly Ripple, Renn Frayne and Cap Britt would hear it before the week was out. Raine Surface would be a marked if not a ruined man.

One of the spectators outside the store was Kiskadden.

"Howdy, Texas. Where'n hell have yu been for so long? Did yu heah our little session in there?"

"Heah yu! Say, cowboy, yu could have been heahed over in the next county. Thet was good, even for Brazos Keene. I reckon they got yu desperate."

"Riled, anyway. What'll they do, Kiskadden?"

"I'll be damned if I can reckon thet. Import some ootfit to get rid of yu, I reckon."

"I've been lookin' for the two men 'an a girl who killed Allen Neece. Cain't find a trace of them."

"Wal, yu will now. Surface will have to kill yu to save his name. It shore was a clever trick, Brazos. Let's drop in somewhere an' talk."

For three days Brazos watched Bodkin unobtrusively. Brazos found nothing tedious in hiding in every conceivable kind of place to get track of Bodkin's movements. The ex-deputy went about with a bold front, but it was evident to Brazos that the man was wearing to extreme perturbation. He never went near Twin Sombreros Ranch. Bodkin was waiting for the terrible news to reach Surface's ears.

On the third night Brazos frightened the proprietor of the hotel where Bodkin stayed into giving him the room next to Bodkin's. Brazos made sure Bodkin was out, then carefully cut a hole through the partition in a corner where it would not soon be discovered. This done, Brazos sat down to wait. Some time Bodkin would be cornered in that room by Surface, or would confer with one or more of the rancher's men. Brazos meant to hide there, going out only after nightfall, until the developments he expected reached their climax.

But as Brazos' luck would always have it, his marvelous patience did not need to be exercised. At midnight, just after the eastbound train had arrived, Bodkin entered his room with two men. Brazos, moving about in his stocking feet, glued his ear to the little hole in the corner.

"Talk low, fellars," Bodkin said, "I'm scared even of the walls in this town. . . . Keene hasn't been seen for three days."

"Sure as God made little apples he's trailin' you," whispered one of them.

"I feel it, Brad. . . . Set down. Hyar's likker an' cigars. I sure got a lot on my chest."

Brazos' frame leaped as if galvanized by a vital current at the name Brad. That night on the road, had he mistaken the name Bard for Brad? He was going to find out, and he stiffened with eagerness. He heard the gurgle of liquor out of a bottle and the striking of matches.

"Panhandle Ruckfall showed yellow clear to his gizzard," spoke up another voice, thin and low, somehow sibilant. "He turned the job down. I raised the ante to two thousand dollars. Ruckfall gave me the laugh. 'A hell of a lot of fun I'd get out of ten thousand after meeting Brazos Keene!' is what he said. . . . He had too much sense to tackle such a deal. He might have killed Keene, but it's an even bet that Keene would kill him. . . . There was not another gunman in Dodge or Abilene who would have any chance against Keene. I advised against that . . . and there we are. Wild Bill was in Hays City—sheriff there. But we couldn't hire him for a dirty job like this. And if we tried Billy the Kid he'd be liable to bore us."

"We're stuck," whispered Bodkin, thickly. "I've been keepin' out of the boss's way. But he corraled me today. . . . Gawd Almighty! I reckoned he was goin' to shoot me."

"You're wrong, Bodkin," rejoined the one with the curt voice. "It's he who's stuck. Serves him right. He's gone too far. That Neece deal was too raw. I *told* him. . . . Now, if Bard and his girl fail . . ."

An eloquent silence gave Brazos time to grasp this new connection.

So there was a Bard as well as a Brad!

"Did you fetch them?" queried Bodkin.

"Yes. And Orcutt with them. They went to Hailey's."

"Now what?" asked the third man.

"We'll lay low till it's over, Brad."

"Listen," whispered this member of the trio. "It'll be over pronto. Brazos Keene will see through thet dodge. Bard's black-eyed wench is a slick one. But I'll bet she fails hyar."

"She's our best bet," returned Bodkin, hoarsely. "Keene is hot after women. The town is full of talk about him runnin' after Lura Surface an' the Neece twins. An' they're all *good* girls. Bess Syvertsen is *bad*—bad from her mother up. Add to thet, she's handsome as hell. Keene can't resist such a combination."

"The hell's fire he can't," retorted Brad. "You don't savvy that hombre. Now here's what I think of your deal. I'm not beholdin' to any of you. An' tomorrow I'm lightin' out of this town an' I'm ridin' far. If you've got an ounce of sense you'll do the same."

"Brad, I can't pull up stakes hyar. I'm goin' to be sheriff of this county."

"You're goin' to be a stiff," snorted Brad.

"Not so loud," put in the third man, with his cool voice. "Bodkin, I'm afraid Brad has it figured. I'd say if we had plenty of time we'd have a sure thing with Bess Syvertsen on the job. She's the most fascinating girl I ever met. But the hell of it is, can we take time? It's got to be done right now."

"We'll have to give her time."

"Every hour adds to the doubt and suspicion already working."

"Even with Brazos Keene dead—which is sure a far-fetched conclusion, gentlemen—this town is going to think on. Henderson, Kiskadden, Inskip, Moore, Hadley, Stevens—all these men are getting their heads together. They are going to buck the Cattlemen's Association. They'll split it wide open. Most of them are honest cattlemen, you know. They've just been fooled. Cattlemen are the easiest of men to fool because they take a little irregularity for granted, even among themselves, and they don't want to think. But when it comes to being robbed by rustlers—they wake up. . . . Look at the Lincoln County War—the Nebraska range feud, the Wyoming Jasper deal, or any of the famous examples, especially that Sewall McCoy-Russ Slaughter combine a few years ago over here in New Mexico. And Brazos Keene is the cowboy who ferreted that out, confronted those men with the fact of their guilt—and killed them both!"

Another pregnant little silence ensued. One of the men got up to move about and breathe hard. A second poured out a drink. That interview was wearing to a close. And Brazos grew tense and stiff with a fast approaching problem of what his next move should be.

"Fellars," said Brad, at length, "I'm pullin' up stakes. An' I don't mind tellin' you I'd take that bag of gold with me, if I could find it."

"Ha! Ha!" laughed Bodkin low and sarcastically. Brad was not the only one who had had that ingenious idea.

"Where did he put it?" queried the unknown man. "He must have banked such a large sum."

"Not much. He hid it," declared Bodkin.

"What was the motive in that?"

"He couldn't bank it. An' it's too soon yet after Neece's holdup. But it runs in my mind that he'll keep it close so he'll be well heeled when he slopes."

"Does Bard know where that money is?"

"No more than do I. . . . It's always stuck in his craw —that bag of gold. He an' Orcutt held Neece up. An' once I heard Orcutt say, 'Why did we let that gold get out of our hands?' "

"Same reason that applies to all of us. The stronger will of a crookeder man! . . . Well, he's run his race. It's not in the nature of things for all the men he has used to stand around now, waiting to be hanged or shot. How about you, Bod?"

"I'll stick around," replied Bodkin, evasively.

"Every man for himself from now on, eh?"

"Let's drink to thet."

Brazos had only a moment more to decide his course of action. All the tiger in him leaped at the thought of confronting these conspirators before they left that room.

He had heard the facts. But the strong heady impulse to kill could not hold against his intelligence, his judgment, his genius for thinking the right thing at the right moment. There would be little to gain in a fight and very much to risk. Wherefore Brazos relaxed from that passionate blood lust. This Brad, and the unnamed man, would go their separate ways, and probably never cross Brazos' trail again. But Bodkin, coward though he was, had some powerful motive for remaining in Las Animas.

Brazos heard the two men depart, treading softly, and he heard Bodkin curse his relief and satisfaction. Something had ended and it was more than that interview. Brazos went to bed and for a long while was aware of Bodkin pacing the floor. Then all sounds ceased. The hour was late. Brazos could address himself to considering the exciting possibilities for the morrow. So he was to be made game of by this Bess Syvertsen—this handsome black-eyed clever little siren whom no cowboy could resist? Brazos confessed to a weakness for meeting Bess and he began to revolve in mind a cunning to match her own. But before he perfected it, he went over the situation as it stood. He had no immediate gunplay to consider. The old range custom of getting rid of an enemy by the common method of provoking a gun fight was going to fail in the case of Brazos Keene. As Brazos' tension of mind eased to that fact he had a melancholy exultation in his reputation. This Surface combine could not find a man to meet him face to face. Wild Bill Hickok and Billy the Kid could not be approached for the simple reason that the great frontier sheriff on one hand and the great frontier desperado on the other would both take Brazos Keene's side. It was something of which to be proud, something to tell June, when he saw her. He had sent word to her by Jack that he might not be able to see her for a day or two. June would understand. The warmth and the softness of the thought of her was an emotion he sternly banished from his mind.

This Bard Syvertsen, with his allies, would proceed with caution and secrecy. They would not risk an open encounter with Brazos, nor would they dare shoot him in the back on the street or in a gambling den. That would bring to a head the already aroused public suspicion. The girl Bess would work on Brazos as she had done upon poor Allen Neece. Brazos thought over every possible phase of such a plot and how to meet it and what invention of his own might not only defeat them but gain the objective he had set himself—a betrayal of Surface.


## Chapter Eight


ON EVERY Sunday, the event of the day was the arrival and departure of the afternoon train. It was about as much of a social gathering as Las Animas saw except at dances and school etnertainments. There was no church. The crowd appeared dressed in their best.

Brazos occupied his old stand against the wall of the station building. His presence, for those who noticed him, served to inhibit somewhat the leisurely pleasure of the hour.

Bess Syvertsen was there with some country folk about whom Brazos was almost as curious as he was about her. He needed only one look to convince himself that no two of the four men could be Bard Syvertsen or Orcutt. The fifth was a woman of rather bold and flashy appearance. Brazos studied them with interest.

He was surprised at this incident. He had not expected the stellar member of Surface's crooked trio to show any interest in people of the community. He had expected them to be strangers. Moreover Bess Syvertsen should be looking for him, which she assuredly did not happen to be doing. The train arrived, and the woman, accompanied by the best-dressed of the men, boarded it. Bess, with the other two, turned away to stroll along the station platform, following the crowd up street. Brazos, from under his sombrero brim, looked that trio over as if his eyes were magnifying glasses. The two men were hangers about town; he had seen them somewhere.

Brazos paid little attention to Bess Syvertsen's cowgirl garb, except to note that she packed a gun somewhat too heavy for her slim build. He looked at her face.

From a distance it appeared oval, of pale olive hue, lighted by piercing dark eyes. As she came nearer he had opportunity to observe more closely. A small face, framed in dark hair which showed well under the small black sombrero, it would have been strikingly pretty but for a hard ruthless hawklike cast that Brazos did not miss. He would have been most thoughtful about it but for the conviction, as she passed, that without doubt she knew him and had all the while been aware of his presence. She was a consummate actress then, which discovery occupied his thoughts to the exclusion of her singular physical attraction. Brazos wended a thoughtful way up street, and though he lingered here and there until nightfall he did not see her again.

Monday brought back the bustle and rising dust and moving color to the cattle town. Brazos felt that this day he would meet Bess Syvertsen and he was on edge for the event. He would give her all the opportunity to approach him, if that was to be her first step. Would she make that move on the street, in one of the stores, at the post office or railroad station, or in the seclusion of a saloon or gambling hall? During the day he saw her twice on the street and once in the lobby of Hailey's hotel, and each time she passed him with different persons and apparently did not see him. Brazos decided that she was making as many chance acquaintances as she could, so that eventually her attachment of him would not appear marked.

"Doggone!" drawled Brazos, to himself. "I'm shore gettin' powerful keen aboot this heah bad girl in cowboy pants. Darn good thing for me I'm in love with June Neece!"

Wherefore Brazos was all primed and set for the momentous meeting when it came about at the post office. Bess had dropped out of the sky, apparently, to follow him up to the window where Brazos was asking for mail. She pressed close to Brazos and asked the clerk for a stamp. What a hot gush ran along Brazos' veins at the sound of that young high-pitched voice! He recognized it, except for the sweet quality, which had taken the place of the nervous shrill note he remembered. For the stamp she tendered a hundred-dollar bill, which the clerk pushed back with a laugh.

"What will I do?" she complained.

"I'll trust you. Go to the bank and get change."

Brazos promptly produced some coins. "Heah, Lady, I'll oblige yu," he drawled.

"Oh, thank you," she replied, suddenly becoming aware of his presence. She took the two cents and paid for her stamp, but she had no letter upon which to put it. Then she turned to Brazos, who had dropped back a few steps. That was the moment and it certainly gave Brazos one of the great thrills of his life. Here was the girl who was the prime instrument in the plot to murder him. Nevertheless, Brazos felt her charm.

"Cowboy, how is it I haven't seen *you?*" she asked, merrily.

Brazos took off his sombrero and stood uncovered before her, with his habitual cool courtesy in the presence of the opposite sex.

"Wal, I was just thinkin' the same aboot *yu,*" he drawled, with his slow smile.

"I am Bess Syvertsen," she said, deliberately.

Brazos made her a gallant bow. "I shore am happy to meet yu," he replied, but he did not mention his name.

While these remarks were exchanged she led Brazos aside from the doorway to the window. They stood there then, looking at each other. She was as sincere as a woman could be. Brazos' interest, a cowboy's sudden flare-up at meeting a new girl, was only a smiling dissimulation. Surprise seemed to be her dominant feeling of the moment, behind which she betrayed a profoundly deep interest. Brazos thought ironically that a girl who meant to murder a man in cold blood would be likely to have some interest in him.

"Put on your sombrero. I'm not used to men standing bareheaded before me," she said, a little irritated by something she had not anticipated.

"Thet's just one of my habits," rejoined Brazos, frankly. "Where I come from men bare their haids to women."

130

"I like it. But it struck me—sort of—of odd. . . . You're from Texas?"

"I reckon yu guessed right."

"Who are you?"

"Aw, I hate to tell yu."

"You needn't be afraid," she said, with a smile that changed the flinty beauty of her face. "I can stand a shock."

"But if I tell yu—why yu'll dodge an' run oot thet door, leavin' me unhappy."

"No, I won't."

"Wal, then, doggone it—I'm thet poor hombre, Brazos Keene."

"No!" she exclaimed. Despite her deceit she betrayed sincerity as well. "Not that hard-riding, hard-drinking, hard-shooting cowboy?"

"I shore am ashamed to confess it, Lady."

"But he's a grown-up man—and a gunman to boot. . . . Not you!"

"Yes—me."

"Oh, no. Not you with your nice boy's face, your sleepy eyes, your curly hair, your wonderful smile!"

"Air yu complimentin' me, Miss Syvertsen?"

"I just can't believe you're Brazos Keene," she declared, seriously, and she flashed those glittering black eyes over Brazos' silver spurs and high boots, his dark garb against which the heavy black gun belt and gun did not show conspicuously, his vest and scarf, to his face where it fixed with as compelling a scrutiny as Brazos cared to meet.

"You forget yore West, my girl," he drawled. "Range talk blames me for a lot thet I'm innocent of."

"Range talk is always true, Brazos Keene."

"Wal, I'm gonna return yore compliment, so far as lookin' yu over is concerned," said Brazos, with his disarming smile, and proceeded to treat her to an examination as keen as hers had been.

The spurs she wore had been used to ride with and not for ornament, though they were of finest Spanish design. Her elegant custom-made boots adorned the smallest and most shapely feet Brazos had ever seen. He felt the creeping fire under his skin. Those little boots had made the tracks in the dust under the tree out at the Hill cabin. Brazos had to keep his gaze lowered so that she might not read the sudden passion that flamed over him. But her slender legs and rounded hips, the grace of which the trousers accentuated rather than hid, were excuse enough to hold the gaze of a woman-mad cowboy such as he was said to be. The gun she packed had too businesslike a look to please Brazos. She wore a gray blouse and a red scarf and a dark leather vest with pearl buttons. It hung open. Brazos noted that it could not have been buttoned over her swelling breasts. And as he permitted his scrutiny to end on her face, he saw that to be beautiful on the moment, warm and radiant, almost sweet with the light of woman's pleased vanity. And smiling into her eyes Brazos could no more believe that she was a hardened frontier dance-hall girl, a lure used to entice men, than she could believe he was the frontier's wildest and bloodiest cowboy.

"Well, how do you like me?" she queried, archly. "You took long enough about it. I felt as if you were undressing me."

"Wal, I like yu too darn powerful much," rejoined Brazos, which outburst was a true statement.

"Why too much? It couldn't be too much to suit me."

"Aw, yu're same as all the rest of them, even if yu have got on pants. . . . Gosh, I'd love to see yu in the clothes yu belong in."

"And what are they?"

"Wal, I reckon somethin' white, with a touch of color—red, like them spots in yore cheeks—an' with yore arms an' neck bare. . . . Yu'd shore slay the cowboys, Bess."

"It's not impossible to see me that way, Brazos," she replied, dreamily. "But the occasion is wanting. . . . When have I been to a decent dance—with a———"

She caught herself before romance, the poor jewel of her soul, betrayed her, and she gazed thoughtfully out of the window at the passing procession. Brazos had struck the right note. No matter what she was—no matter what any woman was—there still abided deep within that something eternally, ineradicably feminine. This girl might be old in border experience, but she could not have been more than a year or two along in her twenties.

"How come I never saw yu before?" Brazos repeated his earlier query.

"I'm sure I don't know. You've got a pair of eyes, cowboy," she replied.

"Wal, fact is I been lookin' for men."

"What men?"

"I don't know. Reckon the hombres who're lookin' for me," rejoined Brazos, gloomily.

"Oh, I see. Have you enemies here? But of course you have. I forget who you are."

"I made some when I hit this burg a few weeks ago. Yu probably heahed aboot thet."

"Why don't you fork your horse and ride back to Texas?"

"I shore been wantin' to an' maybe I will yet. But I was kinda riled. At thet I cain't go, now I've met yu."

"Some things I heard about you are true," she said, brightly.

"Ahuh. Who told yu?"

"It might have been Lura Surface and the Neece twins. Women often help each other to self-preservation, you know."

"Wal, do yu hold it against me thet I tried oot those girls?"

"No. I admire your taste."

"Thet Surface girl was shore provokin'. But she's a destroyin' angel. An' the Neeces air too soft an' sweet. An' besides yu cain't tell them apart." Even though he was playing a game, Brazos had a sense of disloyalty at this speech.

"I would have thought one of them just your kind."

"Yu think a lot wrong aboot me, Bess. . . . For Gawd's sake don't tell me yu're some lucky cattleman's wife?"

"No, I'm not, worse luck. I'm single and fancy free. At least I was until I came into this post office."

"We air gettin' somewhere."

That drawling cool assertion seemed to acquaint Bess Syvertsen with the fact that she was reacting honestly to an intrigue the intent of which had been entirely different.

133

"Where are we getting, Brazos?" she inquired, curtly.

"I leave it to yu, Lady," replied Brazos, just as curtly.

"You just met me, cowboy!" she expostulated.

"Wal, what do yu want? Yu struck me deep. But don't misunderstand me. No Texan ever insulted a girl."

"Insult! How could you insult me?"

"*I* couldn't, thet's shore."

"You like me, Brazos Keene?"

"Like! Why, I think yu're just wonderful. An' I don't care who yu air, where yu come from, or who yu're with."

"You might be taking a risk. My father has no use for cowboys."

"Is he heah?"

"Yes. Bard Syvertsen. He's a cattle buyer. We travel all over from Kansas City to Denver. Father has a deal on with Surface and Miller."

"Who else with yu, Lady?"

"Orcutt, a partner of father's. He's not so young, but he's sweet on me. And he won't take to you."

"Jealous, eh? But air yu sweet on him?"

"Sweet on Hen Orcutt?" she ejaculated, as if the idea was unutterably new and somehow belittling. "Hell no!"

Brazos stared hard at her. "Lady, yore lips air too sweet an' red for cuss words."

"Can't I swear in front of you, Brazos Keene?"

"Wal, yu can, I reckon, but only once."

"You'd turn your back on me?" she queried, in amaze.

"I shore would—an' be most doggone sorry."

"Are you trying to string me? Whoever heard of a cowboy who hadn't played up to dance-hall girls?"

"Yu're lookin' at thet cowboy now, Lady—if by playin' up yu mean more than havin' a drink an' a dance with one."

"I meant more, Brazos Keene."

"Then yu got me wrong, Miss Syvertsen," returned Brazos, coldly. "Good day."

"Wait," she said, and detained him with a hand on his arm. "I apologize. I take your word. But don't hold it against me that naturally I thought you to be like most men. I see you're not. . . . Neither am I a dance-hall girl, though I can swear."

134

"Wal then—where air we?" drawled Brazos, his smile coming slowly.

"I don't know," she admitted.

"I reckon talkin' aboot yore menfolks."

"At this particular moment I wish they were in Hades," she said, with sudden passion that transformed her.

"Bess, does thet mean if it wasn't for them yu'd like to try oot this new acquaintance?"

"Yes—and more."

"Wal, it's just too bad. Always my luck! I ride the ranges an' I meet girls. Reckon I'm hard to please. My mother taught me to respect her sex. I don't care for town hussies or camp trulls. I cain't stand these nice goody-goody spooney little girls, neither. Lura Surface was one to make a cowboy ride high an' handsome. But she was a flirt. An' heah I meet yu!"

"Brazos, I might be a flirt—or worse," she said, as he ended eloquently.

"Shore. I'm only confessin' how yu strike me. An' yu'll have to tell me if yu want to change thet."

"Brazos! The hell of it is I—I don't want to change it," she said, with emotion. "It's got me by the throat. . . . Now doesn't that flatter your cowboy vanity?"

"I don't savvy yu, Bess. I never could savvy a girl who was deep. All the same I feel as if yu were fightin' somethin' yu didn't want me to know. Tell me or not, as yu like. But if I strike yu pretty pronto, yu know, an' bold—it's because I see no sense in holdin' back things. I've a bad reputation an' I'm liable to be shot any time. Life is too short for my kind not to live from day to day."

"Well, I savvy you, Brazos Keene, and I think . . . Never mind what *I* think. . . . Suppose I don't tell you another thing about myself?"

"Thet'll make no difference. It's what yu air to me thet'd count. Take it or leave it. No harm's been done. An' if there's a regret it'll be mine. I'll shore be glad I met yu an' had this little talk—an' I'll ride on always rememberin' what a turrible lot I missed."

"Meaning friendship—or more—with me . . . kisses and all that?"

"I reckon."

"Take you or leave you?" she mused, darkly. "For a notorious gunman you certainly are a strange fellow. You put me in a hard place. . . . I won't let you go. . . . I'd rather you didn't think me as—as good as gold—such a wonderful girl. Yet it's so—so——"

"Wal, Bess, if yu're not sendin' me aboot my business let me dream on," interrupted Brazos. "Yu couldn't change yore looks nor thet somethin' like sweet fire thet I feel in yu."

"But, romantic cowboy, you don't understand a woman."

"Wal, am I the only romantic cowboy yu ever met?"

"All cowboys are full of romance, sentiment, gush and silly nonsense. . . . You're a boy—*a boy,* Brazos Keene, and I simply can't get over it."

They stood at that post-office window for two hours more. Brazos had the advantage over her, inasmuch as he knew beforehand just what she was, while all the characteristics she had conjured up about him were wrong, as well as the ugly, vicious and hard, and matured attributes supposed to mark gunmen. Brazos could not help but be aware that he did not have to put anything on to be fascinating to women. There was a glamour about even his name. If Bess Syvertsen had expected to find him like Panhandle Ruckfall she was suffering for it now. It seemed possible that Brazos' physical person had had the same effect he had known it to have on other girls. He had been swift to find her vulnerable point. If he had taken a cowboy's fancy for her and had chucked her under the chin it would have been diamond cut diamond. But whatever Bess Syvertsen's life had been—and Brazos knew that it had been dishonest and bitter—she was helpless before the terrible fact of being taken for good when she was evil, for fine when she was base, for being loved when she should have been despised. She never got anywhere near telling Brazos this lamentable truth. Yet in her woman's heart she wanted to. If he had fallen in love with her at first sight, that was really more than she had planned. As she saw it, the game was already won. And she found herself in a dilemma. As they talked on, apparently at cross-purposes, little by little this became evident to

136

Brazos. The cruel truth was that she had plotted to lend her beauty and her person to the enticement of this cowboy for the sole purpose of luring him somewhere so that her accomplices could murder him. But now, having met him, possibly fallen in love with him, at first sight, she did not want him murdered. That was how Brazos interpreted her contradictory and ambiguous and strange remarks. The more she talked, the more she listened to Brazos and felt his slow smile warm upon her, the more she became divided against herself. He saw her predicament and augmented it by every word and glance possible. He was relentless, and yet as he had liked her at once, he grew to pity her at the last.

"It's growing late. I'm hungry," she said, finally. "Take me some place to eat."

"I reckon the safest place will be the Twin Sombreros restaurant," he replied, as he followed her out upon the street. "Did yu ever walk with a gunman—when he was kinda nervous aboot the men he met?"

"No. It'll be thrilling," she laughed. "And perhaps make history for Las Animas."

They walked down the street, which at that hour was pretty numerously populated. She was a superb actress and walked and talked as naturally as any ordinary girl accompanied by a masculine friend. But Brazos, out of the corner of his eye, saw the unobtrusive piercing glances she shot ahead. She was pale, too. He could not read her mind then. Nevertheless on the walk from the post office to Twin Sombreros restaurant he made certain they did not meet Bard Syvertsen and Orcutt.

They went into the restaurant, which, fortunately for Brazos, appeared half full of customers. They found seats at a corner table where he could watch the door. On the way to it Brazos had flashed a significant glance to one of the twins, whom he took to be June. Her face had not changed markedly at sight of him, but he read her eyes. This entrance of his with Bess Syvertsen would be an ordeal for her. Brazos regretted that he could not avoid it.

On the other hand he wanted to see how the cowgirl would react to the proximity of the Neece girls. If Bess had any qualms of conscience, if she had any compunc-

137

tion whatsoever she certainly hid them perfectly. She was tense, in the grip of strong feeling, but it had nothing to do with memory of the boy she had betrayed to his death.

Brazos marveled at her cool command of herself and his heart became flint to her. His plot to deceive her and wring a confession from her, one way or another, seemed to grow immeasurably easier. That she had vanity, and could succumb to it, and to love, did not soften him.

To Brazos' relief June sent the Mexican girl to wait upon them; and after that he attended only to the door and to the strange creature opposite him.

"Do you know these Neece girls?" she asked, curiously.

"Yes, I've met them," replied Brazos, easily. "Reckon they didn't cotton to me. . . . Yu see I was arrested by Bodkin for murderin' their brother. But I was innocent an' Kiskadden let me off."

"Bard told me about it," said the girl, dropping her eyes for a second. "About your holding up the posse and driving them to the jail. That was a Brazos Keene trick, he said. . . . You must be sore at Bodkin."

"Tolerable. I'll bore him sooner or later, when I've nothing else to do," drawled Brazos, with an air of detached deadliness that had its effect on her. "It's thet Joel Barsh I'm sore at. The young hombre who put the noose aboot my neck."

"And how about these—these gunmen, or whoever they are—who are on your trail?"

"Bess, when men like them don't come right oot in the open to meet yu, then yu know they're hardly worth considerin'."

"You're not afraid?" she asked, her dark gaze in brooding wonder and admiration upon him.

"Nope. . . . But, Bess, I never talk aboot thet sort of thing. Yu flatter me if yu're worried. An' I kinda like thet. Only don't yu worry none."

"Worry!" she uttered an incredulous laugh, as if suddenly realizing she was concerned about the life of a cowboy whom she had been hired to lure to his death. "It seems to me I'd take a precarious chance with my heart—to fix it upon an uncertain hombre like Brazos Keene."

"Yu shore would, Bess. . . . Wal, heah comes our supper. Air yu hungry?"

"I forgot we came here to eat," she said. During the meal she spoke but little and seemed pondering her growing problem. Once more out on the street she recovered something of her vivacity. When Brazos remarked that he had better be saying good night she took his arm and held it. They walked up and down the main street of Las Animas. She made no move to entice Brazos down a dark side street or into any place.

"Wal, Bess, I hate to be makin' excuses," drawled Brazos, "but I'm a cowboy. I'm used to forkin' a hawse. An' I'm near daid walkin'."

"So am I," she said, and squeezed his arm. "But there's no place *we* can go."

"We might try the railroad station an' set down for a while."

So they went there. Bess appeared less strained when they were among people, though she did not lose her watchfulness. After the train left she rose and said: "Come, I must go now. I'm so tired I can hardly wag. . . . Do you affect all girls this way, Brazos Keene?"

"What way?"

She clung to his arm during the walk to Hailey's where she released it.

"Brazos, I thought I was glad to meet you—at first. But I'm not so sure now."

"Aw, thet's not kind. Is it good-by, then?"

"Where will you meet me tomorrow?"

"Heah. Anywhere—any time."

"Anywhere?" she asked, wth her unfathomable eyes piercing him. "How about out of town?"

"Wal, I reckon it'd better be heah," returned Brazos. And when he said that it seemed a passion wrenched her.

"Tomorrow then. Here at two o'clock. Adios."

Next day Bess Syvertsen was late. Brazos walked to and fro in front of the hotel. She came at length betraying signs of anger and she was all the more handsome for that. She vouchsafed no explanation. But Brazos did not need one. They spent the afternoon together, walking, sitting in the station, standing in the post office. Brazos made violent love to Bess and she drank it up thirstily. She begged off going to supper with him or seeing him that night. When she left him she was apparently again dominated by the attraction he had for her.

This state of affairs continued next day and on the following, with Bess betraying to Brazos' keen eye varying augmenting emotions.

Despite Brazos' knowledge and his ruthlessness, it was quite impossible not to be receptive to her fascination. No doubt her predicament accounted for some of this. She had not done one single thing, since their meeting at the post office, that Brazos could construe to be intent on her part to lure him to his death. That, of course, had been the original incentive; that was what her father, Bard Syvertsen, and his man Orcutt, were waiting for. No doubt when Bess faced them after another day with Brazos she had to lie and plead for more time.

These hours together must have been sweet to the unfortunate girl. She prolonged them. Brazos had begun by dissimulation. But as their affair wore on there seemed to be less and less need for this. The respect, the gallantry, the deference Brazos paid her were things she thirsted for almost as much as love. And as daily, almost hourly, she responded to these, Brazos grew more toward sincerely feeling them. He divined, too, that she was so bound to her father, and perhaps to Orcutt, that she could not accept an honest man's offer of marriage even if she dared risk his love.

On the fourth day of this strange relation Bess came an hour late. Her face was colorless and showed other signs of havoc. For once Brazos failed to read the expression of her piercing eyes. Behind her stalked two men, one tall, the other short. That they were without vests and gun belts Brazos' sharp eye recorded before he paid attention to their features. The little man had a visage that was a map of frontier crime. This should be Orcutt. The tall man then was Bard Syvertsen and he was a splendid specimen of Norwegian manhood, lofty of stature, fair-haired, with eyes like blue ice, and a handsome craggy face. He was all of forty years old.

140

"Brazos," said Bess, hurriedly, as she advanced, "meet my father, Bard Syvertsen, and Hen Orcutt."

"Howdy, gentlemen," drawled Brazos, in his cool voice, and he made no effort to be other than Brazos Keene. At the moment he knew he risked no peril from them, and they had confronted him significantly unarmed. What their idea was, Brazos could not conjecture. Perhaps it was an overwhelming curiosity to see the cowboy at close hand.

"Howdy, Keene. Glad to meet you," said Orcutt, curtly.

Syvertsen eyed Brazos wth a curious intentness that was not all due to the fact of Brazos' status on the frontier. Brazos read that cold blue eye as if it had been an open printed page. The Norwegian did not know fear; he was callous, yet he burned inwardly. He returned Brazos' greeting in a voice Brazos would have recognized among a thousand voices. If Bard Syvertsen had been armed at the moment he would have been some time closer to the death Brazos meant to mete out to him.

"My girl has been spending a good deal of time with you, cowboy," he said.

"Wal, I reckon I know thet, an' how lucky I am," replied Brazos.

"I object to it."

"Yeah. . . . An' on what grounds, Mister Syvertsen?"

"No insult intended. But it's common talk about town— you're a trifler with women. I told Bess, and that she must stop your attentions. She said I could tell you myself."

"Ahuh. Wal, I'm sorry to say I cain't take offense. But in this heah case I'm in daid earnest."

Both these allies of Bess Syvertsen evinced expectation of any other reply save this—evasiveness on Brazos' part or curt assurance that it was none of their business, or a cool denial. Orcutt blazed under his swarthy seamed skin and if Syvertsen's eyes did not glare with jealousy, Brazos was wrong. He loved the girl with a passion Brazos did not think paternal.

"Keene, I did not believe Bess," returned Syvertsen, as if forced. "That accounts for this intrusion. You'll excuse us."

They turned into the hotel and Brazos' keen ear caught

a remnant of a curse Orcutt was bestowing upon the other. Brazos could not gauge the significance of this encounter.

"Bess, what'n hell was all thet aboot?" queried Brazos, turning to the girl in apparent bewilderment. She seemed to be in distress.

"Come. People are staring," she answered hurriedly, and drew him away.

The ensuing hours of the afternoon grew to be something of a nightmare to Brazos. They walked all over town and when too tired to walk more they sat down on whatever there was available.

If Bess Syvertsen had been a fascinating creature on former days, she was on this occasion vastly more. Only late in the day did Brazos gather that the climax had come—that Bess Syvertsen had been driven by her accomplices to end the farce—or that she was a woman being torn apart by love and an evil power too strong for her. After supper, which they ate at Mexican Joe's, she leaned her elbows on the table, her face on her hands and gazed at Brazos with eyes that hid much and expressed more.

"Air yu in love with me, Bess?" asked Brazos, for the hundredth time.

"Terribly. But what's the use? . . . If I give in to it I'll be killed. . . . If I don't you'll be killed."

Brazos noted that she did not grasp it as strange when he asked no explanation of her enigmatic reply. She was beyond cunning. Evil was losing its hold over her. It struck him that she was evading the issue or postponing it, trying to cheat time, to extract some bitter sweetness from the present. Brazos had no doubt that when she had left the hotel with him some hours previous she had bowed to Syvertsen's bidding. But all afternoon she had struggled against that. Brazos knew what she did not guess—that he had seen Syvertsen and Orcutt ride out a side street toward the open country where they expected Bess to make a rendezvous with Brazos. She was a tortured woman. Up to nightfall Brazos expected some importunity of hers—some subterfuge to entice him out of town. But it never materialized, and for that proof of womanliness on her part he swore he would spare her when the worst befell.

142

"Let's go," she said, suddenly, her eyes alight with new impulse too soft to be crafty. They went out upon the street. It was the supper hour and the street was deserted. There was no one in the lobby of Hailey's hotel. "Come!" And she drew him with steel hands and will as steely, up the stairs to the floor above. The lamp had not been lit and the corridor was shadowy. Brazos grew wary. Still he could not sense any relation to Syvertsen and Orcutt in Bess's tense mood and action. She unlocked a door and opened it.

"Wal, sayin' good night early, eh, honey?" he drawled. "It's been a hard day at thet. See yu tomorrow same time."

"Yes—but come in—now," she panted.

"Bess! Air yu loco—askin' me into yore bedroom?"

"Loco, indeed! Come . . . don't be a fool."

"I'm only human, Bess—an' I reckon I'd weaken if we was goin' to marry. But with all yore love talk I cain't see yu'd marry me."

"Brazos Keene! Would you marry *me?*" she whispered, passionately.

"My Gawd! What yu take me for? I told yu I was a Texan an' had respect for a woman I loved."

She threw her arms around his neck and clung to him quivering, appearing to stifle speech as well as sobs upon his breast. It was as if a new emotion had consumed a lesser fire within her. The paroxysm ended in a passionate embrace, in sudden wild despairing kisses upon his cheek and lips. And she tore at his hair. "Go . . . go—before I . . ."

She broke off huskily, and releasing him shut the door in his face.

Brazos heard her fling herself on a bed with smothered sobs. He went swiftly downstairs and out upon the street, where in a shadowed doorway he halted to watch and think. The street appeared less deserted; a wagon rolled by; the clip-clop of a saddle horse sounded at a distance; pedestrians were chugging by with heavy boot tread.

"Before I—before I—" mused Brazos, thinking of Bess's last choked words. Before she what? Before she succumbed to that frenzy which had possessed her and dragged him into her room? No! . . . Before she betrayed herself to be other than the good woman she believed he thought her? No! Before she told him the truth! That was what Brazos felt drummed into his temples. That was what love had done for Bess Syvertsen. She might not betray Surface and she would not betray Syvertsen and Orcutt, but she could no longer deceive Brazos as to herself.

Brazos' morning habit of whipping and rolling his guns—at rare intervals he packed two guns—had infinitely more next morning than the perfunctory practice indulged in by all gunmen. His instinct told him the day had come—the meeting with the murderers of Allen Neece, was not far away. His dark favorite gun made a shining wheel as he rolled it on his finger. And like magic it leaped at his bidding from the gun sheath. He went down to breakfast with his right hand burning, with the thin skin on his thumb feeling almost raw. He was late for this meal, yet he lingered over it, brooding while he watched the street. When he saw Surface drive by in a buckboard he muttered. "Ah-huh. I reckon my hunch was aboot correct."

At length Brazos stalked out of Mexican Joe's tense for the climax, choosing as always to let the moment demand its decision and action of him.

He met Kiskadden and Inskip on the street.

"What's Surface doin' in town?" he queried, bluntly.

"Meetin' of the Cattlemen's Association," replied Inskip. "Surface looked black as a thundercloud."

"Either of yu know Syvertsen an' Orcutt when yu see them?"

"I do," returned Kiskadden. "They ducked in Hall's to avoid meetin' me. Somethin' on their minds, Brazos."

"Will yu fellars do me a favor? Cross the street heah an' walk up thet side an' down on this side. Don't miss seein' anybody, but be particular to locate Syvertsen an' Orcutt. I'll wait heah. Take yore time. Those hombres shore won't be paradin' the street."

Brazos leaned against the wall and watched, while his friends reconnoitred. They seemed to take a long while. It wanted a quarter of an hour to his appointment with Bess Syvertsen. Hank Bilyen came along, apparently casually, but he stepped aside to join Brazos.

"Kiskadden told me you was heah. What's comin' off, Brazos?" he queried, sharply.

"Go into Hall's an' line up at the bar so yu won't look nosey. But if Syvertsen an' Orcutt come oot be shore where they go."

Bilyen's uncertainty ceased. Without another word he walked on to enter Hall's saloon. Inskip was the first of the other two men to get back. He breathed hard, his gray eye glinted.

"Brazos, I got a hunch there'll be hell a'poppin' pronto," he announced, excitedly. "I seen Surface an' Bodkin in the doorway of the stairs leadin' up to the Odd Fellows. Surface was poundin' his fist in his hand, purple in the face. An' Bodkin was the color of sheepskin."

"Ahuh . . . Aboot what time will thet cattlemen's meetin' be comin' off?"

"At two. But I reckon with Surface on the rampage it'll be late."

"Wal, yu an' Kiskadden make it yore business to be there so in case I run in you won't miss nothin'."

"Brazos, are you goin' to brace Surface?"

"Don't stand heah. Go back across the street. Watch Hall's. An' when I go in yu come pronto."

Kiskadden reached Brazos at exactly two o'clock, the time of Brazos' appointment with Bess. The Texan showed no exterior fire, but Brazos felt him burn.

"Surface just went into Hailey's. He stopped Bess Syvertsen, who was comin' oot. I took time to light a smoke. I couldn't heah what Surface said to the girl, but I shore heahed her answer. "

"An' what was thet?"

" 'No——you, Surface! I won't! Get some one else to do yore dirty work!' "

"Ahuh. Short an' sweet. I had Bess figured. . . . Anythin' more?"

"Surface hissed like a snake an' dragged the girl into the lobby. He's there now, ridin' her, I'll bet."

"Wal, he's ridin' for a fall. What else, Kis? I'm rustlin'."

"I peeped into Hall's. Yore men air still there."

"Drinkin'?"

"Not them. Watchin' oot the window."

145

"Wal, thet'll be aboot all. Yu stay heah. An' when I go into Hall's yu follow pronto."

"Brazos, let me go with yu?"

"Nope. The cairds air all oot, but they don't savvy them."

Brazos strode swiftly into the first store, traversed its length, hurried out into the alley and ran to the side street. Here he slowed up, caught his breath, and went on to Hailey's hotel, which occupied the corner at its junction with the main street. Brazos stepped into the side entrance and on to the lobby. Surface stood near the door of the hall, his tall form bent over the girl who was in the act of wrenching free from his clutch. His back was toward Brazos. Bess leaned against the wall as if for support. She looked a defiant hounded creature, game to the finish.

"You can't scare me, Raine Surface," she said, low and hard. "I tell you I wouldn't be in your boots for all your money."

Brazos entered the lobby to confront them.

## Chapter Nine

"WAL, Bess, air yu meanin' daid man's boots?" queried Brazos, as he stepped between them.

"Oh—Brazos!" gasped the girl.

Surface's visage changed instantly, markedly in color, monstrously in expression. The surprise was so complete that had Brazos sought more proof of the man's perfidy he would have seen it with the mask off. Unquestionably for an instant Surface thought his death was imminent.

"What yu raggin' my girl for?" asked Brazos, with a pretense of jealousy.

"Your—girl!" ejaculated Surface, huskily, his jaw ceasing to wobble. "She's deceived you, Keene—same as all of us. . . . She's Syvertsen's——"

"Daughter, yu mean?" interposed Brazos.

The rancher swerved. As his first shocking fear subsided he began to recover his nerve. "Daughter—hell! She's no more Syvertsen's daughter than mine."

"So yu say? Wal, what is she, then?"

"What could she be, Keene? For a cowboy who's supposed to be so damned smart you're sure a fool. . . ."

"That'll do, Surface," cut in Bess, coming from behind Brazos. "I meant to tell him myself and leave Las Animas. Take care you don't drive me to tell him what *you* are!"

Brazos jerked as if stung. That was a liberation of his pent-up force. But the imperative need of pretense still persisted.

"What the hell!" he flashed. "Bess, I don't like this talk between yu an' him. But I trust yu. . . . Surface, I always thought there was somethin' queer aboot yu."

Dealing Surface a powerful left-handed blow. Brazos knocked him flat. The rancher, scrambling up, stuttering maledictions, lifted a bloody, distorted visage. "You'll pay for this—outrage—you——."

"Aw, go for yore gun," snorted Brazos, contemptuously.

But if Surface had a gun on his person he made no move to get at it. Surface now concerned himself about the several witnesses to this scene.

"This cowboy is drunk," he said, thickly, as he faced them, and began to brush dust from his black coat. "Another example for citizens of Las Animas. We've got to have law and order here."

"Bah! Who told yu yu were a citizen of Las Animas?" retorted Brazos. "Yu're not even Western, Surface. Yu don't belong oot heah. An' if yu're gonna stay I advise yu to get law an' order—a hell of a lot."

Surface controlled a malignant rage. He had sense enough to see that he was impotent in the Western creed of man to man. But he could not control his expression, which flamed demonically upon Brazos and Bess, as he lunged away, colliding with the door in his hurry. Brazos watched him a moment. The man was not big or strong in any sense. Brazos marveled that he had lasted as long as he had. To compare Raine Surface with Sewall McCoy, or any of the great cattle thieves, would have been to insult them.

"Come—Brazos," said Bess, low-voiced, and she touched his arm.

"Doggone it, Bess!" complained Brazos, going with her into the street. "I come pretty near gettin' sore."

"You well had reason," she replied, composedly. "I'm sorry you saw me with Surface. You might believe *that* influenced me—to tell you—what I must."

"Ump-umm, Bess. But yu don't have to tell me nothin'."

"I must . . . if it's the last honest thing I ever do."

"All right, if yu put it thet way."

"Will you believe me, Brazos?" she entreated. "Believe me—when I've been such—a—a—cheat and liar?"

"Wal, Bess, yu air upset," he replied, soothingly. But after a swift glance he did not want to look at her again. He had to see every man who approached them, as they walked on down the street. "An' I can make allowance. If it'll do any good to tell me what's on yore mind go ahaid —an' I'll believe yu."

"Brazos Keene, you are the only man I ever honestly loved," she said earnestly.

"Wal, I'm glad to heah thet, but I don't savvy 'honestly'."

"I am proving it right now. If I hadn't loved you— you'd be a dead man right now."

"Yeah? Bess, thet kind of talk has a familiar ring. I've heahed it before."

"I was a cheat and a liar," she went on, swiftly. "Whatever else I am you can guess. Surface told the truth. Bard Syvertsen is not my father. . . . I never had any parents that I knew of. I was brought up in a home for—for illegitimates. . . . Syvertsen did not ruin me—nor Orcutt. Don't hold *that* against them. They were hired to make away with you. . . . I was to work on your well-known weakness for women—entice you to some secluded spot—or my room, where you'd be shot—supposedly by an angry father and lover for attempting to dishonor me. . . . That was the plot. But I give you my word—never once since I met you, looked into your eyes, have I kept faith with them. I

148

double-crossed them. . . . And today—after I say good—good-by to you—I'll tell them. . . ."

"Ump-umm, sweetheart," returned Brazos, enigmatically, and he felt rather than saw her sudden start. They had almost reached Hall's saloon. Inskip stood at his post across the street; Kiskadden remained where Brazos had left him; Bilyen had not come out. Brazos laid hold of Bess's arm with his left hand, so that she could not break away from him. But she appeared unresisting, bewildered.

"Girl, when yu confessed all thet yu proved a lot. . . . Yu won my respect. . . . An' yu saved yoreself a term in prison if not yore life!"

With that he swung her with him into the door of Hall's saloon, and sent her whirling, almost falling toward Syvertsen and Orcutt, who were backing away from the window. Brazos leaped back in front of the door, so that he could face them and all the big room.

*"Everybody in heah freeze!"* he yelled, his voice loud with strident ring.

An instant silence contrasted strangely with the former clink and rattle and hum of the saloon. On the moment Kiskadden came sliding in behind Brazos, closely followed by Inskip. Then they backed slowly to Brazos' left step by step until the tables halted them.

On the other side Bess sagged against the wall, ashen of face, her piercing eyes on Brazos in a terrible comprehension. She knew that Syvertsen and Orcutt were trapped wolves. The staring crowd at the bar, at the gaming tables divined the same, though they did not understand why. But the Norwegian and his swarthy ally divined nothing except the monstrous possibility that they might have been betrayed. Passion, not fear, transfixed them.

"Yu hellcat!" burst out Syvertsen. "What does this mean?"

His base epithet, his cold query, acted upon the girl like a goad. She stiffened as her head swept up and back to the wall, knocking off her sombrero. Then she appeared a white-faced woman at bay.

"I told him!" she cried.

*"What!"* Syvertsen's word, like a bullet, might have been either question or ejaculation. It was Orcutt who

149

flung at her: "You double-crossin' white-faced—! You told him what?"

"You bet your life I double-crossed you," she flashed, further inflamed. "I made love to Brazos Keene. Yes! But I *meant* it. . . . And I've just told him the plot I had been dragged into—that I was your tool—to entice him—to get him drunk—or off his guard so *you* could kill him. . . . To murder him because you had not the guts to fight him! . . . That you'd been hired to do it!"

"You told him that . . . you told him who . . ." gasped Syvertsen, suddenly shaken from his icy fury.

"No—not who . . . but if Brazos Keene has half the sense he's credited with he knows."

"You've been in love with him—all this time?" demanded Orcutt, incredulously, jealousy mastering all else.

"All this time," she said, tauntingly.

"You love this towheaded, girl-chasin' cowboy . . . this snoopin', sneakin', watchin' gunman!" shouted Orcutt, furiously, his leather face no longer swarthy.

"Love Brazos Keene? Yes—yes! Thank God, I had honesty enough left in me to love him!" she returned, with a passion that matched Orcutt's.

"I'll tear out your lyin'——"

*"Stop!"* thundered Brazos. He waited a moment for that command to sink in. "Yu're forgettin' I'm here. Yu ask *me*."

Both Bess's antagonists had actually forgotten the presence of Brazos Keene. They were rudely reminded of it and that the stiffness of the spectators, the silence, the strange position of the cowboy, bent a little, both brown powerful hands extended a little low, and quivering—that all these constituted a tremendous menace. Then the significance of Brazos Keene dawned appallingly upon them. He confronted them. There was no escape. No matter by what incredible means this encounter had worked out, it was a reality. And the reputation of this fire-eyed cowboy might as well have been blazoned on the walls.

"Ask me, yu yellow dawgs," rang out Brazos.

But neither of these trapped men voiced a query regarding what was dawning upon them. Engrossed in their own greeds and lusts, slow-witted and weak-willed, they had been falsely led into a mortal predicament, into an encounter with the very man they had plotted to murder.

"Wal, if yu haven't nerve to ask I'll tell yu," went on Brazos. "Bess told me, but she didn't need to. All the time I knew it."

"There!" boomed Syvertsen, coming out of his trance to point a shaking finger at the wide-eyed girl. "You were the fool. He made love to you. He double-crossed *you*. All the time he knew! So he made *you* the fool. You betrayed us for his kisses."

"That's not true," flashed Bess, a dark scarlet staining her white cheek. "He never kissed me. . . . And I don't believe he made a—a fool of me."

"Ask him. Look at him—an' ask him," shouted Orcutt, beside himself.

Bess swerved her fathomles gaze to the cowboy.

"Brazos, is that true?"

Brazos did not answer, nor shift his narrowed gaze from the two men.

"Let her alone," he called, bitingly. "What difference does it make to yu now?"

"Keene, if she squealed—I'll kill her!" choked out Syvertsen.

"Squealed? . . . Yu mean aboot young Neece an' the dirty job yu hung on me!" queried Brazos, once more in his slow tantalizing drawl with its note of mockery.

"By Gawd!" ejaculated Syvertsen, hoarsely, his eyes rolling. And the content of his words, if not their audible sound, was echoed by Orcutt.

"No! No!" cried Bess, suddenly desperate. "Bard, I swear I didn't. . . . I told him no more. . . . Hen, believe me. . . . I didn't—I couldn't be that rotten!"

Orcutt's white thin lips framed a vile name he could not utter.

"Ah! I see it all now," burst out Syvertsen, tragically. "—your false soul!"

*"Heah!"* yelled Brazos, in a piercing anger. "Let thet girl alone. Yu split on her—shore. She stacked yore deal. But the game's with me now. . . . *Me!* Brazos Keene!"

"You!" echoed the two pale men, in unison.

"Yes. Me! An' I say what's the difference to yu now—
*now?* . . . Haven't yu got sense enough to see thet?"

They had. It struck them like a bludgeon. Orcutt's lips
tightened. Syvertsen began to bluster. By these signs
Brazos read that Orcutt was the more dangerous of the
two. Then Brazos let loose the dammed-up flood that for
weeks had been waiting for this moment.

"I've run into some low-down hombres in my day. But
yu two take the bacon. I wouldn't waste my breath callin'
yu names thet'd fit yu, if I could think of any dirty
enough."

Brazos paused with that. Even in liberating passion he
did not forget his cunning. He knew how to work on such
men—to destroy what effectiveness they might have had.
And the fact that he could rail at them proved his estimate
of their nerve and prowess.

"So what am I callin' yu for? . . . Remember thet
little deal of yore's oot at the Hill cabin? Ah! Yu haven't
forgot thet. Wal, neither have I—an' thet's what I've been
workin' on all these weeks. . . . Orcutt—Syvertsen, if yu
ever got oot of heah alive yu'd swing. But then maybe yu
might have too many powerful friends who'd clear yu of
the rope. Miller, for instance, an' Bodkin, who's runnin'
for sheriff—an' Raine Surface. . . . Ahuh. Thet makes yu
kinda pale aboot the gills. . . . Wal, I reckon yu won't get
oot of heah alive. I'm not trustin' the justice of Las Animas—nor yore cattle combine."

"Keene! You're clean—mad," broke out Syvertsen.

"Bard, I *told* you," rasped Orcutt, in bitter accusation.
"Shut your bellarin' trap an' take your medicine."

"You hombres murdered Allen Neece an' blamed thet
job on me," went on Brazos, relentlessly. "Yu murdered
him because Surface wanted it done. An' yu schemed to
put me oot of the way because Surface was afraid I'd take
Allen Neece's trail. Wal, yu bet yore life I took it an' it
ends right heah. . . . Surface beat Abe Neece oot of Twin
Sombreros Ranch. Yu men held up Neece thet night an'
robbed him of the money he had to pay Surface for his
cattle. An' yu-all sicked this girl on me 'cause none of yu
had the nerve to meet me face to face. . . . Wal, thet's my
say. An' after all yu're meetin' me face to face!"

As Brazos ended he read the desperate intent in Orcutt's eyes and beat him to a gun. Orcutt's heart was split even as he pulled the trigger and his bullet hissed hotly by Brazos' ear. Syvertsen, slow to realize and act, scarcely had his gun free when Brazos shot him through. The ball thudded into the wall. Syvertsen's vitality equaled his terrible fury. He did not fall. He did not lose sight or intent. But his muscular co-ordination had been destroyed. Fire and smoke belched from his wavering gun. His frown of immense surprise, his pale lighted eyes, his incoherent ejaculations of hate were all appalling to see.

Brazos had to end them all, though the man was mortally struck, by blowing out his brains. Syvertsen swayed from his lofty stature, to fall across a table, to slide from that into another, and to crash down.

The smoke cleared away disclosing Bess, back against the wall, her arms wide spread, with her gaze fixed terribly upon the fallen men.

"He—killed—them?" she panted, as if dazed. *"Brazos Keene!"*

Suddenly she sprang out from the wall, an incarnate fury, formidable as a tigress.

"Bess," called Brazos, who had feared her reaction to the tragedy.

"You fooled me—to kill them!"

"Don't draw, Bess. . . . *Don't!*" warned Brazos, shrilly.

"I'll kill you!"

As she whipped out her gun Brazos had to be quick to save his life. He took a shot at her arm, high up. The heavy bullet spun her around like a top and sent the little gun flying. Shrieking wildly she collided with the wall, bounced out to fall beyond the two dead men, where her boots pattered on the floor.

As Brazos sheathed his gun and knelt to lift her head she ceased the cry of agony. She gazed up at Brazos, fascinated, suddenly bereft of all hate and passion.

"Brazos—you shot me," she whispered accusingly.

"My Gawd, I did, girl! But why did you draw on me? Why did yu, Bess?"

"You made a fool of me."

153

"No. I swear I didn't. At least I didn't intend to. Yu did all the foolin', Bess."

"You've killed me—Brazos?"

"I'm terrible scared, Bess," replied Brazos, and he did not lie. He saw that he had hit her in the breast or shoulder, instead of in the arm. Blood was pouring out. He was afraid to open her blouse.

"It's better so. I deserve it. . . . But to be killed by you, Brazos Keene—for loving you! Oh, what irony! . . . Oh, my wasted life! . . . the pity of it!"

Bilyen knelt beside Brazos. Kiskadden, Inskip—the others crowded around, shocked and silent.

"Bess, if you have to go—make it a clean job," said Brazos, earnestly. "Confess. Tell the truth aboot this deal."

"The truth?" she whispered.

"Yes. Of Allen Neece's murder."

"Oh, I will, Brazos."

"Hank, Kiskadden—somebody get paper an' pencil. Take down what she says. . . . An' all of yu listen. Yu'll be called to prove some things important to this range."

"I'm fainting. . . . Whisky!" called the girl, almost inaudibly. Somebody fetched a glass, and Brazos, with bloody hand, held it to her ashen lips. She drank. "All right," she said, smiling up at him. "My right name is Bess Moore. I am not Syvertsen's wife. . . . We belonged to Raine Surface's crooked outfit at Abilene. Surface is a man of two sides. One of them is black as hell. . . . We were called here to put Allen Neece out of the way. I got him to drink—coaxed him to ride out of town with me. . . . Orcutt roped him from behind bushes on the road—jerked him off his horse. . . . As he lay on the ground Bard shot him—in the back. . . . They carried him to the Hill cabin —left him in the loft. . . . Then Brazos Keene rode up. Bard had a few words with Brazos—thought he deceived him. He rode back to town and fastened the crime upon Brazos. . . . But our own plot miscarried . . . and lately— Surface called us again—to do the same job—over . . ."

"Thet'll do, Bess. Give me the paper, Kiskadden. Bess, can you sign yore name—heah?" importuned Brazos, with strong feeling.

Bess signed her name and then fell back fainting.

Brazos, with shaking hands, tore open her blouse, shivering at the white swelling breast. He pulled the blouse down over the blood-stained shoulder to feel for the wound, frantic in fear that it would be too low. But it was not low. He found it high up, just where the arm met the shoulder, a bad painful wound, but not in any sense dangerous to life.

"Aw!" Brazos burst out. "She's not bad hurt at all. She's only fainted. . . . Hank, get somebody to help carry her to Hailey's. Call the doctor. An' when she comes to, tell her she's not gonna die an' I'll be back pronto."

Brazos snatched the paper from Bilyen and relinquished the girl to him. Then he stood up, tense and eager.

"It's aboot all, men, but not quite," he said, as he carefully folded the confession. "Come with me. Yu too, Kiskadden, an' fetch somebody with yu."

At the foot of the Odd Fellows stairway Brazos halted to load his gun and wait for the followers he had outstripped.

"Brazos, is yore haid cool?" asked Kiskadden, breathing hard. "I ain't presumin' to advise yu. I'm just askin'."

"Speak oot, old-timer."

"It might look better to hold yore hand at Surface. Yu know the range—an' he has friends. Don't let them call this a gunman's spree."

"Wal, onless he goes for his gun—which he won't. Only I hope to Gawd he does! Come on an' step easy."

Inskip arrived with thumping strides, followed by men in twos and threes.

"Did yu search them?" asked Brazos, facing around from the stairway.

"Yes. Both well heeled. Bilyen took charge of money, papers, guns."

Brazos went up the stairs three steps at a time, and his followers strung after him, trying to step softly on heavy boots. The door of the hall stood open. Surface was holding forth with resonant voice.

"Gentlemen, all our fellow citizens were invited to participate here. Evidently those who stayed away were satisfied to leave important matters to us. . . . We have all voted and the results assures Bodkin's election as sheriff of

Las Animas. Formerly he was appointed by the Cattle-men's Association. That is a distinction with a difference."

Surface halted impressively for a moment, then resumed in strong voice:

"There remains to invite undesirable loafers, gamblers, dissolute women, suspected cowmen, and at last one no-torious cowboy to leave Las Animas."

Brazos drew his gun and stepped into the hall.

"Wal, Surface," he called, ringingly, "heah's yore last named undesirable—tò talk for himself."

Surface stood on a platform facing a room full of men, sitting in rows. A stiffening jerk appeared to run through them, but all of them turned to look.

"Set tight, everybody," ordered Brazos. "Surface, the jig's up!"

No noticeable change showed in the rancher's pale face. He had begun to weigh this intrusion. Kiskadden, Inskip, and other filed in with grave grim visages. They must have meant as much, or more to him, as the advent of Brazos.

"Gentlemen, you come too late to participate in this election," he rolled out, sonerously.

"Ump-umm!" retorted Brazos. "Surface, did yu heah me? I said yore jig was up."

"What do you mean?" shouted Surface, harshly.

"I just shot yore ootfit."

"Wha-at! . . . Who?"

"Bard Syvertsen . . . Hen Orcutt . . . an' Bess!"

*"Dead!"*

"Wal, the girl lived to sign her confession."

Then a startling transformation made Surface another man.

"Yu're gonna heah thet confession read."

With left hand, watching the cattleman like a hawk. Brazos extracted the paper from his vest and held it back.

"Somebody read this."

Kiskadden took the paper and with slow deliberate voice, somehow more telling and inflexible for the cool Texas accent, he read it solemnly.

When he had finished, Surface seemed actually to have shrunken in stature. He opened his mouth several times as if to speak, but no words issued forth.

"Surface, I shore hope yu got the guts to throw yore gun, but I'm gamblin' yu've not," called Brazos, in cold scorn.

The rancher flunked that challenge, and as that fact became manifest the stiff occupants of the seats began to scrape their boots nervously, to squirm and mutter, and at last to gaze at each other for angry confirmation.

"All right, Surface. I cain't waste time waitin'," went on Brazos. "March down heah."

Without protest Surface obeyed and when he reached the open space behind the chairs Brazos ordered him to halt and had him searched.

"Wal, so yu was packin' a gun!" drawled Brazos, in derisive exclamation. "I wonder what'n hell for. . . . Surface, yu're aboot as low-down as they come. If we was in New Mexico yu'd be strung up an' bored while yu was kickin'."

This speech from Brazos precipitated expression of the pent-up astonishment and wrath of the men whom Surface had addressed.

*"Shet up!"* yelled Brazos, suddenly inflamed. "Yu're hollerin' a little late against this man. Maybe most of yu air honest. But some of yu air crooked! . . . An' it'll shore be best for yu'all, an' for Las Animas, to swaller the disgrace yu all gotta share."

Then he punched Surface in the back with his gun.

"Mosey along, yu! An' don't forget I'd jump at the chance to try oot yore specialty of shootin' men in the back."

Brazos marched Surface down the stairway to the street, and into the rancher's buckboard. Brazos climbed into the back seat.

"Drive oot to Neece's ranch," he called, loud enough for the gathering bystanders to hear.

"Neece's ranch! . . . Where's that?" choked out Surface.

"Where do yu reckon, yu—robber? . . . Twin Sombreros Ranch!"

The crowded sidewalks of Las Animas were then treated to another of Brazos Keene's peculiar actions. And it was of the most prominent citizen of that frontier town driving his team of black horses down the middle of the street with a gun at his back and behind that gun the cold-faced cowboy.

Brazos did not look to right or left, and he was too grimly concerned to enjoy that ride, or the gathering whoop which rang along the street and out of town with him.

In short order the spirited team arrived at the ranch.

"Surface, I want thet bag of gold."

"What—bag—of gold?"

"Yu know. Syvertsen held Neece up an' robbed him of it."

"That! I haven't got it," replied Surface.

"Wal, thet'll be too bad. Think again an' maybe yu'l remember. I heard Bodkin an' Brad an' another man talk aboot thet bag of gold. Yu got it. Find it—or I'll bore yu pronto an' find it myself."

"All right. I—I'll get it," rejoined Surface, thickly.

At the point of Brazos' gun the rancher led the way into the ranch house, and into his room, where from under the floor of a closet he dragged up an extremely heavy satchel.

"Open it," ordered Brazos, eagerly.

Surface complied to expose packs of greenbacks and bags that gave forth a musical clink of precious metal.

"All right. Carry it oot."

Brazos had Surface drive him back as they had come. Groups of men stood on corners and in front of saloons. There was a crowd in front of Hailey's.

"Drive to the station, Surface. It's aboot time for the afternoon train."

With gun in hand Brazos saw that the deposed rancher bought a ticket to Abilene—saw him stand on the platform a target for all eyes—saw him mount the platform of the passenger coach of the train. Then he delivered himself of a final word.

"Surface, yu're gettin' off turrible lucky. Maybe it'll make yu think when I tell you thet it's due to yore daughter. . . . Get oot of Colorado an' stay oot. . . . If I ever run into yu again I'll kill yu."

Brazos stalked back to the buckboard as the train pulled out. Through a window he saw Surface, white and haggard, stare out with unseeing eyes.

Bilyen came hurrying across the tracks carrying heavy gun belts.

"My Gawd—cowboy, but yu're hard to keep track of," he panted.

"Hank, I let him off," said Brazos, as if the fact was incomprehensible. "First low-down rustler I ever weakened on . . . all 'cause of thet green-eyed, red-haired girl of his!"

"Best thing you could have done," rejoined Bilyen, heartily. "Brazos, it may have been yore weakness for women, but it'll look different to hardheaded men of this range. . . . But where'd yu go—what'd yu do?"

"Hank, I got thet bag of gold an' bills Syvertsen stole from Neece," declared Brazos, triumphantly. "Heah, under the seat."

"You—dod-blasted amazin' son of a gun of a Texas cowboy!" ejaculated Bilyen, utterly confounded.

"Listen. Take this bag oot to Neece. An' yu drive him right in this heah buckboard oot to Twin Sombreros. Today! . . . Tell June an' Janis their home is ready for them—an' no blood spilled oot there to spoil their homecomin'. Tell them they won't have to sling hash over the counter any more. . . . An'—an' tell them I'll be goin' oot in the country for a spell, but I'll come back shore."

"Brazos, no man on earth but yu should tell Neece thet an' the twins. Cowboy, think what yu'll miss!"

"Hank, for a Texan yu're plumb thick. I just got through some bloody gunplay, didn't I—an' damn near killed a woman?"

"I savvy. Mebbe yu're right. But the girl Bess ain't bad hurt. . . . We carried her to Hailey's an' Doc Williamson fixed her up pronto."

"Ahuh. Any bones broke?"

"Wal, she won't try to throw any more guns. . . . Gee, wasn't she wild, Brazos? Funny how a woman can love you an' kill you almost in the same breath. . . . Heah's her little gun—an' the hardware we found on them hombres. . . . Money, too, Brazos. Both of them had stacks of bills. Here, you better take charge of that. You sure earned it, ha-ha!"

Brazos slung the gun belts on his left arm, and gazed

with a grim smile at the little gun Bess had drawn on him. "Doggone! Yu gotta hand it to her! She would have bored me, Hank. . . . Right in thet weak spot I had for her! All right, I'll take charge of these an' the money if yu think I'd better. . . . Gosh! what a wallet!"

"Thet was Syvertsen's," said Hank, "an' heah's Orcutt's."

"Ahuh. Money was easy for those hombres. Wal, they won't need any of it where they're goin'. Bess will."

"An' so will you, Brazos. You should keep Orcutt's wallet yourself, and if I know you, everyone but yourself will be gettin' the good out of it."

"Well, we'll see. . . . So long, Hank."

"Look us up soon, Brazos," called Bilyen after him. "Oot at Twin Sombreros!"

There were two windows in Bess's room, letting the sunlight flood in, to show her white, strained face on the pillow. But the fire, the hate, the passion were gone.

Brazos advanced to the bed as he spoke to the woman in attendance. "Leave us alone a little, nurse."

"Howdy, Brazos Keene," said the girl, looking up with her unfathomable eyes.

"Howdy yoreself, girl," he replied, and carefully sat down on the bed. "Air yu in pain?"

"Not so bad now. It did hurt like hell, though."

"Close shave, Bess. . . . Gosh, I was scared."

"You didn't mean to kill me?"

"Heavens no! I had to do somethin' pronto an' tried to wing yu."

"I wish you had killed me."

"Shore, yu mad girl. But I didn't. An' yu're gonna get over this, an' somewhere far from heah, live yore—yore trouble down, an' turn oot fine."

"Brazos! You believe that's in me?"

"Yes, I shore do."

"But won't I have to go to prison?"

"I should smile not. . . . Bess, have yu any relatives or friends yu could go to?"

"Some friends back in Illinois. No kin, Brazos. . . . Oh,

160

how good you are! Back of all your deviltry. . . . Brazos, if I can go I should go at once. This town will hum."

"I reckon. Yore mix-up with cattle rustlers was not so bad. But thet deal of Surface's—hirin' yu an' yore pards to do away with young Allen Neece. . . . Pretty raw an' low-down, Bess! Yu'll do wal to get oot of Colorado pronto."

"I'll leave on the night train," she returned, hurriedly. "I can be carried. This woman will take me—across the line, anyway. . . . But, I'll need money, Brazos. I have none. Bard had a wallet full of big bills. Did they find that?"

"Heah it is, Bess," answered Brazos, and slipped the wallet under her pillow. "An' I reckon it'd be wise for yu to go pronto. Nothin' might come of yore stayin', but when yu recover—wal, men air queer, Bess. An' whether yu were forced or not, yu had somethin' to do with Allen Neece's murder. Thet'll come oot."

"Oh, yes, I know. It's horrible," she returned. "I was forced. But that's no excuse. They tried harder to force me in your case. It didn't work."

'Wal, it damn near worked, at thet," said Brazos.

"You wonderful, terrible cowboy! . . . You're lovable, too. I'm going to remember you that way—instead of . . . God! it all came to me like a flash—when you dragged me into that saloon to spin me before Syvertsen and Orcutt. There was death in your face. But I was thick—I couldn't figure your dodge. . . . I know now. Orcutt had you figured. Too late! I'm glad it's over. I think—if I was sure of one thing—I could go straight now."

"Shore of what one thing, Bess?"

"I could stand your—your fooling me—if you really cared," she said, unaware of her strange inconsistency.

Brazos took her little tight cold hand in his and held it close. He did not need to perjure himself to help this girl, but he would have done so and thought it justified.

"Bess, I knew yu was in with a bad ootfit," he said. "But I thought yu was Syvertsen's daughter, an' I was plumb loco aboot yu until I found yu wasn't. Thet hurt like hell, Bess. Yu're not atall like one of these dance-hall girls. Yu've got class, Bess—an' I mean thet as I'd mean it when I called a hawse thoroughbred. Yu're the prettiest darn thing I ever saw. The other night—heah at yore door—when yu got yore arms around my neck I was scared plumb stiff."

"Scared!" she echoed, wondering. She was softening. Her face lost its pallor. "Don't tell me you thought I had it planned for Bard and Hen to catch you in my room—or coming out of it—and use that for an excuse to shoot you? Not *then,* Brazos!"

"Ump-umm, sweetheart, I didn't——"

"Brazos, say that again."

"Ump-umm, sweetheart. For once I forgot Syvertsen an' Orcutt. I was plumb scared 'cause I feared yu might mean—wal, what yu *did* mean—an' scared wuss 'cause I wanted to. . . . Thet would have ruined all. Bess. How I got away from yu I don't know."

"You loved me then, Brazos?"

"Wal, what would yu call it?"

"But after you had time to think . . . and *now,* Brazos?"

"It's different, Bess. Somethin' to despise yu aboot—yet sweet an' regretful. . . . I'm gonna remember yu, Bess. I'll forget, after a while, yore—wal, yu know, an' think of yu as yu made yoreself for me. Thet's all."

"Kiss me, Brazos."

He bent over and kissed her as he might have if she were indeed what she had tried to deceive him into believing.

"Oh, Brazos! What have you—done to me!" she cried, brokenly, clinging to him.

"Wal, wearin' yu oot, for one thing," he replied, gently disengaging himself and rising. "I'll go now, sweetheart. Yu look most as turrible as when yu lay on the floor at Hall's an' I reckoned yu was dyin' . . . I've excited yu too much."

"You've broken—my heart . . . and made me bless you—for it—and want to—to live."

"Wal, think of breakin' a girl's heart an' makin' her the better for it!" drawled Brazos and he bent to kiss her again. "Thet's somethin' for a hombre like me to remember. I'll come down to the train an' see yu off."

She whispered something too faint for him to hear and her dark eyes followed him to the door.

# Chapter Ten

BRAZOS sat his horse and gazed with mingled feelings of relief, pain and gladness down into Coglan's valley nestling between the last foothills and the rugged barrier of the mountains.

Though only early September, the altitude provided for the frost that had begun to gild the aspens and fire the oaks. Brazos had been there years before. Time did not make much difference with nature if man did not come to despoil it. He could see no change. He remembered the lone dead pine that stood like a sentinel along the trail which crossed over into New Mexico.

The hour was near sunset, with thunder rumbling among the heavy cumulus clouds along the black horizon. Through rifts, bars of gold shone down into the green valley, with its squares of alfalfa, its gray pastures, dotted with horses and cattle, its meandering stream of shining water.

"Doggone!" soliloquized Brazos, pensively. "Thet was the kind of a nook I was gonna homestead some day. An' now I reckon I gotta ride for a big ranch."

This valley was forty miles up in the foothills from Las Animas, a secluded spot once inhabited by Ute Indians, who still came down from the mountains occasionally. The tribe had moved on into a more inaccessible spot, driven farther by the advance of their unscrupulous foe—the white man. They were friendly to Coglan, Brazos remembered.

"Wal, I reckon it was aboot time for me to hole-up a spell," went on Brazos. " 'Cause I'd shore got in a wuss fight somewhere. . . . Them hombres with Bodkin thet night—Brad an' the other fellow—they kinda worry me. The job wasn't finished. I've a hunch I'll look up Bodkin someday, anyway. . . . Heah I am, an' it's aboot time— or I'd been lookin' at red likkèr. Already I feel sorta loosenin' up around my gizzard. I'll chop wood 'till I drop, an' I'll pack a rifle up on those slopes—an' after a while maybe I'll let myself think—"

It was over—the long strain, the uncertainty, the continual need of watchfulness and sleeplessness, the drain on his reserve force, the hard cold expectancy of a fight— the blood lust. He was sick now, with that ice in his bowels—the gnawing remorse of the man who was not a killer by instinct. And his gladness was that of freedom to work and rest and dream, and presently to think of the splendid girls he had served and the love he had won.

Brazos rode on down into the valley and up to the log cabin among the firs. Two little girls were playing about the door. They ran like Indians. Presently a buxom, rosy-cheeked young woman looked out. The sight both startled and pleased Brazos. Coglan had gotten himself a wife.

"Evenin', lady," said Brazos, taking off his sombrero, "is Coglan anywhere aboot?"

"He was. Get down an' come in, stranger."

Brazos had scarcely dismounted when Coglan appeared, ax in hand. He was a strapping man, still young, half hunter and half trapper, brown as an Indian.

"Howdy, Coglan," drawled Brazos, "I shore am glad to see yu."

"Brazos Keene, by Gawd!" ejaculated the mountaineer, with a whoop. "You pestiferous, long-legged cowpuncher! Put her thar!" And he nearly crushed Brazos' hand.

"Hey, man, be careful of thet paw," yelled Brazos, trying to extricate it. "I just had to use it an' I might be needin' it bad."

"Haw! Haw! I figgered thet. Nothin' else would fetch you up hyar to see me. But you're welcome, cowboy, as the flowers in spring. . . . Rose, this is an old pard of mine. Brazos Keene! We rode together in the Panhandle . . . an' but for him you wouldn't have me for a husband. Brazos, hyar's the little wife you always told me to get."

They made Brazos welcome and the little girls, owl-eyed and shy, came forth to capitulate.

Later Brazos and Coglan walked down to the corrals leading Brazos' horse.

"Coglan, I want to hang about heah for a month or so,"

Brazos was saying. "Chop wood an' hunt an' load, An' be alone. Yu know!"

"I savvy. Tell me when you feel like it or not at all."

"Wal, I'll get it off my chest," replied Brazos, and briefly related the Las Animas tragedy.

"So thet was it," said Coglan, soberly. "I thought you looked kind of pale an' peaked. Another McCoy-Slaughter deal, eh? ... I've heerd of Surface. An' I've lost cattle this summer. I had about a thousand head."

"Wal, I reckon rustlin' will slow up for a spell," said Brazos, thoughtfully.

"Hope you winter up hyar with me, cowboy," returned Coglan, warmly.

"About a month will be all. I'll sweat oot this poison. Gosh, I haven't had enough to eat lately to keep a grub-line rider alive. Yu'll have to feed me up, Coglan. An' I want yu to ride in town once a week an' fetch me the news. Yu can make some excuse to call on Neece. Bilyen knows I'm gonna be heah. Yu can talk to him. I'll be powerful interested in all thet's goin' on. But don't tell anybody, especially the Neeces, thet I'm up heah."

Brazos erected a bough shack for himself under the pines on the bank of the brook. He made a mattress of fir boughs and spread his blankets upon that. Later he returned to Coglan's cabin and ate a bountiful supper, among the good things of which were venison and wild turkey. He did not linger long with the hospitable Coglans. To the children he said: "We're gonna be friends after a bit." Then he sought his bed in the darkness of the pines and stretched out on it as if he wished never to move again. The mountain air was cold and rare; the brook rushed murmuringly over the stones; the wind moaned through the pine tops; and the old familiar lonely wail of coyotes came thrillingly at long intervals.

He had it out then with the dark forces that had actuated him. This time Brazos did not have a drunken spree to bring oblivion and to dull memory. That ruthless side of him was only a part of his nature. Like a demon in the night it passed out, leaving him free to sleep.

Next day he awoke to new life, but he could not let himself revel in perfect solitude, in the colorful beauty of the autumn morning, in the songs of bird-travelers that had halted in the valley on their way south. He must drive himself physically to make the hours and days string out behind him with their softening influence.

As a boy in Texas he had been a great hand with an ax. Here at Coglan's woodpile, where logs of dead aspen and oak lay heap on heap, Brazos went to work. He wore gloves because it was one of his melancholy cares to keep his hands, especially the right one, soft and flexible. He heaved and he chopped and split wood until, as if by magic, that day was gone and he was spent.

Days passed swiftly then until the evening of one came with Coglan returning from Las Animas. Brazos saw that he was bursting with news which he did not care to impart before his wife.

"Brazos," he said, after supper, "I got a couple two-bit cigars thet was give to me. Let's go out an' smoke them."

They went out in the mellow gloaming. The red was fading off the ramparts; cool air was blowing down from the heights; the late crickets were at their autumn requiem.

"Brazos, I heerd so damn much thet I'll never remember it all," began Coglan, enthusiastically.

"Talk, man, or I'll bounce somethin' off yore haid," retorted Brazos, impatiently.

"Listen to this. The very day you rode out hyar Raine Surface was killed on the street in Dodge City."

"No!" ejaculated Brazos, amazed.

"Fact. An' it caused a heap of talk from Dodge to Denver."

"Who?" flashed Brazos, in sudden sharpness.

"Nobody in Las Animas could say just who killed him. But talk laid it to a tall man with a queer voice. He was heerd to cuss Surface an' after the shootin' he left Dodge pronto."

"By thunder! I'll be doggoned. It was thet third party I heahed the night I spied on Bodkin with his two cronies. The other was called Brad. He an' this unknown hombre was nursin' a grievance. . . . Wal! So Raine Surface got his just deserts pronto."

'He sure did. I wonder if they don't all get it, sooner or later."

166

"Nope. They shore don't. I've known more than one cattle baron who was respected by most an' known only by a few to be a bloody thievin' rascal. I know one now over heah in New Mexico who'll die in his bed surrounded by family an' friends. But there air only a few great cattlemen of thet stripe. . . . Go on, Coglan. Talk! You haven't told me nothin' yet."

"Wal, there's Bodkin," resumed Coglan. "He's taken office as sheriff. No one in town cared to dispute his claim. An' some of the Cattlemen's Association appeared to be back of him."

'Yu don't tell me!" ejaculated Brazos. "Wal, thet's a sticker. Coglan, shore as yu're smokin' thet punk cigar. Surface was stronger than I guessed. An' his combine was stronger. . . . I'm a son of a gun."

"Brazos, is Bodkin crooked?"

"Crooked! Say, man, a Missouri rail fence would be straight alongside Bodkin. . . . But come to think aboot it I didn't implicate Bodkin. Neither did Bess in her confession. . . . Wal, of all the nerve! I wonder what Kiskadden an' Inskip said aboot thet."

"I'll tell you, Brazos. I know them both well. An' you bet this trip to town I was meetin' everybody, buyin' drinks an' smokes, an' thirstin' for news. . . . Kiskadden said the situation was by no means cleared up. An' Inskip said it never would be until the cattle range was all plowed up. Neither of them came out blunt about Bodkin. But Bilyen did. He said Miller had stepped into Surface's boots an' the new Cattlemen's Association was as strong as ever, with fewer dissentin' voices. What did Bilyen mean by thet, Brazos?"

"I don't savvy. It's got me buffaloed."

"Wal, the town people are inclined to lay hands off. An' the cattlemen are waitin' to see what Bodkin makes out of his job."

"Ahuh. Wal, I'm not predictin'," said Brazos. "Let thet pass. . . . How aboot the Neeces?"

"I rode out to Twin Sombreros," returned Coglan. "Thet's where I seen Bilyen. Neece remembered me. He was sure a new man—if what I heerd was true. Same keen-eyed cattleman I knew, busy as a bee. Asked me if

I had any stock to sell, an' I said yes—what the rustlers left me. An' he said, 'Drive it down before the snow flies.' . . . Bilyen took me all over the ranch. Surface had spent a pile of money on improvements. It sure is a wonderful ranch. I met the twins, June an' Janis. Couldn't tell them apart! But who'd want to? They 'peared to me like girls in a trance."

"Trance! Wal, no wonder. . . . What'd they do with their restaurant?"

"Kept it, by golly. It's a money-maker. They put in a manager—a woman whose name I forget—an' they'll run it as before."

"Good idee. But I reckon all the young buckaroos will stop eatin' there. . . . What'd Neece do with Surface's ootfit?"

"Let 'em go pronto. He's hired a new bunch of riders an' he's waitin' for you to come back an' be his foreman."

"Aw!" gasped Brazos, and in his collapse he bit his cigar almost into two pieces.

"What ails you, cowboy?" queried Coglan. "Don't be a damn fool now, an' go ridin' away! Yu should have seen the eyes of them twins when their Dad said thet."

"Aw!" repeated Brazos, in greater volume.

"Cowboy, I'm givin' you a pointer," replied the puzzled homesteader. "Some of the young bucks around Las Animas would like to be in your boots. You might marry one of them twins. It wouldn't make any difference which one. You're a hero down thar, an' you ought to make hay while the sun shines. Young Henry Sisk is throwin' in with Neece on some pardnership deal. An' Jack Sain is temporary foreman of the outfit. Them two boys ain't lettin' any grass grow under their feet. Bilyen says they make life miserable for the twins."

"Aw, hell!" burst out Brazos, and unable to endure more he flung his cigar away and strode to the solitude of his camp.

Brazos sawed and split all the wood Coglan had hauled in for winter use. When he surveyed the cords of neatly stacked billets he could scarcely believe his own eyes. He belonged essentially to that class of cowboy who rode and stood guard, and handled ropes and guns. To have set

Brazos Keene to the task of digging fence-post holes would have been to invite disaster. Yet there stood the evidence of his toil—a long winter's firewood.

After that job was completed Brazos took to the slopes with a rifle. He climbed. He hunted. Deer, wild turkey and elk fell to his unerring aim; and it took strenuous work to pack the meat down to the valley. When to kill more would have been wanton slaughter, Brazos still climbed and hunted, but did not shoot again.

Brazos had the prairie range rider's love for slopes and hills and peaks—all high places. Not since he left Don Carlos' Rancho had he indulged in mountain climbing. Here he satisfied a long-felt want—a climbing and a hunting for he knew not what. It was perhaps the epitome of solitude.

As September wore on toward October he unconsciously grew to returning to certain places that fascinated him. One was a sunny open swale thickly carpeted with high silver grass and yellow daisies, and marked by clusters of aspens burning dead gold against the blue sky. Pines and firs walled this swale about. Deer and elk browsed there paying little attention to the lonely watcher.

Brazos went there every day, to cast himself on the thick grass just at the edge of the pines where sun and shade met. And here he would rest and dream for hours.

Another favored spot was a rocky glen, heavily timbered, and full of huge moss-covered boulders. At the bottom rushed a mountain brook, clear as crystal, falling white here and eddying there, filling the glen with melody. Such experiences were rare in a cowboy's life. Brazos idled there the sleepy noon hours, when only a low moan of wind stirred the lofty tree tips, and the brook seemed to grow drowsy and tarry in its descent.

At length Brazos came to frequent more and more a lofty promontory and to linger there longer and longer. It looked down upon the fastnesses of the mountain gorges, the gray rock ridges, the green thickets and yellow patches, out through a grand gateway to the vast plateau to the south. Somewhere across that dim purple stretch Brazos had ridden the Old Trail from Dodge to Cimarron. Coglan had been twice again to Las Animas to return with pleasant, disturbing, thought-provoking news and gossip. Brazos grew increasingly eager to ride down to Twin Sombreros. Yet he was loath to leave this high country. He would stay on into October. It seemed long since he had first arrived in Coglan's, and though rest and change had come in full measure, the transformation he had hoped for had not materialized. Perhaps Brazos had longed for a miracle. He found that unless a man-killer retrograded toward the beast he would never be free from remorse, from doubt, from the consciousness that fate must await him with another encounter, that his past inevitably militated against his chances of making a wife and her children happy. But Brazos had to face that gamble.

He got back one October night to the valley to find Coglan home a day earlier than he had expected him. The rancher lacked his usual geniality.

"Bilyen says you're stayin' away too long. Bodkin is braggin' he will arrest you if you ever come back."

"Good Lord!" ejaculated Brazos, incredulously.

"Wal, thet oughtn't to surprise you, Brazos," said Coglan, tersely. "Sure we know his breed. Bodkin ain't very bright. He's like an animal. He soon forgets when the danger is gone. . . . But I reckon Bilyen is keen about your reputation. He's sore. He knows soon as you come back to Las Animas thet Bodkin will shut his loud mouth."

"Gosh, I hope he does," replied Brazos, ponderingly.

"There's a stranger lately dropped into town. Calls himself Knight an' says he's a cattle buyer for a big Kansas City firm. He an' Bodkin got thick pronto. Bilyen remembers seein' this man with Bodkin once last August."

"Wal, I'll ride down soon. Gosh, I hate to leave this valley. . . . What else did yu heah, Coglan?"

"Not much. I didn't go out to Twin Sombreros. But I met Neece in town. No one would think he'd ever been down an' out. The Neece-Sisk-Henderson cattle deal went through. They're runnin' eighty thousand head."

"Thet's a solid combine. Reckon they're gonna buck the Miller ootfit. Neece is not goin' to get caught again. I reckon Bilyen is behind thet deal."

"They're buildin' a big barn at the ranch. Hauled in

170

a sawmill. Hank says it'll be the biggest in Colorado. They got the roof up an' the floor down when the twins stopped work with an idee. To give a grand dance!"

"Twins—idee—dance?" echoed Brazos, suddenly intensely curious.

"So Hank said. An' thet if you didn't rustle down you'd miss a hell of a time."

"Aw, June wouldn't give a dance withoot me!" exclaimed Brazos, vaguely disbelieving.

"Girls are queer critters. You'd better rustle, Brazos."

Nevertheless Brazos had to have one more climb up the scarlet and gold slopes to the heights.

The morning was frosty. The meadows and fields shone white. Over the valley hung a gray fog curtain through which faint blue patches and streaks appeared. Soon Brazos was lost in the cloud. At length when he emerged above it into the open sunlight the roof of this canopy resembled a soft pearly sea of rounded ripples with island crags lifting their tufted heads. And it was as if the sea circled the black base of a huge mountain with its peak rosy with the flush of sunrise.

Brazos climbed on into the forest and lost himself in the great windfalls and the jumbles of avalanche, where to cover a short distance he had to travel a meandering course through a labyrinth of ruined walls and fallen timber, until he came out upon the promontory which had been his favorite retreat.

The grassy mossy ledge with its swaying columbines lay warm and dry and fragrant under the sun, its background a forest and its foreground a leap into the abyss. Far below hung the silver fog curtain, dissolving in places, moving slowly, split by spear-pointed firs and shining-faced rocks.

Brazos had not yet found out why he came so often to this almost inaccessible spot. And now he divined that probably he never would know. He reveled in its color and beauty and wild grandeur, but these were only a part of what he felt. It was the nearest he could come to being an eagle, which boyish wish had persisted in him. The secret, perhaps, abided mostly in the solitude that seemed never to have been broken.

He sat down in his accustomed place and gave himself over to the influence of these lonely heights, feeling it magnified by the fact of this last visit and the need to carry it away with him, back to the haunts of men. Nature was lavish here with its magnificent ruggedness of cliff and peak, its ghastly bones of bared rock and bleached dead pines, its hundreds of perches that only an eagle could reach, its belts of scarlet, its patches of gold, its black fringe of fir high up and its purple clefts of canyon low down.

As Brazos gazed, a golden eagle crossed his vision, sailing on broad still wings across the void, dominant in his command of his kingdom of the heights. Suddenly he bowed his wings and shot like a thunderbolt into the depths.

The eastern wall of that colossal amphitheater was shrouded by shade, a blank mountain page, mysterious with its dim letters. Brazos followed the western fall, blazing with sunlight, to where it stepped down and down, in endless broken line, to the foothills below. These, black-domed and high, billowed away and down, losing height and color, until they sloped out into the world of plateau range.

Hours afterward Brazos wended a thoughtful way back to Coglan's valley. He gathered from all his vigils up there that he had found a strength to lose himself in solitude and be at peace should his dream of love fail him. There was just one little ineradicable drop of bitterness in his cup and that was a strange vague doubt of the enchantment which burned like a rainbow in its promise of love, happiness, fortune.

Then he put it out of his mind and next morning at dawn he left Coglan's and rode the downhill journey to Las Animas in eight hours.

Brazos installed himself again at Mexican Joe's and sallied forth to visit the barber and to make purchases.

"Howdy," he drawled to everybody. "I shore am glad to see yu-all again. Been holed-up in the hills, choppin' wood an' huntin' deer. Looks like the old burg got along withoot me."

Brazos walked into the big general store and said: "I

172

want the doggonedest best ootfit yu have in this heah store." Despite the most various and ample stock of cowboy garb short of Denver, Brazos seemed inordinately hard to please. "I gotta look handsome, which is shore a turrible job for me." At last he chose a soft gray blouse and red scarf, a huge light sombrero, and the finest of high-top boots, soft as a glove and as snug. In addition to this principal outfit he bought low shoes and black socks, shirts, scarfs, underwear, a shaving kit, and altogether so many things that he forgot what they were. By the time his purchases had been brought to his room, darkness had set in. Brazos had supper with Joe and then went out to let the saloons and the gambling halls know he had returned. He went everywhere, even into Hall's saloon, where they had printed "Brazos Keene" under bullet holes in the wall, and he was the same cool, easy, drawling cowboy as of old.

Next morning Brazos paid vastly more attention to his appearance than was usual with him. His clean-shaven face, tanned with a hint of red, did not show a line nor a shadow. "Doggone it! I could look better," he soliloquized, dissatisfied. "But at thet I'm not so pore." When he buttoned up his new gray coat he found that only the tip of his gun sheath, belted high, showed beneath it. That afforded him great satisfaction, but when he went out to ride to Twin Sombreros he left that coat open and hitched the gun sheath to its old place.

## Chapter Eleven

BRAZOS turned off the road at the brook and rode down to the pine-skirted glade where he had once met Lura Surface. Almost he saw her red hair and green provocative eyes and enticing lips. Impossible to help a little twinge of regret!

"Doggone it! Where women air concerned no man is

any good," he soliloquized. "Heah I am burstin' with love for the girl I'm goin' to see—an' yet regrettin' I didn't kiss thet red-haided cat!"

He forded the brook and rode through the pines down to the lane that came up from the pastures to the corrals and barns at the back of the ranch house. Presently he came upon the skeleton structure of a new barn, huge in dimensions. The floor was clean and shining. Benches had been built and set all around the wide square floor.

"By golly, I'm in time for thet dance."

Another new structure, probably of Surface's engineering, was a bunkhouse that almost could have rivaled Holly Ripple's at Don Carlos' Rancho. Saddle horses stood bridles down, and cowboys watched Brazos' slow approach. He reined in before them. How many times in his range life had Brazos surveyed such a group with narrowed gaze! On this occasion it left him favorably impressed.

"Howdy, cowboys. Is this heah Twin Sombreros Ranch?" he drawled.

"It sure is, cowboy. Get off an' be at home," answered one young fellow.

"Where's them twins? I want to hit them for a job ridin' heah."

"Fact is, stranger, we got so many bosses thet we don't know who's boss," said another clear-eyed youth, with a laugh.

"How many bosses?" queried Brazos, in pretended alarm.

"Mr. Neece, Henderson an' Sisk, Hank Bilyen an' Jack Sain."

"Doggone! Thet's an ootfit of bosses. I'll take my chance askin' the twins."

"Say, cowboy, you can't fool us. You're Brazos Keene," spoke up another.

"Who'n hell said I wasn't?" inquired Brazos, mildly.

"Hey, Jack, come here," called Brazos' first interrogator sticking his head into the door of the bunkhouse. "You're wanted."

Whereupon Jack Sain emerged to look, to start, to

give a whoop and thump clinking off the porch. No doubt as to his gladness! It shone in his eyes.

"Brazos! What you doin' on that hoss? Git down!" he yelled, leaping to meet Brazos' outstretched hand.

"Howdy, Jack. Gosh, but yu look fat to what yu was. . . . *Heah!* careful of thet hand! . . . I'm tolerably glad to see yu, Jack."

"Maybe I'm not. Why, cowboy, if you hadn't come, there would have been a dance. Bilyen was sore an' Neece was worried. An' the twins! They don't *ask* about you any more. They're mad!"

"Aw, thet's too bad. I'm doggone sorry."

"Where you been? You look great—young an' pert—somehow different."

"I been workin' oot. . . . Jack, introduce me to these heah boys."

"Damn! Excuse my manners, Brazos, I clean forgot. This is Neece's outfit, picked by Bilyen. . . . Fellars, walk forward an' meet Brazos Keene."

"Shore glad to meet yu-all," replied Brazos, and shook the hand of each in turn. They were the youngest, cleanest bunch of cowboys Brazos had seen for years. Then Hank Bilyen appeared on the scene.

At sight of Brazos he swore lustily. But the cloud left his tanned face. He beamed.

"Yu Texas ghost! . . . I was scared stiff. Reckoned yu'd pulled yore old trick of ridin' away. Pile off so I can hug yu!"

Brazos warmed to this welcome, yet it gave birth to an incalculable regret. Was he not going to ride for Twin Sombreros Ranch?

"Come on to the house," said Hank, eagerly. "Neece was just hollerin' aboot yu. He wants to go on puttin' up thet barn, so to get it done before the snow flies. An' he cain't go on with it because June and Janis wouldn't give the dance 'till yu come."

"Wal now, thet's doggone nice of them. . . . Hank, do I look all right to yu? I'm kinda nervous."

"Nice? My Gawd! Yu look like Brazos Keene ten years ago—a pink-cheeked, curly-haided cowboy of sixteen, which you was when I met yu first at Doan's Post."

"Only ten years? I feel turrible old, Hank. But if I don't look it, what the hell? . . . Say, isn't thet Henry Sisk on the porch?"

"Yep. One of Abe's pardners. Fine chap, but so love-sick he cain't be himself."

"Aw! Lovesick? Who with?" ejaculated Brazos, in alarm.

"Janis. An' is she leadin' him a merry chase!"

Brazos' keen perception never had been any stronger than when he met Henry Sisk again. The young rancher was a gentleman but his courtesy did not deceive Brazos. He was not glad for the return of the cowboy. Then a resonant voice, dry and crisp, gave Brazos a thrill.

"By the Lord Harry! It's Brazos Keene."

Brazos turned on his heel to meet Neece, a transformed man he scarcely recognized.

"Howdy, old-timer," drawled Brazos, feeling his heart swell. Not since Cap Britt had bade him good-by had any man looked at him like that.

"Son, there ain't any use to try—tellin' you . . ." began the rancher, with strong emotion.

"Wal, then, don't try," interrupted Brazos, with his old slow smile. "I'll take yore word for it. . . . Neece, yu shore look—wal, like what yore twins' Dad ought to look."

"By Gad! I forgot. If we're ketched talkin' to you before *they* have their turn . . ."

The call of an excited girl cut Neece short. It came from the front of the ranch house, no doubt through the open door of the sitting room.

"Henry . . . *Henry!*" called the same voice, imperiously. "Come in here!"

As young Sisk, hurried across the porch to enter the room, Brazos had a glimpse of a pale sweet face with wild dark eyes drawing back from the door.

"Girls, don't be bashful. Come out," called Neece, gaily.

Henry reappeared precipitously, as if vigorous arms had given him impetus.

"Keene, you're wanted inside," he said, gruffly. Apparently the ordeal was painful for him.

176

"Who wants me?" queried Brazos, both to gain time and to see what further puzzling effect this circumstance had on Sisk.

"June—and Janis. They want you alone."

"Aw!" exclaimed Brazos, and his heart leaped. Yet he had leaden feet as he crossed the porch.

Sombrero off, Brazos crossed the threshold. One of the twins stood in the center of the room: the other closed the door behind him. Then they both met in front of him, pale, tremendously excited and inhibited, amber eyes darkly dilated. Brazos could not tell one from the other.

"Howdy—girls," he said, huskily. "It's shore turrible good to see yu—heah."

"Oh—Brazos!" gasped one.

"Cowboy!" cried the other.

Manifestly they knew him, yet it was obvious he appeared strangly at variance with what they had expected. Brazos bore little semblance to a wild and ruthless cowboy; none at all to a bloody gunman. Even his gun did not show. His tanned face wore the old guileless smile. The month of labor and solitude, with their weaning him from the dark and deadly mood, had removed years from his face. Youth shone upon him.

He had every reason to be happy that he was Brazos Keene.

"Wal, I reckon I feel a little queer, too," he drawled, and laying his sombrero upon the table he made pretense of interest in the big sitting room. "Gosh, what a fine place! Most as nice as Don Carlos' Rancho. I shore——"

*"Brazos!"* Twin voices in unison, deep, rich with emotion, drew him as a magnet. If it had been a feminine shrinking or a check to impulsive feeling that had momentarily frustrated the twins, it went into sudden eclipse. They were upon him, murmuringly, and soft cool lips touched his cheek at the same instant that sweeter lips, on fire, met his own. Then Brazos, in a trance, found himself with two girls in his arms, and he felt throbbing breasts against his. The room whirled around him for a moment. If he thought at all, he did not care which was June and which was Janis. He did want to prolong that

177

moment. It ended, presently, however, with the girls drawing back, one of them scarlet, the other white. And Brazos, recovering his equilibrium, made the observance that the white-faced twin was the one who had kissed his mouth.

Then they both talked at once, with identical voices that spoke different meanings, not any of which gave Brazos a clue to which was his fiancée. But he gathered that their great and measureless gratitude had to do with the salvation and rejuvenation of a dearly beloved father. For the rest, the ranch had not meant so much at first but had grown to be home—the relinquishment of actual work in their restaurant had been strangely regretted —the pleasure of fixing up rooms and changing the ranch house—the fun, at first, of seeing innumerable cowboys who applied to their father for jobs—the troops of horses and mustangs and colts—the building of the huge barn and the idea of a dance destined to make history on the range —all these and more poured out upon Brazos until the twins exhausted breath.

"Ahuh. Grand—just grand!" ejaculated Brazos, bewildered. "But will yu tell me which of yu is June an' which is Jan?"

"Guess," cried one, with radiant smile.

"Does it make so much difference who is who?" asked the other, wistfully, with a devil in her eyes.

Brazos suffered a flash of that old recurrent havoc. He sensed, if he did not realize, that only a hair's breadth separated him from something appallingly nameless and incredible.

"Doggone if I'll guess!" he replied, stubbornly.

"Foolish boy! Don't you wish we were just one girl? ... I am June."

At that juncture the girls' aunt entered to welcome Brazos; and she was so sincere and kind, so apparently oblivious of his status and the violence which had reinstated them at Twin Sobreros, that Brazos found himself at last.

"Wal, it was aboot time somebody rescued me," he drawled. "Miss Neece, yu just couldn't guess how glad I am to see yu."

178

"Thank you. I'd scarcely have known you, Brazos Keene."

"Isn't he wonderful, Aunt Mattie?" asked June, with a blush. "*I* discovered him."

"Well, little Jan was around when it happened," said her sister, subtly. "Come, Brazos, let me show you my room."

"And mine, too," added June.

One at each arm they dragged the bedazzled cowboy from one beautiful room to another, then all over the house, and out into the yard, out toward the corrals, past the group of gaping cowboys, at last to the barn. June held forth on what a marvelous place it would be for her horses when winter came and Janis dilated on its desirability for their dance.

"Now you're here we can have it! When?" exclaimed June, delightedly.

"June Neece, were yu gonna have thet dance withoot me?" demanded Brazos.

"You bet she was," declared Janis. "She and Jack Sain were keen on it."

"Why, Jan Neece!" contradicted June, red as a rose. "I wasn't. . . . It was you and Henry who got Jack to nag me."

"Wal, never mind thet," interposed Brazos, seeing he had struck a discordant note. "I'm heah—an' ararin' to dance. . . . Doggone! I'll bet I've forgot how."

"Everybody is waiting," concluded Janis, who was the dominating one. "Let's say Friday night. That'll give us two days to decorate the barn with autumn leaves and flowers. And get the supper ready. Dad has a surprise for us—I don't know what. This will be the welcome home he had planned for us, June."

"Friday night—two days?" queried June, dreamily, her eyes on Brazos. "It will be full moon."

They marched Brazos back to the house to announce with gay acclaim the date for the dance. Henry Sisk reluctantly obeyed their command to take the cowboys and go into the forest to fetch an abundance of autumn leaves and pine cones and ferns for ornament. The girls rushed in to confer with their aunt. Janis poked her head out to call: "Cowboy, don't you go riding away!"

"Son, when will you take charge?" asked Neece.

"Yu mean of yore ootfits? Gosh!"

"I mean of mine. Henderson has his own foreman. An' Sisk his. They've got pretty good outfits, in my judgment. But I depend a lot on Bilyen."

"What's Hank's job gonna be?"

"Hank will buy an' sell cattle."

"Fine. He's a shrewd hombre an' honest as noonday. Coglan told me yu was runnin' eighty thousand haid. Is thet so, boss?"

"More by a few thousand."

"Ahuh. I don't know as thet is so good," rejoined Brazos, thoughtfully.

"Hank wasn't so keen about it, either. But I am. I'd rather have Henderson in with me with all his money an' bankin' interests, an' young Sisk, than tackle it alone with only the ten thousand head Surface left me."

"Neece, yu're an old-timer. It'll mean drawin' rustlers like molasses draws flies."

"There won't be any more wholesale rustlin'. I've been thirty years on the frontier. An' I've seen the cattle business grow. It's about at its peak now. An' I've never seen big raids on any range but once. Did you?"

"Wal, come to think aboot it—I reckon no. But all the same a steady stealin' of stock in small bunches cain't be sneezed at."

"Brazos, I'll lose less throwin' in with my pardners, an' runnin' a hundred thousand head, than if I stay out an' run one-tenth of that number."

"Sounds sensible. Why isn't Hank keen aboot it?"

"Bilyen is not against it, but he's not crazy about it. Says such big herds invite all kinds of range trouble from stealin' by rival combines an' out an' out rustlers to corruptin' cowboys."

"Wal, Hank is shore right."

"Brazos, we're goin' to find out before the snow flies."

"Heah comes Hank now, in a buckboard. . . . Gosh, them blacks look kinda familiar!"

180

"Where you goin', Hank?" queried the rancher, as Bilyen drove to a halt.

"Town. Got a list longer'n yore laig—all for thet darn dance."

"Hank, I've been talkin' with Neece heah. He says yu're not keen on his combine an' the big herd."

"Wal, air yu, Brazos?" parried Bilyen.

"Shore I am. The more the merrier." Brazos deliberately contradicted his opinion to Neece for reasons of his own.

"To be honest I feel all right aboot it now, 'cause yu're heah, Brazos."

"Ahuh. Wal, what was on yore chest before I got heah?"

"Mebbe I'm a little personal. I got a grudge against Bodkin. An' I ain't so damn friendly toward this new cattleman Knight."

"Bodkin kinda rubs me the wrong way, too, boss," returned Brazos broodingly. "He was crooked. I know. I heahed him talk with two men I didn't know. But all of them was in thet deal, an' all of them was ready to double-cross Surface. It was from them I heahed aboot the bag of gold I got back for yu. They were all huntin' for thet. . . . An' Coglan told me the talk had it thet this man Knight is the hombre who shot Surface."

"Wal, they've side-tracked thet talk. . . . Brazos, do yu reckon Bodkin's bein' elected sheriff will make him go straight?"

"Not in a million years!"

"Thet will simplify the problem for Neece," declared Bilyen, gathering up his reins. And he drove off without another word.

"What'd thet sore-haided Texan mean, anyhow?" queried Brazos, irritably, when he knew perfectly well what Bilyen meant.

"Drive Bodkin out of Colorado," replied Neece, grimly. "Thet'd break up this range ring."

"Yu cain't drive thet hombre oot of Las Animas."

"Brazos, you can't *kill* him," declared Neece, seriously. "Bodkin has been elected sheriff by the citizens of this

181

county. This time he wasn't appointed. He's our first elected officer. If you kill him you'll be an outlaw."

"Ahuh. I was thinkin' aboot thet."

"Bodkin is not goin' to be caught brandin' calves or dealin' with rustlers. He's going to play safe from now on."

"All the same, he's crooked, Neece. An' half the town knows it if the other half is blind. . . . Even if none of them—not even yu or Hank— *I* know. Absolutelee! . . . An' it makes a rotten situation for me, if I go to ridin' for yu."

"If! . . . For land's sake, Keene, don't say you might not. Why, I'm relyin' on you. Thet's what got Henderson to throw in with me. . . . Besides you're goin' to be a son to me, aren't you?"

"My Gawd—I'd like to be," gulped Brazos.

"June told me thet she'd guarantee your ridin' for me. An' Jan said *she* could get you if June couldn't."

"Help!" cried Brazos, in a weak voice. Then after hanging his head a moment he looked up to speak feelingly. "Neece, I'm thankin' yu for yore trust an' likin'. An' I'm shore proud thet June—an' Janis, too—wants me heah. . . . I'll come, boss, an' ride my damndest for yu."

"Good! Thet relieves me. An' it'll make the girls happy," replied the rancher, with great satisfaction. "I reckon it's a delicate situation for you, Brazos. Wild cowboy an' gunman thet you are—thank God!—you still have pride an' honor. You might feel compunctions against askin' me for June or Janis, because you are who you are. But I'll declare myself before you ask me—I'd like you to take Allen's place. . . . Don't worry about decidin' between the twins. They'll settle your hash pronto, an' it doesn't make any difference to me. . . . Now thet's off my mind. Let's go in an' drink to it."

"Wal, I'm kinda in need of a bracer myself," replied Brazos, rapt and troubled, following his host indoors. Evidently Neece considered the moment propitious for more than one drink. The result was, that when Brazos came out again, his natural reserve was somewhat lessened. And his worry about telling the twins apart did not seem so monumental. Fortunately for Brazos, however, there was a sort of general conference about the dance, in which he and Neece were consulted. After that came dinner, which was a festal board for Brazos. Everybody except Henry Sisk, who sulked over some real or imagined grievance, appeared wonderfully happy. Brazos was lost in the brightness of two pairs of eyes. He was asked, presently, what he thought about their having a huge bowl of punch in the living room the night of the dance.

"My Gawd, thet's a turrible idee," quoth Brazos.

After the merry howl had subsided one of the twins asked him gravely:

"Good or bad?"

"Bad."

"Brazos Keene," interposed the other twin, "do you think *any* cowboy would *dare* drink too much at *our* dance?"

"Aw, no, not any cowboy," returned Brazos, rising to the occasion, "but yore Dad will be heah, an' Hank, an' Henry——"

"I don't drink," snapped Sisk.

"We'll take a chance on everybody," concluded Neece, rubbing his hands. "It won't be an ordinary dance."

"I should smile it won't," agreed Bilyen.

"Holly Ripple gave a dance an' dinner once years ago," said Brazos, reminiscently. "Her Dad had kept open house like the old Don, Holly's grandfather. Thet was a party, folks, believe me. The whole range was invited. Why yu couldn't find any cowboys for cattlemen, trappers, Injuns, soldiers, freighters, bandits, rustlers, desperadoes. An' the wonderfullest thing aboot thet party was there wasn't one single fight."

"We could not hope to emulate Miss Ripple," said one of the twins. And the other fixed Brazos with inscrutable eyes. "One range celebrity will be quite all June and I can take care of."

Amid the laughter Brazos subsided, as much from this retort as from the conviction that he had for the hundredth time taken Janis for June.

After dinner they dragged Brazos, Neece, Henry, Bilyen out to the barn, and collected Sain and the cowboys on the way. Already heaps of evergreen, boughs of pine with the cones intact, and branches of different colored autumn leaves lay upon the floor.

"Not half nor a quarter enough," declared Janis. "Henry, take the wagon and the boys out for more."

Henry demurred and made a weak suggestion to the effect that Brazos go.

"Brazos can stay here and show us how to balance on a ladder," replied Janis, demurely.

All that wonderful afternoon Brazos climbed and balanced and nailed, pounded his thumb, made mistakes, fell off the ladder, and proved according to Hank that he might be Brazos Keene but he was the locoedest decorator who ever came over the range.

For once Brazos was meek, so far as taking criticism was concerned. Brazos scarcely heard his old comrade nor any of Neece's dry remarks. He tried to do the bidding of the twins, blandly oblivious of his limitations for the job, and thought only of the delicious and bewildering intimacy to which they admitted him. Half the time he was hidden with Janis or June, or both of them, behind great flaming boughs of maple leaves or golden aspens or russet oaks. And Brazos daringly took advantage of his opportunity to make love to June when he was sure he was with her. But, as the afternoon grew apace, in the excitement of fleeting moments, he would not always have staked his life upon a certainty that he was right. Then he was in too deep to get out and he did not care. And they did not help him to discriminate between them. That was the strange fiendish weakness of the twins. They had perpetrated this innocent mischievous prank since childhood.

Nevertheless, the work progressed rapidly, especially as Neece and Bilyen lent a hand to close the open ends of the barns with brilliant foliage. Then the two kindly men took it upon themselves to attempt more without consulting Janis, which omission brought dire disaster upon their heads, and the patient cowboys from their other tasks. It also left Brazos alone with June in one of the foliage-screened stalls.

184

"June, this shore has been a thrillin' day," said Brazos.

"Indeed it has. But you haven't been a thrilling good cowboy, not for me," she observed. "Here—hold this—*not* my hands!"

"June! I've been as good as—as I know how to be," protested Brazos, aghast.

"Perhaps that's not very good."

"What have I done?"

"Led poor Jan on—for one thing."

"Led pore Jan on!" burst out Brazos, suddenly on fire.

"Brazos, I—I haven't told Jan or anybody we—we're engaged. . . . I'm afraid Jan—l-likes you."

"Good Lord!—'course she liked me. Why not? I've been nice to her—an' I shore——"

"Do you think it's *nice* to make sheep's eyes at her—to smile that devastating smile of yours—to hold her hands—to let your hands. . . . Well, Brazos, your hands have dexterity aside from bridles and guns."

"June, I hope to die——"

"Don't play so terribly on words. Women take words seriously from any one they—they like. You don't hope you may die and heaven knows *I* don't want you to. . . . Brazos, I'd be glad if you—you loved Jan too—only not as you do me—and me best!"

"Child! I don't love Jan atall," cried Brazos, as one who rushed to his doom. "Leastways—only as a sister—as *yore* sister."

"Do you swear that—Brazos?" asked the girl, emotionally.

"On a stack of Bibles a mile high," declared Brazos, again possessing himself of her hands, and drawing her a little closer.

"Oh, dear Brazos—I'm happy again," faltered June. "Yet I—I'm almost sorry you don't love her, too. . . . If only she just *likes* you! Jan is strange these days."

"Aw, she's in love with Sisk."

"Like hob she is! She likes Henry, better than any of her beaux, and she might have——"

"June, don't waste so much time," expostulated Brazos. "Heah we've been alone only a minute—the first time—an' yu waste it."

185

"But Brazos! We can't spoon right under the noses of Dad—Jan—Jack——"

"Shore we can. An' why Jack? June, I'm scared yu—yu like thet cowboy."

"I do. Very much since Allen was—is gone. He was Allen's best friend. But Jack is not *you*."

"Darlin', yu gotta do two things or I'll go clean loco," importuned Brazos.

"And what are they?"

"Wal, be more of a sweetheart—an' wear somethin' or give me some kind of a hunch yu're June."

"Brazos, I've been the—the faithfulest sweetheart you ever had. If you only knew!"

"June, I mean a lovin' sweetheart. I'm the kind of a hombre thet's got to have kisses—millions of kisses."

She uttered a little laugh, easy to misinterpret. "I rather guessed that. You're so sure of the number—I wonder if you're as sure of where they're *all* to come from."

But she yielded easily to his tender clasp and shyly held up her lips. Her kiss was cool—sweet—quick, gathering something as it ended.

"There! one on account . . . Wait! they're calling me. I'll be back soon."

"June!" came the clamoring cry from outside the leafy bower.

She slipped away from Brazos, with a touch, a look that convinced him she wanted to stay there in his arms. Brazos stood staring after her in the gathering rosy gloom of the great barn. He did not attend particularly to the argument going on at the other end. He was still under the spell of June's shy surrender, her half promise, and he waited with strong impatience for her return. There would surely be a moment more. Dusk was falling. The cows were lowing in the fields. Then the supper bell put an end to the animated discussion that had disrupted Brazos' moment of bliss.

"Come on, Brazos," yelled the merry voice of Jack Sain.

"Doggone!" muttered Brazos.

"Hey, Texas, we're knockin' off for supper," called Bilyen.

Brazos stood there with a sense of blank disappointment, a letting down of his expectant mood, listening to the voices and footsteps receding. Then his heart leaped at a quick light patter of feet that slowed, halted significantly outside the booth.

A slender form in white stood framed in the darkening doorway of foliage.

"Aw, heah yu air!" whispered Brazos, with a passionate regurgitation of feeling.

"Oh, I couldn't see you. . . . They sent me back. . . ."

Perhaps it was his sudden looming right over her that checked her gay voice. He saw her face, pale against the background of leaves, her eyes unnaturally large and dark.

"Yu near found a daid man," said Brazos, snatching her off her feet.

*"Brazos!"* All her slender form appeared to leap with a divinely startled convulsion, but it did not strike Brazos that it was resistance. His surprise attack gained something from his disappointment. He gathered her up tight in his arms and as he kissed her eyes shut she cried out: "Oh! . . . please don't! . . . Mercy! . . . Ah!" And with that Brazos' thirsty lips closed hers and he spent his ardor in long, lingering kisses.

"There! Thet shore was—comin' to yu—Lady," panted Brazos, as her head dropped back, her eyes closed under mystic lids.

They opened. "Cowboy devil!" she whispered, both tone and look impossible to read.

Nevertheless Brazos translated them in his own behalf.

"No—more," she cried, frantically, and surprising Brazos with sudden strength she freed herself and fled.

Brazos followed, still in a transport. But as he got out of the gloom of the barn into the open where it was light he sustained a return of rationality.

One of the boys had waited and in a moment more Brazos recognized Henry Sisk.

"What'd you go back for?" he asked, in low voice.

"What'd you—drag June—away for?" panted the girl, as she reached him.

"I took her for *you!*" returned Sisk, in anguish.

"Ha! Ha!"

Janis' sweet laugh not only silenced Sisk but also made a stone image of Brazos. The couple hurried on to catch up with the others down the lane. Brazos stood there in the summer twilight as suddenly stiff and cold as if he had been turned to stone, his consciousness capable of only one thought: "My Gawd, if it wasn't Jan!"

Brazos had faced bad men, rustlers, wild beasts, outlaw mustangs, fire and flood with far less fear than it took to walk into the Neece dining room. But he had to go. To flee would have been a fatal blunder. Like a man going to his execution Brazos faced that merry table.

"Brazos, what made you so late? I called and called," said one of the twins, her dark eyes full of laughter. That had to be June.

"I went back after him," said the other twin, with her dark eyes lowered. "He's no plains cowboy. He's a woodland faun."

"Wal, I reckon I don't know what thet is," Brazos drawled, in his old cool lazy voice. "But in the fall when the leaves air all gold an' red I get kinda loco!"

## Chapter Twelve

THE rest of that evening Brazos sought the safety of numbers. But just the same, he was conscious of June's observance of him, as if she knew what a fool he was, and of Janis' smiling radiance, as if she had a secret not to keep long from the world. One other shared it, of that Brazos was sure, and he was Henry Sisk. Jack Sain betrayed a curiosity beyond jealousy, but something that would eventually probe to the bottom of the mystery. And as the evening wore on Brazos began to grow suspicious of the others.

"Wal, folks," he said at an opportune moment, "I'm gonna say good night an' ride back to town."

"What's the sense in thet?" spoke up Neece, quickly.

"This is your home. An' Hank can fetch your pack to-morrow."

"Please don't go, Brazos," added June, suddenly anxious.

"Brazos Keene, you've got a job," piled on Janis, with a merry subtlety impossible to interpret. "This Neece outfit is getting obstreperous. You can't run it gallivanting to town."

"Wal, I reckon I cain't run it if I stay," replied Brazos, for whom the humor of the situation had ceased.

"I was only fooling," said Janis, hurriedly.

"Why must you go?" pouted June.

"Wal, since yu call my hand," drawled Brazos, exaggerating his cool habit of speech, "the fact is there's a couple of hombres in town thet I forgot aboot shootin'."

Blank surprise and silence ensued upon Brazos' reply. As Brazos had intended they could not tell whether he was in jest or earnest.

"So long. See yu-all in the mawnin'," he concluded, and left the room. Hank Bilyen followed him out on the porch, and one of the twins caught up with them.

"Brazos—wait," she faltered.

"Cowboy, I'll have yore hawse heah in a jiffy," said Hank, and thumped off the porch.

Brazos had taken a step down, but turned to look at the girl, whose face was on a level with his.

"You are—angry?" she asked.

"Not atall. . . . An' which one of these heah Neece girls air you?"

"Brazos! I'm June. Don't look at me like that. We were only in fun—and they coaxed—nagged me into it."

"Into what?" queried Brazos, bluntly. June's distress told him there was something in the wind of which he had had no inkling.

"You've guessed it—haven't you?"

"Ump-umm. I'm a pore guesser. An' I'm a pore social cuss, too. I reckon I don't belong heah."

"Oh, Brazos, you *are* angry," cried June, and she looked back to beckon Janis, who stood with white face and wide eyes in the light of the door. But Janis did not come. "See! Jan leaves it all on my shoulders. . . . And look at

189

Dad and Jack! Laughing like hyenas. . . . Brazos, I don't blame you. . . . But forgive *me,* darling."

This was so astounding and delicious that Brazos could not resist prolonging it.

"Wal, June, I'm not a forgiving cuss, either—when I see I'm bein' made fun of."

"Now they're making fun of me, too," protested June. "They put up a job on us, Brazos."

"Ahuh. Suppose yu tell me aboot it."

"Darling!"

"Awful sweet talk, June, but not gettin' us anywhere."

"But don't be such a stranger to me," she wailed. "Brazos, would—would you be terribly angry if—I—confessed something I said about—about you and me?"

"No. If it was true I'd like yu the better."

"You remember tonight before supper—when you and I were alone in the stall?"

"Wal, I'm not liable to forget."

"We must have been there a long time. It was almost dark. They teased me unmercifully. Even Dad! I got mad. Jan didn't help it any, believe me. So I said: 'I guess no one has a better right to be alone with Brazos Keene. And if *this* is all you called me for, I'm going back.' . . . Well, Jack Sain grabbed me. They dragged me out of the barn. Oh, they were full of mischief. And then they sprang the joke on me. That same old trick that has got me into a peck of trouble lots of times! . . Sent Janis back. Let her pretend to be me. She would string you along until we got in to supper. I objected. I didn't like it. I didn't want to. But *Jan did!* And always I'd do anything under the sun for her. So I weakened and she went. Henry was the only one who was sore. He *was* sore. He waited. And Jan kept you there in the barn so long that all of us but Henry ran off. . . . When Jan came in alone with Henry, who was black as a thundercloud, and you didn't come—then they guessed the joke hadn't gone so good. Jan was mysterious. She kept mum. She didn't care a whoop how mad Henry was. But she couldn't fool *me.* Jan doesn't have that white look and those black eyes for nothing. Something had hap-
190

pened while she was pretending to be me. . . . And I've been frantic ever since."

"Wal, I shore took Jan for yu, all right," declared Brazos, with a grim satisfaction.

"Oh, Brazos—you—you didn't——"

"Let yore imagination run high, wide, an' handsome, June, an' maybe yu'll get somewhere."

"Brazos! I'll bet you were too smart for them. You knew Jan!" exclaimed June, hopefully. "You played up to them. Poor Jan! No wonder she was so strange—so tense. Served her right! Oh, Brazos, I'm horribly jealous, but if you guessed the trick I—I can stand it. . . . Only Jan worries me. . . . Do you forgive me, Brazos?"

"Shore, sweetheart, I'd forgive yu anythin'. But I'm not so shore aboot Jan an' Jack an' yore Dad."

"Now you're my old Brazos again," murmured June. "I'll be a match for them next time. . . . Brazos, let's play a terrible joke on them."

"I should smile. How aboot elopin'?"

"Oh! . . . Brazos, you're not serious?" cried June, aghast yet intrigued at the idea.

"Shore am. We could slope off in the mawnin'—get to Dodge City long enough to slip thet bridle on yu—then come back to the dance."

"Glorious! But—but——"

"Then it wouldn't make so much difference whether or not I took yu for Jan," drawled Brazos, dryly.

"Wouldn't it though?" flashed June. "Brazos Keene, I agree with Jan. Nobody can be quite sure of you."

"If yu were my wife, wouldn't yu feel tolerable safe?"

"Don't tempt me, Brazos. If we eloped it'd hurt Dad. And there's no need of hurry. I—I'd like it! But I mustn't. Another thing—Jan would never forgive me."

"For marryin' me!" ejaculated Brazos.

"No. For not telling her. We'll wait, Brazos dear—if you can be true to me."

"I shore can if yu'll only wear somethin' or do somethin' so I cain't mistake yu for Jan again."

"I guess you don't really want to," she said, reproachfully. "It must be great fun for a cowboy, especially when his fiancée's sister doesn't run away from him."

"About as funny as bein' piled off yore hawse. June, will you promise to give me a hunch, so I'll know yu?"

"Yes. I promise, Brazos. I'll think up something that no one else can tell."

"June, do yu reckon they-all took yu to mean we air engaged?" asked Brazos, wistfully.

"No, they didn't. Dad never mentioned it. And Jan laughed in my face. Then she tried to pump me. Oh, she worries me, Brazos."

"Wal, if yu had my state of mind aboot thet girl yu'd be loco. . . . Have yu got any nerve, darlin'?"

"Nerve? Yes. For what?"

"Jan has backed into the room. Gosh, her eyes look like burnt holes in a blanket. They're all peekin' oot at us. Makes me kinda sore. How aboot kissin' me good night? Thet'll fix them."

"Oh, I haven't that—much nerve," faltered June. "I might——"

"Jan would have in yore place," interrupted Brazos, a little bitterly.

"If I had your nerve I know what *I'd* do," retorted June.

"Aw, heah comes Hank with my hawse."

"Pooh! Who cares for Hank. . . . Brazos, Brazos, you may grab me—hug me like a bear—kiss me good night, then run."

"June!"

"Yes—and explain to Dad tomorrow."

Dared thus and spurred by June's provocative smile Brazos brazenly availed himself of the sweet privilege. It made his head whirl so that he nearly fell down the steps.

"Say, cowboy, what'n hell's got into yu?" queried Hank, in mild concern, as Brazos swung into his saddle.

"Gawd only knows, Hank," drawled Brazos, with his cool laugh. "I might be ridin' away from Don Carlos' Rancho. So long, Texas."

Brazos had a fleeting glimpse of the disheveled June standing slim and lovely in the light with her hands over her face.

Riding furiously away down the dark road Brazos'

192

sheer joy crowded out his other emotions. June, the little minx, had challenged that sweet madness. Janis had seen it, her father, Sain, and all of them. They would tease June into a confession of their plighted troth. Brazos thought himself not only the happiest of men but the most fortunate.

When he neared the town he slowed the spirited horse to a walk and his rushing mind slowed proportionately. Any cattle town had a quieting effect upon Brazos. And suddenly it struck him that he had never gone back to any town where he had engaged in a serious shooting fray. The cold stars, the breeze off the range, the dark avenues into the hills, the pale light that located Las Animas, these told him that love and happiness could not change the merciless truth that he was still Brazos Keene. He was hated by men he had frustrated. He would ever be marked by them and their allies. He could never enter that town without reverting to the hard steely vigilant gunman. The creed of border rustlers was that dead men did not find or trail their tracks.

Brazos left his horse at the accustomed corral and walked up the side street into the main thoroughfare. That element of Las Animas which did not sleep at night, and the cowboys and cattlemen upon whom they preyed, were out in force. Saloons, dance halls and gambling dens hummed with their peculiar low ominous roar. Las Animas was growing. The hour was midnight and Brazos met many men, some accompanied by women. He peeped into the dives. He stood back in dark doorways and watched. His conclusion was that Las Animas would never compare with Dodge, or Abilene, or Lincoln in the viciousness of those cattle towns in their heyday, but it was a hard town, and a center for rustling activities that no one man could clean up.

Brazos at last went to his room at Mexican Joe's, and after lighting the lamp he broodingly unbucked his gun belt and sat down on the bed.

"Better men than I am have been in the same kind of fix." he mused, darkly. "I'm supposed to marry and settle down to quiet home life. An' forget the men I've killed an' thet there's some left I ought to kill. . . . Ha!

193

Thet's the idee. Thet for Brazos Keene! . . . Wal, I'll do even thet for June if they only let me. . . . Pore kid! It's tough on her. She really never ought to have fallen in love with me. If I'd been half a man I'd never let her do it. But I did an' she did! . . . Bless her lovin' heart! . . . An' I gotta hide this secret fear an' watch as I never did in my life, hopin' time will change things."

Brazos slept late, a luxury he seldom indulged in. And after he awakened he lay in bed, realizing that in broad daylight, with the sun pouring golden in at his window, he could not feel the same as he did in the black midnight hours. He was wonderfully happy. And that exalted mood lasted until, booted, spurred and gun-belted, he walked out up the street of Las Animas.

He had not taken a dozen steps from Mexican Joe's when a cowboy, a lean hard-faced youth, sauntered out of a doorway.

"Howdy, Keene," he said, as if in casual greeting. "I been walkin' the street for an hour watchin' for you."

"Howdy, cowboy," returned Brazos, slowly.

"Gimme a match. Make this look natural," returned the other.

"Ahuh. Heah yu air. Talk fast, stranger."

The cowboy took the match and lighted his cigarette leisurely, but he spoke rapidly.

"Last night at Hall's—heerd two men talkin'—Brazos Keene in town—Knight swears we're to git him at any cost—Bodkin's rarin'."

The cowboy raised his young hard visage, puffed a cloud of smoke and turned away.

"Thanks, pard," said Brazos, and went on as before. "Doggone! Thet's hot. I reckon thet cowboy risked his life an' knew it. . . . They're gonna try to shoot me in the back. Bodkin again!"

Brazos went in the first store and out the back way, where he proceeded along the alley to a side street from which he reached the corral where he had left his horse. The Mexican boy, Pedro, had fed and watered Bay. Brazos lost no time riding out of town. The conclusion he reached was that Bodkin had taken up with this Knight—that they were going to proceed on the lines Surface had developed—and that such operations were retarded because of the unwelcome existence of one Brazos Keene.

The approach of winter might have necessitated renewed activity on the part of cattle rustlers. Cattle had gone up in price to forty-three dollars on the hoof with increasing demand. Neece had seen this coming and he had bought wholesale, getting some small herds for as low as thirty dollars a head.

When Brazos arrived at Twin Sombreros he rode in with little thought of the distracting sisters and the gala supper and dance to be held that evening. As luck would have it June or Janis called gaily to him from the house, but Brazos only waved without stopping. He found a merry bustling crowd of cowboys working to enhance the autumn effect desired by the girls.

"Heah, one of yu rollickin' gazabos," he called. "Tell Neece an' Bilyen I want them pronto."

The rancher was the first to reach Brazos and he wore the warm smile he had acquired for this cowboy.

"Mornin', son. You look pretty serious. Scared of bracin' Dad after last night, eh?"

Brazos had to grin. No fear of this father's censure or criticism! Neece was on his side.

"Scared as hell, Dad, now yu make me think of last night. But thet wasn't on my mind atall."

Hank Bilyen joined them at this juncture. "Mawnin', Brazos," said the Texan, his gray gaze studying Brazos' face.

"Come heah," returned Brazos, and drew the two aside.

"Aw, yu're gonna bust up the party," complained Hank, a sense of calamity evidently striking him.

"Ump-um. Not atall. I've got a tip, though. . . . Cattle gone to forty-three dollars. It'll be forty-five in less's a week, an' goin' up."

"You don't say!" ejaculated the rancher, eagerly. "Hank, my hunch was correct."

"Wal, I was holdin' at forty for this fall. But forty-five! Say, Neece, we're settin' with a powerful good hand."

"How many haid can yu drive in an' ship pronto, inside the week?" queried Brazos, thoughtfully.

"Close to twenty thousand if the railroad can handle them," replied Neece, promptly.

"I saw hundreds of empty stock cars as I rode oot. Neece, yu can beat the other cattlemen to it, an' save, I reckon, half thet twenty thousand—if yu rush the ootfit."

"Save! What yu mean, cowboy?" asked Bilyen, darkly suspicious of his young friend.

"Wal, there's a lull in rustlin' just now, but it won't last long onless this ootfit Surface left behind gets ripped up the back. Neece, it'd be a good bet to sell all the railroad can handle."

"I'll grab it pronto, Brazos, thanks to you."

"How aboot Henderson an' Sisk? Can they grab it pronto, too?"

"No. Henderson's stock is scattered all over the range. Sisk's is on his ranch forty miles out. Rough country. It'd take a month to round up a big bunch."

"Too late for the top price—an' too late to beat the rustlers."

"Hank, I tried to get Sisk an' Henderson to see this very thing—that is, the price of beef goin' up. I didn't figure on rustlers. . . . Brazos, how can they get away with any large numbers of cattle?"

"Wal, it does seem ootlandish, with law an' order in Las Anamas," rejoined Brazos, with a grim laugh. "Boss, ten hard-ridin' rustlers can move a heap of stock. None of thet stock would come heah. They'd shove it along the line, an' have it shipped the day it got to the railroad, long before the owners found oot. Some of it would be throwed in with the shipment of cattlemen we reckon air crooked. Aw, it's easy enough. Too damn easy!"

"I'll go write telegrams to my buyers an' order all the stock cars available. Hank, you can ride in with these at once," said Neece, decisively, and hurried away.

"Come oot with it, darn yore pictoors," demanded Hank, gruffly.

"Wal, it's nothin' new, but kinda worrisome, considerin' the mix-up I'm in heah," answered Brazos, and he gave Hank the information he had received from the strange cowboy in town.

The Texan swore mightily and to no purpose, which verbiage Brazos received in silence.

"I knowed somethin' was in the wind, else yu'd never advise Neece to sell stock so pronto. Doggone lucky for Neece! We can ship thet number of cattle before the price drops or a hoof of it can be rustled. . . . But what'n the hell air yu gonna do?"

"Me? Aw, I better lay low."

"Bodkin! —— his yellow gizzard! All Bodkin! Brazos, do yu reckon thet hombre *knows* yu can't kill him?"

"He's just aboot smart enough to figure it," admitted Brazos.

"Who ever heahed of such a —— muss!" growled Hank. "If this was only Texas!"

"But it's not Texas. It's Colorado, where they got law an' order," declared Brazos, bitterly.

"Where's layin' low gonna get yu, cowboy?"

"I don't know. It's all I can think of."

"They'd reckon yu was scared an' rustle the hair off this range."

"Shore. But they'd hang themselves sooner or later. Las Animas won't stand it forever."

"No, I reckon not. All the same they're daid slow."

"Slow? Say, Texas, they're not alive. The trouble is each cattleman heah suspects his neighbor. Yu know, Hank, thet kind of deal is hard to handle. It just might last until this range has seen its best days."

"Nope, it won't, 'cause the haids of this combine, Bodkin an' Knight, Miller mebbe, whoever they air, don't stock up enough gray matter."

"Hank, I just oughta ride away," said Brazos, tragically.

"Shore. Thet old dodge of yores would fit in heah," rejoined Bilyen, with sarcasm that made Brazos flinch.

"Only I cain't."

"An' why cain't yu?"

"It's not humanly possible for me to leave this girl."

"Brazos, I'd be damned if I would, either."

"If only June would run off with me! . . . We could come back after these hombres peter oot."

"June? Say, cowboy, we reckoned it was Janis."

*"We?* Who'n hell air we?" jerked out Brazos, with a start.

"Why, me, an' Neece—an' some of the boys. Leastways Jack."

"Jack Sain? The two-faced son of a gun! He's crazy aboot June himself. Thet's why he——"

"Jack is honest," interposed Bilyen. "An' Neece reckons yu're sweetest on Janis."

"Neece? Aw, my Gawd!" ejaculated Brazos, throwing up his hands.

"Cowboy, ain't yu kinda mixed up yoreself aboot *which* one of the twins yu're daid set on."

"Mixed up? I'm standin' on my haid this heah minute. . . . Hank, I love June, honest an' true—but—aw! it's orful. . . . I cain't tell her from Jan."

The Texan laughed so hard that Brazos wanted to punch him. "Haw! Haw! Haw! . . . doggone—me," he choked, trying to talk. "Yu're not in any mix-up. Oh—no! . . . Yu reckon it's June, but yu cain't tell 'her from Jan! . . . One's the same as the other. . . . Thet settles yore hash, Brazos Keene."

"Hank, I could get mad at yu—yu —— old muddlehaid," declared Brazos, red in the face. "Now what'n hell do yu mean by thet last crack? Yu saw me kiss June last night."

"Shore Brazos, but thet only proved yu're in love with them both."

"Yu're a damn liar."

"An' yu're plumb lucky," returned Bilyen, curtly. "There's safety in numbers. Yu been playin' fast an' loose with two fine girls. Don't forgit yu're from Texas."

"Wal, I'll be dod-blasted," muttered Brazos, as his friend strode away, plainly offended. "What the devil did he mean by lucky—an' safety in numbers?"

Brazos sat there trying to puzzle it out, but the more he thought the deeper in he got until he grew hopelessly bewildered. Presently Bilyen reappeared leading his horse.

"Doggone it, Brazos, I cain't be mad at yu," he complained.

"Wal, I can be at yu, old-timer, an' don't yu overlook thet."

"Have yu got anythin' in town yu want fetched oot?" queried Hank, ignoring Brazos' rudeness.

"Yes. Go to Mexican Joe's an' pack my ootfit. An' don't yu muss thet new gray suit thet I got to wear to the dance."

"So yu're gonna be there," said Hank, pretending surprise.

"I should smile I am. . . . Hey, who yu wavin' to?"

"Heah come June an' Jan," observed Bilyen. "Air they lookin' for one Brazos Keene? They air! . . . Gosh, look at them! Two sweeter, purtier, nicer, finer, gooder girls never before graced this range. . . . Brazos, I'd be only too glad to be in yore boots."

"Yes, yu would, yu brute! . . . Where air they? I'm gonna slope."

"They see yu. Take yore medicine, Brazos."

"Fork thet hawse, yu grinnin' ape," yelled Brazos, and then, at the sight of the twins, he sank back with a groan. "Aw! Was there ever such a miserable cuss as Brazos Keene? . . . But this is never gonna do. I gotta make a bluff as big as Pikes Peak, or bust."

He assumed a lolling lazy pose, and leisurely began to roll a cigarette, well and tinglingly aware when the girls stopped before him.

"Mawnin', Brazos," mimicked one.

"Air yu heah again?" mimicked the other.

Brazos slid off his sombrero, and sprang erect, his old cool smiling courteous self.

"Good mawnin', twins," he drawled. "I shore am glad to see yu-all this mawnin'."

They stood hand in hand before Brazos, demure and arch, shy and provocative, dressed exactly alike as always and looking hopelessly more alike than ever, surely the sweetest pair that had ever distracted a poor cowboy. Brazos viewed them with a grim smile, vainly searching for some tiny bit of distinctive apparel on one different from the other's, waiting vainly for a wink or sly glance that would proclaim one to be his sweetheart June.

"Come, Brazos."

"You're going to help us."

199

"Shore, if yu stay together," said Brazos, doggedly. "But I'm not gonna ever be alone with one of yu again."

Laughing merrily they separated and one at each arm they led him across the grassy plot to the barn.

The rest of that day flew as if by magic. Late afternoon found all available ground space at Twin Sombreros Ranch occupied by saddle horses, and vehicles from fine buckboards to muddy-wheeled wagons.

Two hours before sunset the girls had run off to dress and Brazos had had all that time to satisfy himself with his appearance. But he just could not arrive at that. All the same he had a sneaking idea that he had never looked better. The new gray coat seemed better buttoned, which was very desirable, as it hid his gun belt and all but the extreme tip of his gun sheath. His feet, in the new low shoes, felt as light as feathers, only Brazos imagined they looked too small for a hard-riding cowboy. Lastly he put a wildflower in his coat, and strode forth to do or die.

Brazos ran into Jack Sain, slim, dark-garbed, shining of face.

"Hello, Brazos. Have you forgotten anything?"

"Gosh, I reckon my haid," replied Brazos, but he clapped his hand to his hip to feel if his gun was there.

"It's time for us to light the pine cones. Henry an' his gang have to take care of the fires. We get off easy. . . . Gee, what a night, Brazos! Look at the moon, peepin' over the mountains. . . . The orchestra is here. From Denver! Think of that, cowboy. An' the dancin' begins at eight sharp."

"Wal, it ought to be aboot thet now," drawled Brazos, affecting a calm he did not feel.

They lit the rustic pine-cone lanterns up and down the lane leading from the barn to the ranch house; then the oil lanterns in the colorful barn and the big locomotive lamp that had been fastened high on a post. The huge bonfires added to the cheerful night scene. And the moon soared above the black range, full and white and radiant. Then the crowd of girls, some in white, and most in bright hues that matched the autumn leaves, flocked down the lane with gay voices and merry laughter, to meet the eager young men waiting at the barn. Last came the older folk, less brilliantly garbed, but quite as merry and as happy. Voice and mirth of all were drowned in a burst of rhythmic music.

Brazos was surrounded by the glad throng, although none appeared to notice him, and he drew to one side, with a feeling of detachment. He was beginning to lose something of the thrill and uncommon pleasure that possessed him, when a soft little hand slipped inside his. Brazos turned to find a vision in white beside him, with lovely face uplifted to his and dark eyes the dullest of men could have read aright.

"It's June," she said, simply. "How do you like my New York gown?"

"Girl—I never knew yu were so beautiful," replied Brazos, rapturously.

"Cowboy, you look stunning yourself. Jan, the old hawk, saw you first. She was making for you when Henry grabbed her." All at once he felt her other hand moving lightly down his coat on the right side, to stop on the bump that was his gun. "Brazos, you would pack a gun at my party," she concluded, reproachfully.

"Darlin', I cain't go withoot it," explained Brazos, poignantly. "Only last night I heahed there were men lookin' for me."

"Oh, how terrible to be in love with a desperado!" she exclaimed, her warm cheeks blanching.

"June! Thet hurts."

"But how terribly more sweet to be in love with a handsome cowboy whose very name makes girls' hearts beat fast!" she added quickly, voice and look making amends. "Come. This first dance is yours. I chose a long waltz, because you told me you liked waltzing."

They had whirled scarcely more than a quarter way round the big barn when June looked up to whisper: "You said you were a clodhopper on your feet."

"Wal, I am—in my boots."

"Brazos, you can dance . . . but you hold me a little too tight—for public——"

"Aw, I don't know whether I'm dancin' or ridin' or sailin'. . . . An' June, if I didn't hold yu like this—I'd not know I had yu in my arms—yu're so like a fairy."

"Don't talk—flatterer!"

They danced on and Brazos thought that he was indeed sailing around an enchanted glade in the autumn woods. Yet he preserved his equilibrium enough to lead her through the whirling throng of dancers. But toward the end the sense of rhythmic dreamy movement, the murmuring voices of girls, the bright dresses, the scarlet flare of autumn leaves, and the entrancing feel of June so soft against his breast—these went to Brazos' head like wine.

"Brazos—you're—hugging—me," June whispered, pantingly.

"Am I? . . . Doggone! I hadn't noticed it," he drawled, loosing his hold ever so little.

"Everybody—else—has."

"June, if my eyes air not pore, they're all doin' the same."

"Jan saw. She looked—daggers at me."

"Wal, don't yu look. . . . Aw, it's over! How could thet happen? . . . June, I reckon I never had so wonderful a dance."

"Not even at that famous dance of Holly Ripple's—with *her?*"

"Wal, thet was wonderful, too. But not like this one with yu. Yu see, Holly wasn't my sweetheart."

"I don't see. I should have thought she'd be mad about you. . . . Brazos, do you want to please me?"

"More than anyone."

"Make yourself agreeable to the girls who haven't beaux, and some of the older women. You can be so nice! It's a chance. It'll make them like you—and help our party to success. Will you, Brazos?"

"Goodness only knows how I can, but I'll manage. But how aboot Janis?"

"Jan will have three partners for every dance. But you must get a part of one, at least. She'd blame me if you didn't."

"I'll bet I cain't get within a mile of her . . . or yu, either, after this. Look at these buckaroos pilin' over each other to get at yu!"

"Brazos, I'll hunt you up," she flashed, and was whirled away.

Glowing and eager, with all his doubt fled, Brazos turned to the duty imposed upon him. He gave himself such an impetus that he found real pleasure in dancing with an unattractive girl no longer young. Thus launched, Brazos bent all his efforts to helping make the party of the Neece twins a success. Now and then, when a moment offered, he would stop to gaze among the circle of dancers, who grew grayer as the evening wore on, to pick out the lovely flushed face that flashed like a flower and then was gone. Once out of that same face, or its counterpart, he met dark reproachful seductive eyes, and he drew up with a sharp breath. They must have belonged to Janis. That fleeting glimpse was the first Brazos had had of her. He did not look again after that incident.

The hours fled like the dances; the pine cones burned out; the big bonfires were replenished; many of the young men and some of the girls went often to the great bowl of punch that Neece had ordered must be kept full; and the moon climbed high to burn white in the blue dome above.

At midnight supper was served for the younger folk on the wide porch, and in the long sitting room of the ranch house for the elders. Brazos ate his food standing, as many thousands of times he had done beside a chuck wagon on the Old Trail.

Soon the dancers flocked back to the barn, lured by the strains of music. Brazos watched them from the porch, a little wistfully, wondering when June would hunt him up. Then a white hand slipped under his arm.

"Come, cowboy," called a challenging voice.

"Aw, heah yu air!", cried Brazos.

"Quick. They're after me. Run!" she said, with a giggle, and led him into the pines instead of down the lane. In a moment they were out of sight of the ranch house, the lights, and in another almost out of hearing of the merry hum.

Then they walked hand in hand. Brazos' heart seemed full to bursting. There was no need of talk. The pines black-barred the silver glades. The girl stopped to confront Brazos, though she did not let go of his hand.

"Where have you been all these hours?" she asked. The moonlight enhanced her loveliness, blanched her oval face, darkened her unfathomable eyes. Brazos divined that she had given him the opportunity he had longed for.

"I've been helpin' make yore party a success. Didn't think it was in me! Dancin' with old maids, doin' the elegant with the wives and mothers, makin' a waiter oot of myself. But it was fun, an' did me good."

"Brazos, that was sweet of you," she returned, warmly.

"Wal, don't yu want to reward me?" he drawled, softly.

"Yes." As she spoke that forceful word Brazos caught a hint of something as strange as lovely about her. In the magic of the moonlight all her charm and mystery appeared magnified.

"Would a—a kiss be too much?" he asked, hesitatingly.

"Too little!"

Brazos kissed her and trembled on the brink of the unknown. She stood there, slender and white in the silvered radiance, eyes intent on him, lips upturned.

"Girl, don't look at me like thet . . . you said yes."

"I also said 'too little'!"

Brazos' restraint broke at that, and he took her in his arms, but did not avail himself of the repetition of that challenging surrender. Still she held back from closer contact with him, somewhat stiffly.

"Tell me yu'll marry me?" he demanded, suddenly strong and vibrant with released emotion.

"Ah-h!" she gasped, and as if the strength had left her limbs she sank upon his breast. Brazos held her closer and closer, bending his head over hers, to put his cheek upon her fragrant hair.

"Did thet surprise yu, darlin?"

She stirred her head in soft motion Brazos took to be affirmation.

"But it shouldn't have?"

"Who could be sure of—Brazos Keene?" she whispered.

"Wal, yu should be. . . . I love yu turrible, lass. . . . Say yu love me."

"I adore—you!"

"Say when yu'll marry me?"

"Oh, what will Dad and sister say?"

"They'll be glad. But never mind them. Honey, I cain't wait much longer. Yu blessed twins air drivin' me crazy... Say when, precious?"

"When do you—want me?" she whispered, very low.

"Aw! . . . Why, I hate to rush yu, darlin'. But there's a reason, yu know. I'm a marked man in Las Animas. I oughta go away 'till those hombres forget they wanted to kill me."

"*Brazos!*" She roused to passionate life in his arms.

"I told yu, darlin'," he expostulated.

"Oh, my Brazos! I—I will marry you."

"When? The sooner the better."

"We'll elope!" she cried, thrillingly.

"Wal, thet'd be easiest an' safest for me. Yore Dad wouldn't hold it against me."

"We'll do it!" Suddenly she appeared transformed into a little whirlwind, throwing her arms around his neck, rumpling his hair wth furious little hands, at last to draw his head down to kiss him with lips of sweet fire. "Oh, Brazos! I've been dying for you," she burst out with inarticulate cry. "You won me—even though I thought you a devil with girls . . . a trifler! . . . All the time—all the time I thought it was June you loved!"

## Chapter Thirteen

FOR an appalling instant, Brazos, in his realization of catastrophe, stiffened so violently that he almost crushed the girl in his arms.

"Don't kill—me," Janis managed to utter, faintly.

"Aw—I'm sorry. I—I just went off my haid," replied Brazos, in a smothered voice, as he released his clasp.

But Janis did not let go her clinging hold of him nor take her head from his breast. "Oh-h! . . . Brazos, a girl in love—even as terribly as—I am—has to breathe."

"Wal, I didn't know yu loved me—turrible."

"I do—I do! . . . I was aching with love—burning with jealousy—dying with fear. . . . But at times I *knew* you loved me."

"My Gawd, how I know it!" exclaimed Brazos, huskily, horror-stricken with a sense of his guilt and the exultant madness that enveloped him.

He bent his head over her and again enfolded her slender form, while he gazed unseeingly out into the silver-black shadows of the woods. The white pitiless moon looked down upon him like an accusing eye. The night breeze moaned pitifully in the tips of the pines. Only a soft strain of music in the distance gave that strange solitude reality.

"Darling, this is perfect," said Janis, stirring, and trying to look up at him. "It pays me for my anguish. It sustains me—until the next time. But we mustn't stay longer."

"No," agreed Brazos, and stood like a stone.

She pressed back from his breast to look up. "Oh, Brazos! You're so white and stern! Was it to choose between June and me? . . . My poor darling, you could have had *me* for the asking!"

Brazos wrenched his gaze from the shadows to look down upon her, fully conscious now that he was as weak as guilty, that he loved her the same as June, that she had a devastating power he had never felt in the shy sister. And suddenly she manifested it again, flaring up like a flame, to cling with round arms as strong as steel, to tear her fingers through his hair, to lock them behind his head and draw him down to those lips of fire that he would have faced doom to meet. Brazos surrendered to a moment of transport. Whatever came of this mad folly, he would have that to dream of. Janis was intensely alive. He could feel the bursting swell of her breast, the throb of her heart, the burn of her blood through the skin of her bare arms. He could hear her broken utterances of endearment, low, deep, with a strange rich hoarseness. And he spent all the passion of his lonely unsatisfied heart—the endless hours of longing by day and night in the saddle—the bitter fatality that a fulfillment of love was not for him—in his response to her kisses.

Then it seemed somehow that this ecstasy waved away and she was smoothing his hair.

"I was always crazy to muss your hair like that," she was murmuring, her eyes like dark stars.

"Jan—I've kinda—mussed yu—too," he replied, hoarsely.

"If you haven't! . . . Oh, dear, this dress wasn't made for grizzly bears. . . . Come, I'm as bold as a lioness. But I'd just as lief not meet Henry. This was his dance. I saw you on the porch. I sent him after something. . . . But it was *our* dance, Brazos. Now we will pay the piper, come what may!"

All down the lane she held his hand, while he strode fast to keep up with her tripping steps. Even the blazing bonfire did not deter her. Twice she turned to look at him with wonderful eyes, the secret of which was for him alone. The music grew louder. Brazos saw as in a dream the moving figures, pale, unreal, like disembodied spirits. Then he heard Janis' sweet mocking little laugh: "Henry! how did you ever miss me?"

"I did. But this cowboy didn't," growled Henry, at which Brazos awoke to life and reality.

"Wal, Sisk, what one man misses, another hits," drawled Brazos, caustic in his sudden awakening.

"Never mind, Henry. We will dance this. . . . Adios, Brazos, until——"

And Brazos stood watching in a light that had lost its dim unreality—watching the girl as she glided away with Henry, her lovely face turned, piquant and moon-blanched, lit by great dark alluring eyes. The crowd swallowed them up. And Brazos plodded away, his head bowed, like a man lost on an endless shingle of shore, in the weird pale night, aimless and hopeless.

Corrals, fences, gates, gardens, orchards, ditches and woods and rocks were as if they were not. Brazos' new gray suit, of which he had been so proud, became a tattered muddy garment. He came out into the road and heedless of direction he walked on. Miles west on the hill he saw the cabin where he had slept that fatal night Allen Neece was murdered. He had no thought for himself now. He would have been an easy prey for novices at the game of killing. But he turned at the hilltop and plodded back.

The moon slanted low and its dimming light showed

the road winding pale between black borders of trees and brush. Coyotes began their hue and cry. In open places Brazos saw faint streaks of gray over the eastern range. Dawn was not far away. Brazos walked on slower and slower. His feet became leaden. This was not his accustomed mode of locomotion. Sunrise found him skulking through the woods and fields, up the corral lane, to the little cabin he shared with Bilyen.

Brazos heard the music end; he saw the thinned crowd of dancers file in couples out of the barn; he saw June and Janis, dragging homeward on the arms of their escorts. And bitterly he recognized them to be Janis with Henry Sisk and June with Jack Sain. Sick with anguish, numb with cold, staggering with exhaustion Brazos turned from that sight into the cabin, to divest himself of his ruined clothes and crawl into his blankets.

Bilyen snored like a man seldom used to keeping late hours. But that did not keep Brazos awake. He did not hear it. He was trying to free his brain from unbearable thoughts. What was it that had happened?

June and Janis Neece! They were twin sisters, nineteen years old. It had been the ambition of a proud and loving father to send them east to give them an education. They had come back unspoiled, still Western, beautiful as the dreams of cowboys beside lonely prairie campfires. They were amber-eyed, and no cowboy could look into those eyes and tell the twins apart, or ever have any peace of mind again. They were perfectly, absolutely, damnably alike. Their shapely forms, their pearly skin, their brown hair, their voices, looks, smiles, mannerisms, all were enhanced irresistibly by this marvelous likeness. They had an infernal habit, or coquetry, or some instinct of self-preservation, to dress precisely the same.

But to the cowboy who had been blessed or cursed by fate to be loved by both of them, this similarity so unsupportable to him did not extend to character. They seemed as far apart as the poles. One was the south and the other the north. June was cool, sweet, shy, reserved, deep as the sea, adoring and unselfish, strangely and passionately devoted to her sister. Janis was fire hidden under a cold provocative exterior, selfish in her need of conquest, vain where her twin was modest, conscious of her alluring charm, a little devil in her chary practice with it, maddeningly irresistible and royal in her final abandonment to love.

Brazos knew them both now—knew them to his doom. He worshiped them both. He could not have made a choice. June called to all the courage, nobility—to the unplumbed depths of his power to help, to serve, to protect, to the cowboy's dream of range and ranch, home and happiness, to tranquillity and peace after his hard life on the trails. And he would not have had that otherwise. Janis enveloped him in a flame, as he had seen prairie fire race through the windy grass. She had brought out in him a side he had not known he possessed, a tremendously strong primitive self, impossible to resist, a dark demanding master, up from the savage, engendering a yearning and a need stronger than habit, more compelling than any force he had ever experienced.

At last Brazos saw the situation in all its stark naked reality, and he voiced it to himself, as was his habit. "Wal, Brazos Keene, heah's where yu get off the woman trail for good. Yu love this June Neece. She's yore ideal—the girl of the long trail's dreams. An' yu're engaged to marry her. . . . Yu love her sister, too, this bewilderin' Janis—an' yu wouldn't stop lovin' her if yu could. An' yu told her you'd elope with her. . . . Yu love them both. . . . Yu wouldn't have it different. . . . . Yu cain't tell them apart . . . Wal, it's aboot time to go oot an' get yoreself shot!"


A voice pierced dimly into Brazos' sleep, stirring old associations so intimately related with dead slumbers and early calls.

"My guard? Awl-l right. . . . A cowboy's life is ha-ard."

"Wake up, Brazos. If I don't miss my guess, yours this evenin' will be harder than hell."

"Huh?"

"It's four o'clock an' you're wanted," said the curt voice.

Brazos rolled over and opened his eyes to see Jack Sain standing beside his bunk, a quite different person from the usual cheerful cowboy.

"Who wants me?"

"June an' Jan. They sent me. They're waitin' for you where the trail turns off the lane into the woods."

"Ahuh. . . . An' yu have a hunch my life is gonna be harder'n hell pronto," drawled Brazos, sliding his long legs out of bed.

"I'll bet you get the spur-rakin' of your ridin' days."

"Boy, yu shore look like life was kinda hard for yu this mawnin'. . . . I mean this evenin' after the dance."

"I'd just as lief be dead," returned Sain, hopelessly. Then Brazos took a second look at him, and felt remorse gnaw at his own heart.

"What's yore trouble, cowboy?" asked Brazos, kindly.

"You know. It's the same as yours."

"Ump-um. Don't yu get thet idee. Mine is double yores. . . . All the same I can help yu."

"Thanks, Brazos . . . I just can't help likin' you—though you've ruined my life."

"Turrible extravagant talk, Jack. . . . Yu mean June hasn't been so—so nice to yu since I rode along?"

"Brazos, she al-almost loved me before you came," replied Sain miserably. "Since then she's been— Oh, hell! nice an' kind, yes, but different. It just hurts, Brazos. I'm not sore at you. I think you're the grandest fellow I ever knew. An' even if you wasn't I'd have to feel square toward you because of what you've done for June—an' all the Neeces. It's only——"

"Only what, Jack?"

"I'm afraid to tell you, Brazos, but—but they all say it. An' you're bound to hear it."

"Go ahaid. My gun is way back under my pillow, so I cain't bore yu."

"Brazos, they say you're playin' hell with the twins," replied Sain, huskily—"that you're payin' them up for their fun—their lettin' us all take one for the other."

"Wal, who says thet?"

"All the outfit. Even Neece. He told me it served the girls 'good and damn right.' . . . But, Brazos, I *know* that's Jan's fault. June worships her. She'd give her very soul for Jan."

"Jack, I kinda had thet hunch myself," replied Brazos, pulling on his boots. His mind seemed to scintillate with the sparks of an inspiration Sain had given him. He stood up, reached for his gun belt and buckled it on. Then he stepped to the little mirror, and had a look at his face. "My Gawd! what a mug! . . . Did yu ever see a pictoor of thet gazabo Lucifer? . . . Wal, I shore look like him this mawnin'."

"It's evenin', Brazos. Everybody has been up since noon. Bilyen rode to town, worried about somethin'—an' the girls are waitin' for you."

"Let 'em wait," said Brazos, and he turned piercing eyes upon his friend. "Jack, yu're a good boy. I like yu heaps. An' I'm damn sorry I upset yore courtin'. But thet was only an incident in yore romance. Let me give yu a hunch, boy. Don't be sick an' jealous an' black. Be yore real self to June. Thet girl is gonna rebound into yore arms like a rubber ball off a dobe wall."

"Oh, Brazos. Don't lie—don't rave just to cheer me up."

"Keep this under yore sombrero, cowboy. I did give the girls a dose of their own medicine. I shore played a low-down trick on them. Why, Jack, it was apple pie for me to tell them—one from the other. An' I let on I couldn't. . . . Wall heah's what no one else but yu will ever know—except Neece, an' I give yu leave to tell him. . . . I got burned turrible bad in thet little game of makin' love."

"June an' Jan—both!" gasped Jack, suddenly enlightened.

"Boy, yu hit it plumb on the haid."

"Oh, Lord! . . . But, Brazos, damn it, I'm not glad. I couldn't stand your—that you didn't really care!"

"Gosh, Jack, yu're a heartless hombre," drawled Brazos. "Wal, I'll trot along to my little rendezvoo."

But Brazos knew in his heart, with grim anguish, that no man ever presented such a false exterior. His mind was set on one thing—to look and act and talk the character the cowboys at Twin Sombreros had given him. To make June and Janis hate him! He caught sight of them before they saw him, and then his thoughts raced, and his feelings kept pace. They were waiting in a grove of pines off the lane.

He flipped his cigarette away and leisurely took off his sombrero.

"Mawnin', girls—aw, I mean good evenin'," he drawled, as true to his frank careless winning way as ever in his life. "I shore am glad to see yu so—so fresh an' pretty after thet all-night dance."

But his conscience smote him as with a terrific mace. Incredible as it seemed, he recognized instantly which girl was June and which was Janis.

"Brazos, Jan—we have something serious to ask you," said June, sad searching eyes on his. She was pale, composed, surprisingly strong. Brazos divined he was to learn the depth of her. Janis was white as snow and her eyes were great black baleful orbs of fire. She had no reserve. She was ready to burst into flame.

"Brazos," she whispered, hoarsely. "I—I told June."

"Ahuh. I reckon yu girls been comparin' notes . . . what'd yu tell her, Jan?"

"About last—night . . . that you begged me—to elope with you . . . and I promised."

"Wal, June, what'd yu say to thet?"

"Brazos! Oh, it's true—then. . . . I told Jan that I was in love with you—and engaged to marry you."

"What happened then?"

"We had a terrible quarrel."

"Brazos Keene, is she telling the truth?" flashed Janis, furiously.

"Shore she is," drawled Brazos. "I'm enjoyin' the honor of bein' engaged to June an' plannin' to elope with yu."

"Oh, you devil! . . . You lying flirt of a conceited cowboy! . . . You ought to—be horsewhipped. Making game of us—making a fool—of *me*! . . . For I—I was in—earnest—horribly in love with you. . . . Oh, I ha-hate you! . . . the shame of it! . . . You've broken—my heart!"

"Jan, did it ever occur to yu thet yu've broken some hearts yoreself?"

"Don't add insult to injury," she cried, passionately.

"Wal, I figured thet yu an' June needed a lesson—a dose of yore own medicine," said Brazos slowly. But he felt June's eyes upon him and inwardly he began to weaken in this preposterous deceit. "This game of yores—bein'

212

one girl when yu air really two girls—thet's shore not fair to us boys. We never could tell yu apart. An' you built yore house of mirth on thet. Yu were havin' fun at our expense. Yu dressed exactly alike an' talked an' looked an' acted thet way. Yu played tricks on us. . . . I reckon thet would have been all right when yu were kids—but yu're grown girls now—women in face an' form an' feelin', an' most distractin' lovely. An' thet makes yore trick pretty damn low-down, in my way of thinkin'. . . . Every cowboy on this range, an' I'll gamble a lot of older men, air love-sick over yu two. . . . So little Brazos rode along an' thought he'd break up yore game."

"If you hadn't saved Dad—made him happy again— I'd kill you!" burst out Janis, in helpless rage.

"Jan, you see," interposed June, gravely, her hands going out to her sister. "I always told you it would get us into trouble."

"It has—ruined me," sobbed Janis, covering her face. "June—I'm sorry. But it was such fun—until this devil came. . . . He never played any game—for fun. . . . He was deadly earnest—and he m-made me l-love him so— horribly. . . . I know now—maybe he served me right. . . . But that doesn't help—this—this——"

She left off and suddenly uncovered her convulsed face, to fasten a gaze on Brazos that appeared to blaze through tears.

"You carried your poor joke too far. . . . You're a heartless villain—a shameless trickster. You disgrace the very name of cowboy."

Brazos winced under that last jibe, the justice of which he recognized; and he was fighting to keep up his shallow pretense when June confronted him with soul-searching eyes. She came close. She laid a steady hold on him, looking up with the clearest, the most solemn eyes he had ever met. Their expression changed on the instant. In their amber depths came a shining little glint of woman's divination.

"Brazos Keene, you lie!"

"Aw—June!"

"You're lying. You're trying to save us—to make us despise you. But you can't do it."

213

Brazos sat down on a log as if his legs had weakened as had his will. His cigarette fell from shaking fingers—his sombrero rolled on the grass. And he dropped his head unable longer to stand June's look of love and pity. His very life seemed to fall a wreck about him.

"Shore. I'm—a liar . . . an' a miserable hombre."

*"Brazos!"* Janis darted to him and knelt, one hand on his shoulder. "What did she mean? What do you mean?"

"Aw, Jan, it's no use. June saw through me. . . . I fell in love with yu both. I cain't tell you apart. . . . I've been honest with June—an' with you, too. I did ask her to marry me. An' when—those times I'e been alone with yu—I thought *yu* was June! . . . But now I know yu, it doesn't make no difference. I love yu just the same—just as turrible. . . . An' after last night—when yu let yoreself go—Aw! I'm a gone goslin'."

"You loved me—thinking I was June?" she asked, her voice breaking.

"I reckon I did."

"But you love me, too?"

"Yes, I love yu, Jan."

"Just as much as you do June?"

"I cain't tell my love apart any more than I can yu girls."

"But Brazos," cried Janis, frantically. "We can't be absolutely the same to you."

"Yes, yu air. Only June makes me happy, quiet, shore of myself—an' yu drive me wild with yore kisses. . . . Jan, I'd go to hell for one of those kisses."

Janis slipped her other arm around Brazos and embraced him passionately, as if she could never let him go. Then she looked up at her sister in anguish. "June, I forgive him. We—*I* am most to blame. But I can't hate him now. . . . I can't bear to let him go. . . . Oh, merciful heaven, what *can* I do?"

"Jan, you need not give Brazos up," said June, her voice strong and sweet. "You shall marry him."

Brazos heard aright and he sprang up, almost lifting Janis with him.

"What's thet?" he demanded, roughly.

"Jan shall have you, Brazos."

214

He stared at her, only conscious through sight of her drawn face and wonderful eyes that for the first time he was realizing the true June Neece.

"I cain't consent to thet."

"Nor I, June," added Janis. "It wouldn't be fair. To cheat you of everything? No, no! All my life I have let you put me first. I won't do it here. . . . But I'm not big enough to give him to you. . . . We must be broken-hearted together."

"Janis, neither of us needs be brokenhearted. He shall marry you and we'll all be happy."

"But—but—" faltered Janis.

"What yu got in yore haid, girl?" interposed Brazos, sternly, and letting go of Janis he squared toward June, studying her pale face with narrow piercing eyes. She was proof against his scrutiny. She was the strongest of the three.

"Brazos, I'd give my very life to make Jan happy."

"Shore. But it cain't be done."

"Jan shall be your wife, Brazos . . . and you can have me, too."

Janis leaped to her. "June! . . . I—he— Oh, if it could only be!"

"It can, sister."

Brazos seized her shoulders in rough grasp. He felt the blood rush back to his heart leaving his skin tight and cold.

"What air—yu sayin'?" he demanded, huskily.

"I said Jan shall be yore wife . . . and you can have me too. We're twins, you know, almost the same as *one* girl. . . . I'd never marry. I'd always be true to you, Brazos. No one would ever know."

"My Gawd!" gasped Brazos and he fell back overcome. June's solution to their problem was as dazzling and blinding and shocking as a thunderbolt. It caught him unprepared. He had no time to think, to weigh, to reason before he was caught in a tumultuous wave. The blood that had crowded back to his heart, numbing his senses, suddenly leaped like wildfire through his veins. Burning, dizzy, he saw the twins through dim reddened sight. "Aw, June! for Gawd's sake! don't say thet!"

"I do. I mean it."

"But girl! . . . listen. I'm only human. I love yu turrible. . . . I love Jan wuss. An' I cain't stand up—like a man—against such temptation as thet. . . . I beg yu—June——"

"No! I will be yours—too."

"Jan, yu cain't accept thet. . . . Say so. . . . The girl is mad . . . yu heahed her say she'd give her life for yu. . . . An' now she'd give me—her all—for *me!* Jan, if yu love me, save me from myself. I'm only a pore lone-ridin' cowboy. . . . I'm——"

Shaken, spent, Brazos faced them in eloquent importunity, holding out his hands, mute with the appalling thing he divined.

"Oh, Brazos—how can I save you—when I'm lost myself?" cried Janis, rapt with ecstasy, scarlet with guilt. "If June can be happy, so— Oh, Brazos! . . ."

Brazos bowed to that, utterly beaten. A man might contend with one woman—fight to save her from the havoc of love—but two women—twin girls, young, beautiful, physically perfect and equally fascinating, one of them deep, the other shallow—one of them sweet and noble, the other sweet and bad—how could he ever beat down the insupportable fact of being loved and desired by both? It was too much for Brazos Keene. He had lived unloved and lonely for this miracle. He bowed to what he could not break. And even the arraignment of self and fate could not detract from his transport.

"Wal, girls, yu've knocked the pins oot from under me," he said finally, after he had recovered his sombrero and stood brushing it when it did not need brushing. Then at length he stood erect with steady eyes on them. They stood each with arm around the other, and though one face was opal white and the other glowing crimson he again had the sense of confusion as to their identity. "Yu wonderful girls! I've shore had glorious fortune thrust upon me. . . . I'll slope along now an' see if I cain't find the Brazos Keene who used to be."

## Chapter Fourteen

BRAZOS' first intimation that there were other men in the world, other dramas than his own, came as he slid off his horse at Pedro's corrals, when the Mexican said something about a shooting fray in town.

"What's thet, Pedro?" queried Brazos, blankly. He had ridden all the way from Twin Sombreros in a chimera in which, if a still small voice of conscience made itself heard, a clamor of passionate exultance howled it down.

"Thar ees beeg shoot' in the town thees day."

"Ahuh. Yu see it, Pedro?"

"No, señor. I hear the gun—the yell. Then thees men she run."

"Who got bored?"

"I don't hear, señor."

"Take my hawse, Pedro."

Brazos wended his way uptown in a gathering thoughtful mood. Shooting frays were not uncommon. To be sure, Las Animas was not Dodge or Lincoln, where seldom a day passed without a smell of brimstone, and never a week without some man biting the dust with his boots on. Nevertheless this news of Pedro's stuck in Brazos' consciousness. He argued that it was because, for very long, it seemed he had forgotten the vital relation of guns to Brazos Keene. But before he turned into the main street he had a regurgitation of keen perception. After midday the street appeared mostly deserted and the warm autumn air drowsily hung upon the stores and saloons.

"Wonder who?" muttered Brazos, and somehow the query concerned itself more with who had done the shooting than with the person who had been shot. A little somber cast came over him. Mexican Joe's would be the place to find out. But he had not gone halfway down the block when he encountered Inskip emerging from a store. The instant Brazos met Inskip's gray eyes, he understood the strange creeping shadow that had come between the vividness of his emotion and his thought. Inskip wore the look of hard Texas brotherhood.

"Howdy, Brazos. Talk aboot the devil an' he pops up."

"Howdy, Inskip. Yu been talkin' aboot me?"

"No. But I jest heahed a man gamble yu wouldn't be long comin'."

"Wal, I been pretty long at thet," said Brazos, ponderingly.

"Yu're lookin' for Knight?"

"No. Not particular just this minute."

"Then yu haven't heahed?"

"Inskip, fact is I haven't heahed nothin' but thet waltzy music oot at Twin Sombreros."

"Knight shot Hank Bilyen this mawnin'."

"Aw!" A rending pang in Brazos yielded to leaping fire. "Hank! . . . Daid?"

"No. Pretty close call, though. Doc says Hank ain't in danger."

"Wal, thet's a relief. Shore was sweatin' cold. . . . This hombre Knight? He shot Surface, yu recollect. . . . What was it all aboot?"

"Hank ain't tellin'. But Knight has been roarin' aboot town. He was drunk when he did the shootin', so I heahed."

"Drunk! What'n hell was Hank doin' all the time?"

"He wasn't packin' no gun."

"Ahuh. I'll shore cuss him. . . . An' what's this gun slinger Knight roarin' aboot?"

"Wal, it sobered him, I reckon. But he's mad or pretendin' to be. Tellin' everywhere he thought Bilyen had a gun an' was drawin' it . . . thet he told Bilyen he was goin' to hold Neece for cattle Surface owed him . . . thet Bilyen began to curse an' threaten."

"Ahuh. An' what's the talk aboot town?"

"Wal, there's not much talkin', but a lot of lookin'. . . . What I heahed, though, was daid agin Knight. He's not liked by the substantial residents of Las Animas, thet's shore."

"Any talk connectin' Knight with Bodkin?"

218

"Not thet I heahed. But they're thick as hops, Brazos. Take it from me."

"Bodkin is the nigger in the woodpile. Inskip, how yu reckon thet nigger has lasted so long with Texans?"

"Meanin' me an' yu an' Kiskadden? . . . Wal, Gawd only knows how he's lasted with yu. But Kis an' I have responsibilities—business an' family. Then Bodkin had a strong followin', for a while, long enough to elect him. Sooner or later everybody heah in Las Animas will know he's crookeder than a rail fence, same as we know now."

"Where is Hank?" queried Brazos, his brow knit heavily.

"At Gage's. I'll go with yu."

"Reckon yu'd better locate Knight for me."

"No need. He's been walkin' the streets. In stores an' oot. Shy of saloons. All yu got to do is wait somewhere 'till he comes along."

Brazos found his friend Bilyen lying on an improvised bed of blankets on the floor of a room back of Gage's store. The Texan's rugged visage lacked color and was clammy.

"Would yu men mind leavin' us alone with Bilyen?" queried Brazos, to the group present. They left and Brazos knelt by the prostrate man.

"Wal, old-timer, how yu makin' oot?" he drawled, with deep feeling.

"Howdy, Brazos. I been wonderin' when yu'd roll in. . . . Me? What's a gunshot to a Texan? . . . I'm all right. I ducked when he shot, or he'd killed me shore. If ever I seen red murder in a man's eyes it was Knight's. An' I dropped like I was bored plumb center."

"Ahuh. Yu're pretty smart when yore hawse has got oot of the barn. . . . Let me see. . . . Right side. . . . Hank, don't tell me it's low down."

"Right under my collarbone an' clear through. Sorer than a stubbed toe! . . . But it's nothin' atall, Brazos. I wouldn't lie to yu, boy."

"Spit any blood?"

"Nary a drop. Thet forty-five slug just missed my lung. Doc Williamson says I can be moved tomorrow."

"Gosh, thet's fine, Hank. I was kinda worried. . . . How come yu wasn't packin' yore gun?"

"June an' Jan—they been coaxin' me to lay it off," replied Hank, visibly confused.

"Hank Bilyen, yu listened to those little softies?"

"Hell yes! What're you gonna do?"

"Wal, yu're gonna listen to some plain talk. Yu——! ——! . . . ——!!"

"Thet'll do, pard," ejaculated Hank, no longer pallid. "An' I'm askin' yu—couldn't them twins wind yu around their little fingers?"

"Not at all, old-timer," replied Brazos, imperturbably.

"Humph! Yu're such a liar, Brazos. . . . I had it figgered—an' so did Neece—thet yu was the plumbedest, locoedest, lovesickest damn fool there ever was over June an' Jan."

"Yu don't say? Funny aboot how men think! . . . Hank, I'm doggone glad yu're not in a bad way. . . . Now let's get down to business, onless yu reckon yu better leave off talkin' for a little an' rest."

"Cowboy, I shore won't rest or sleep till yu shoot the gizzards oot of thet black buzzard."

"Good. If yu talk short an' sweet I reckon yu can have a sleep in less'n two wags of a lamb's tail . . . what was it aboot?"

"Nothin' I said or did. Knight braced me. Said he was demandin' two thousand haid of yearlin's. From Neece through me I gave him the laugh till I seen thet red light come to his eye. Then if I'd only had a gun!"

"Did yu say anythin'?"

"I cussed him right pert."

"Anythin' more than cussin'?"

"Wal, I was riled. An' before I seen he meant murder I told him to lay off Neece or he'd have yu to deal with. At thet he gave me the hawse laugh. Said he an' Bodkin (he's not smart atall, Brazos. He gave Bodkin away) knowed yore hands was tied. Thet yore gunnin' for sheriffs was over!"

"An' what did yu say to thet?"

"I told him we knowed he an' Bodkin was in cahoots— thet *yu* knowed he was the rustler Brad yu heahed with Bodkin thet night at Hailey's. Brazos, it was a random shot, but it shore went home. I jest guessed it . . . an' thet crack of mine almost settled my hash. For murder leaped to Knight's eyes. I seen it an' shet up pronto. But I was too late. When he drew I ducked."

"So . . . I'll shore know if he's thet Bard the instant I heah his voice. Not thet it matters. But it sort of dovetails in. . . . An' thet's what I got on Bodkin."

"Brazos, this man Brad must have ruled Surface an' Bodkin both. He struck me strong, cunnin', vicious. But he's no gunman. I could have shot him three times runnin'. . . . But Bodkin. I told yu before to lay off him."

Inskip interposed here. "Right, Bilyen. Unless Brazos has proof—material proof, or a witness, he'd better let Bodkin alone. For he has been elected sheriff by the citizens of this country. He's an officer of law in this territory."

"It cain't be done," drawled Brazos.

"Have you anythin' on Bodkin thet'd clear yu in court?"

"I know him."

"But your word only is not enough, Brazos," declared Inskip, impressively.

"Pard, Inskip is talkin' sense," added Bilyen, earnestly. "Listen, cowboy. If—if things oot at Twin Sombreros air the way they seemed to Neece an' me—an' the way we hoped—for Gawd's sake, leave Bodkin alone. He'll hang himself pronto."

"It just cain't be done. I see thet now," replied Brazos, strangely.

"Boy, think of June—if it *is* June," importuned Hank.

"I am thinkin' of June—an' Jan, too," responded Brazos, as he pressed a strong hand upon Bilyen's. And Brazos knew, if Hank did not, that gesture was one of affection and farewell. "So long, yu Texans."

Brazos strode out leaving Inskip there. He passed the group of men, and went through the store to halt to one side of the open door. He wanted another moment to think before he gave all consciousnes to a deadly set of faculties. All in an instant, kneeling there beside his friend, Brazos had received a revealing illumination. By its light he saw the unmistakable, the inevitable part left for him to play. A bitterness, a sadness, and yet an ecstasy waved through his soul as he accepted the gauge. It had all been plotted out beforehand for him. He had had his paradise and he had left it fine and pure, the better for his blunder, his love, his renunciation. The truth had been long hidden. He was Brazos Keene. He never could be anyone else but Brazos Keene. And he strode out that open door Brazos Keene again, cold and ruthless, with all his peculiar gifts magnified.

Brazos had in mind an image of this man Brad—tall, heavy, dark of face with beady black eyes—black garb—forceful presence. He was not the first man Brazos had tracked without ever having seen him in the flesh. It was possible for him to be mistaken in a description, but never in a voice. He had heard Brad talk.

The sidewalks were deserted. A farm wagon, drawn by big horses, appeared at the end of the street, raising slow clouds of dust. At the opposite end two horsemen rode out of town. The stillness seemed unusually pronounced, oppressive, full of suspense. But Brazos knew his mood—how it magnified his senses.

Halfway between Hall's saloon and the Happy Days there stood an unoccupied adobe structure, one of the old landmarks of Las Animas, yellow and crumbling with age. Brazos took his station there in the doorway, from which he could not readily be seen except from a point almost directly opposite. Answering to Inskip's suggestion he meant to wait there a little while.

So Brazos waited with hawk eyes alert, wholly now in the grip of this strange mood that had become a part of him—of faculties which made him so dangerous. He was conscious of enhanced physical activity, a strain, a gathering of nerve forces, of augmented heartbeats and throbbing pulse, of his tight cool skin. In fact, except for his keen thought and cold resolve, he was a tiger in ambush.

He did not have long to wait for the quiet of Las Animas to be broken. There came a movement of vehicles up and down the street, and of boot-thumping, spur-jangling pedestrians along the sidewalk. Two cowboys went by with their awkward gait and they saw Brazos, started to check their talk; and when Brazos made a slight gesture, they hurried on whispering, their heads together. It would not be long from that moment when a wave of expectancy would run along this street.

222

Brazos decided to forestall that, and he was about to start out when a tall man emerged from Hall's. He answered to the description Brazos had in mind as fitting Knight. Three men followed him out of the saloon. They talked. And Brazos detected a nervous excitement in the way they stood and spoke. Then Knight turned his dark face in Brazos' direction. One of his comrades accompanied him, a lean man apparently used to the saddle. He was in his shirt sleeves and his vest was open. Knight wore a long black frock coat. It bulged over his right hip. Brazos smiled scornfully at the folly and blind arrogance of a man who packed his gun like that. The lean man took no such chances.

They came on. It looked to Brazos as if Knight was on parade for the benefit of Las Animas. The other man showed nothing of such a mien. He would bear watching.

As they came on, Brazos made his final estimate of Knight. In another moment, Brazos stepped out to confront them.

"Howdy, Brad," he drawled.

If that name did not belong to this man, it certainly had power to halt him with a stiffening jerk.

"My name's—Knight," he rasped out.

"Aw, hell!" ejaculated Brazos in cold derision. The voice was the one he expected.

"Who are you?" demanded the other, suddenly.

"Wal, if you don't know now, yu haven't got a long time to get acquainted."

The lean man, staring hard at Brazos, said quietly: "It's Brazos Keene."

"Good guess, stranger. . . . Slope damn pronto or I'll bore yu," returned Brazos, just as quietly.

The man wheeled as on a pivot and his boots rang on the hard sidewalk.

"Wal, Mr. Knight, yu've met up with Brazos Keene at last."

"What of that?" retorted Knight.

"I cain't say for yu, but I can guess tolerable wal what of it for me."

"You're this Texas cowboy I hear so much about?"

"How much do yu heah?"

"I'm fed up on it."

"Ahuh. Wal, yu kinda look like it disagreed with yu. Bad stomach, I reckon. . . . An' yu don't strike me very healthy in yore mind," drawled Brazos, sarcastically.

"Is that so?" snapped Knight, his queer voice whistling.

"Shore. Cause if yu were very bright yu'd savvy what yu're up against."

"Brazos Keene, ah? Ha! Ha! It doesn't impress me, you bragging cowpuncher."

"Wal, it's agonna, Brad."

"Damn you! My name's Knight," burst out the other, fiercely. Brazos saw the leap of thought in those beady black eyes. It was a steely red glint, a compass needle wavering and fixing—the intent to kill. Brad would attempt to draw on him, Brazos knew, and he felt profound amaze at this man's ignorance of real gunmen.

"Wal, it's Brad too."

"Who told you that?"

"Nobody. I just heahed Bodkin an' thet other hombre call yu Brad."

"When and where?" queried Brad, heatedly, but he had begun to whiten.

"Thet night at Hailey's. Just after the midnight train had pulled in from the East. I was in the next room an' had a hole cut in the wall."

"You meddling cow hand!"

"Shore. . . . Brad, I shore got a hand to draw to—an' I got one to draw *with!*"

Knight vibrated to that. He blazed with passion. It was fury, not fear, that dominated him.

"An' I'm packin' a gun, too! Which is what yu knew my Texas pard, Bilyen, wasn't."

"To hell with you Texans!"

"Ump-umm. Texans don't go to hell for depletin' the West of such two-bit hombres as yu. . . . Brad, yu an' Bodkin an' Surface—all yore ilk air nothin' but a lot of blood-suckin' cattle ticks."

Knight appeared to be beyond speech, clamped in his rage, slowly awakening to the inevitableness of something sinister that loomed like a specter. Still he had no fear. But it was rage, not nerve.

"Why, man alive!" went on Brazos, in his cold taunting voice of absolute assurance. "I've met up with some real men in my day. Yu're nothin' but a low-down coward that shoots unarmed men. . . ."

With a grating curse Knight jerked for his gun.

Brazos stepped through the drifting pall of smoke to look down upon the fallen man. But he was too late to see Brad die. The rustler boss lay on his back, his right arm pinned under him, clutching his half-drawn gun, his visage distorted in its convulsive change from life to death. And at that instant his sombrero, which had rolled on its rim off the sidewalk, tilted and flopped to a standstill.

It was not until then that the blood lust in Brazos, the passion to slay, his implacable hatred of these parasites of the cattle range, all of which had been developed by circumstances over which Brazos had no control, leaped out of his controlling restraint to make him terrible.

He slipped a fresh cartridge into the one empty chamber of his still smoking gun. A crowd blocked the sidewalk in front of Hall's. Across the street white faces appeared at doors and windows. A noise, like a single expelled breath, arose among the men outside, to augment and swell into voices. It expressed release of suspense, a tragedy enacted.

"Atta boy, Brazos!" yelled a lout at the back, in hoarse venting of his passion, and a laugh, nervous, not mirthful, ran through the crowd.

Sheathing his gun Brazos whirled on his heel to stride rapidly in the direction of the sheriff's office.

It was locked. The dispenser of Las Animas justice wasted little of his valuable time there. Brazos burst into three places before some one told him where to locate Bodkin.

"Seen him go in Twin Sombreros restaurant," called out this individual.

Brazos laughed. Of all places for Bodkin to be cornered by Brazos Keene! There was a fate that waited upon evil men. Bodkin, on the hour that his ally Knight had tried to murder Bilyen, and himself lay dead in the street, should have been in his office surrounded by his deputies and guns, or in the saloon where he drank and gambled and planned with members of his secret contingent. It boded ill for him that he was entertaining visitors from Denver and business men he desired to impress.

Brazos opened the door of the restaurant, slipped in, then slammed it behind him. This eating house of the Neece twins was full of customers. On the right side, facing the street from which Brazos had entered, several of the small tables had been placed together, round which sat ten or a dozen men. Brazos' lightning eye had scanned them to locate his victim.

*"Everybody set tight!"* yelled Brazos.

His appearance had as much to do with the sudden petrified silence of those present as had his stentorian voice. He surveyed the men at table. Miller he recognized. His passion was such that even the presence of the banker Henderson among them occasioned him no surprise. Several other faces were familiar, evidently belonging to new business men of Las Animas. The rest were strangers.

"Haw! Haw! Haw!" laughed Brazos, lustily, wild as a maniac. But a keen observer would have noted that the cowboy swerved not the slightest hair from his slight crouch—that his hands were low and the right spread a little from his body. Far removed indeed was Brazos from irrationality. He was a death-dealing machine, as impersonal as a lightning stroke. "Haw! Haw! Funny aboot findin' yu heah, Bodkin!"

The guests at that table rose so hurriedly that half their chairs turned over. They split, some on each side, leaving Bodkin alone at the head, his ox eyes rolling at Brazos, his leather visage losing its swarthy line.

"Keene, this hyar's an intrusion. . . . Insult to my guests. . . . I——"

"Haw! Haw! . . . yore guests, huh? Wal, they must be crooked as you or the damnedest fools in Colorado."

"Drunk again! Same old Keene! . . . You get out or I'll clap you in jail."

Brazos spat like a cat. "Jail? . . . By Gawd, yu make me remember I got thet on yu too! . . . Wal, Bodkin, my rustlin' sheriff, yu'll never clap me in jail again . . . or any other cowboy!"

226

Still it did not quite dawn upon Bodkin that he was in for more than abuse at the hands of Brazos Keene. There must have been a very strong conviction locked in his dense mind—no doubt the gossip that if Brazos was to marry into the Neece family his gun-throwing days were over in Colorado.

"Get out, Keene. You're drunk an' you're blowin' off. Why do you pick on me?"

"Wal, I didn't feel full of talk when I busted in heah," drawled Brazos, bitingly. "But seein' yu all dressed up, throwin' all this bluff, I just feel like crowin'.'"

"Well, you can go out in the pasture an' crow," replied Bodkin, angrily. "Let me alone. You can't want anythin' of me."

"Hell, I cain't!"

There ensued a pause of suspense, fraught with the significance of the cowboy's icy voice.

"What you want—then?" demanded Bodkin, hoarsely.

"Wal, first off I wanted to tell yu, Bodkin," drawled Brazos, with irritating slowness. He paused. Then he leaned a little more, like an eagle about to strike, to launch words swift as bullets. "Yore pard Brad is layin' oot there in the street daid!"

"Brad?" Bodkin choked out the name.

"Yes. Brad. He calls himself Knight. He's yore new man. I savvy thet empty chair I seen heah next yu was for him. Wal, he couldn't set in yore little game. . . . He's daid!"

"Who shot him?"

"Some hombre from Texas."

"You!"

"Bodkin, yu're so good a guesser maybe yu can guess some more."

"Well, that's no great concern of mine," returned Bodkin, harshly. "You're one of these even-break gunmen, so I can't arrest you. I knew him as Knight. Now get out——"

"Aw, Bodkin, yu're all lie," flung out Brazos, and in two long strides he reached the table. He lifted his boot against it and shoved powerfully. The laden tables slid

227

and tumbled with a crash, overturning Bodkin and half covering his burly form.

"Come up with yore gun!" ordered Brazos.

Bodkin floundered to his feet and would have made a ludicrous figure but for a stark and ghastly terror that was etched on his face. He made no move for his gun, which swung free without coat to hamper it.

"I'm not fightin' you—gun slinger," he panted.

"Yes, yu air—or be the first man I ever bored withoot it."

"Let me by. If you're spoilin' for a fight I'll find men——"

"Bah, yu chicken-hearted greaser! Cain't yu make no better stand before yore guests? Cain't yu die game?"

"Brazos Keene, I'll not add another notch to your gun handle."

"Wal, I'll break my rule an' cut just one notch for you, Bodkin. An' wherever I ride I'll show it an' say thet's for the yellowest, dirtiest skunk I ever shot."

"I tell you I won't draw," shouted Bodkin, desperate in his fear.

Brazos' gun twinkled blue. *Bang!* . . . Bodkin screamed like a horse in agony. His leg gave way under him and he would have fallen but for the chair he seized. Brazos' bullet had penetrated the calf of his leg.

"Air yu gonna take it by inches?" demanded the cowboy.

Bodkin gazed balefully, with wobbling jaw. Horribly plain his love of life, his fear of death! And still it eluded him—the destroying truth of this cowboy.

"Bodkin, yore game is up. Yu've dealt yore last hand at cairds. Yore lyin', cheatin', stealin' days air over. . . . Yore murderin' days air over. . . . For *yu* was Surface's tool in Allen Neece's murder. Yu tried the same deal when yu set Bard Syvertsen an' his girl Bess to murder me. . . . Yu're a menace to this range. These Las Animas fools who elected yu sheriff air crazy or crooked."

"You're the crazy—one," gasped Bodkin.

"Listen man. Cain't yu see thngs? I could kill yu on a personal grudge. But I'm gonna kill yu for better reasons."

"Keene, you can't prove. . . . You have no case. . . ."

"Hell! . . . Heah's one yu cain't deny. I was in the

228

room next to yore's at Hailey's. I had a hole cut in the wall. I heahed yu come in at midnight, with two men. One of them this Brad hombre I just shot. . . . An' I heahed yu talk. About Brad's failure to get the gunman, Panhandle Ruckfall, to come heah to kill me. . . . Aboot the gold Syvertsen stole from Neece an' gave to Surface. . . . Aha! yore memory is comin' to, Bodkin, old-timer! . . . Aboot how yu reckoned yu would hang on heah an' get elected sheriff. . . . An' last, how the third man of yu three thet night—the one whose name I never heahed—how *he* said the cattlemen of this range was wakin' up an' he was gonna slope."

Damning guilt worked upon the lessening fear and agony in Bodkin's visage.

"Now will yu go for yore gun?" added Brazos, sardonically.

"No—you—hydrophobia-bitten cow hand!"

*Crash!* Brazos shot the other leg out from under Bodkin. Still the sheriff did not fall, nor this time did he scream out. He sagged a little, until his knee on the chair upheld him. Then the horrid expression faded, smoothed out of his face, and into it came a vestige of the realization of death and a dark desire to take his merciless adversary with him. He let go of the chair with his right hand and drew his gun. Brazos let him swing it upward. Then Brazos leaped aside and shot. Bodkin's gun boomed so close afterward that the two shots seemed simultaneous. But Bodkin's bullet crashed through the window and Brazos' reached its mark. Bodkin slumped over the chair, his arms hanging, his head drooping, and on the instant his grip on his gun loosened to let it clatter on the floor.

Then the cowboy faced the ill-assorted group of men who had assembled there as Bodkin's guests. There was not the sign of a movement among them. They stood as if petrified.

"Henderson, yu're in bad company," rang out Brazos, "an' no matter what yore excuse, it'll be remembered in Las Animas. . . . Miller, I'm brandin' yu as hand an' glove with this Surface ootfit. . . . Yu business men an' yu strangers all know Bodkin now for what he was. . . . An' I reckon thet'll be aboot all for Brazos Keene in Colorado."

## Chapter Fifteen

BRAZOS rode away from Las Animas at dawn, as the sun was reddening the gray landscape, without ever once looking back, as he had done so often in his tumultuous range life.

His heading for the south, however, with the lean eager nose of his horse Bay turned toward Texas, had an air of finality. Thirst for adventure and even for romance, had been effectually killed. As Brazos took to the well-worn cattle trail, he felt sick and old and unhappy. He reflected that he would recover from the former, which was mostly revulsion at the shedding of blood, but he doubted that he would ever be young or happy again.

For long days he rode alone, shunning the cow camps, going around several little towns, camping at water holes and living upon the food he had packed. He made a gloomy and strange traveler. The gray miles filed past and every one of them seemed a dropped fetter. And in due course the bitter dregs of his last killing orgy wore out of his stomach. But the sense of loss still pressed heavily upon him. He forgot that it had been wise for him to ride away from the scene that had outlawed him, however unjust the law was, and despite the multitude of friends he had left behind.

Brazos knew his despair had to do with a broken heart. That susceptible member had been broken often before, and the time he had ridden away from Holly Ripple he thought it could never be mended. Nevertheless he had been mistaken.

Despite the stress of his emotions, however, Brazos could not prevent the influence of the open and the solitude. There was something healing in the waving grass, the swales and green flats, the winding tree-bordered river bottoms, and the distant uplands. Autumn, his favorite season, met him with its golden and gorgeous Indian summer. The dry fragrant breeze soft in his face, the poise of hawk and bound of jack rabbit, and the slipping away into the willows of deer, the gradual drawing from sight of cattle herds, the warming color in the distance, the smell of dust that at times rose from the clip-clop of Bay's tireless hoofs, the cottonwood grove where he had once camped, the great sycamore tree on the bank of the Purgatory where he had helped to hang a horse thief, the subtle essence of the lovely land which had been so much in his life—these wore upon him more and more until his old philosophy got hold of him again, and reason made clear the change in his life, and that with his marvelous memory he could not be anything else but appreciative even with his broken heart.

The day came when Brazos' trail led to the sleepy village of Hooker, where he purchased a blanket and as much food supply as Bay could carry. Once over the line into the Panhandle, towns would be few and far between. When he rode across the Texas line it seemed as definite a break as riding out of Las Animas. He was in his beloved Texas land. Yet how he had loved Colorado!

Thereafter travel became leisurely. There was now no need of hurry, if there had ever been, and he could think of Bay and be easy on the great horse.

When one late afternoon Brazos rode down toward a gold and scarlet creek bottom, he experienced a singular revivifying sensation. All that Texas range beyond he knew as well as if it had been a treasured book. Camp that night was one of divided memories—the old trail-driving days vied with the poignant experience he had left behind in Colorado. He sat up late before his ruddy little campfire, remembering, dreaming, yet unable to banish the thought of June and Janis. It would not be long now, as days went, until he arrived at Camp Supply on the Chisholm Trail. After that there would not be much more lonely traveling for him. He would meet cattle trains coming north across Texas on their way to Abilene and Dodge. And he would meet trail drivers riding south. He would find company. At the posts he would be unknown.

The deep wide rut in the prairie that was the old Chisholm Trail, which he had ridden so often with cowboys as wild as himself, led on and on down through the gray vastness of Texas. There was a comradeship in the old trail. One day was like another. He continued to make wide detours around settlements and wagon trains and herds of cattle.

Brazos came at length to Doan's Crossing. He was amazed to find himself so far down in Texas, arriving at one of the famous old posts of the frontier. Hungry and travel-stained, with Bay gone lame and needing rest, Brazos was forced to a halt.

"Jest as wal," he soliloquized. "Reckon I cain't be a lone wolf forever. I gotta live. A little more of this lone prairie will make me dotty."

Turning away from the great trail at the crossing, Brazos rode toward the post. It stood back from the river and appeared different. Then he saw that Doan's Crossing had grown to be a settlement. The huge rambling trading post, its adobe walls red in the westering sun, appeared the same as the picture in his memory. But it fronted on the corner of a wide street that stretched far between gray flat houses and red-walled buildings. Back from this typical Western street, full of dust and vehicles and houses, scattered cottages and shacks and tents grew up to the rise of the gray prairie.

"Wal, doggone me!" ejaculated Brazos, mildly. "Tom Doan has shore thrown up a metropolis."

If there were a trail herd in from the south it would account for the saddle horses standing bridles down, and the lounging riders, and the sloe-eyed swarthy Indians, but hardly for the life and bustle of that street. As Brazos slid wearily out of his saddle a lanky young Texan met him with a keen gaze.

"Howdy, rider. Air you stayin' over?"

"Howdy, young feller. I reckon. My hawse is lame. Will you put him up and look after him?"

"Yu bet," replied the lad, taking the bridle.

"Tom Doan heah yet?"

"Shore, Tom's heah, big as life. Yu been heah before?"

"Say, Tex, this old dobe post wouldn't be heah now but for me," drawled Brazos, as he untied his coat and saddle bags.

"Wal, you don't say?" queried the lad, his keen blue

eyes taking Brazos in with Texas perspicuity. "Mister, there's Doan comin' oot."

Brazos' glance lighted upon a tall Texan approaching. Same old Tom Doan! Brazos could have picked him out of a hundred Texans, though they all were sandy-haired, sallow-faced, with slits of gray fire for eyes. Brazos was used to scrutiny and he met it here in full measure. It gave him the first quick beat of pulse for days. He was home in Texas all right.

"Howdy, stranger. Git down an' come in," was the greeting. "Haven't I seen you before?"

"Tom, I reckon I'm starved and thin and black with this heah dust and beard. But it's a downright insult for you not to know me," drawled Brazos.

Doan straightened up from his close scrutiny. His still lined visage broke into a broad smile.

"Wal, talk of the devil an' heah he is! Brazos Keene!"

"Yep, it's Keene all right, only not the boy you knowed. How air you, Tom?"

The warm smile, the glad flash of Texas eyes, the hard grip, and the hand on his shoulder thrilled some of the cold weariness out of Brazos.

"I reckon I'm downright glad to see yu, Tom," he responded, hoarsely.

"Say, yu're spittin' cotton. Come in, boy, an' hev a drink."

"Wal, I need one, Tom. But not red likker."

Doan led Brazos through a lane of curious riders, into the post. The huge interior, its adobe walls decorated with Indian designs and ornaments, the colored blankets and utensils hanging from the rafters, the counters laden with merchandise, and the shelves packed with a miscellaneous collection of stores, and especially the great open fireplace at the end—all these appeared just the same as if he had seen them yesterday. But there was a wide door that Brazos did not remember. It led into a saloon full of smoke and noise. Dusty-booted and shirt-sleeved Westerners stood at a long bar; Indians in buckskin lounged back along the wall; gamblers sat intent at their tables.

"Tom, what the hell has come off about heah?" asked Brazos, after he had quenched his thirst.

"Brazos, we've growed up. Doan's Crossing is a town," replied the host, proudly.

"Hell, Tom, I ain't blind. But how come? There never was nothin' heah. Wal, nothin' but buffalo, Injuns, and trail herd rustlers."

Doan laughed. "So we used to think, cowboy. But we was blind. There's rich land heah. Lots of farms. Plenty ranches. Fine grass an' water. We've got a growin' town. A dozen stores an' more, too many saloons, a school an' a church an' a doctor. I've added a hotel to my post. Turnin' 'em away some days. Two stages a week, herds still trailin' north, travel heavy. Aw, Doan Crossin' is boomin'.'"

"Wal, doggone! I'm shore glad, Tom. But who ever would have reckoned on it?"

"I did for one, Brazos. . . . Where yu headin'?"

"West of the Pecos," replied Keene, ponderingly, his gaze averted.

"Aw! Don't tell me yu are on the dodge, Brazos?"

"Not atall. I reckon I did get in bad up Colorado way. But thet country I cleaned up will be so glad about it they'd fire any sheriff who put oot strings for me."

"Ah-huh. Wal, I hain't heerd nothin' an' I ain't askin'."

"Good. . . . Tom, I want a room and hot water. Last time I was heah I slept on the counter oot there. Recollect thet?"

"I shore do. An' you didn't need no bath, 'cause yu an' Herb Ellerslie got piled off in the river."

"Gosh! Tom, yu do remember heaps. Did I by any chance owe you some money?"

"Nope. Anyway thet's too long ago to remember."

"Tom, yu're a liar. What become of Herb Ellerslie?"

"Shot, Brazos. Shot at Dodge by a gambler named Cardigan."

"Aw, no! . . . I'm sorry. Herb and I were pretty thick on the trail. . . . Cardigan? . . . I'll remember thet name. . . . How aboot Wess Tanner?"

"Jest fine. Wess drove through—let's see—along in August. He raved aboot one of them electric storms. Come to think of it Wess will be along any day now."

"Wouldn't I like to see Wess!" ejaculated Brazos, dreamily, following his host out of the saloon into a long corridor. The whitewashed walls were colorful with Indian blankets, as was also the earthen floor. There were windows on one side and doors on the other. Doan halted at the end of the corridor, which apparently opened into a green and flowery patio. Brazos heard the tinkle of running water. He was ushered into a room that spoke eloquently of the advance Doan's Crossing had made toward civilization.

"Doggone! . . . Tom, this heah is mighty stylish for me. Wonder if I can sleep in thet bed."

"Wal, you look like you needed to," replied Doan, with a laugh. "I'll send some hot water. You got about a half hour before supper."

Brazos laid off his sombrero, his gun, spurs and chaps. Then he opened his saddle bags to take out his last clean shirt, scarf and socks, and also his shaving outfit "Heigho!" he sighed, and sat down on the bed. "Doan's Crossing. . . . Jesse Chisholm's Trail. . . . And I'm a broken old man!"

A Mexican lad brought a bucket of hot water and towels. Then Brazos indulged in the luxury of a bath, a shave and some clean clothes. He was scrutinizing his lean brown face in the mirror, shaking his head dubiously, when the supper bell rang. Brazos did not forget to strap on his gun belt. Then he went out. He had to be directed to the dining room, and found a dozen or more men ahead of him. Most of them were merry riders. Finding an empty seat Brazos stepped across the bench and sat down. The fellow next to him on the right was friendly, though not curious. Still Brazos found himself the cynosure of all eyes. That Doan had mentioned his name seemed evident. A middle-aged man, surely a rancher, sitting at Brazos' left, made himself agreeable. But presently Brazos discovered that he was a starved wolf, and that the meal was sumptuous. He ate until he felt ashamed of himself, and was the last to leave the table.

After supper he went outdoors to walk a little. In the cool darkness Indians had a fire burning. It was pleasant for Brazos to watch and listen. The night wind was cold. He heard coyotes out on the prairie. Presently Brazos went into the post, to lounge around in the background listening to the gossip of the trail that had once been his world. He shunned the saloon with its bright lights and gay riders. Then he strolled down the wide street, along the broad walk, from one end to the other, finding it like any other promenade of a frontier town. The brightly lighted stores, the passers-by, a few of whom were giggling girls who made shy eyes at him, the rattle of a roulette wheel and the metallic clink of silver coins, the sound of music and gay song, loud voices, the bang of a gun, and then silence—all these things left Brazos uninterested and he returned to his room with the pang in his breast more laden and heavy than when he had sat around his lonely campfires.

He went to bed. But tired as he was, he could not sleep. The bed felt too soft, too comfortable. He lay awake, thinking. It was as dark as pitch in his room. Only a hum of noises penetrated the thick walls. And June and Jan Neece filled his mind.

Strangely, though, of all the nights he had been riding away, this one began to assume different and tremendous importance. Perhaps contact with men again had dispelled the dream, the fantasy, the unreality. Something had clarified his clouded mind. It seemed that through all these days and nights he had been nearing the truth of his problem without being conscious of it. Jan and June Neece no longer existed in his consciousness as a single entity—one girl. He had separated them into the twins once again, as they had been at first.

In the dead of night in the blackness of his room at Doan's post, hundreds of miles from the scene of his downfall, he at last saw clearly. All the time, it had been June, and June alone. He had worshiped her, and worshiped her still. At the very onset both girls had won his sympathy, his championship. But it had been June who had uplifted and inspired him, called so deeply and poignantly to the finer side of him, that he had never known really existed. He had thought of June as a girl to work for, to change his nature, to make a home for him and be the mother of his children. All dream! but he saw through it clearly now.

Jan, the devil, the sweet counterpart of her twin sister,

236

the natural coquette, had stimulated all the physical and the wild in Brazos. He had loved her, too. It was impossible not to. Yet he saw it now as singularly different. If it had been possible, failing to get June, he would have chosen Jan for a wife, realizing that instead of peace he would have found turmoil.

The truth seemed to be a relief. He was not so ashamed as he had been. What chance had he had against those lovely girls, both in their way equally devastating? Not one man in a hundred, not one cowboy in a thousand, similarly situated, could have resisted the apalling temptation June Neece had visited upon him. Brazos shook in his bed. That old wave of fire passed through every fiber of his being. He feared that he would feel that until he was old, perhaps to his grave. And yet he would not have had it otherwise. There had been something great in his downfall. Yet what folly to call it downfall or ruin! Those twins had been his salvation. He had to be worthy of what they had made him.

Yet all this did not make clear to Brazos the subtleties of the present. For days he had traveled more and more slowly. It seemed the reverse of that old step on his trail. Doan's Crossing marked some kind of a dividing line for him. Had his subconscious mind been harboring a hidden thought for him to take the stage north? This query shook Brazos anew. How was he to know what he might do? But that was unthinkable. Still there was something that haunted and mocked him—something which seemed to hold aloof inexplicably, to damn him with vague conviction that he had no control over his wretched destiny.

Sleep came very late to Brazos that night. He was awakened from a dead slumber of exhaustion by a pounding on his door. He sat up rubbing his eyes.

"Hey, Mister Keene, air yu daid?" called a voice Brazos recognized as belonging to the Texas lad.

"Mawnin', Tex. No I ain't daid yet. What's the row about?"

"I been tryin' to wake you."

"Say, Kid, don't tell me you called me more'n once."

"I have, though."

"What time of day is it?"

237

"Long after midday. I reckon two o'clock."

"Wal, what's the idee? Injuns or fire?"

"Wuss, for *yu*, Mister Brazos."

"Hell you say! Look heah, Tex, I'm liable to bounce somethin' off yore haid. What you mean—wuss?"

"I—yu .... fact is, Brazos, the Dodge City stage rolled in—with . . . an'—some old friends of yores rode in with it."

The lad's voice betrayed excitement if not confusion.

"Friends?" flashed Brazos, his slow blood quickening.

"Tanner an' some of his riders. I heerd Doan tell him to come wake yu up. An' Wess said: 'Me wake Brazos Keene? Mebbe out on the trail, but not heah. Umpumm!' . . . They was afraid to wake yu, Brazos, An' I wasn't so damn happy about it, nuther. Yu see. . . ."

"What'n hell you all think—thet I ain't human?" yelled Brazos, as he leaped out of bed. "Tell Wess I'll be there in a jiffy. Rustle, you towhaid."

Brazos laughed at the quick footfalls of the lad fading down the corridor. He washed and dressed as swiftly as if this summons had been a trail call. Warm thoughts attended his actions. He wagered that he would be as glad to see Wess Tanner as Wess. . . . Afraid to wake him? That was a good one. The damned old maverick hunter. Brazos belted on his gun belt and strode out into the corridor. He halted at the door of the saloon. There were a dozen or more men at the bar, all strange to see, facing the corridor entrance. All unknown to Brazos, he noted at a glance; but that keen glance registered also that they knew him and looked uneasy. Brazos swore under his breath and strode on into the trading post. A hubbub of voices stilled as he entered. That also stilled Brazos' pleasant sensations. What was amiss? Even if he was Brazos Keene. . . . Indians and riders grouped around the wide door. Outside there appeared to be a crowd. At the far and lighter end of the big post Doan appeared to have stopped waiting on a customer. Brazos saw him jerk a thumb toward the entrance, and following that cue Brazos espied half a dozen riders, standing a little to the left of a tall blond fellow, lean and intent of face, with eyes like daggers. Brazos recognized Wess Tanner and saw him suddenly jerk as if frozen blood had sustained a hot release. One other of the riders Brazos recognized in that quick glance. They all appeared under a restraint. It irritated Brazos. Why should friends act like strangers when he stalked in? That was one bitter price Brazos Keene had to pay. But he shook it off and advanced. When he reached Tanner only genuine gladness possessed him.

*"Wess!* . . .You lean hungry-lookin' old trail driver!" burst out Brazos. "My Gawd, I'm shore glad to see you!"

*"Pard.* . . . You damned ole brown-skinned *vaquero!"* replied Tanner, unsteadily, as he met that proffered hand. "Brazos—I never expected to see this day. An' am I happy?"

They clasped hands and locked glances. It was a meeting between tried and true Texans who had slept and fought and toiled together through unforgettable days. Whatever had made Tanner strange and backward vanished the instant Brazos faced him.

"Brazos—meet my ootfit," said Tanner, presently. "Yu ought to remember Sam heah."

"Sam Jenkins. I shore do. Howdy, Sam," replied Brazos, offering his hand to the sleek dark Jenkins. "It shore is good to meet you again. Can you palm aces like you used to and sing the herd quiet?"

"Howdy—Brazos," replied Jenkins, warming brightly. "Darn glad to see you. . . . Shore I can do them same old tricks."

Brazos was introduced to the other riders, most of them striplings such as he had been when he first started herd driving. Obviously they were overcome at this meeting, and though pleased and excited, they did not succeed in throwing off the restraint.

"Wal, Wess, I reckon you're ridin' back to Santone for the winter. No more trail drivin' this year?"

"Not till spring, Brazos. An' mebbe not then. Pard, I shore have the grandest ranch bargain there is in all Texas. If I can only raise the backin'!"

"Same old Wess. Always dreamin' of thet grand ranch. I shore want to heah about it. Reckon you'll lay over heah today?"

"We ain't in any hurry, Brazos."

"I'd kinda like to ride south with you, for a while. It's been lonely."

Tanner gave him a keen kindly glance that baffled Brazos. He expected a warm response to his suggestion that he accompany Tanner and his boys down the Old Trail, and as that was not instantly forthcoming Brazos sustained a little shock of surprise and disappointment.

"Don't be hurt, pard. It ain't likely you'll want to ride with us. But I'd shore like thet. . . . Brazos, come aside over heah. I've news for yu. . . . I'm scared stiff, yet——"

Wess led Brazos to a corner beside a window and faced him there hopefully yet apprehensively, with a pale face full of suppressed agitation that nonplussed Brazos and gave rise again to his former irritation.

'Scared stiff, you?" he queried darkly, almost bitterly. "Wess, I know I'm an ootlaw—an' unfairly, by Gawd—but you, my old pard who wouldn't have thet blond scalp but for me——"

"Shet up, you fire-eater," interposed Wess. "I couldn't be no more ashamed of yu, Brazos Keene, than of my own brother."

"Sorry, old-timer. Reckon I'm kinda testy. . . . What's on yore mind?"

Manifestly Wess labored under some stress than rendered liberation extremely difficult. He lit a cigarette with visibly unsteady fingers and he swallowed a lump in his throat. But the paleness under his tan had begun to tinge with red.

"Hell, man!" exploded Brazos. "You didn't use to be so damn squeamish. . . . You've heahed about thet little Las Animas mess."

"Shore, Brazos—shore," agreed Wess, hurriedly. "Only it didn't seem little to me. Fact is—it was big—big as Texas."

"Yeah? An' what of it?" rasped Brazos.

"Wal, for one thing Dodge City took it fine. Wild Bill hisself said to me: 'Wess, thet's the sheriff for Dodge when I get mine!' "

"Hell he did? Wild Bill Hickock! . . . Kind of a compliment at thet."

"Mebbe you shouldn't have rode away from Las Animas so quick."

"I reckon you think I should have got up a party and swelled around town," said Brazos, sarcastically.

"Nope, not jest thet, though the deal shore called for some red-eye. Where'd yu stop an' soak up a load of likker?"

"Wess, I haven't taken one dod-blasted drink," de-cleared Brazos.

"Thet settles it. Yu air crazy. I been afraid of it ever since—since——"

"Since what, you tongue-tied hombre? I'm gonna get sore pretty pronto."

"Brazos, for the life of me I cain't see why. If I was in yore boots I'd be so dod-blasted happy——"

"You been afraid since what? Since what?" flashed Brazos, grasping Wess's wrist with fingers of steel. There was something wrong about this old friend—something that had to be solved.

"Wal, then, old pard—since—since Miss Neece braced me on the street in Dodge."

"*What?* . . . Miss—Neece?" Brazos' voice sounded faint in his thrumming ears. His hand fell away from Wess.

"Shore. Yore fiancée," replied Wess. "Pard, if I'd never heerd of yu I'd have been stricken by sight of thet lovely gurl."

"My—my fiancée? . . . How'd you know—thet?"

"She told me."

"Good Gawd! . . . Wess, wasn't she ashamed of thet?"

"Ha! Ha! I should smile she wasn't."

"Aw! . . . But what for? . . . How come? Was she visitin' Dodge with her Dad or friends . . . and heahed you might know me?'"

"No, she shore wasn't visitin' an' as for her Dad . . . Wal, never mind about him. . . . Miss Neece was hot on yore trail, Brazos."

At that Brazos began to shake. What was this? His mind began to whirl. "Hot on my—trail?" he echoed, in a whisper.

"I said hot, pardner. . . . It was this way. I happened to run into the Hotel Dodge to see Jeff—you cain't have forgot Jeff Davis? He shore hadn't forgot you. Wal, before I could say howdy even, Jeff grabbed me an' turned to a gurl standin' there. I went stiff at sight of her. 'What luck!' burst out Jeff. 'Heah he is now. . . . Wess, this is Miss Neece. She has been askin' if any Texas trail driver might know Brazos Keene. An' I told her yu—Wess Tanner—was an old pardner of his.' . . . The gurl's white face went red, then paled again. 'Please come,' she said, and led me off out of the lobby into the parlor.

"  'Yu know Brazos?' she asked, and she was trembling.

"  'Wal, I used to, Miss,' I said.

"  'Yu've heerd about me?'

"  'No. Sorry to confess I haven't,' I had to tell her.

"  'But yu *have* heerd about—what he did at Las Animas?'

"  'Yes, Miss. Thet's town talk heah. But I never believe range gossip, much less about Brazos Keene.'

"  'Oh! But it is all true . . . and I am his—fiancée.'

"  'Miss Neece, whatever Brazos done it was justified. He is a true blue Texan, as fine a boy as ever forked a hawse. . . .' Wal, she thanked me with tears streamin' down her lovely face. An' then she told me yu an' she had had a lover's quarrel. She was jealous of her twin sister. Yu had left her an' gone to town, where yu shot her Dad's enemies, one of them the sheriff. Then yu rode away, thinkin' yu'd made yoreself an outlaw, which yu hadn't. She said she knew yu'd ride down into Texas an' she wanted me to undertake to find yu. Brazos, thet scared me to death. But no livin' cowboy could ever hev resisted her eyes, her voice. . . . 'Could you find Brazos?' she asked. I said it was about a shore thing thet I could. 'Will yu?' she pleaded with me. 'No matter what time it takes—what it'll cost. I have money. I'll pay.' I interrupted her there. I jest couldn't stand thet anguished face. An' I said: 'Lady, I cain't take yore money. I'll find Brazos for yu. An' thet hombre will shoot my laig off for my pains.' 'Shoot yu?' she cried. 'He'll bless yu all the rest of his life!' "

"Right you were—Wess," mumbled Brazos, thickly, fighting the wave on wave of emotion that swayed him. How terrible and sweet this news! "I'll shoot—yore laig off. Damn you! Wasn't I miserable enough? . . . But tell the rest now, if there is any."

"There's plenty, pard. Let's have a drink first."

"No! Plenty? . . . Wess, I cain't stand much more. . . . But the idee? What was her crazy idee—coaxin' you to find me?"

"What do you think, old pard?" queried Wess, drawing a deep breath.

"Think? I cain't think. Only thet it was sweet of June. . . . Tell me, or I'll choke it out of you."

Wess clapped a heavy hand on Brazos' shoulder.

"Pard, Miss Neece's idee was to come with me—till I found you," replied Wess, his voice ringing.

"Come with—you? . . . Heavens above!"

"Thet was her idee, Brazos. An' she did come."

Brazos could only stare in fearful stupefaction into the pale face of his friend.

"She's heah!" rang out Wess.

Brazos went blind. His shaking hand groped for Wess, who met it with his own and steadied him.

"Heah—*now?*" gasped Brazos, rousing to sensations that had almost disrupted his consciousness.

"Right now, pard. She's in with Mrs. Doan."

"Right now! She's heah!" echoed Brazos, huskily. His legs went unsteady under him. He had to hold on to Wess. These were his physical reactions, which possessed him momentarily. Then, his mind released, wonder and joy followed, to lift him to seventh heaven.

"Brazos! For the good Lord's sake!" Wess was saying in faraway voice, as he shook Brazos. "What ails yu? Man, yu should be the happiest man in all Texas. Why, I never seen yu like this. An' how many gurls have I seen yu crazy over? Shore, pard, this is different. This gurl is the real an' the last one. . . . But . . . hell's fire, Brazos, yu haven't held up a bank or stole a hawse? Somethin' bad to clinch thet outlaw name?"

"Which—one?" whispered Brazos, his eyes closed tight.

*"Which one?* Say, the boy's dotty. No wonder. . . . Which what? Which gurl, yu mean? Why yu pore locoed ghost of yore old self. It's yore sweetheart. Yore fiancée. The gurl yu're engaged to."

243

Wess's piercing whisper penetrated Brazos' tortured consciousness. The stupefying shock passed, if not its wake of emotion. Brazos let go of Wess and turned to the window. Gradually his dim sight cleared. Outside he saw Indians and horses, a sweep of gray slope leading up to the horizon. He found himself. What was this that had happened? The nameless thing he had felt had held him here at Doan's Crossing. For what? Retribution had caught up with him. One of the Neece twins had followed him. He had imagined it was June—the good and quiet—the sweet and noble girl whom he had worshiped. But June could never have undertaken this wild chase. She would never have deserted her father for an outlaw. It was Jan. It was Jan—that passionate little devil who at last had given rein to the wildness in her.

"All right, Wess," declared Brazos, finally, turning to his friend. "What's the rest?"

"Wal! Thet's more like my old pard," replied Wess greatly relieved. "There ain't so much more. Yore gurl had a lot of baggage, Brazos. Easy to see she wasn't goin' back home. Ha! Ha! . . . Wal, we loaded it on the stage. An' we rode with thet stage all the way from Dodge. There were several other passengers off an' on. They an' my boys, an' me too, fell turrible hard for yore sweetheart. I reckon the stage come purt' near bein' held up once by road agents. At least Bill Hempstead, our driver, said he know thet outfit. But we was too many. Afterward Miss Neece confessed she had a lot of money with her an' thet it was great luck for her thet we happened to be her bodyguard. . . . I reckon thet's about all. Yu bet I never enjoyed the Old Trail like I did this time."

"Lot of baggage and money!" exclaimed Brazos, bewildered again. "Wess, tell me this is a nightmare."

"Nightmare, my eye! Look at thet—where yu bruised my wrist, squeezin' it so hard."

"I'm sorry, pard. Thanks for everythin'. I reckon I won't shoot yore laig off."

"Wal, I'm tolerable glad about thet. Brazos, I got a gurl myself, an' when yu've time yu must heah about her."

"Aw, thet's fine, Wess. I'll be glad to heah."

"Brazos, there's Mrs. Doan," went on Wess, quickly.

"She's lookin' for yu, I'll bet. Come, pard, yu better get it over. I cain't help sayin' I wouldn't mind bein' in yore boots."

Doan introduced Brazos to his wife, a comely sturdy pioneer type, blonde and buxom. She certainly gave Brazos a looking over before she relaxed into friendliness and sympathy.

"I think you had better see your fiancée at once. She is under a strain. I hope—nothing's wrong. She is sweet and she must care greatly for you."

"Cowboy, I seen thet an' I had it figured when she stepped off the stage. Such eyes! Black an' hungry as a starved Indian's!" added Doan, with his hearty smile.

"Wal, friends, she must think a lot of me," replied Brazos, gravely. "It's too late now for me to worry about not bein' good enough for her an' ridin' away like I did. . . . Take me to her."

"Wal, cowboy," interposed Doan, impressively, "take it from me. A Texan like you is worth any two Yankee gurls thet ever was!"

Two girls! Brazos suffered a piercing stab. His quick flash of eyes assured him that the frontiersman was just bragging in the simplicity of his loyalty and pride.

"Tom, if Brazos is good enough for *one* girl—and half good enough for *this* one—we have a lot to be thankful for. Come, Brazos," added Mrs. Doan.

She led him to a door at the south end of the post. "This is my room, Brazos. You'll be secluded there. Make it up to her. Try to realize your great good fortune."

In the moment before he stepped into the room, Brazos faced his ultimatum. It was June he loved most and wanted for his wife, but it could never have been June who had the adventurous spirit to follow him. So Jan must never know. And love her he did, too, but not as he did June. In all humbleness, he told himself that he was lucky to have either of the twins give up everything to come to him.

Brazos was tense and tingling when he opened the door. The room appeared large and bright. Sunlight streamed in the several windows, to give the furnishing a touch of warmth and vividness. He heard a gasp. Then he wheeled.

"Bra-zos!" whispered some one, tremulously. She had been standing almost behind the door, waiting, her face white, her lips parted, her eyes wide and dark. Brazos had not expected to see her in a white dress, but of course she had had time to change. Jan would never have let him see her travel-stained or disheveled. Her face was lovely, despite the havoc he read there. That mark of grief drew him as subtly as the gratitude and love which welled up upon sight of her.

"Jan! You sweet devil," he cried, huskily, and held out his arms.

She had been already on the way to him. Apparently his poignant exclamation, or the welcome of his gesture suddenly halted her for a moment, while a spasm crossed her face. It passed, and she flew to him, swaying the last step to his arms. She hid her face and clung to him.

"Brazos—darling. I—I had to come," she said, in smothered tone.

"Wal, I couldn't be shore till I felt you—like this," he replied, hoarsely, and he held her close and tight to his breast while he bent his head against her rippling hair. On the moment he could not see well. He seemed to float in that dim room.

"Don't—hug me—so," she whispered, almost inaudibly, "unless you—don't want me—to breathe. Brazos, you're not—angry?"

"Angry? No, Jan. I'm sort of buffaloed. My Gawd, child, it was sweet and good—and bad—of you to trail me heah."

"Bad?" she queried, quickly.

"For you, dear. I'm an outlaw, you know. You've disgraced yourself, and all of them."

"But for *you,* Brazos, darling?"

"I reckon it's near heaven again."

"Oh! . . . Then you forgive me."

"I probably will—if you kiss me like you did thet turrible night."

"Same old Brazos! Only you look. . . . Brazos, tell me you won't send me back," she importuned, softly.

"No, Jan. I cain't do thet."

"But you *want* me?" she flashed, with a show of her old fire.

"Yes. I'm mad about you, Jan. I reckoned I'd got over it, a little. But I hadn't."

"Darling! . . . And J-June?"

"Wal, *she* didn't trail me, did she?"

It appeared then that a convulsion waved over the girl. She clung to Brazos with her face hidden against him. He felt her breast throb upon his. She did not weep. Her arms slid up round his neck. Blindly she raised her face, flaming now, with tears coursing from under her closed eyelids, and she found Brazos' lips with her own. And she kissed them again and again, left them for his cheeks and eyes only to return, until it seemed to Brazos that her kisses gathered strength and fire and passion as they multiplied. But suddenly she sank limp against him, her arms sliding down. Holding her close Brazos leaned against a table and tried to separate conflicting tides of emotion from tumultuous and overwhelming thoughts. Presently he could see clearly through the window, the blue sky beyond the green trees.

"Jan, I reckon we—might sit down," he said huskily, and half lifted her to the couch. But she would not let go of him. Weak and nerveless now, she still clung. "You must be kinda tired . . . all thet long stage ride."

"No. I wasn't tired," she said, lifting her head. "Just overcome at meeting you. . . . Scared weak. I was afraid you'd send me back . . . that—you—you love J-June best."

Brazos took her face between his hands and studied it gravely. The havoc he had seen appeared warmed out and the dark eyes had lost their strain. But there was a difference. Tiny blue veins he had never noticed before shone through the white of her temples there were dark shadows under her eyes, magnifying them; her cheeks were thinner. Beauty abided there imperishably, but it was an older, nobler, sadder face.

"Let us talk—now," he voice had quieted. "First I have much to tell."

"I reckoned you had, darlin'."

"Brazos. . . . Dad died suddenly less than a week after you left," she began, with tragic force.

"Aw! . . . Jan! How awful!" cried Brazos, shocked to his depths. "My Gawd, I'm sorry! . . . Thet fine up-standin' Westerner—not old atall—just got his home and daughters back! Aw! but this is a tough one on me. I was turrible fond of yore Dad. . . . Jan, I don't know what to say."

"Brazos, you've said enough. It comforts me. We knew you loved Dad—J-June and I. It was partly what you did for him that made us love you. But Dad is gone. And if I hadn't had you to think of—to save, I'd sunk under that blow."

"Save? Jan, you think I have to be saved?"

"Indeed I do. Thank heaven I caught up with you in time. . . . Brazos, that is the saddest news, But there's more—not sad—yet it'll hurt you."

"Go ahaid, darlin'," replied Brazos, simply. "I reckon I can stand anythin' now."

Jan averted her face. Her breast rose and fell, indicating oppression. Her hand tightened on Brazos'.

"It's about J-June."

"Shore, I reckoned thet. Don't keep me in suspense."

"She eloped with Henry Sisk . . . came home married!"

"What're you tellin' me, Jan Neece?" ejaculated Brazos, fiercely.

"You heard me, darling." Her voice was low, but perfectly clear, carrying a note unfamiliar to Brazos.

"Jan, you lie!" Brazos leaped up in a perfect frenzy of amaze and fury.

"What motive could I have in telling you a lie?" she returned proudly. If she were lying it had all the guile and subtlety of a woman behind it. Brazos turned her face around so that he could see it in the light. Its pallor, the proud dark eyes, that peered straight and unfathomably into his, the set lips, almost stern now—these to Brazos were not eloquent of falsehood.

"Jan, I beg—yore pardon," he went on, haltingly. "But that knocks me cold and sick, to my very gizzard. Worse than when I kill a man! . . . But damn June's fickle heart!

248

She loved *me*. She proved it . . . and then, all in no time —she shows yellow. . . . Henry Sisk? Fine chap, shore, but he was sweet on you, wasn't he?"

"I thought so. He swore it."

"So he throwed you down for June?" demanded Brazos, hotly.

"Something like that, darling."

"Did you care?"

"Yes, I did. It hurt. I'm a vain creature. But *I* couldn't marry Henry. On my soul of honor I couldn't."

"Why couldn't you, Miss Neece?"

"Because I loved you. I never knew how well until you ran away."

"Ahuh. You must forgive me. I'm shore upset. . . . And how did June take my runnin' away?"

"I think—I *know* it broke her heart, too. . . . Then Dad died. That changed the world for us. J-June and I must be separated. All at once I found out. I had to find you—or just lie down to die."

"Jan, I've misjudged you. I never gave you credit for bein' so deep and true and fine. I reckoned you was the flirt and June the steady one. What a fool I was! . . . Gimme a little time to cuss this thing out of my haid."

Brazos fell to striding the room, yielding to his jealous wrath, to the incredible thing that had happened. He had wanted to reverence June Neece all his life. Yet in a day, almost, she had betrayed him. She was not worth Jan's little finger. And he cursed under his breath at her and her inconstancy. He had not expected June to remain loveless all her life on account of him. But hell! if she had loved him as she had sworn and he believed, like any locoed cowboy, she would not have married Sisk or anyone so soon. It was hardly decent. She was shallow. And he raged there for he knew not how long, until his wounded vanity and bitter heart had taught him another lesson of life. Then he turned to Jan, finding her watching him with what appeared an incomprehensible contrast to grief. Could Jan, being human, be glad to see her sister toppled from her pedestal?

"Wal, Jan, yore bein' heah to tell me—to sustain me— keeps me from fallin' to a low-down hombre of a greaser.

Thet news would have just plumb knocked me forever."

"Oh, Brazos—darling. Can I make up for the loss of June?"

"I reckon. But let me be straight with you, Jan. If June hadn't turned out faithless and whatever else it was —neither you, however sweet and lovely you air, nor all the rest of the girls in the world, could have made up for the loss of her. Can you stand to heah thet?"

"Yes, Brazos, I—I can stand it," faltered Jan, her face drooping.

"Don't take it too hard, honey. I'm a queer duck. I always make amends. I always pay. You won't never be sorry thet I worshiped June—reckoned she was an angel. After all she was a part of you."

"Brazos, there's more to tell," went on Jan, hurriedly. "I'm afraid again. You are such a strange fellow. So honorable and fine and true! I'll never forget you when, that night, J-June solved our problem by telling you to marry me—and you could have her, too."

"I wish to heaven I could forget it. Mebbe I can now— thet she's turned out so pore."

"Brazos, can you stand another surprise?" asked Jan, fearfully.

He eyed her askance. But Jan did not look formidable just then or anything to be dubious about. He drew her into his arms, yet held her back, so he could study her face.

"Shoot, Jan. You cain't knock me out again."

"I'll bet I can."

"Ha! I won't bet. But tell me. . . ."

She leaned back, toying with his scarf, provoking and adorable, but hiding her eyes.

"Could you stand a sweetheart—an'—and a—a wife— who is very, very rich?"

"Good—Lord!" exploded Brazos, and then succumbed to incredible fate.

"Could you?" she repeated. "Just because you 'air a pore lone prairie cowboy,' you won't be too honorable and proud—to—to make those amends you spoke of?"

"What you got up yore sleeve?"

"Brazos, if I'm a very rich girl—that won't make any difference to you?"

"You're talkin' riddles. But I reckon—if you *was* a very rich girl—I wouldn't feel turrible bad about it."

She let out a sweet peal of glad laughter and caught him around the neck. "Brazos, listen. Henry bought my share of Twin Sombreros Ranch and two thousand head of cattle."

Brazos sat mutely staring at this apparition—this angel of fortune—this living refutation of his vain judgment of women.

"You see it hasn't turned out so badly, even if you have lost June."

"How much?" queried Brazos, faintly.

"How much what? Oh, how much I love you? Oh, more than any girl ever loved any man."

"Jan, my heart is weak. Don't tease no more. . . . How much did you sell out for?"

"I made a pretty good deal, Hank Bilyen said. For the cattle I got forty dollars a head. Figure that out."

"I cain't—darlin'—I cain't figger, or add—or anythin'."

"Well, that comes to eighty thousand dollars. And I sold my half of the ranch for twenty thousand. I brought the money with me."

"Mercy!" begged Brazos.

"I got a few thousand in cash. Bilyen said 'Lord only knows what it'll cost to find thet feller.' And the rest in drafts on the Las Animas bank. Mr. Henderson fixed it up for me. I wasn't worried about the drafts when those road agents almost held us up. Those drafts cannot be negotiated by anyone except your little girl. Savvy? But I was afraid I'd lose the cash. . . . Now, Brazos, darling, now what are we going to do?"

"Now, Jan, darlin', what air we goin' to do?" mimicked Brazos, in consternation.

"You're not exactly a poor cowboy down at his heels. You can do things."

"Jan, I cain't do nothin' but love you," replied Brazos, abjectly.

"Well, that's grand. But I prefer you do a *little* besides

loving me. . . . Brazos, those boys with Wess Tanner, especially the dark handsome lad, they were sweet on me. And you know I'm unreliable. It seems to me you had better put a halter on me while you have the chance. Dad always said that once I was haltered, I'd steady down."

"Jan, at thet I believe you've changed—grown. But still the same old sweet devil."

"Brazos, we were engaged, you know," said Jan, seriously. "I told everybody. I don't know how you really regarded our engagement. But if it hadn't been for that I never could have followed you."

"I savvy. And now thet you've come up with me . . ."

"You're perfectly free, Mister Keene, unless you want me as terribly as you wanted June," she interposed, her chin lifting and level searching eyes on him.

"Jan, will you take my solemn word?" asked Brazos.

"Yes, Brazos, I will."

"Wal, before I entered thet door I knew I'd ask you to marry me—first, because thet old love came thunderin' back—second, because I would have asked you if I hadn't loved you, I was struck so deep by yore trailin' me— and last because I could never let one word of range gossip get started about Jan Neece."

She appeared enraptured, almost satisfied, yet there was a restraint, a doubt about her that puzzled Brazos. He caught his breath and asked her to marry him.

"Yes, darling," she replied, and hid her face upon his shoulder.

"When?" he flashed, tense and keen, succumbing to the current of the great river that had swept him off his feet.

"Need we wait?" she asked. That indeed betrayed this frank and devilishly sweet Jan Neece at her truest.

"If I had my way we wouldn't wait atall," rang out Brazos.

"Your way is my way—and always shall be," declared the girl, eloquently. And she arose to go to the window, where she peered out upon the prairie. Brazos saw that there was nothing soft and tremulous about her then. "If it is possible I will marry you here."

"Jan! . . . It's shore possible. Dean told me they had a church heah. Course they'd have to have a minister."

"Run darling—and find out. . . . Jan, you know, can change her mind." She did not turn away from the window. Brazos leaped up, to forget his sombrero, and rush from the room. He encountered Doan and Tanner, both of whom received his onslaught in alarm.

"Tom! You said—you had a church—heah?"

"Yu bet we have."

"Then you've got a pastor."

"Naturally. An' a fine chap he is."

Brazos gulped. "Can he marry—Jan an' me—right away?"

"Wal, pard, yu're-shore ridin' high, wide an' handsome now," declared Wess, his bronze face shining.

"Go fetch him," cried Brazos, excitedly, hanging on to both his friends. "Fetch him. Tell him to bring papers . . . and whatever I gotta have. . . . Wess, you go with Tom. And call me when you get back."

"Brazos, I always knowed when yu got this way over a gurl yu'd be a ravin' lunatic," drawled Wess. "An' holy mavericks, am I glad?"

"Cowboy, air yu shore yu won't go out of yore haid before we can get back?" asked Doan, half in earnest and half in jest.

Not waiting to reply Brazos ran back to Mrs. Doan's door, halting when he came to it. He sensed a mysterious portent beyond that threshold. It checked him—held him with abated breath. But he knocked. There was no reply. Uncertain and strangely agitated he entered the room. Jan was lying face down on the couch.

Brazos ran to kneel beside her, his hands eager to gather her up, but lost their strength when they came in contact with her quivering form.

"Jan, dear, what ails you?"

"Oh, Brazos. . . . I—I can't go through with it. I can't. . . . I'm a little fourflush. I have none of the nerve you—you credited me with," burst from her in smothered tones.

Brazos' heart sank like lead. He suffered a moment of despair. But she must be overwrought. . . . The suspense, the long trip, the ordeal with him had been beyond her.

"Darlin', you cain't what?" he asked, tenderly. "I reckon you mean—marry me?"

"No! No!" she cried, frantically, raising her face, to disclose it tear-wet and shamed, with tragic eyes dark upon him. "I'm crazy to—to marry you. I'll die if you won't have me. . . . And, oh, misery, you'll hate me now!"

"Ump-umm, honey. I cain't hate you, no matter what you've done, so long as you're crazy to marry me."

"Brazos, I didn't know it'd be so hateful. I was just wild for you. I'd have done anything . . . anything. But now, you've been so sweet—and wonderful—I can't go through with it."

"Jan Neece, will you come out with it?" demanded Brazos, in desperation.

"That's—just—it. . . . I'm not Jan Neece. . . . I'm *June!*"

"Lord Almighty! Am I drunk or crazy?" burst out Brazos, tearing his hair, and staring incredulously at her. "Who air you?"

"Oh, Brazos! Don't look so—so awful at me. . . . It's I! June—June Neece! Not Jan. . . . I couldn't live without you. It was Jan who eloped with Henry. And I thought you loved her most—that *she* could do anything with you—and I came down here to find you . . . make you marry me first—then tell you afterward."

"You damned—devilish little cat!" declared Brazos, astounded beyond passion. "I don't believe you."

"Oh—Brazos," she wailed.

"I—don't—believe—you."

"But, darling, I *am* June. I swear to heaven I am. Jan couldn't have done this rash thing. She hadn't the nerve. She didn't love you enough. Why, I'm ashamed to admit she was on Henry's neck as soon as you left. . . . Brazos, you must see I'm telling the truth. If I *were* Jan, intending to get you by hook or crook—would I be betraying my plot now? No! I'd wait till we were—married."

There was incontestable logic in this passionate confession. But Brazos chose to hide the ecstasy which was waving through him. He believed her now. Only those kisses had deceived him. She had acted them faithfully enough, though perhaps, once June had cast restraint and decorum aside, they had at last expressed her true fervor.

254

"I cain't believe you," said Brazos, solemnly.

"But you *must*. Brazos, no girl ever before did such a thing. Oh! I'm not ashamed. I'd glory in it, if you just—just. . . . Didn't I offer to let you marry Jan, and *give* myself to you, in the bargain. . . . Brazos, darling, for God's sake, don't say you won't marry me now!"

"I will if you prove you're June," replied Brazos, relentlessly. "I've had about all I can stand of takin' Jan for June—and June for Jan."

"Prove I'm June?" she echoed. "Of course I can. I *am* June. My name June is on the drafts for all that money."

Brazos sagged desperately under that potential proof. Bank presidents did not make colossal mistakes about making out drafts, especially when Henderson knew the Neece girls.

"Aw, you could fool Henderson just as easy as me. Haven't you fooled everybody under the sun? Yore own Dad even. . . . No, Miss Neece, you gotta prove you're June."

"Wait till we're married," she pleaded, so sweetly and humbly that Brazos smothered another wild desire to snatch her to his breast. Then an idea flashed into his rapturous mind.

"No. And let me remind you thet pastor with Doan and Wess, and I reckon everybody heah at this post, will be comin' pretty pronto."

"Beloved! Trust me!" she whispered, beseechingly. "I would die of shame if they came now."

"Listen. June Neece had a birthmark like a bluebell . . . on her laig. . . . didn't she?"

"Who told you that?" cried the girl, blushing scarlet.

"I heahed that when I first came to Las Animas. Everybody knew about it. The *only* way the Neece twins could be told apart! . . . Wal, if you air June you shore have thet birthmark. Now haven't you?"

"Yes, Brazos Keene. I have," she retorted, at bay. "Will you trust me—until . . . ?"

"I'll trust you afterward, forever. I reckon you deserve to suffer a little shame."

"Shame! *I* have nothing to be ashamed of, unless it's chasing an unchivalrous cowboy all over the south."

"Thet's a heap, I'm bound to admit. . . . There! Girl, I reckon I heahed Wess's loud laugh out there. They've come with the parson. You better rustle or you may lose a husband."

"Brazos Keene, if you force me I—I won't have you for a husband," she cried, loftily. She was white of face again and her eyes burned with reproach.

"I'll risk thet, darlin'. You cain't get out of marryin' me now, if only to save yore good name and yore pride."

"Very well, cowboy! Come over to the light," she returned, with what seemed a calm disdain. Brazos followed her haltingly to the window. He felt her gaze upon him and dared not meet it. Moreover his eyes were glued to her shapely capable hands as they grasped her gown at each side. She lifted it and her white skirts. Her trim ankles, her slender graceful legs, her rounded knees and pink garters sharply outlined against her black stockings led Brazos' fascinated gaze to her white thighs.

"You should know this would be apple pie for Jan," she said, with a suppressed giggle that belied her haughty scorn of this exacting lover. "I've forgotten which leg it's on . . . the left, I'm sure. Look. . . ."

Merry voices outside preceded knocks on the door. Brazos, with the wonderful swiftness of that right hand, snatched her skirts down.

"Aw, darlin', I was only foolin'," he whispered.

"Yes you were," she taunted. "Did you see it?"

"No. I couldn't see nothin'. Besides, June, I shore knew you all the time."

"Liar! I could have fooled you . . . I wish . . . Oh!"

Louder and more impatient knocks sounded upon the door. June smoothed her ruffled gown.

"Brazos, we're heah, all ready to make yu the happiest cowboy in Texas," called Wess, his voice ringing.

"Can we come in?" Doan's booming voice attested to the joy he felt. "Parson, papers, witnesses, an' all."

"Just a minnit more, Tom," drawled Brazos. "The lady has consented to become Mrs. Keene. But, doggone it! she hasn't proved yet which one of the Twin Sombrero twins she really is!"

256